Tree-House Comix Proudly Presents

DOG MAN

A Tale of Two Kitties

WRITTEN AND ILLUSTRATED BY DAV PILKEY

AS GEORGE BEARD AND HAROLD HUTCHINS

WITH COLOR BY JOSE GARIBALDI

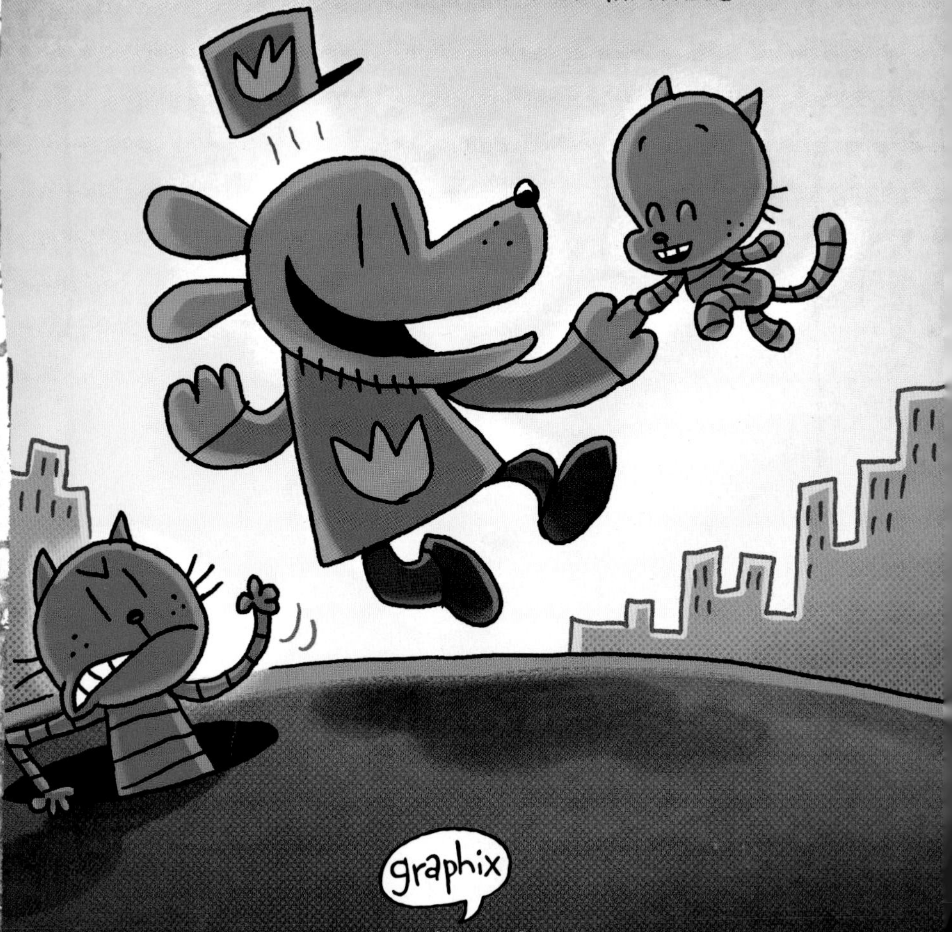

graphix

AN IMPRINT OF

SCHOLASTIC

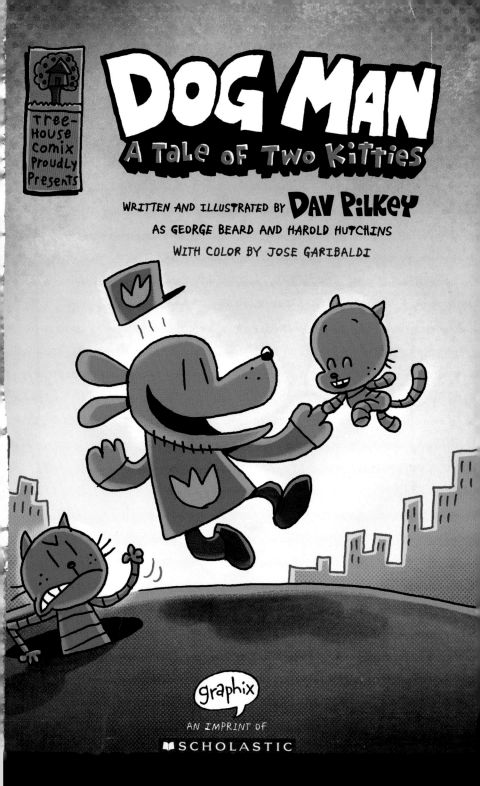

HERE'S TO YOU, MR. ROBINSON!
(THANK YOU, DICK.)

With thanks to Charles Dickens, whose novels, particularly A Tale of Two Cities, still resonate with readers today.

Library of Congress Control Number 2016961907

978-0-545-93521-0 (POB)
978-1-338-61199-1 (Library)

10 9 8 7 6 5 4 3 2 1 20 21 22 23 24

Printed in China 62
First edition, September 2017

Edited by Anamika Bhatnagar
Book design by Dav Pilkey and Phil Falco
Color by Jose Garibaldi
Creative Director: David Saylor

ChapTers

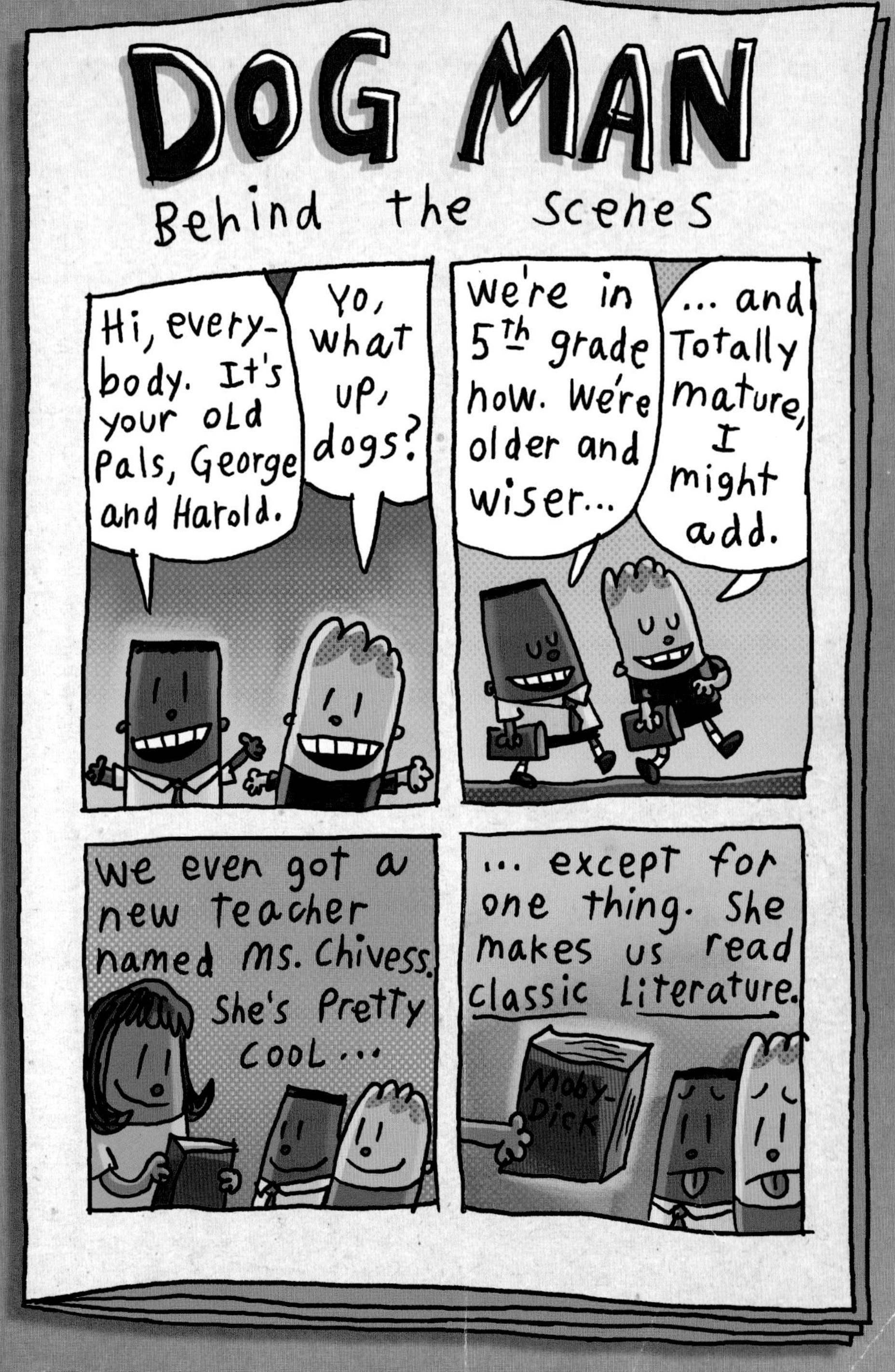
DOG MAN
Behind the Scenes
Hi, every-body. It's your old Pals, George and Harold.
Yo, what up, dogs?
We're in 5th grade now. We're older and wiser...
... and Totally mature, I might add.
We even got a new Teacher named Ms. Chivess.
She's Pretty cool...
... except for one thing. She makes us read classic Literature.
Moby-Dick

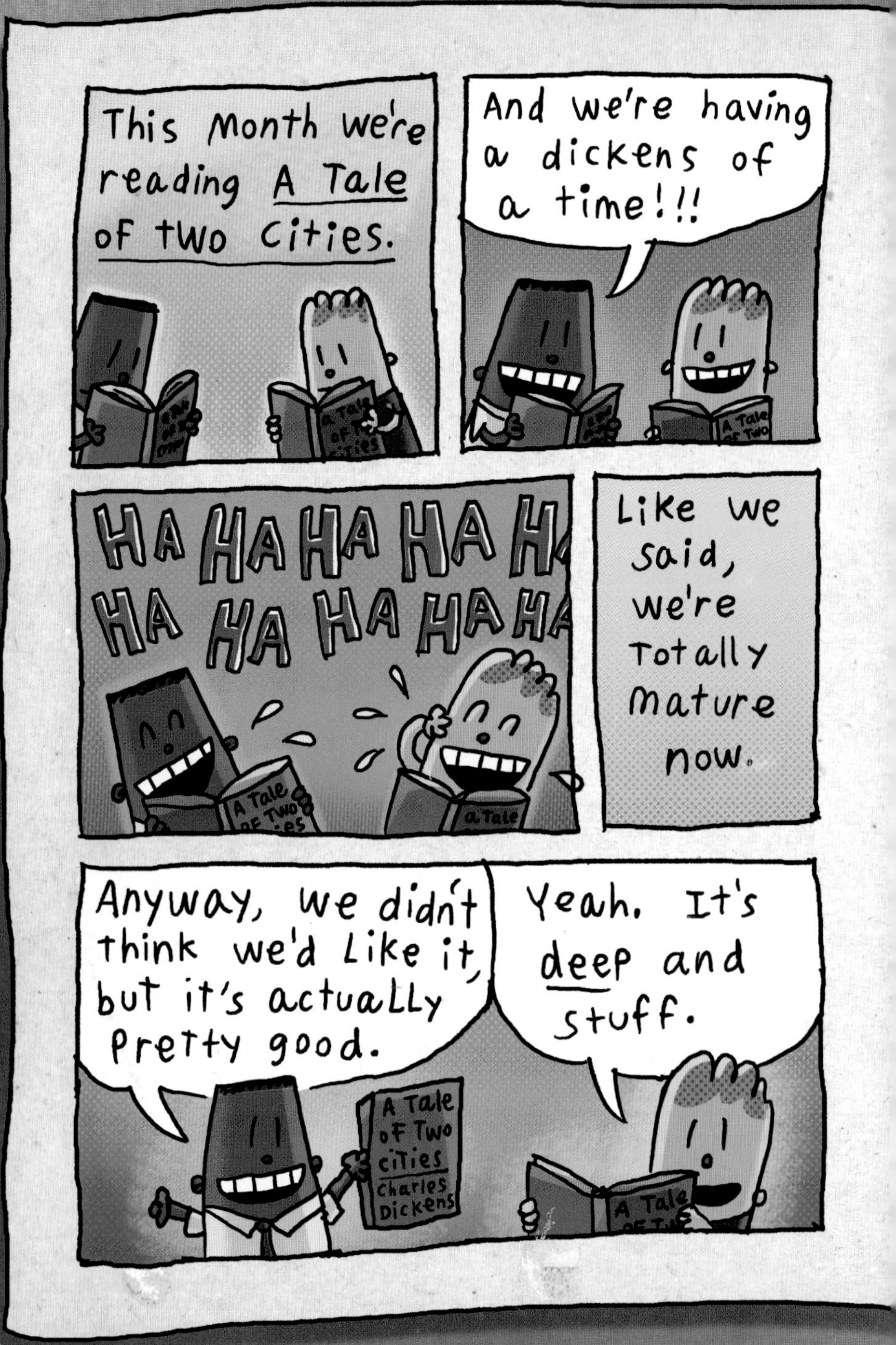
This Month we're reading A Tale of Two Cities.
A Tale of Two Cities
And we're having a dickens of a time!!!
A Tale of Two
HA HA HA HA HA HA HA HA HA HA HA HA
A Tale of Two
a Tale
Like we said, we're Totally mature now.
Anyway, we didn't think we'd Like it, but it's actually pretty good.
Yeah. It's deep and stuff.
A Tale of Two Cities Charles Dickens
A Tale

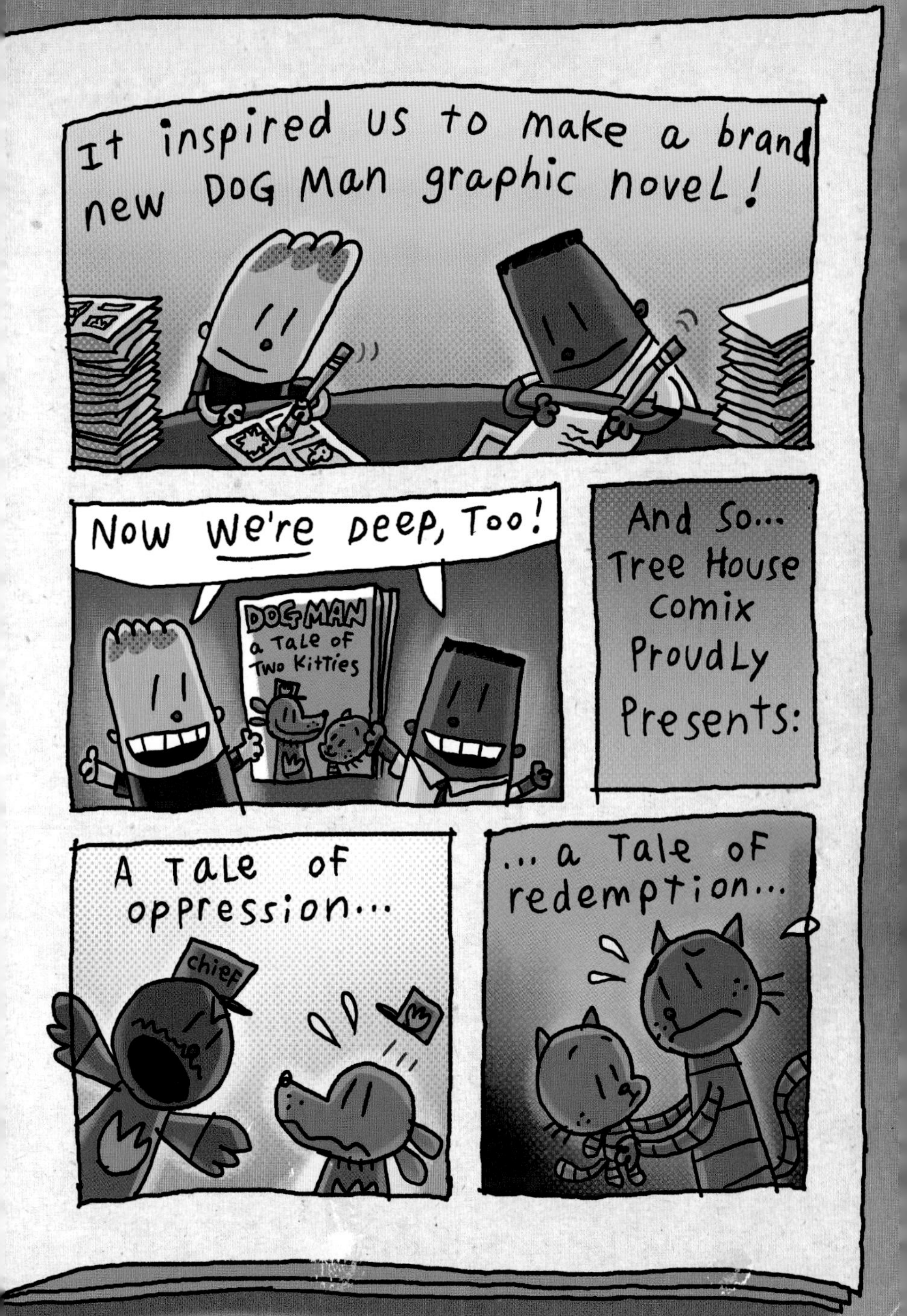
It inspired us to make a brand new DOG MAN graphic novel!
Now We're Deep, Too!
DOG MAN
a Tale of Two Kitties
And So... Tree House Comix Proudly Presents:
A Tale of oppression...
chief
... a Tale of redemption...

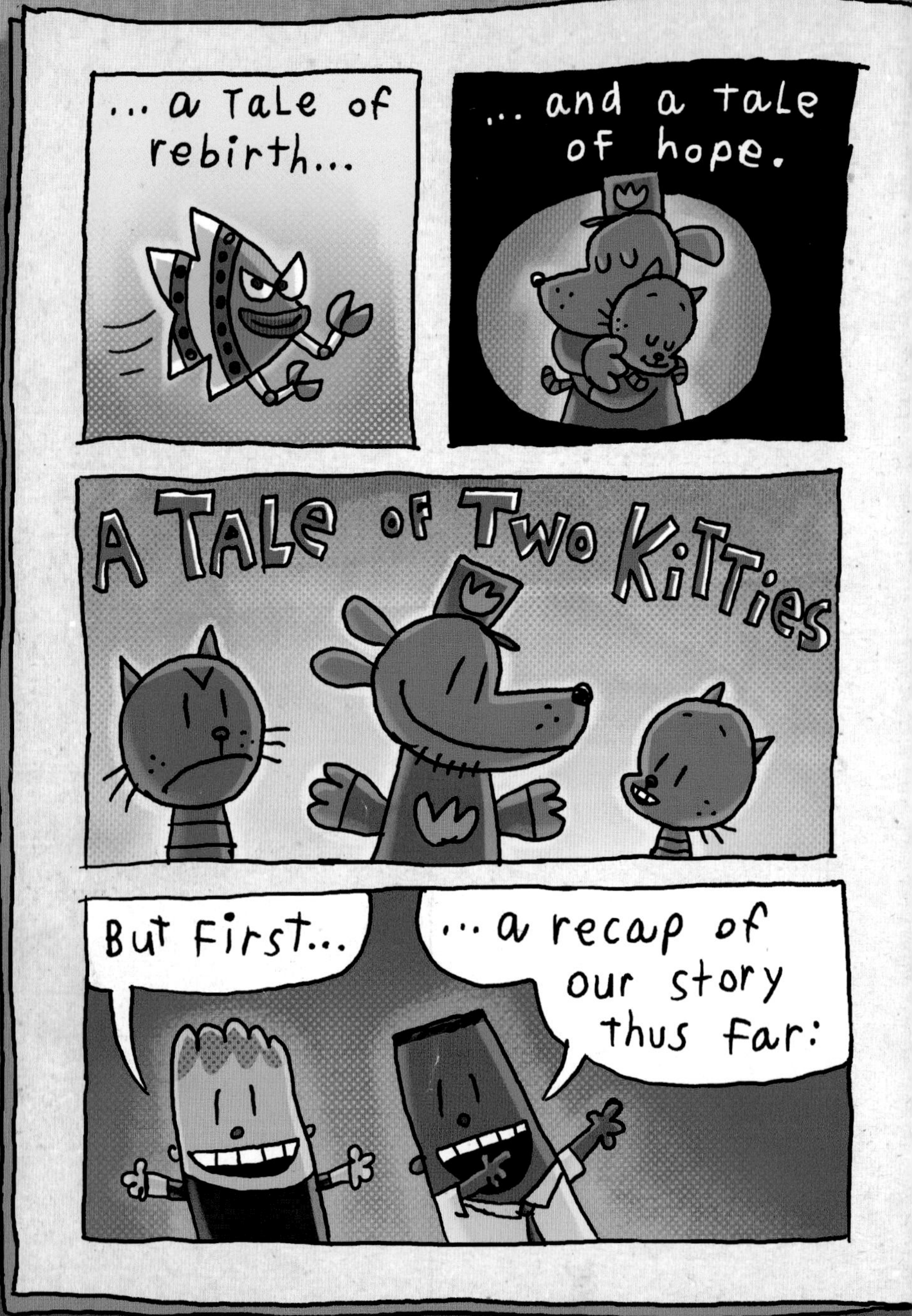
... a Tale of rebirth...
... and a tale of hope.
A TALE of TWO KiTTies
But First...
... a recap of our story thus far:

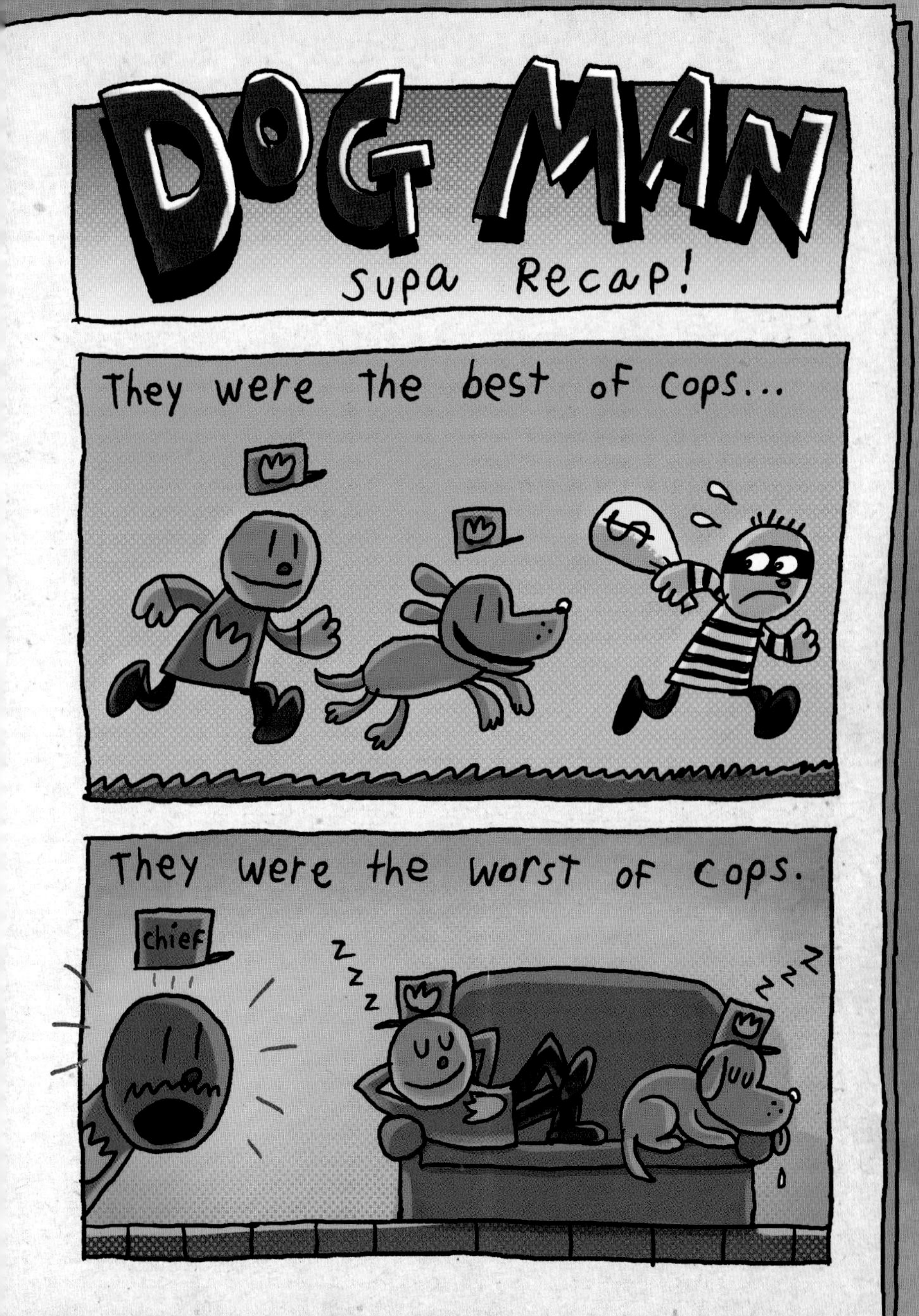
DOG MAN
Supa Recap!
They were the best of cops...
They were the worst of cops.
chief
Z Z Z
Z Z Z

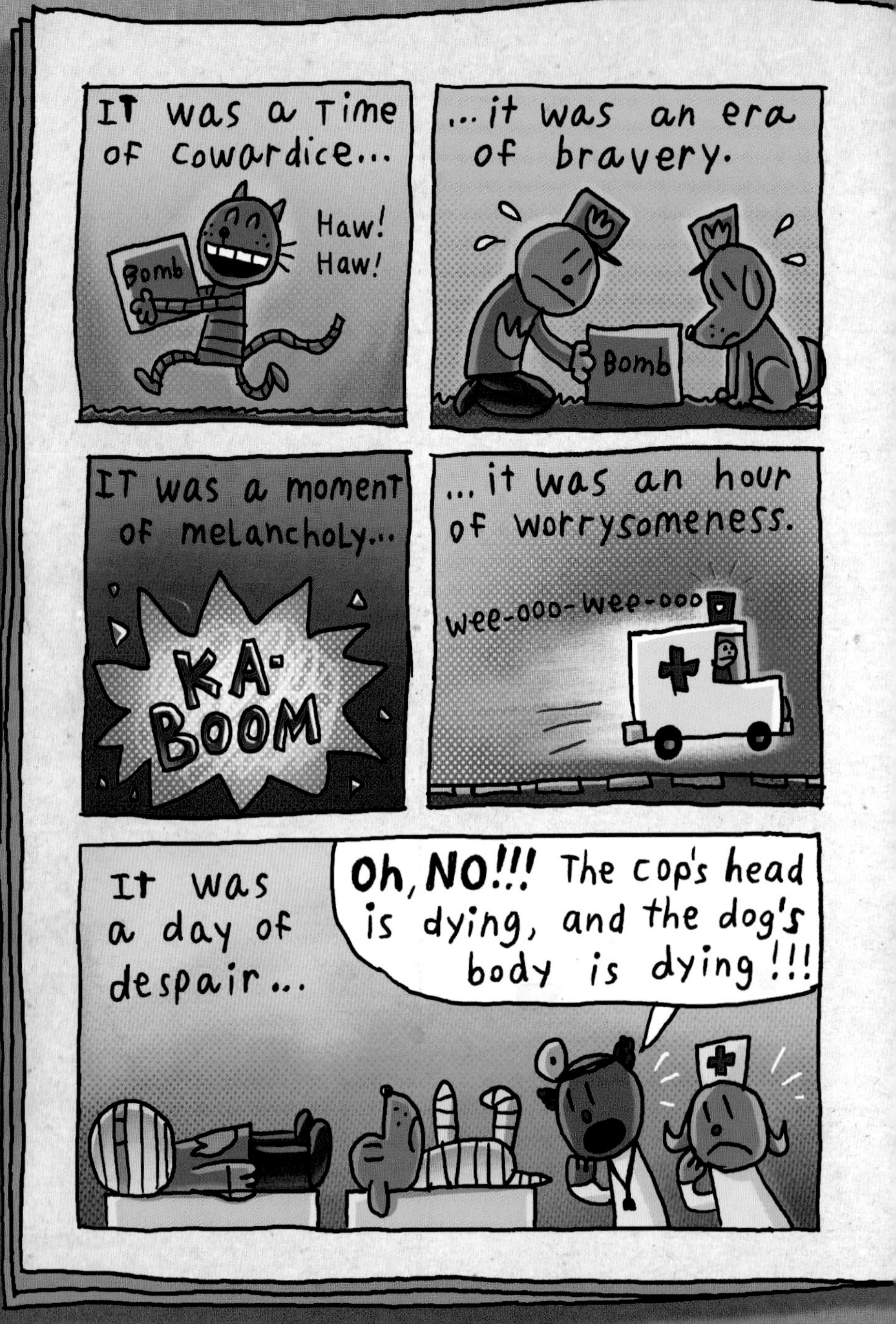
IT was a Time of cowardice...
Bomb
Haw! Haw!
...it was an era of bravery.
Bomb
IT was a moment of melancholy...
KA-BOOM
...it was an hour of worrysomeness.
wee-ooo-wee-ooo
It was a day of despair...
Oh, NO!!! The cop's head is dying, and the dog's body is dying!!!

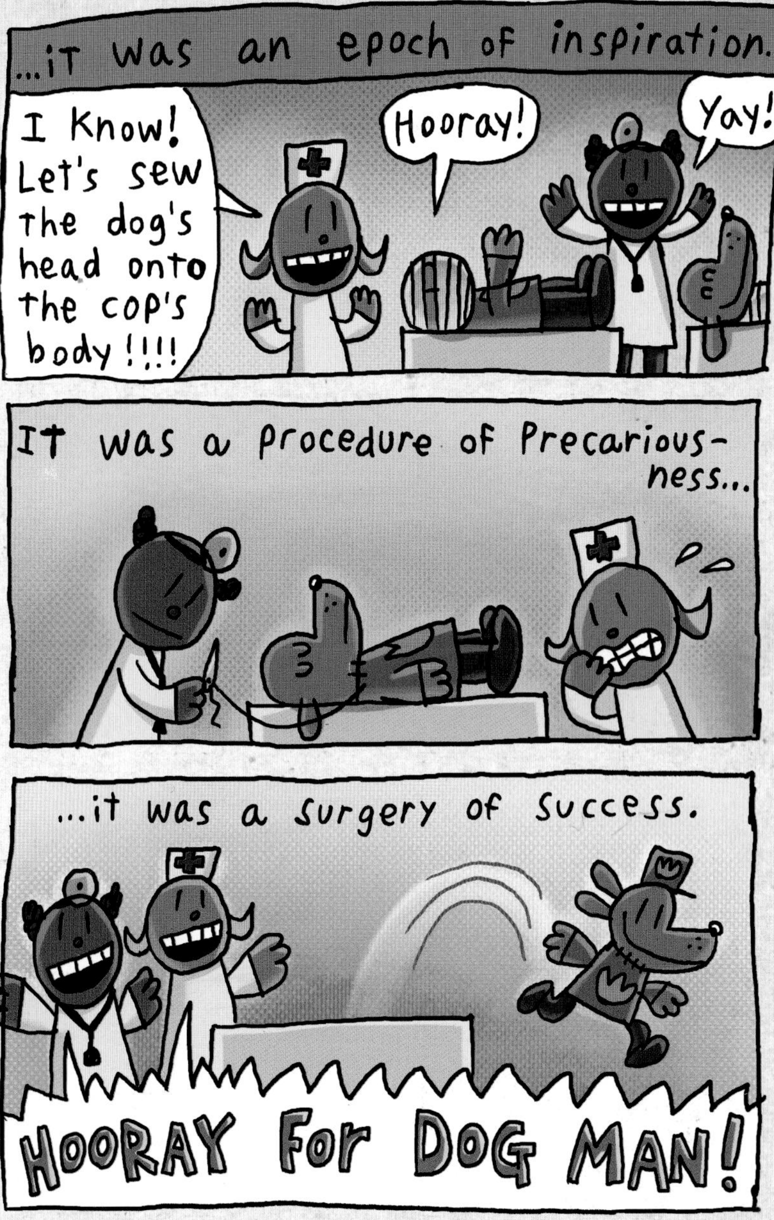

...iT was an epoch of inspiration.
I Know! Let's sew the dog's head onto the cop's body!!!!
Hooray!
Yay!
IT was a procedure of Precarious-ness...
...it was a surgery of success.
HOORAY For DOG MAN!

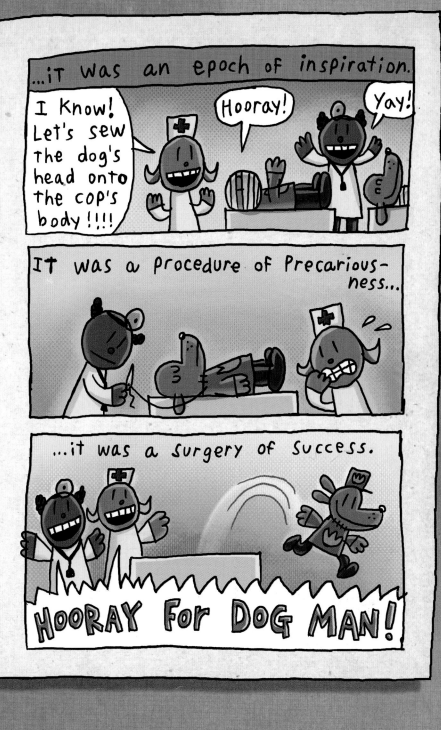

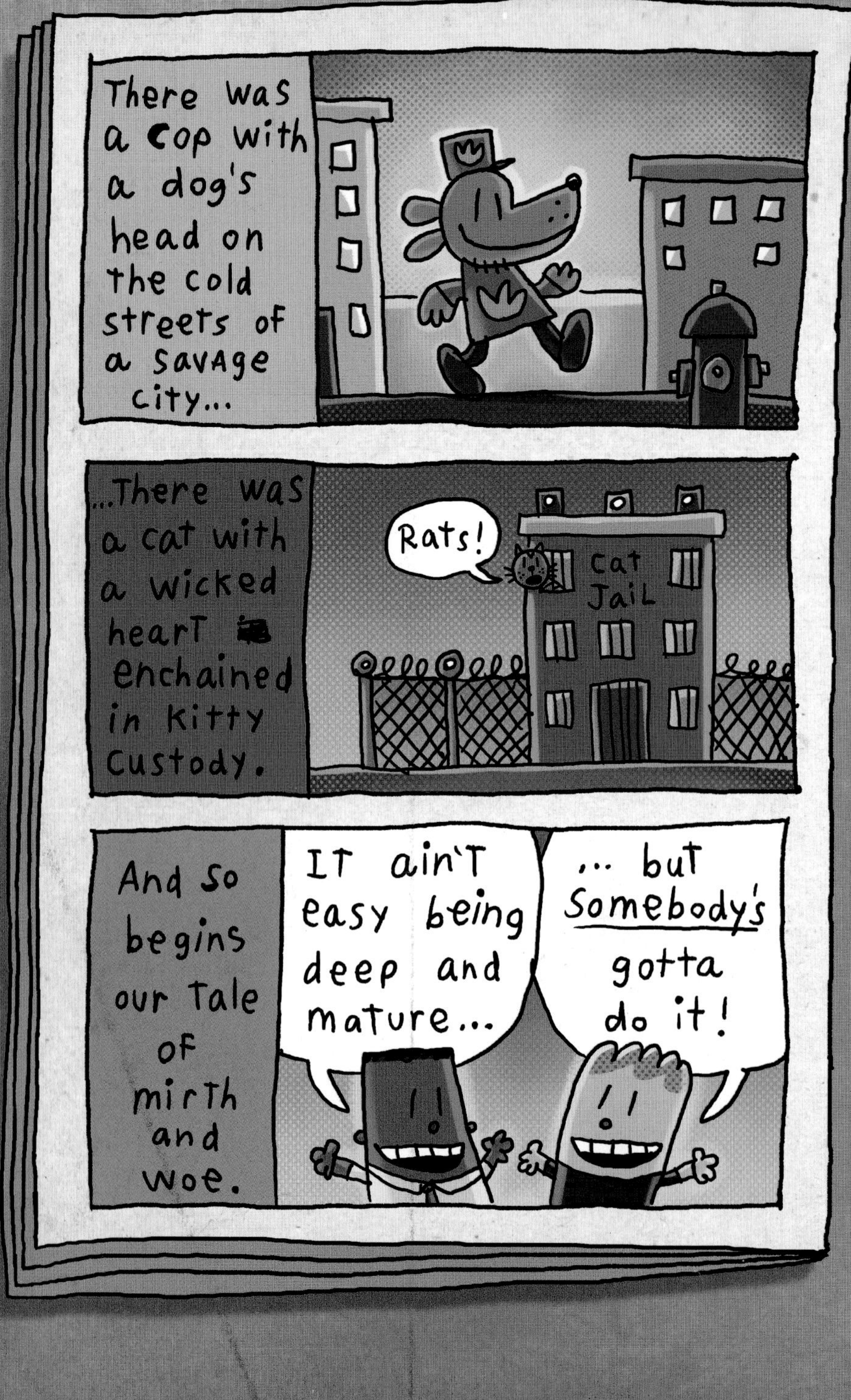
There was a cop with a dog's head on the cold streets of a savage city...
...There was a cat with a wicked heart enchained in kitty custody.
Rats!
Cat Jail
And so begins our tale of mirth and woe.
IT ain'T easy being deep and mature...
... but Somebody's gotta do it!

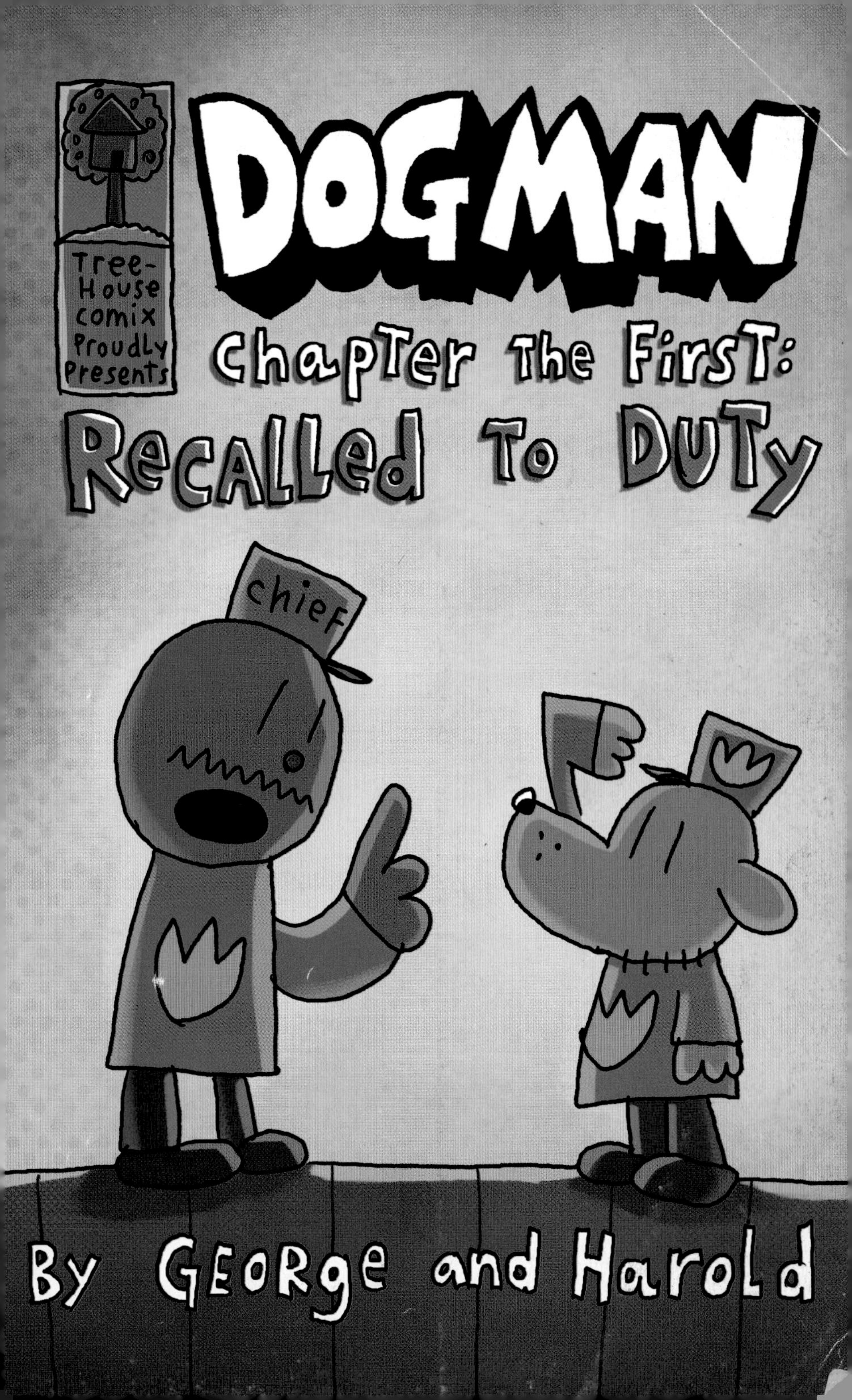
Tree-House comix Proudly presents
DOG MAN
Chapter the First:
Recalled to Duty
chief
By George and Harold

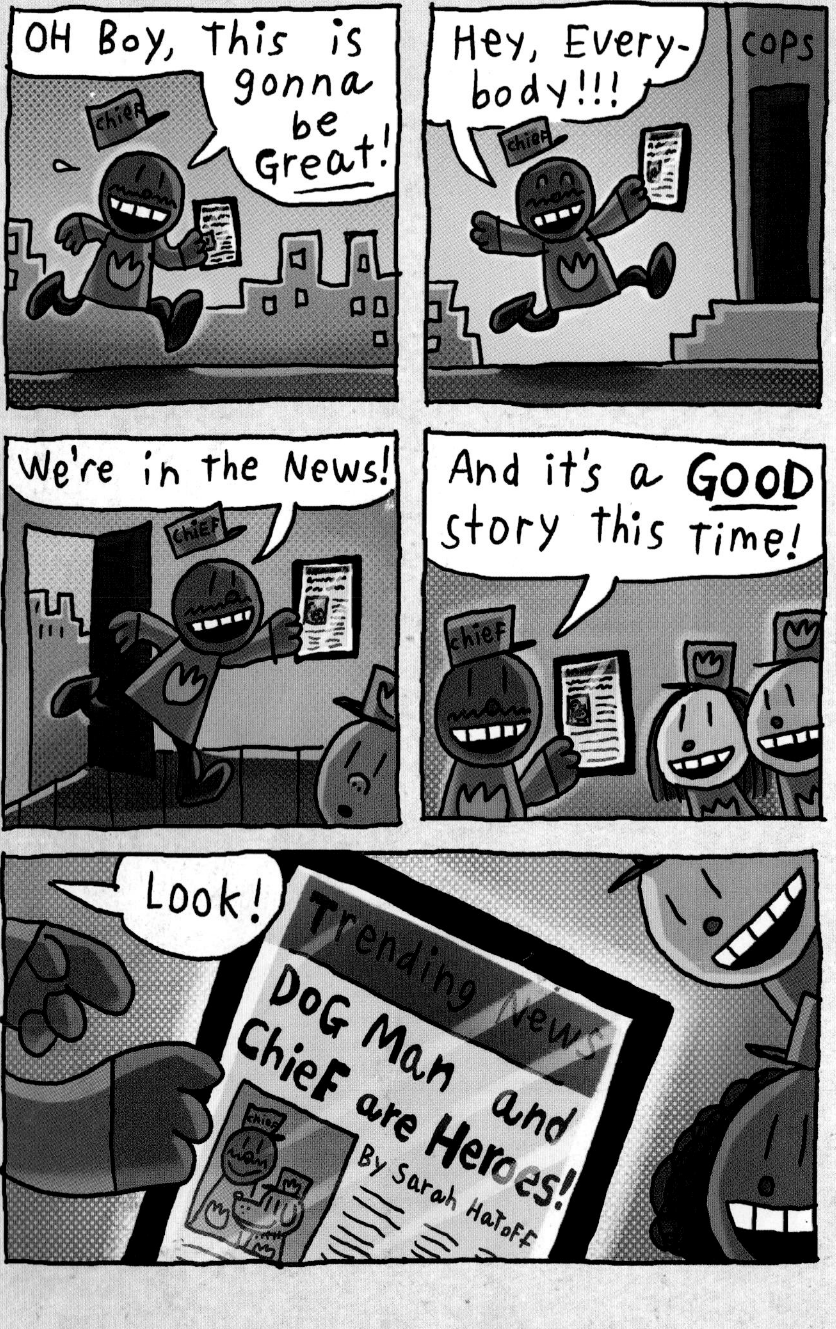
OH Boy, this is gonna be Great!
chief
Hey, Every-body!!!
COPS
chief
We're in the News!
chief
And it's a GOOD story this time!
chief
Look!
Trending News
DoG Man and ChieF are Heroes!
By Sarah HaToff

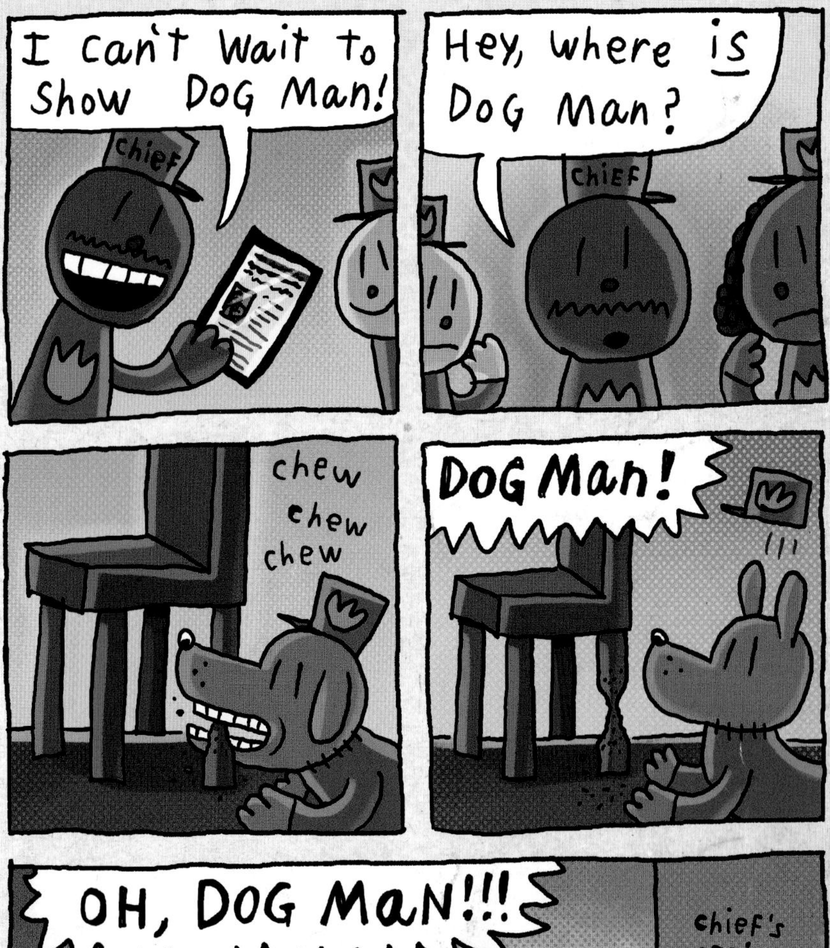
I can't wait to show DOG Man!
chief
Hey, where is DOG Man?
chief
chew chew chew
DOG Man!
OH, DOG MaN!!!
chief
chief's office

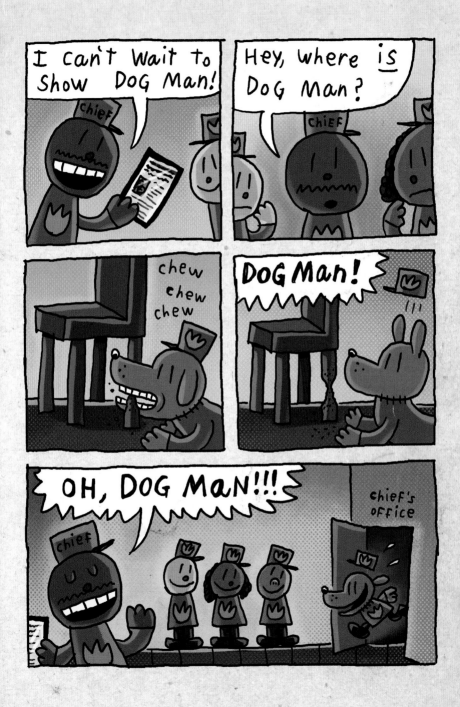

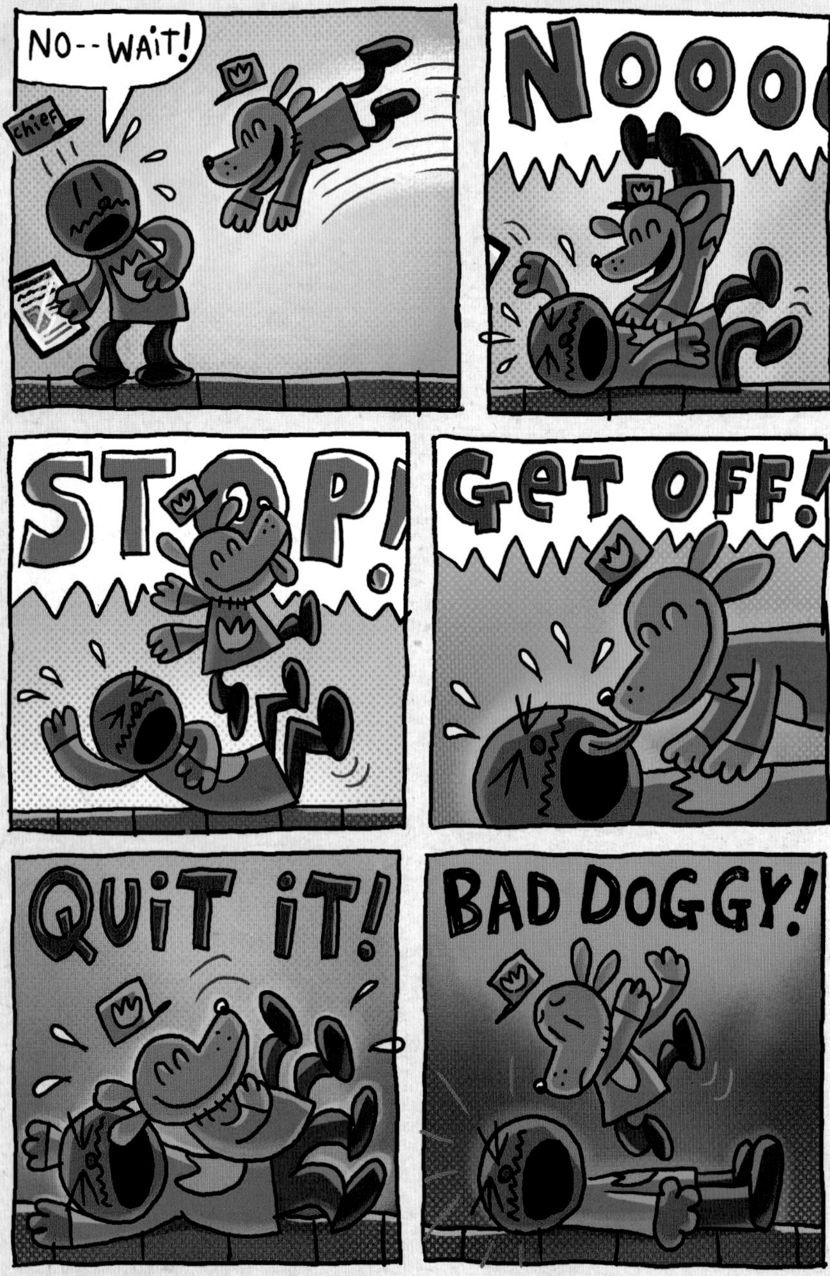
NO--WAIT!
chief
NOOOO
STOP!
GET OFF!
QUIT IT!
BAD DOGGY!

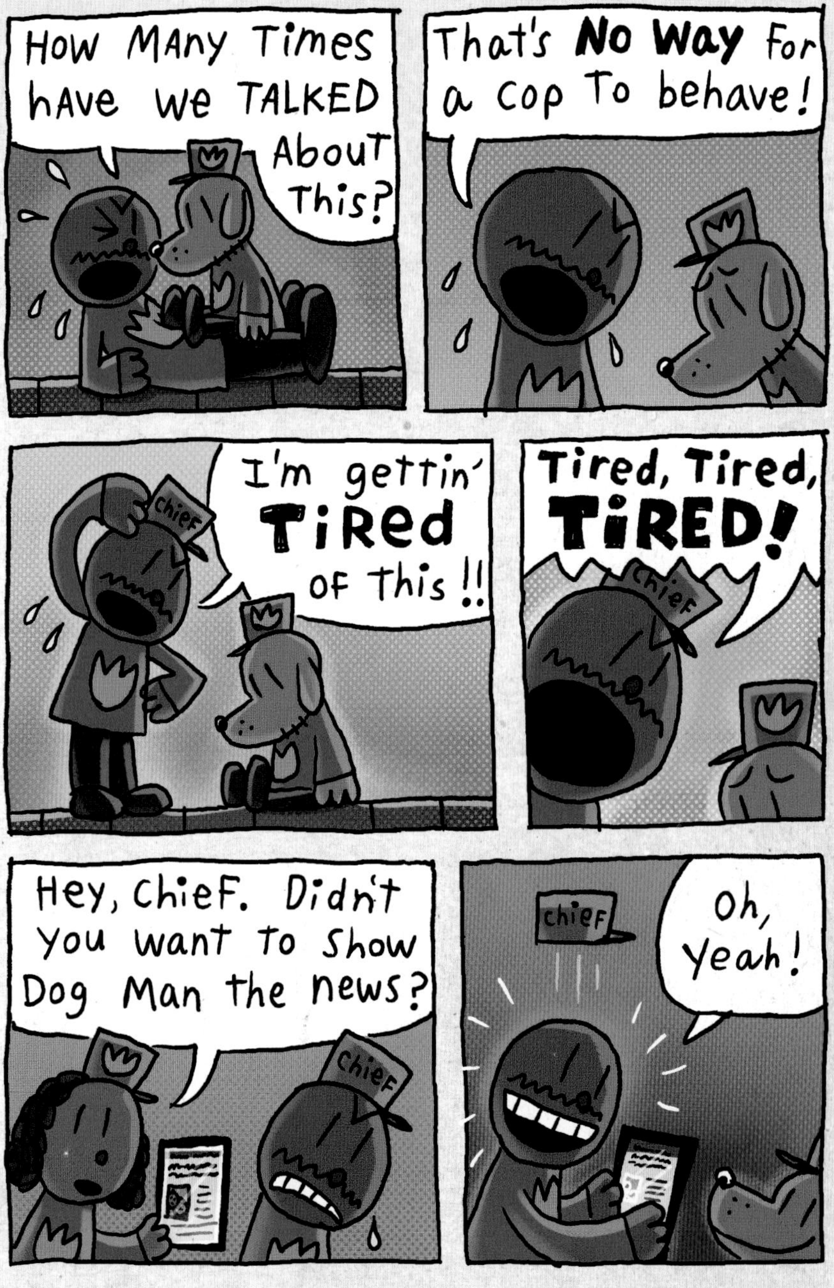
How Many Times have we TALKED About This?
That's **No Way** For a cop To behave!
I'm gettin' TiRed of this!!
Chief
Tired, Tired, TiRED!
Chief
Hey, Chief. Didn't you want to show Dog Man the news?
Chief
Chief
Oh, Yeah!

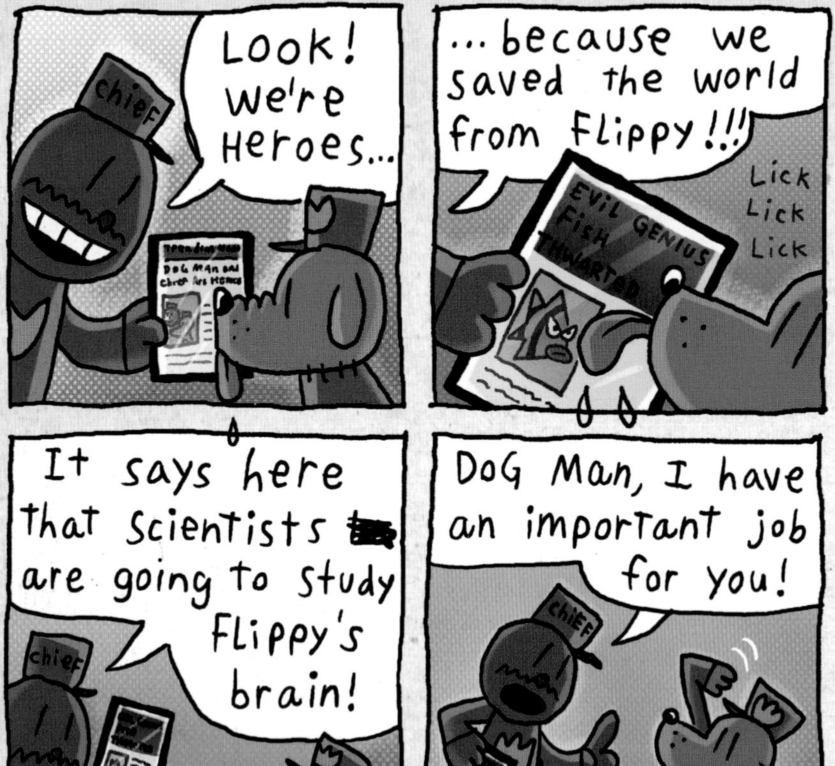

Look! We're Heroes...
...because we saved the world from Flippy!!!
EVIL GENIUS FISH THWARTED
Lick Lick Lick
It says here that scientists [redacted] are going to study Flippy's brain!
Dog Man, I have an important job for you!
I'm putting you in charge of security!
Who wants to protect the scientists?

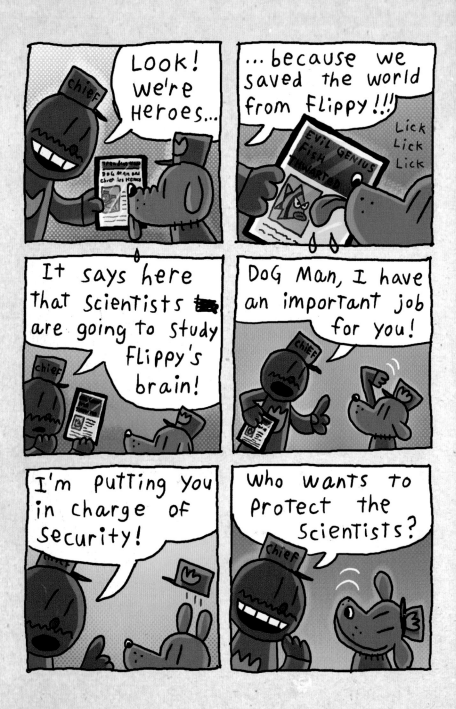

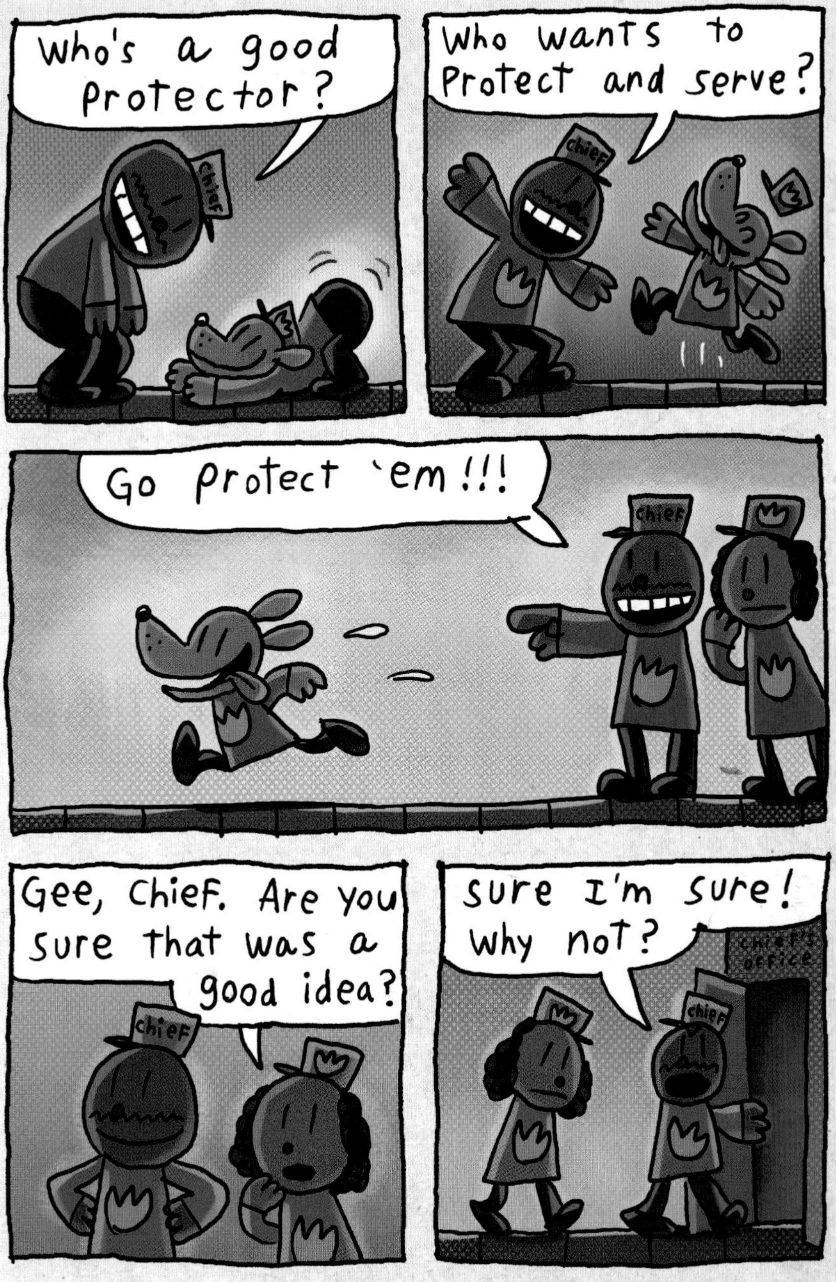
Who's a good protector?
Who wants to Protect and serve?
Go Protect 'em!!!
Gee, Chief. Are you sure that was a good idea?
Sure I'm sure! Why not?
CHIEF'S OFFICE

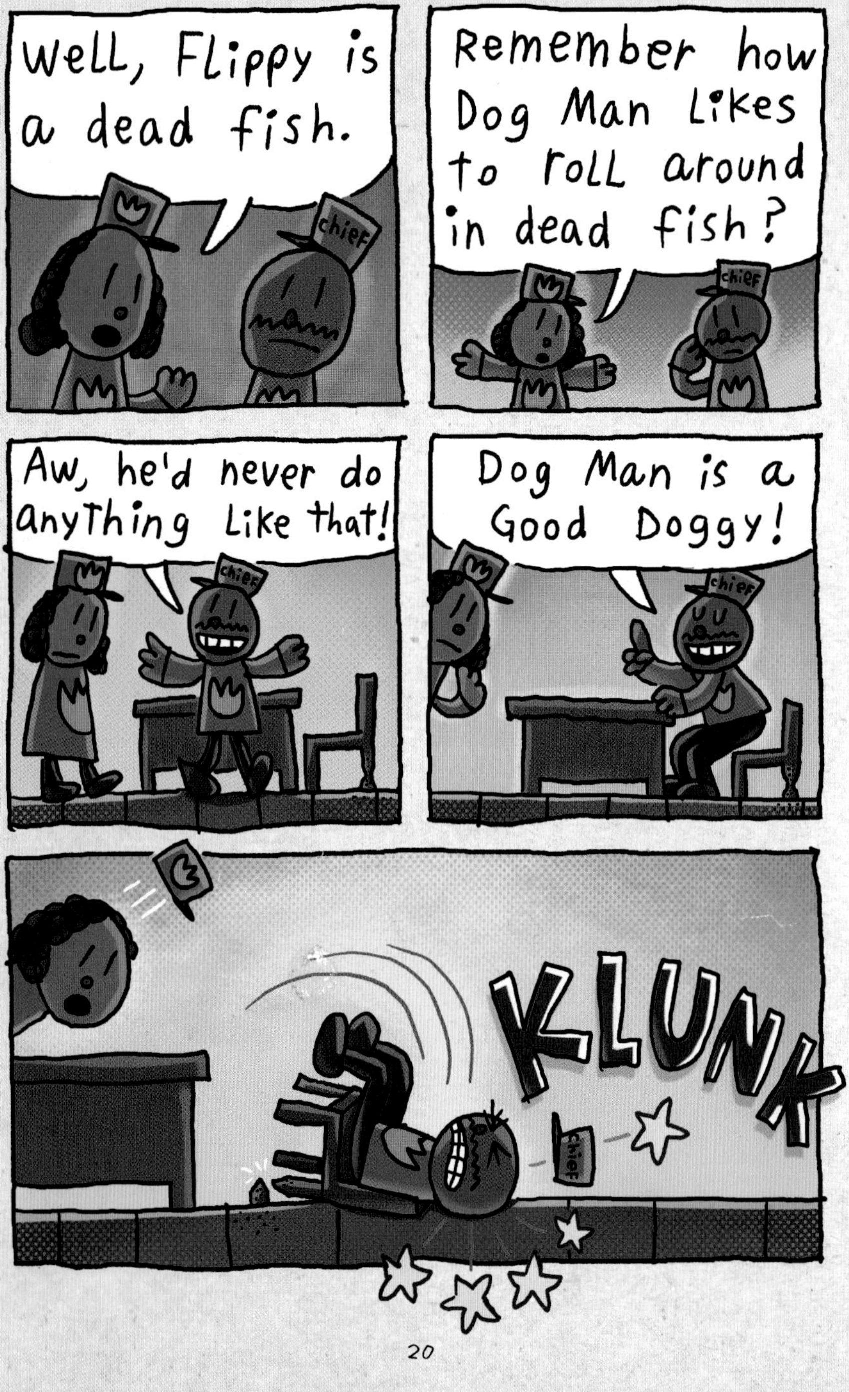

WeLL, FLippy is a dead fish.
Remember how Dog Man Likes to roLL around in dead fish?
chief
Aw, he'd never do anyThing Like that!
chief
Dog Man is a Good Doggy!
chief
KLUNK
chief

Chapter the Second: You've Gotta Be Kitten Me!

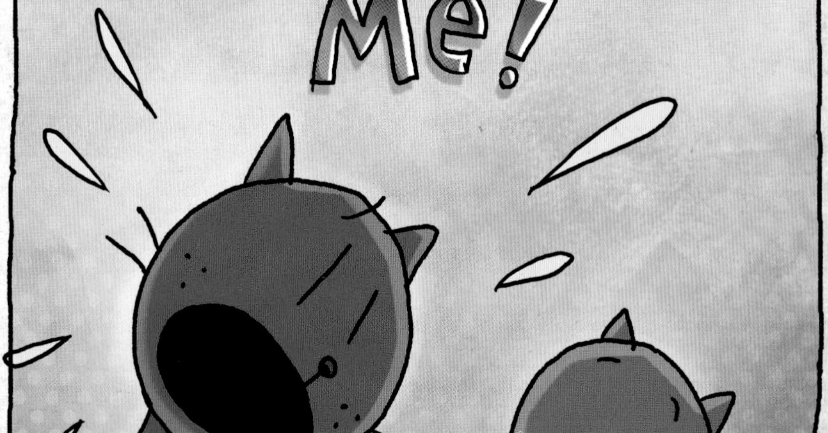

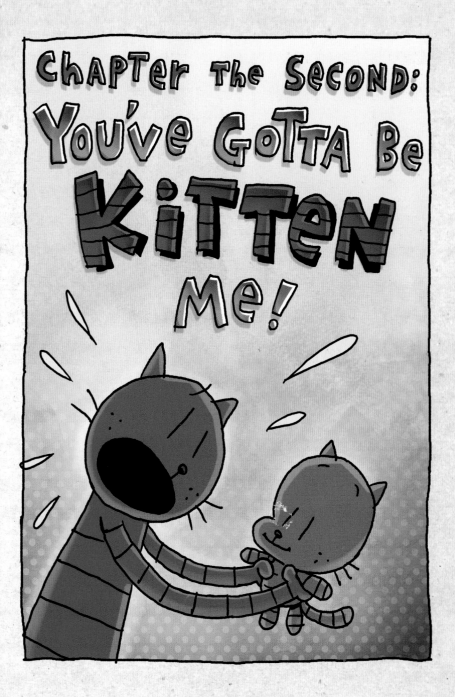

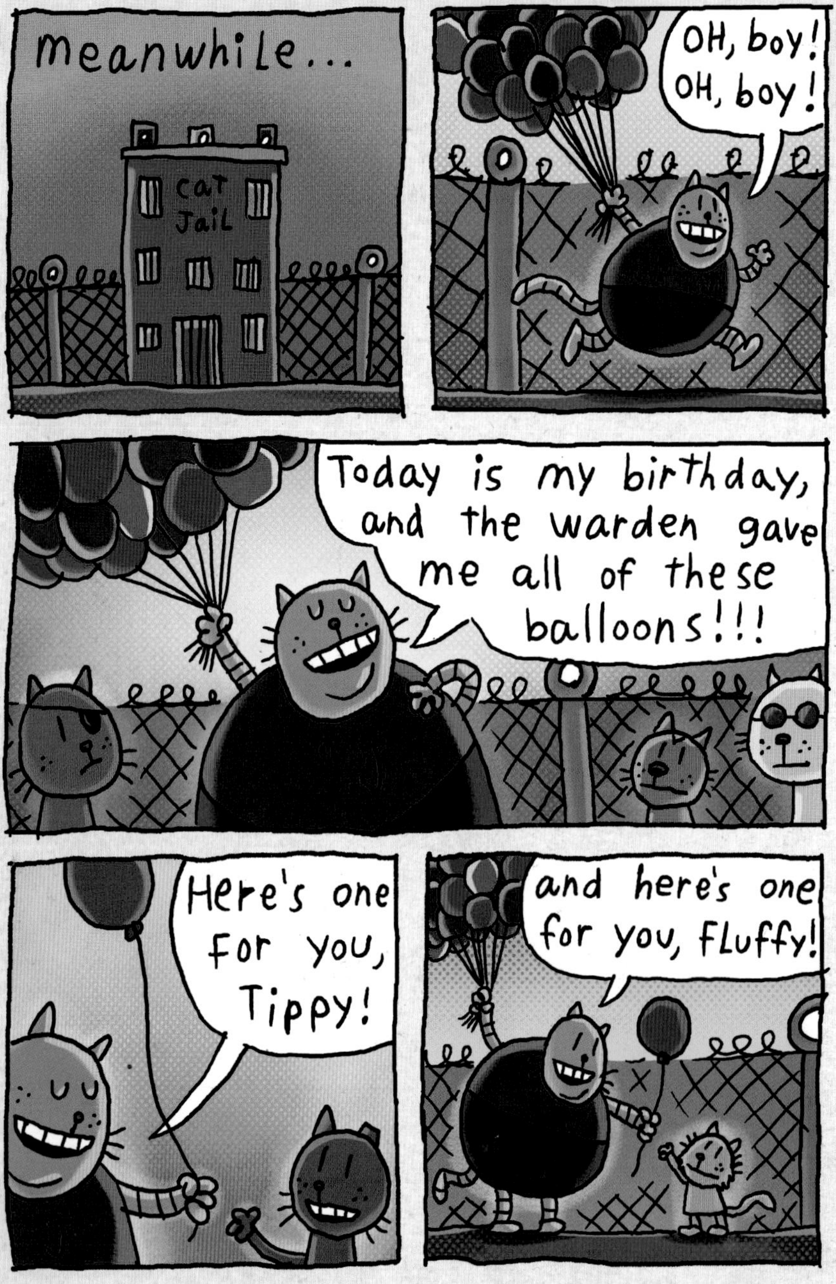
meanwhile...
Cat Jail
OH, boy! OH, boy!
Today is my birthday, and the warden gave me all of these balloons!!!
Here's one For you, Tippy!
and here's one for you, Fluffy!

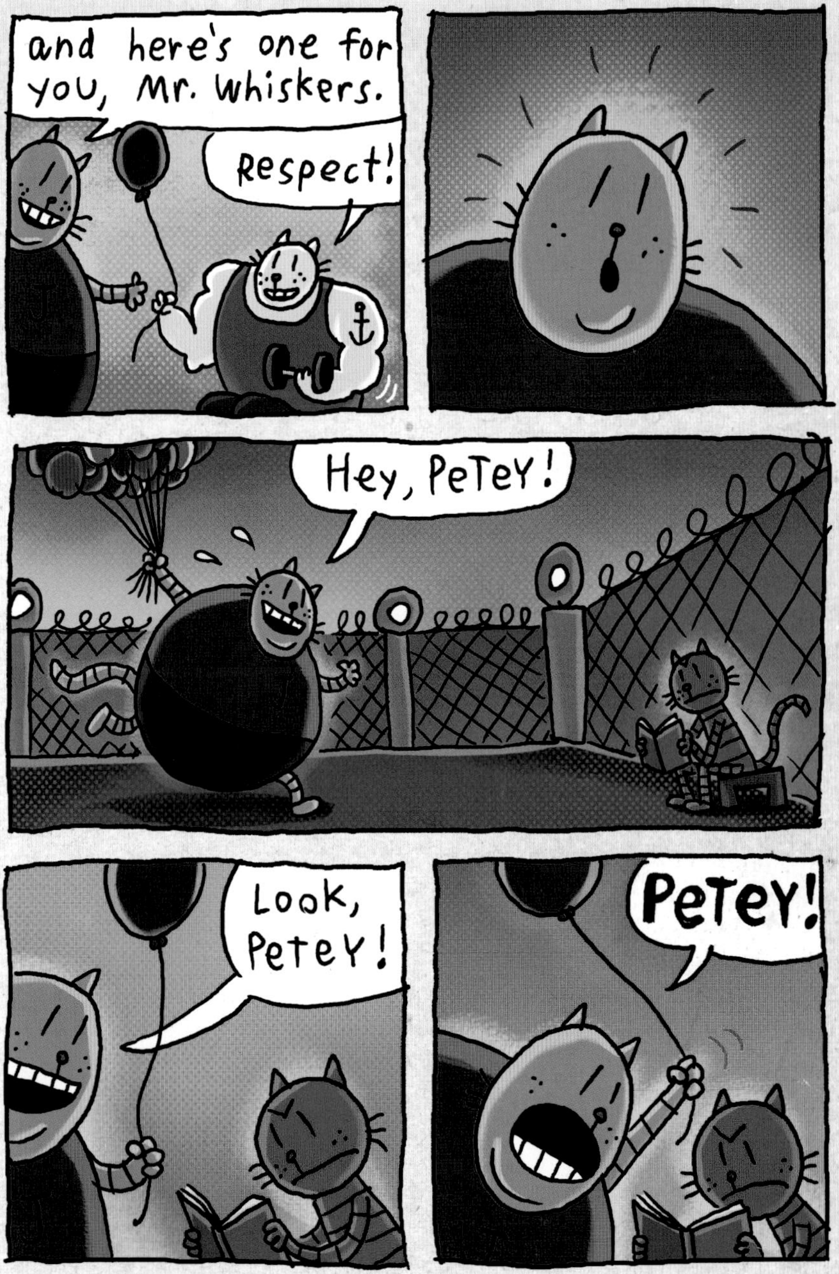

and here's one for you, Mr. Whiskers.
Respect!
Hey, PeTeY!
Look, PeTeY!
PeTeY!

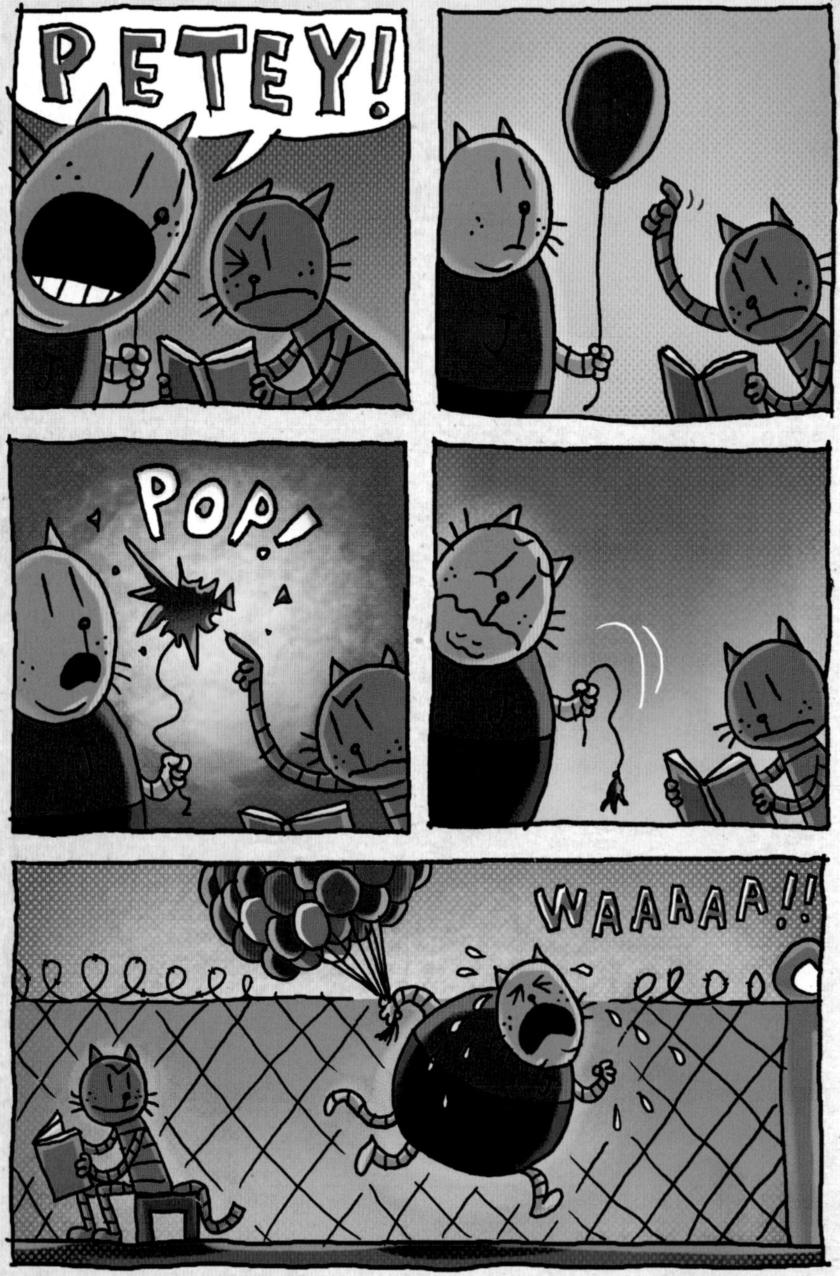
PETEY!
POP!
WAAAAA!!

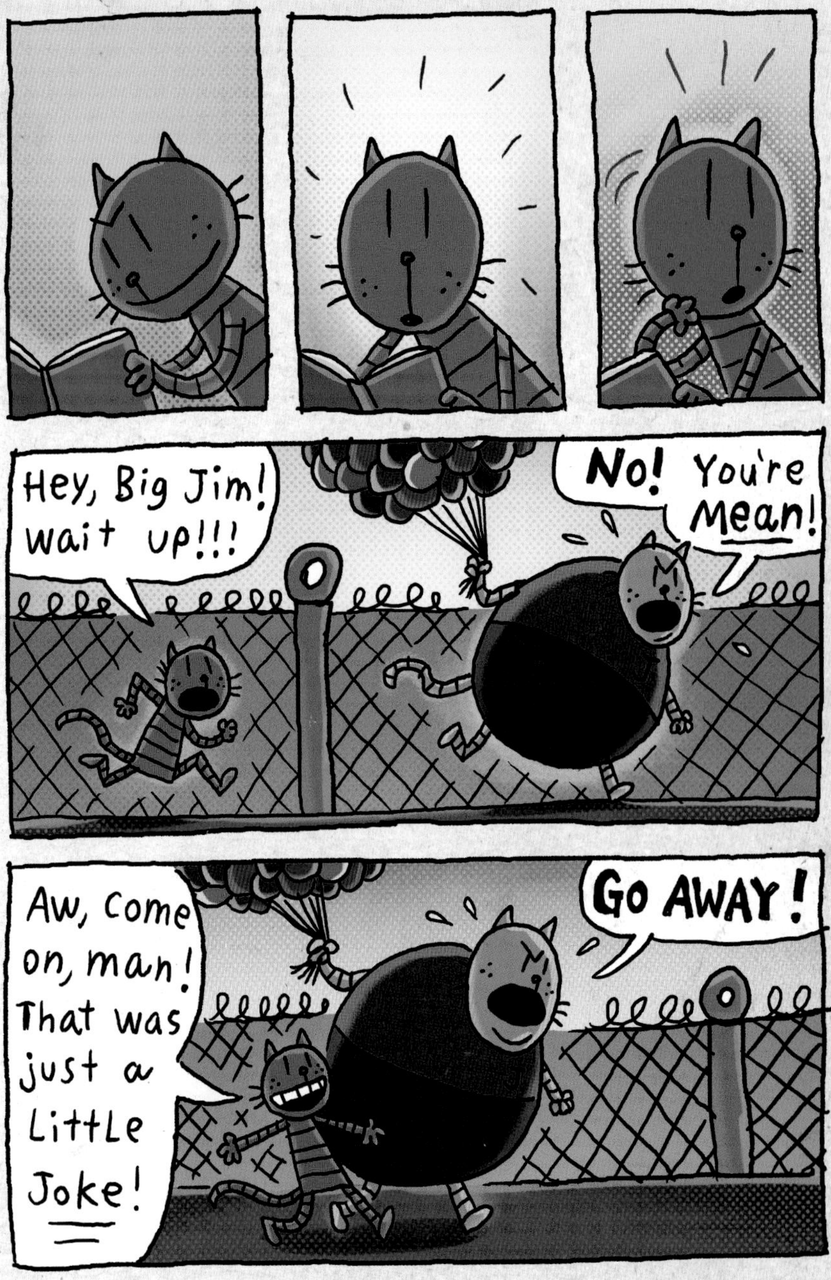
Hey, Big Jim! wait up!!!
No! You're Mean!
Aw, come on, man! That was just a Little Joke!
GO AWAY!

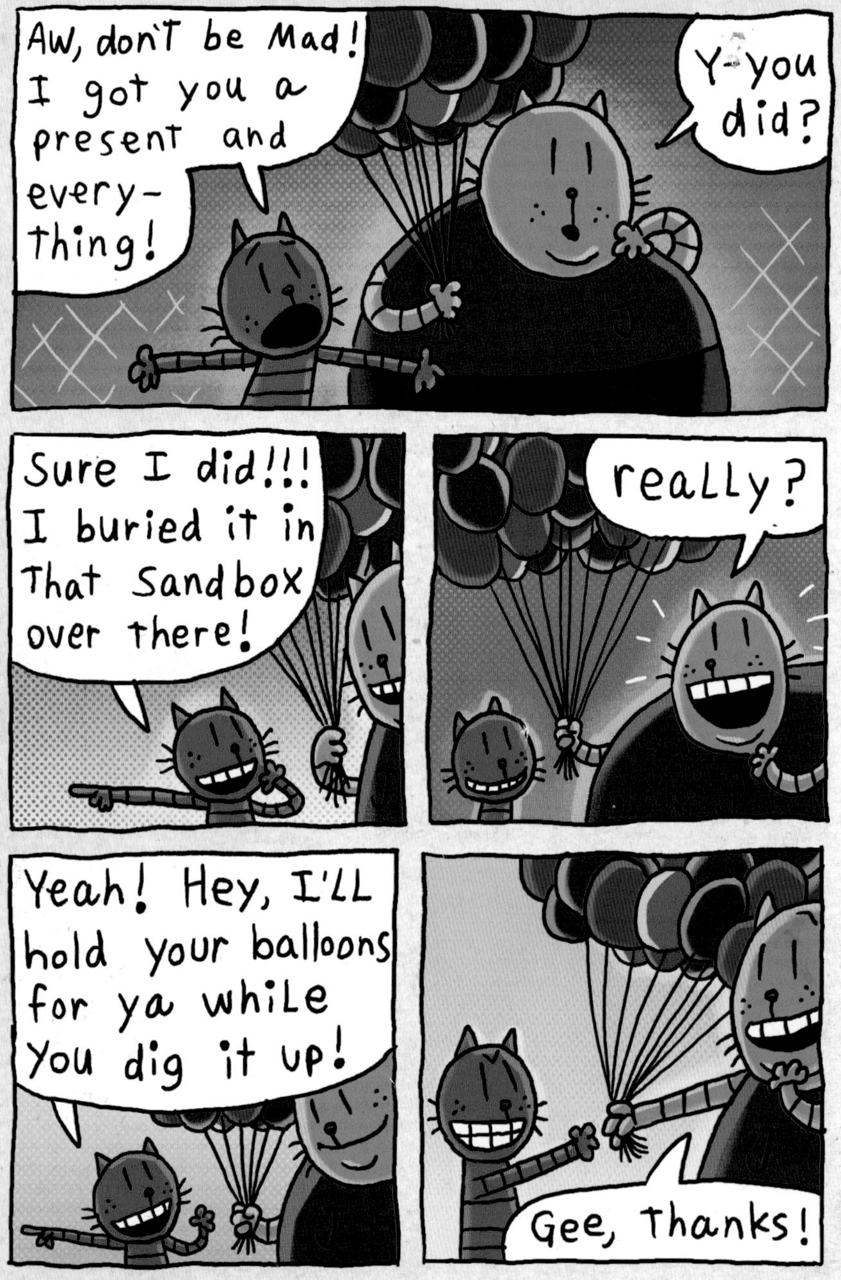

AW, don't be Mad! I got you a present and every-thing!
Y-you did?
Sure I did!!! I buried it in That Sandbox over there!
really?
Yeah! Hey, I'LL hold your balloons for ya whiLe You dig it up!
Gee, Thanks!

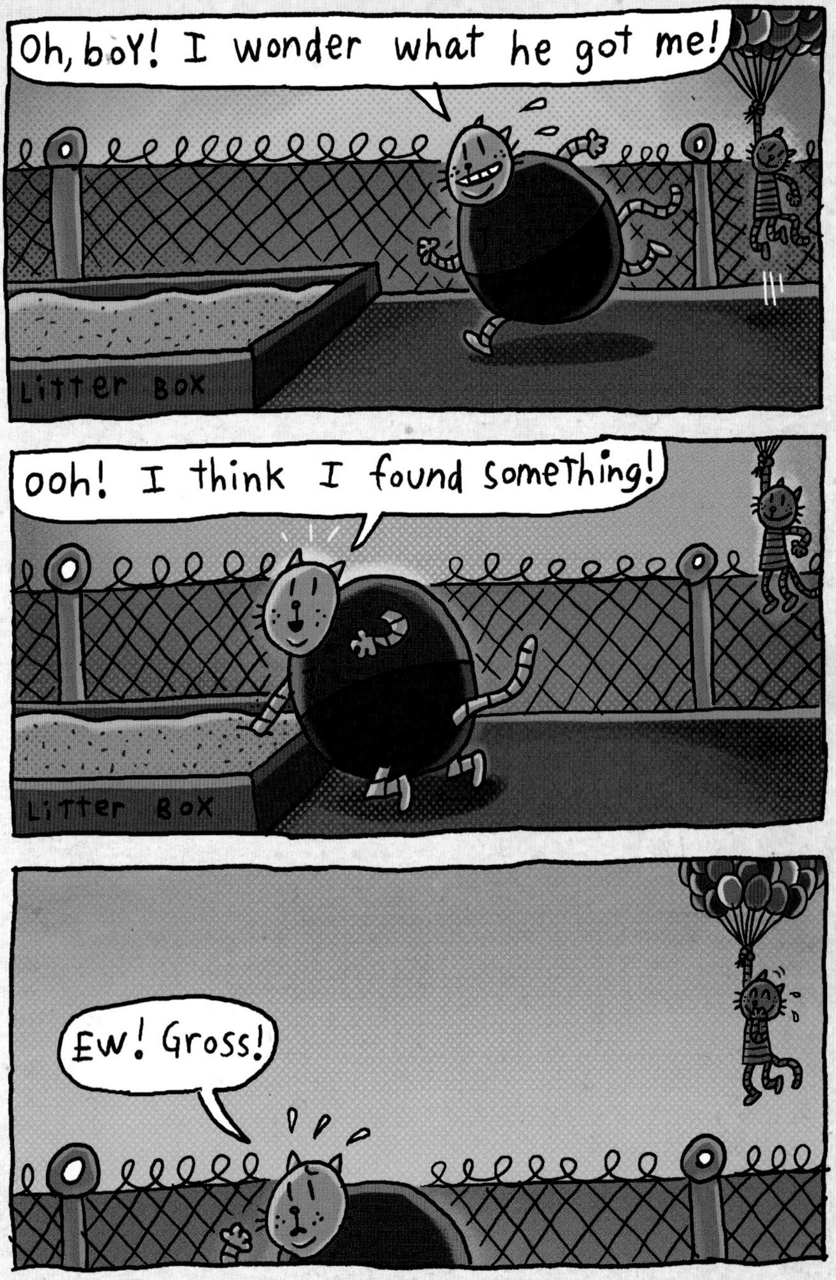
Oh, boY! I wonder what he got me!
LITTER BOX
ooh! I think I found something!
LITTER BOX
Ew! Gross!

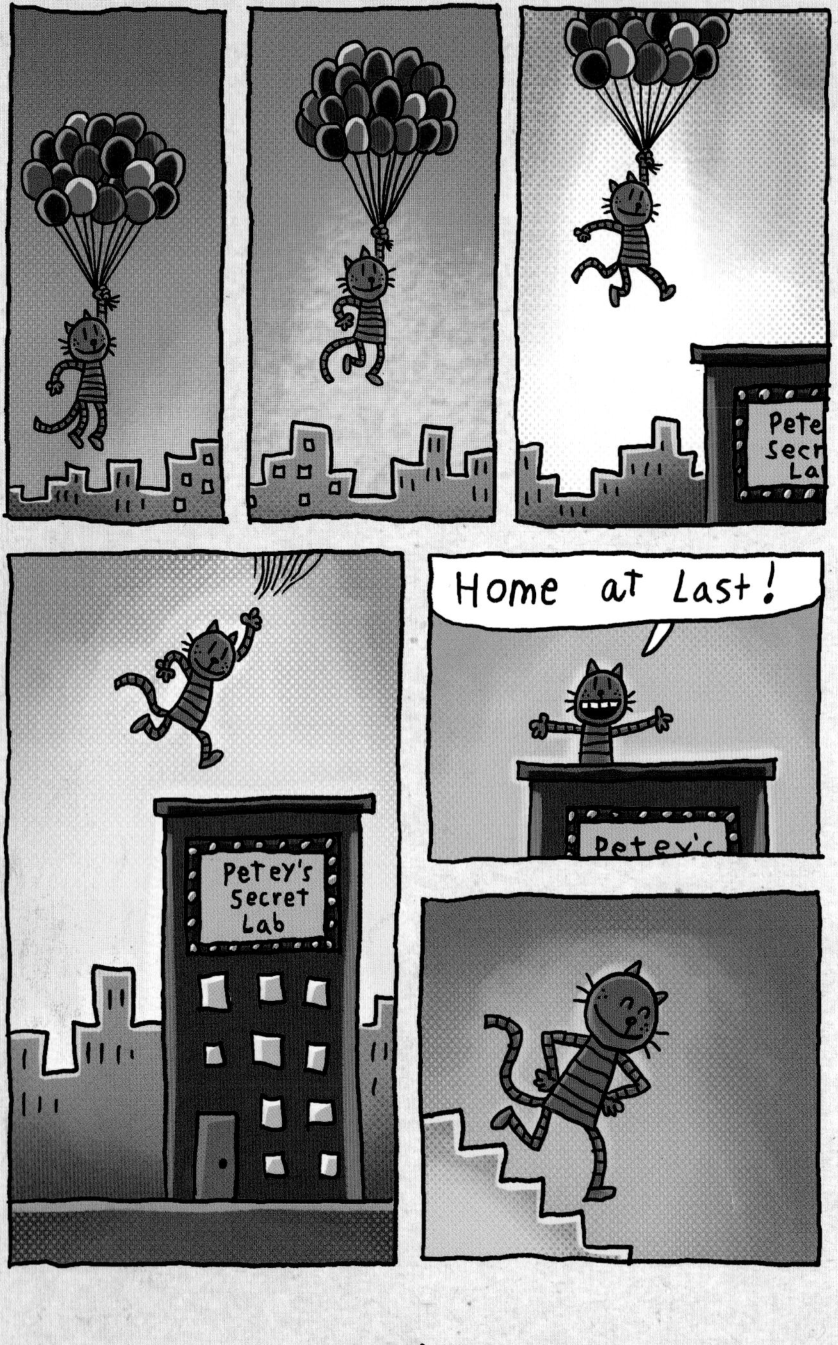
Pete
Secr
La
Petey's
Secret
Lab
Home at Last!
Petey's

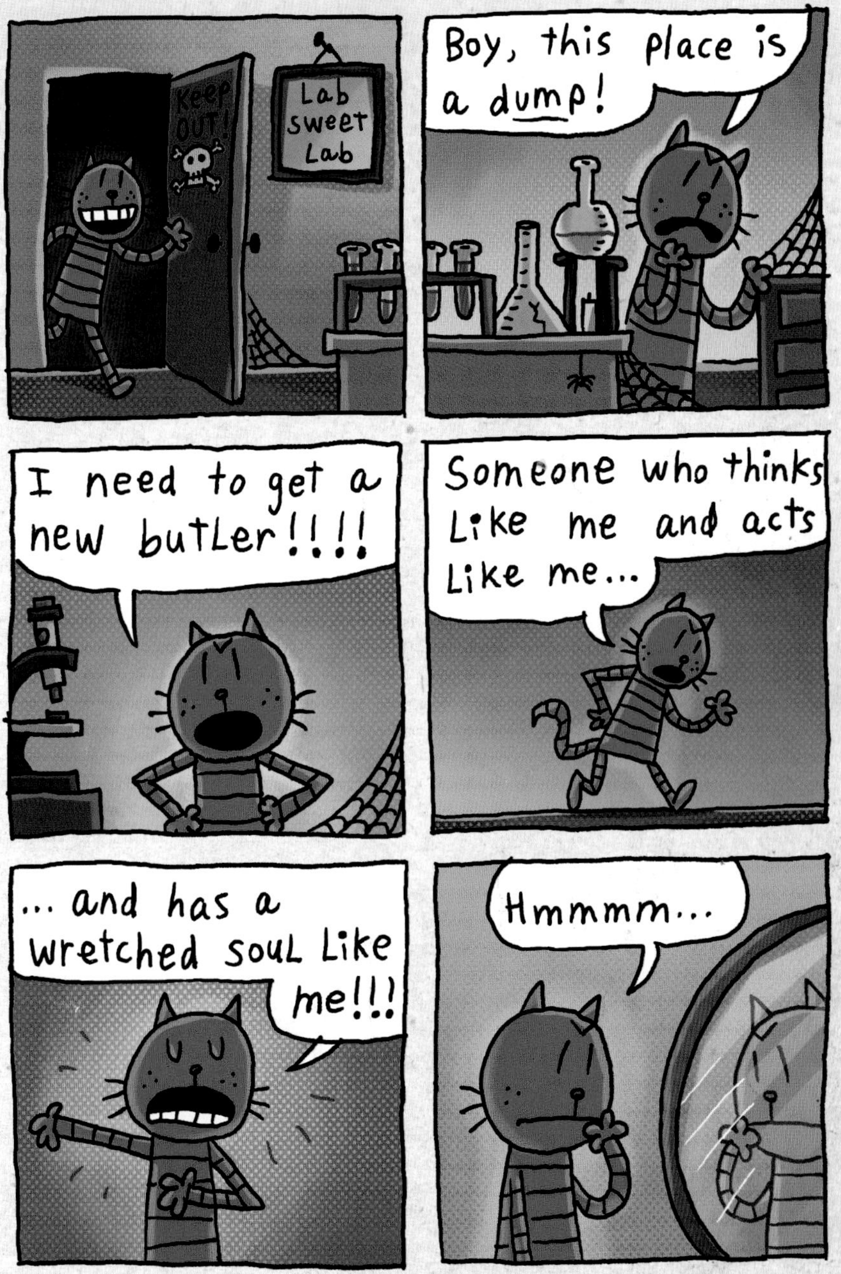
KEEP OUT!
Lab Sweet Lab
Boy, this place is a dump!
I need to get a new butler!!!!
Someone who thinks like me and acts like me...
... and has a wretched soul like me!!!
Hmmmm...

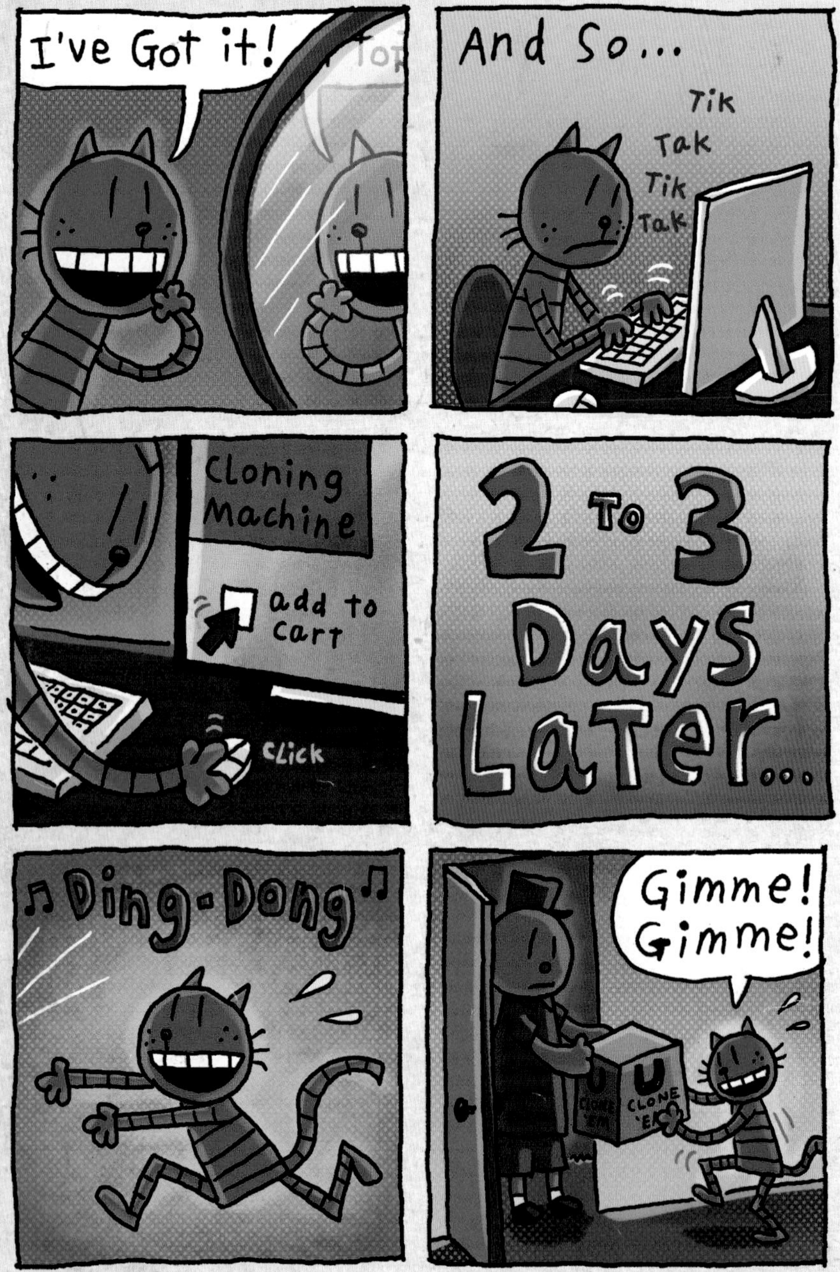
I've Got it!
And So...
Tik
Tak
Tik
Tak
Cloning Machine
add to cart
Click
2 To 3 Days Later...
Ding-Dong
Gimme! Gimme!
CLONE 'EM
U CLONE 'EM

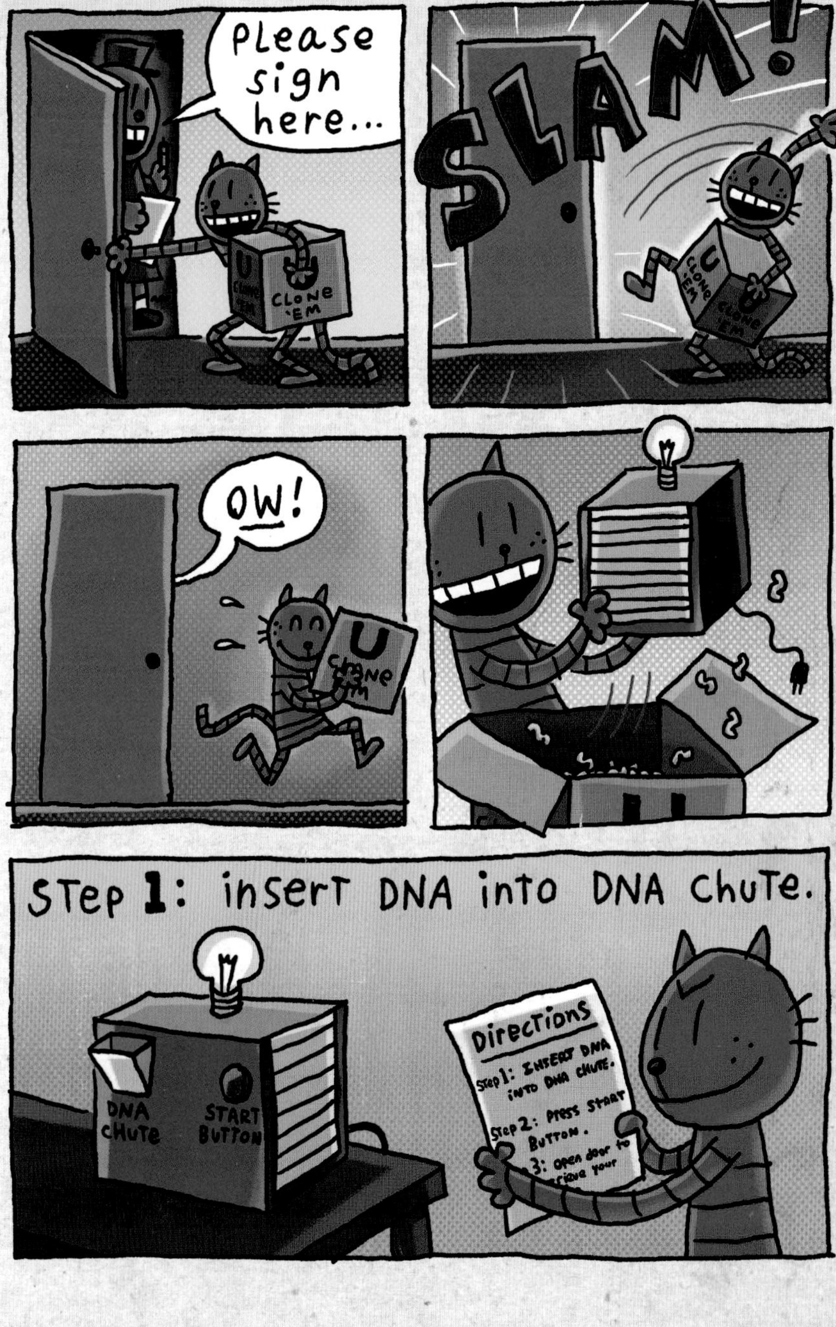
Please sign here...
U CLONE 'EM
SLAM!
OW!
STep 1: inserT DNA into DNA ChuTe.
DNA CHUTE
START BUTTON
DirecTions
Step 1: INSERT DNA INTO DNA CHUTE.
Step 2: Press START BUTTON.

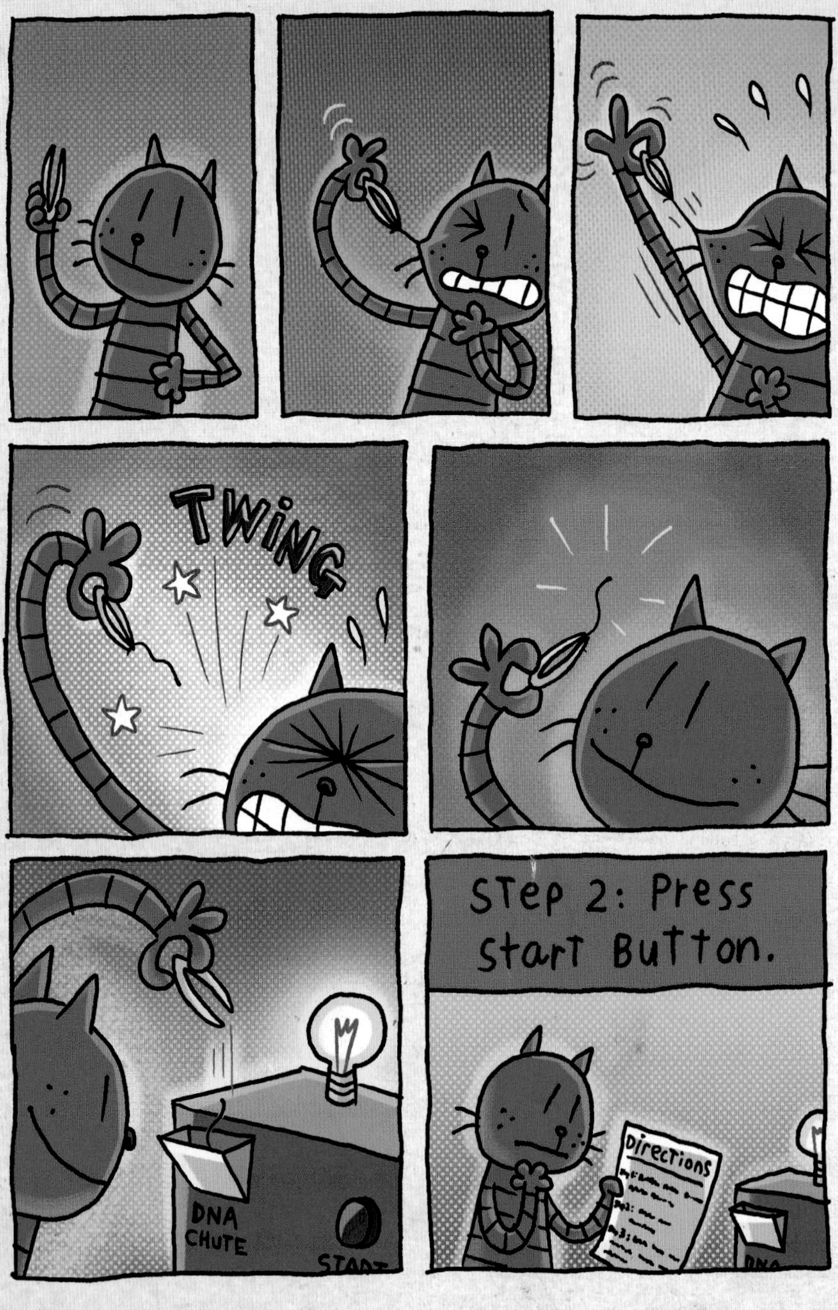
TWiNG
DNA CHUTE
STep 2: Press start Button.
Directions

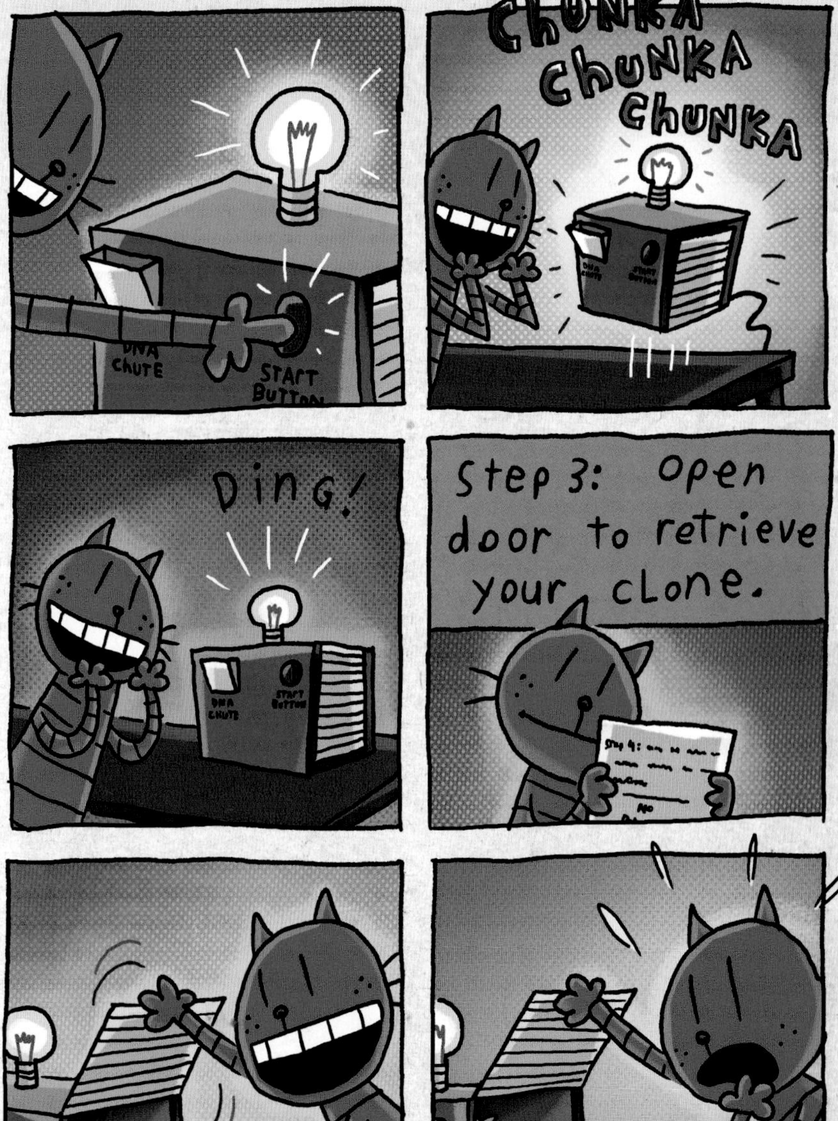
DNA CHUTE
START BUTTON
CHUNKA
CHUNKA
CHUNKA
DING!
Step 3: Open door to retrieve your clone.
START BUTTON

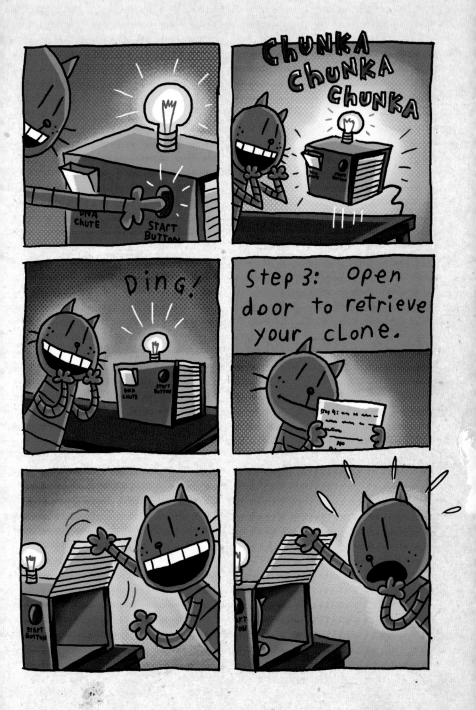

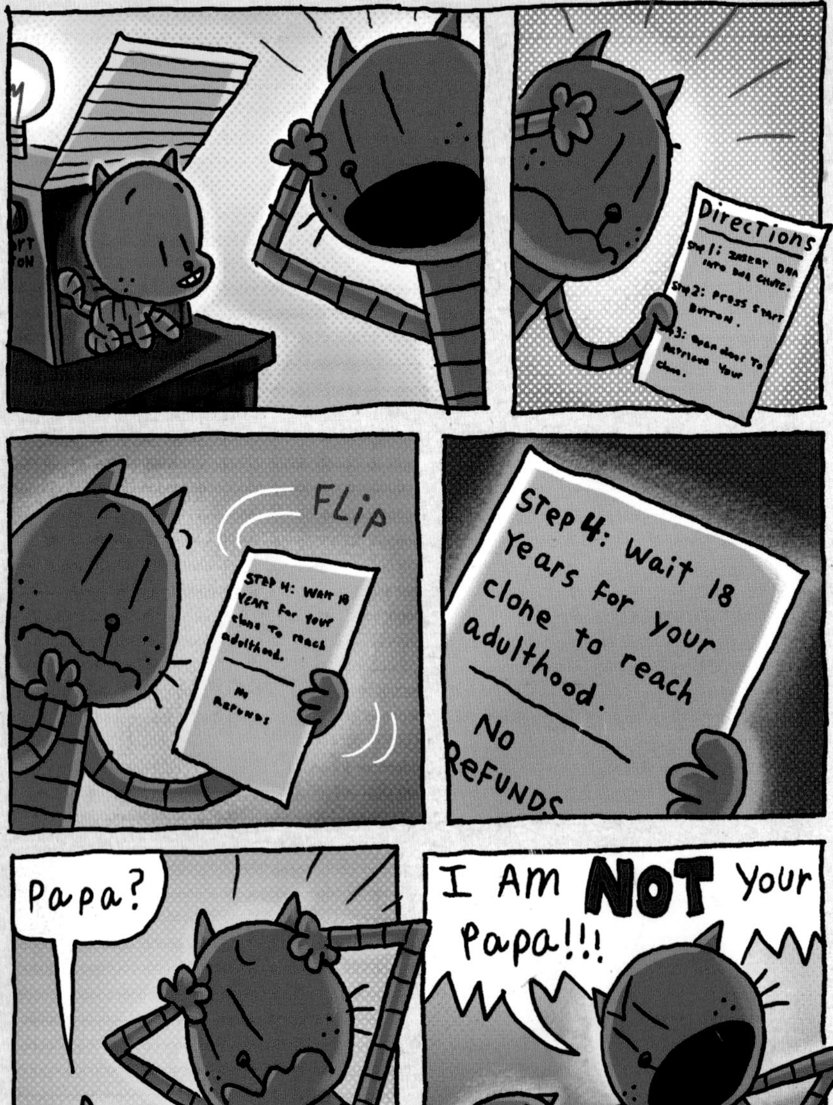

Directions
Step 1: Insert DNA into DNA chute.
Step 2: Press Start Button.
Open door to Retrieve your clone.
FLip
Step 4: Wait 18 Years for your clone to reach adulthood.
No Refunds
Step 4: Wait 18 Years for your clone to reach adulthood.
No ReFUNDS
Papa?
I Am NOT your Papa!!!

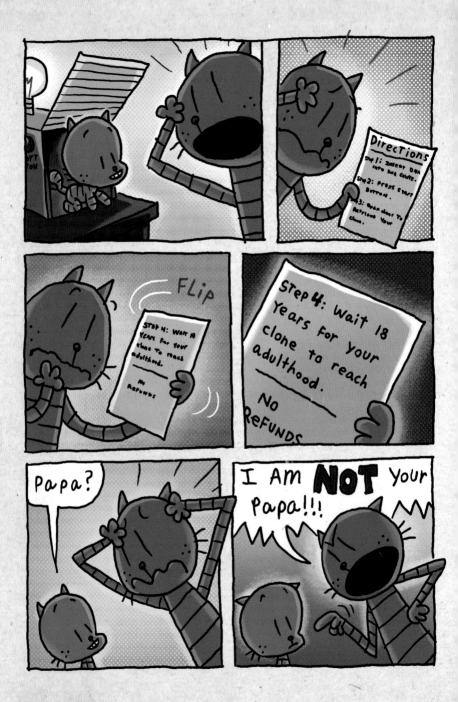

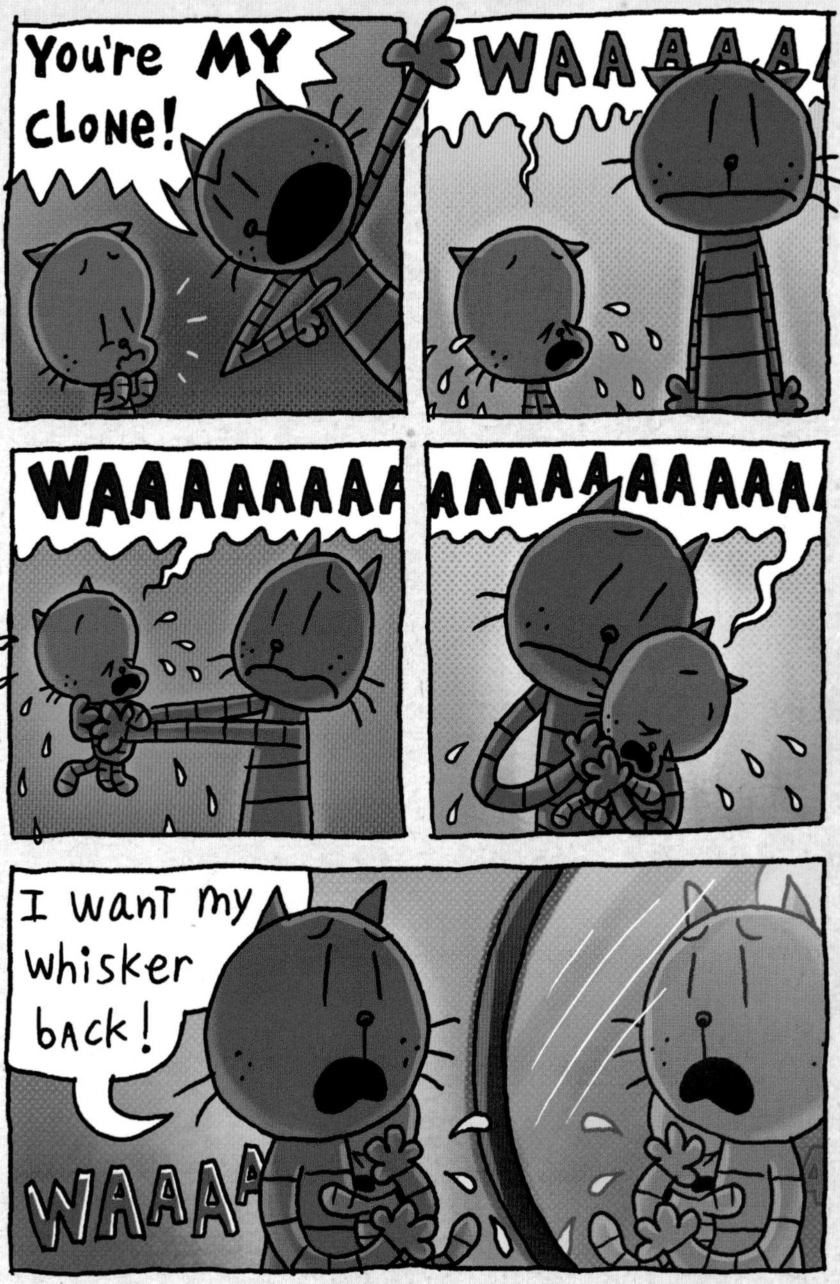
You're MY CLONE!
WAAAAAA
WAAAAAAAAA
AAAAAAAAAA
I WANT my whisker BACK!
WAAAA

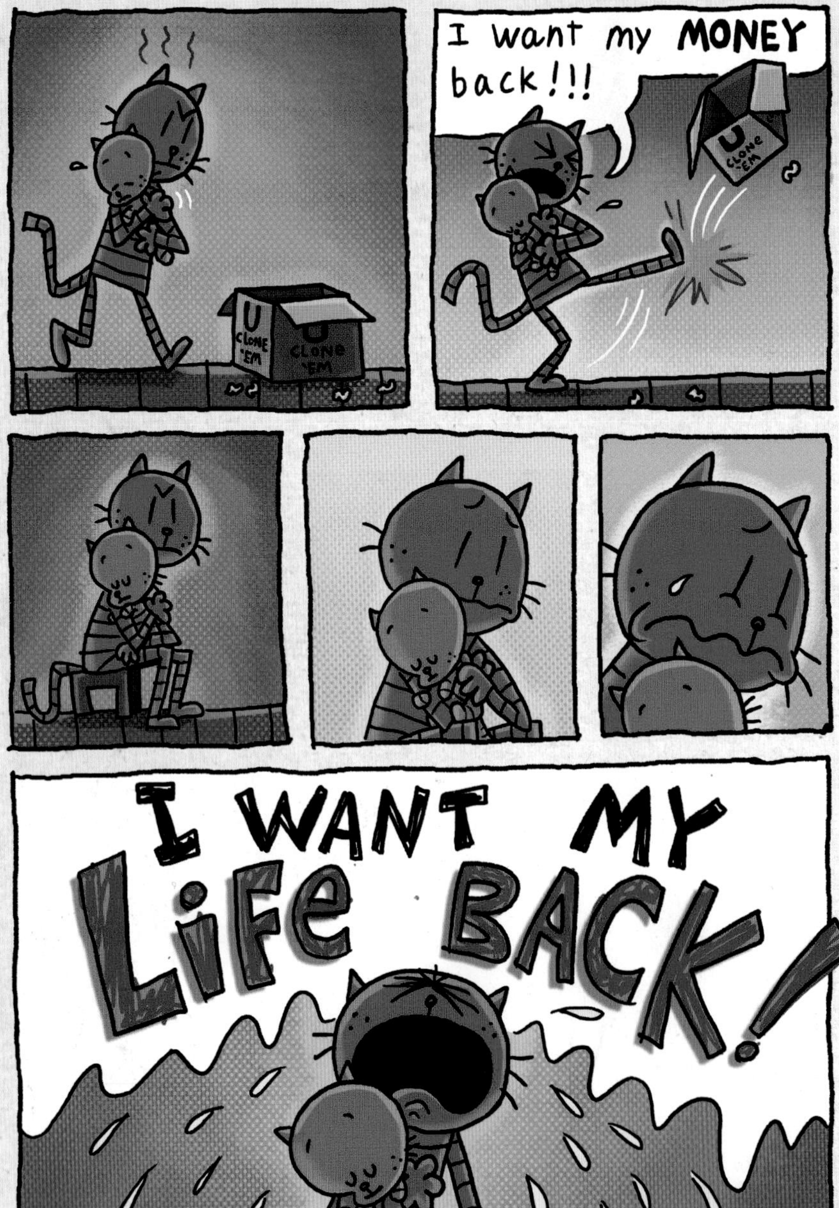
I want my MONEY back!!!
U CLONE 'EM
I WANT MY LIFE BACK!

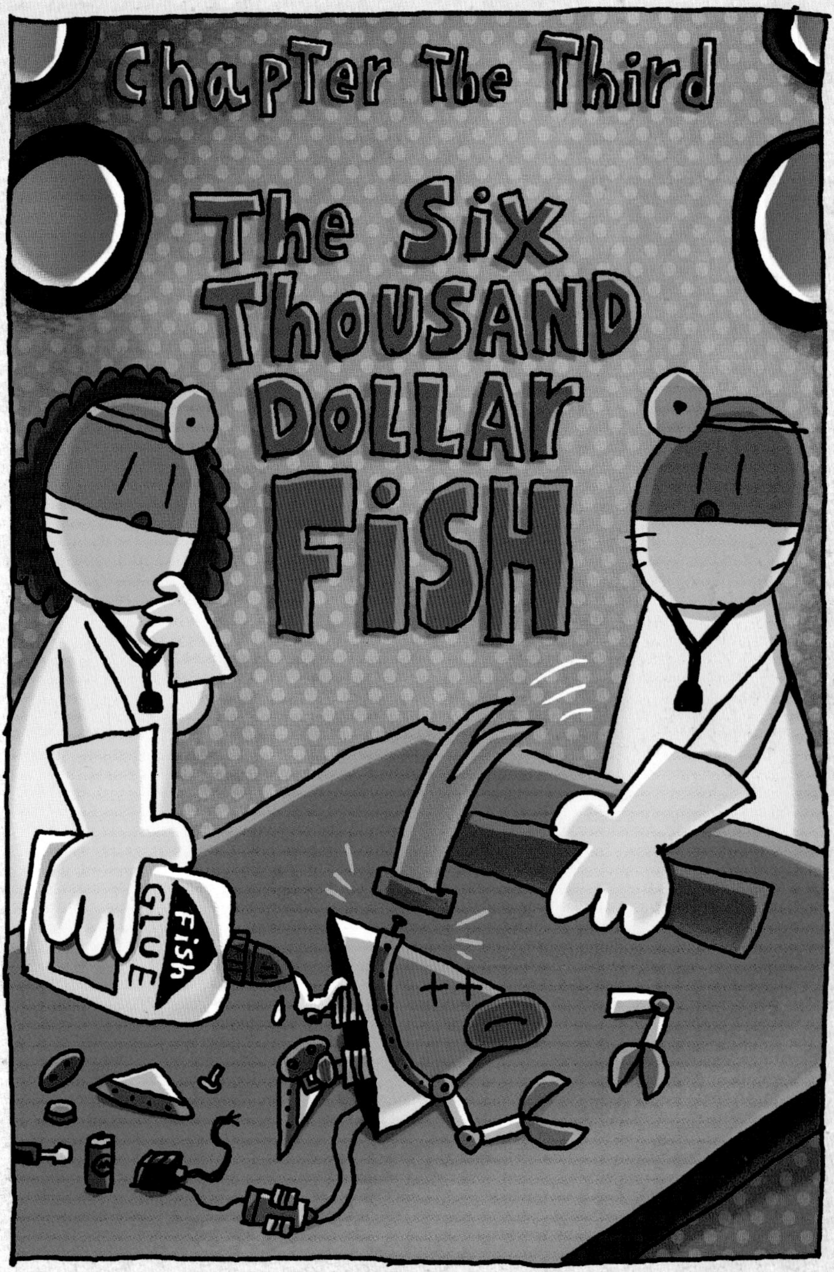
Chapter The Third
The Six Thousand Dollar Fish
Fish GLUE

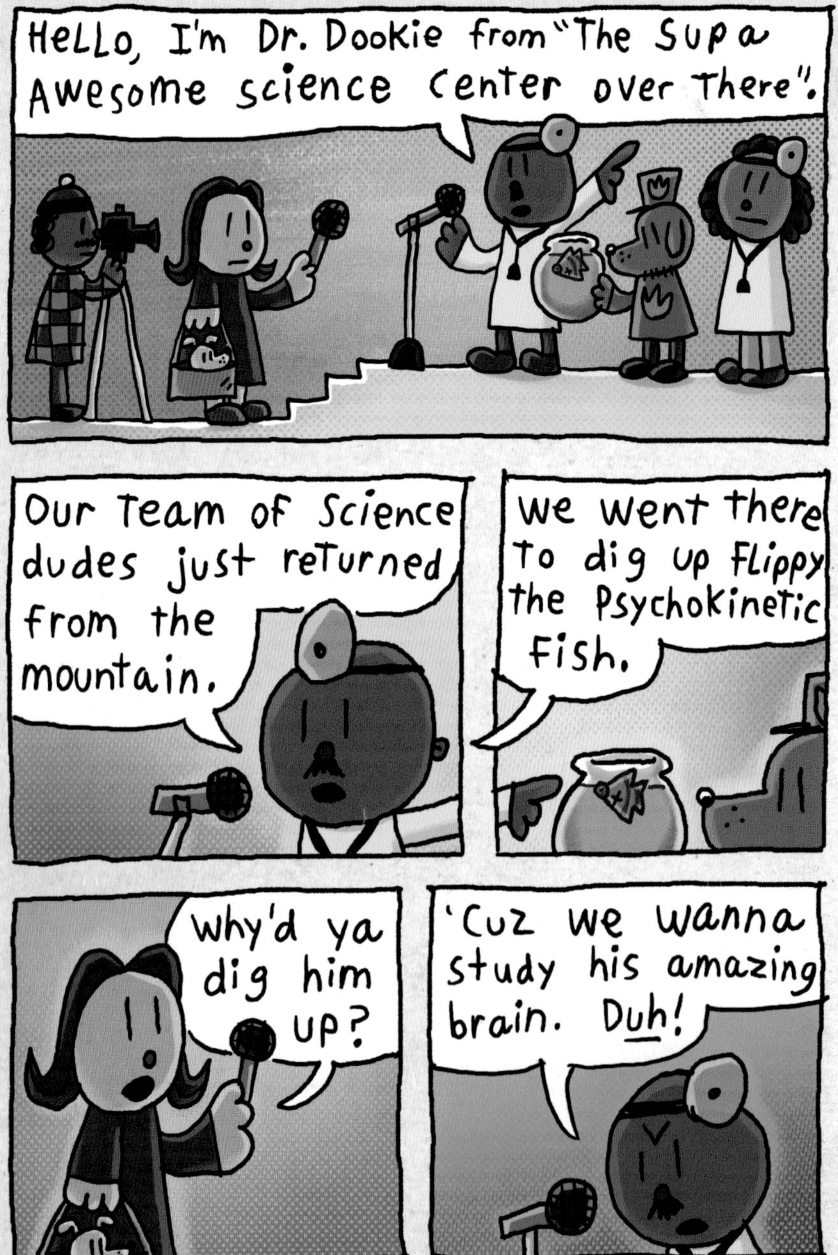

HeLLo, I'm Dr. Dookie from "The Supa Awesome science Center over There".
Our Team of Science dudes just returned from the mountain.
We went there to dig up Flippy the Psychokinetic Fish.
Why'd ya dig him up?
'Cuz we wanna study his amazing brain. Duh!

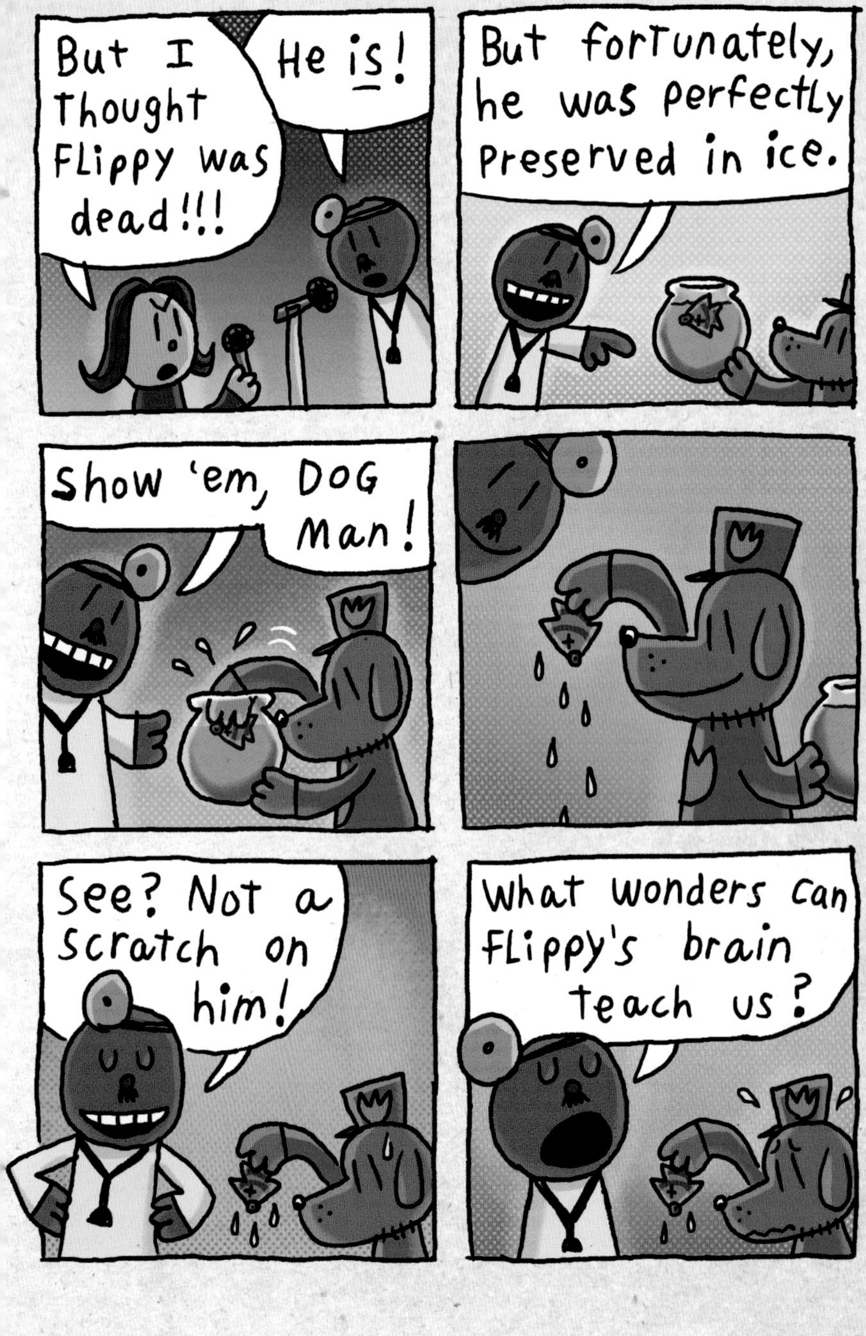
But I Thought Flippy was dead!!!
He is!
But fortunately, he was perfectly preserved in ice.
Show 'em, DOG Man!
See? Not a scratch on him!
What wonders can Flippy's brain teach us?

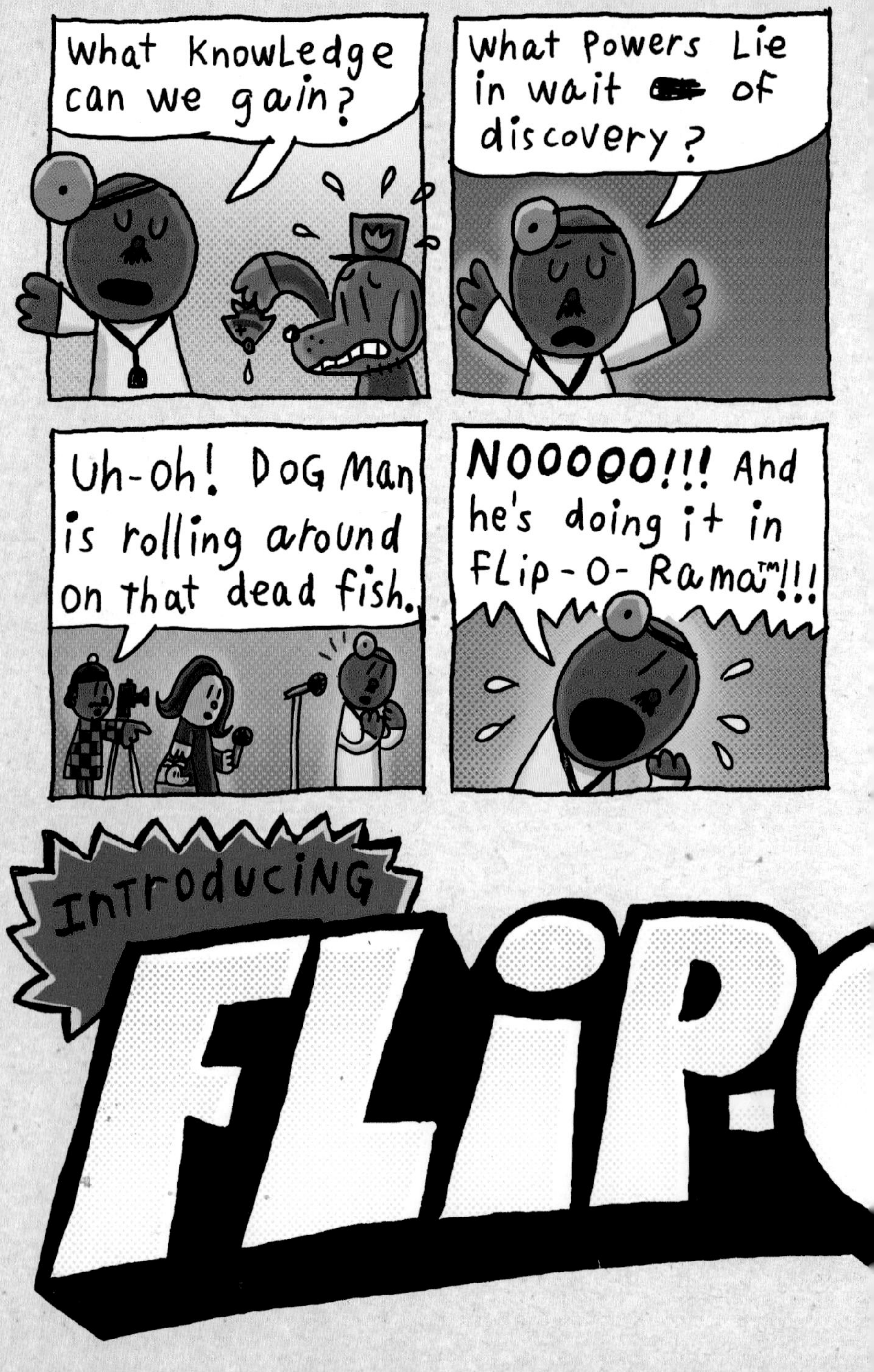
What KnowLedge can we gain?
What Powers Lie in wait of discovery?
Uh-oh! DOG Man is rolling around on that dead fish.
NOOOOO!!! And he's doing it in FLip-O-Rama™!!!
Introducing
FLIP

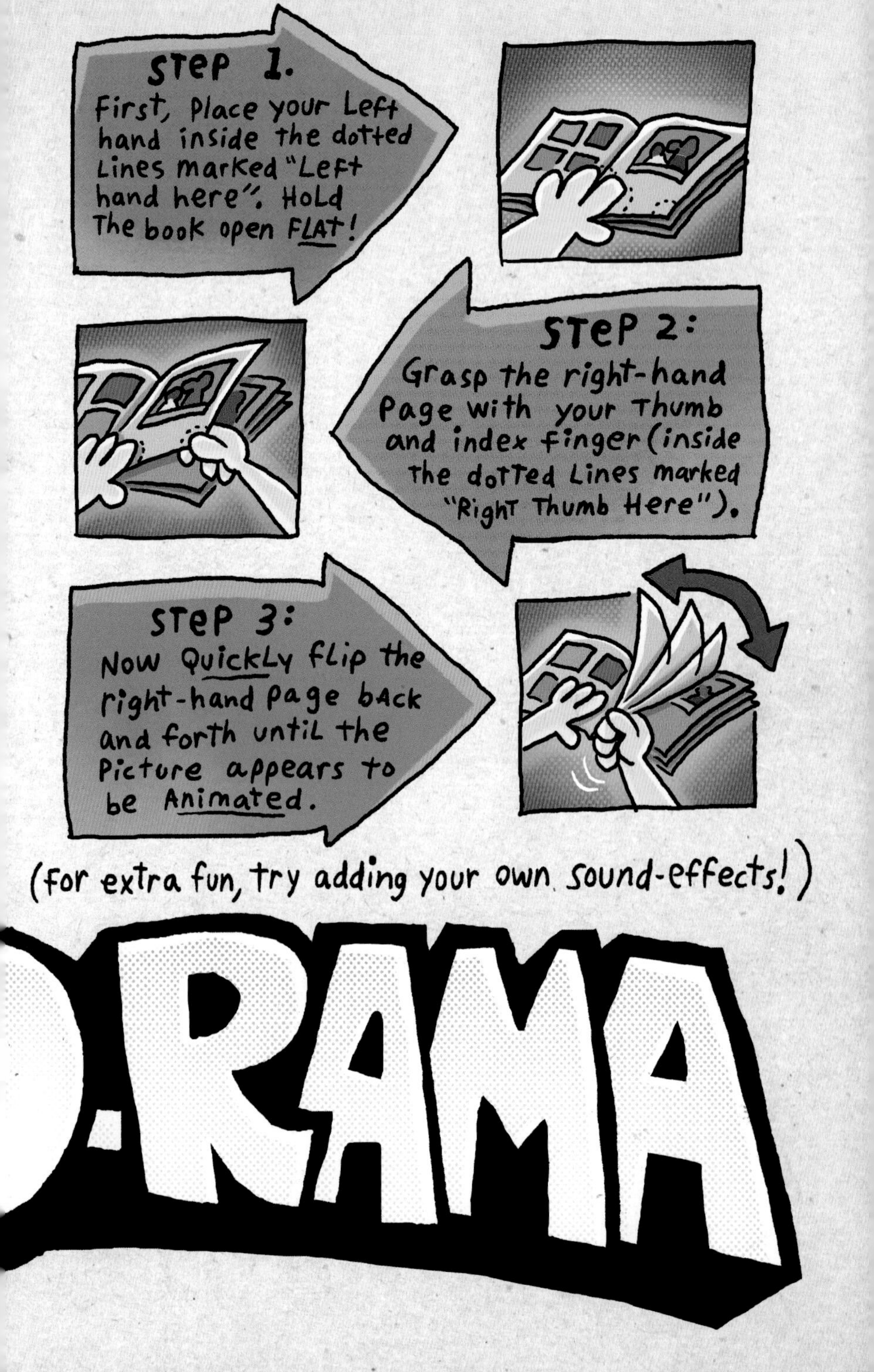
STEP 1.
First, Place your Left hand inside the dotted Lines marked "Left hand here". HoLd The book open FLAT!
STEP 2:
Grasp the right-hand Page with your Thumb and index finger (inside the dotted Lines marked "Right Thumb Here").
STEP 3:
Now QUICKLY fLip the right-hand Page back and forth until the Picture appears to be Animated.
(For extra fun, try adding your own sound-effects!)
.RAMA

Remember,

while you are flipping,
be sure you can see
the image on page **43**
AND the image on page **45**.

If you flip QUICKLY,
the two pictures will
start to look like
one **ANIMATED** cartoon!

Don't forget to
add your own
sound-effects!

Left
hand here.

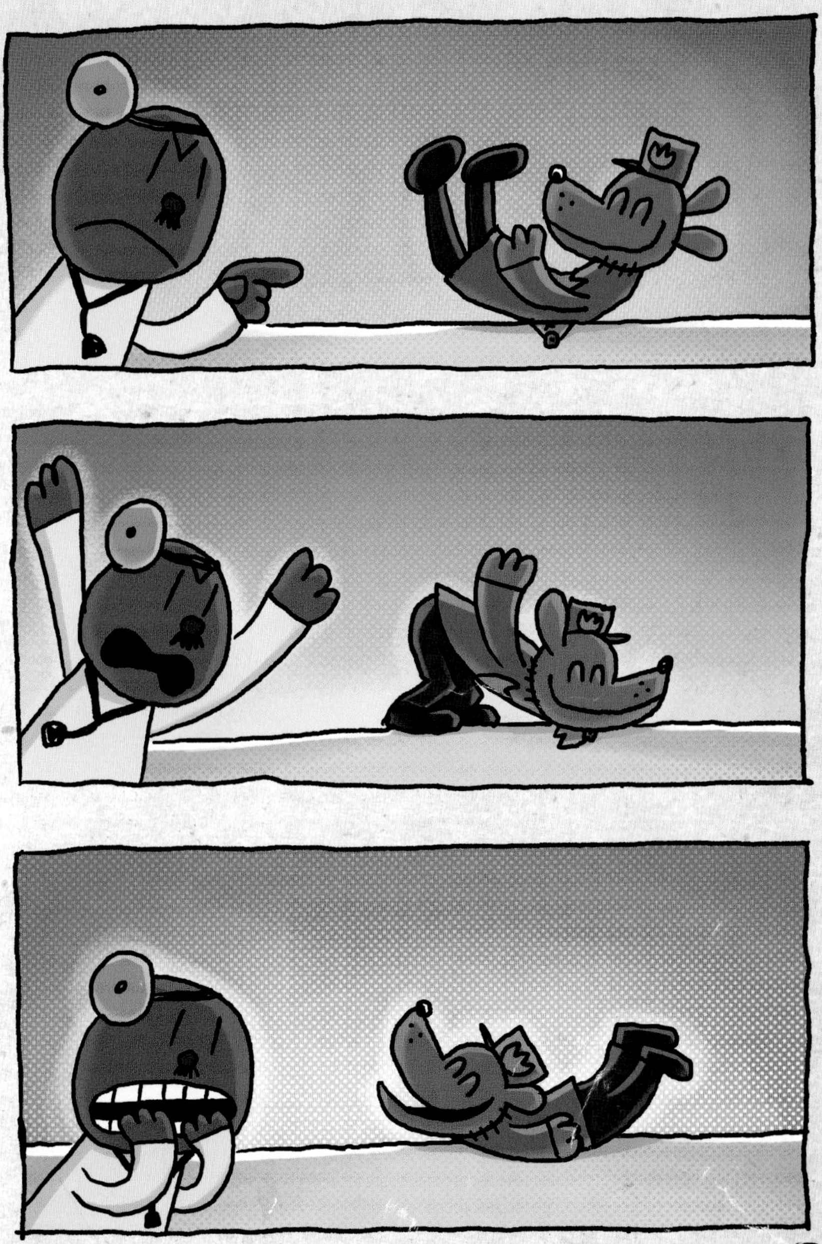

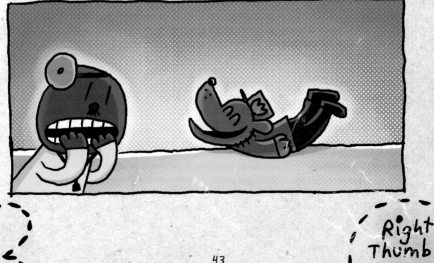

Right Thumb here.

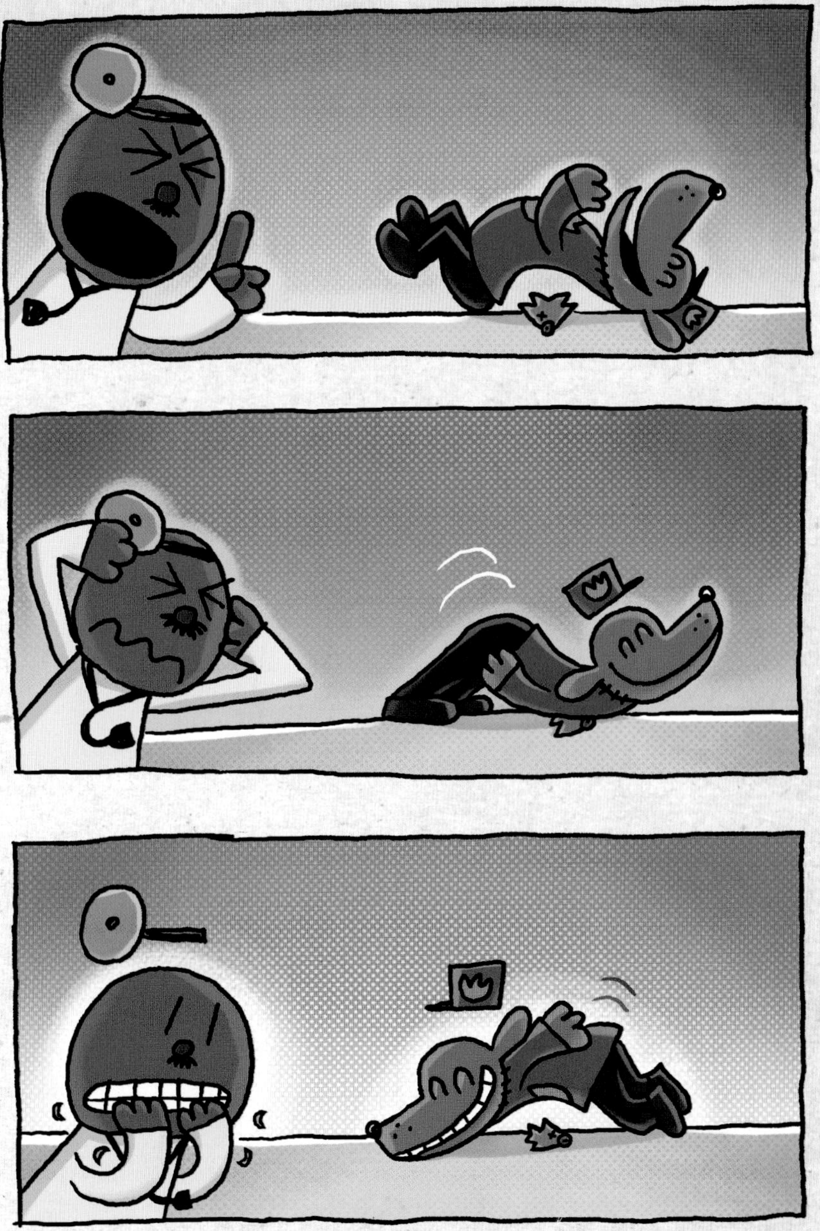

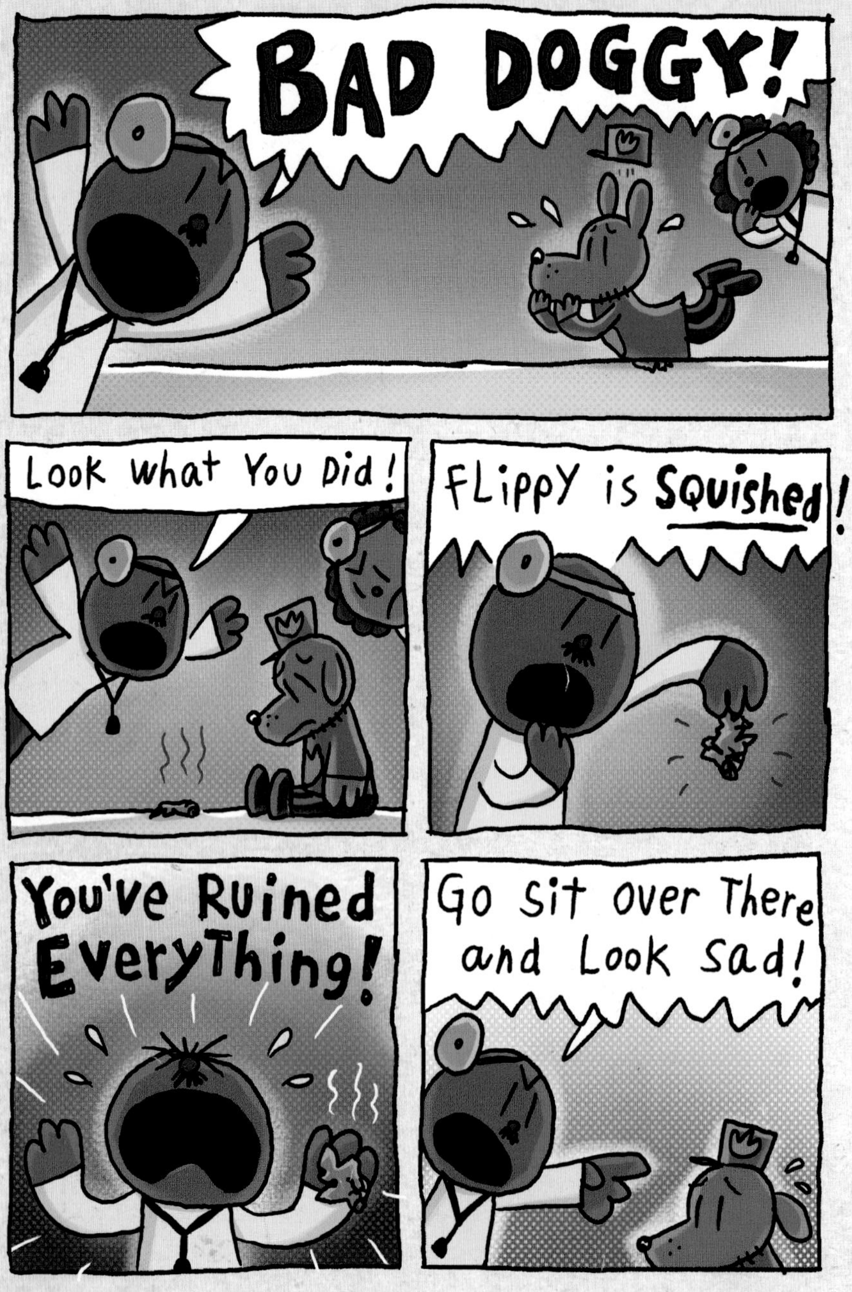
BAD DOGGY!
Look What You Did!
FLippy is Squished!
You've Ruined EveryThing!
Go Sit over There and Look Sad!

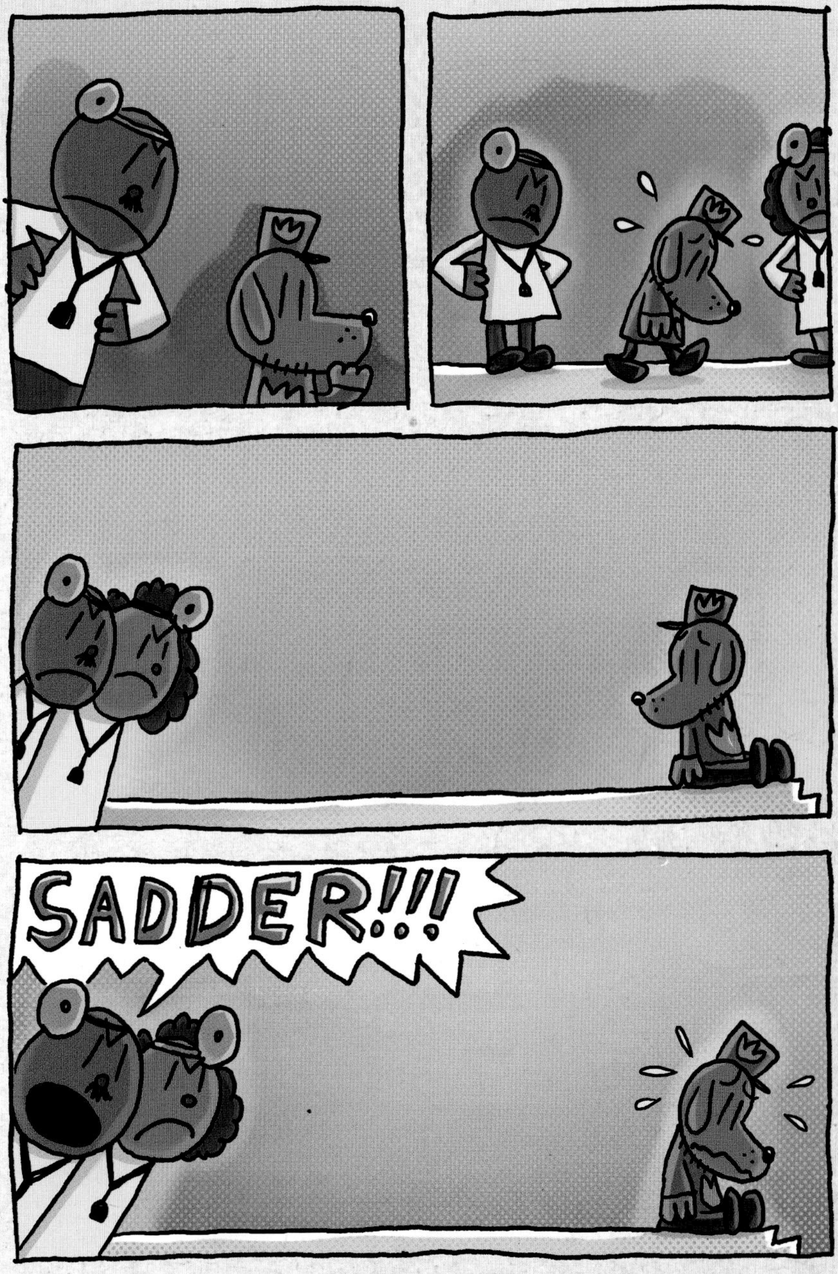
SADDER!!!

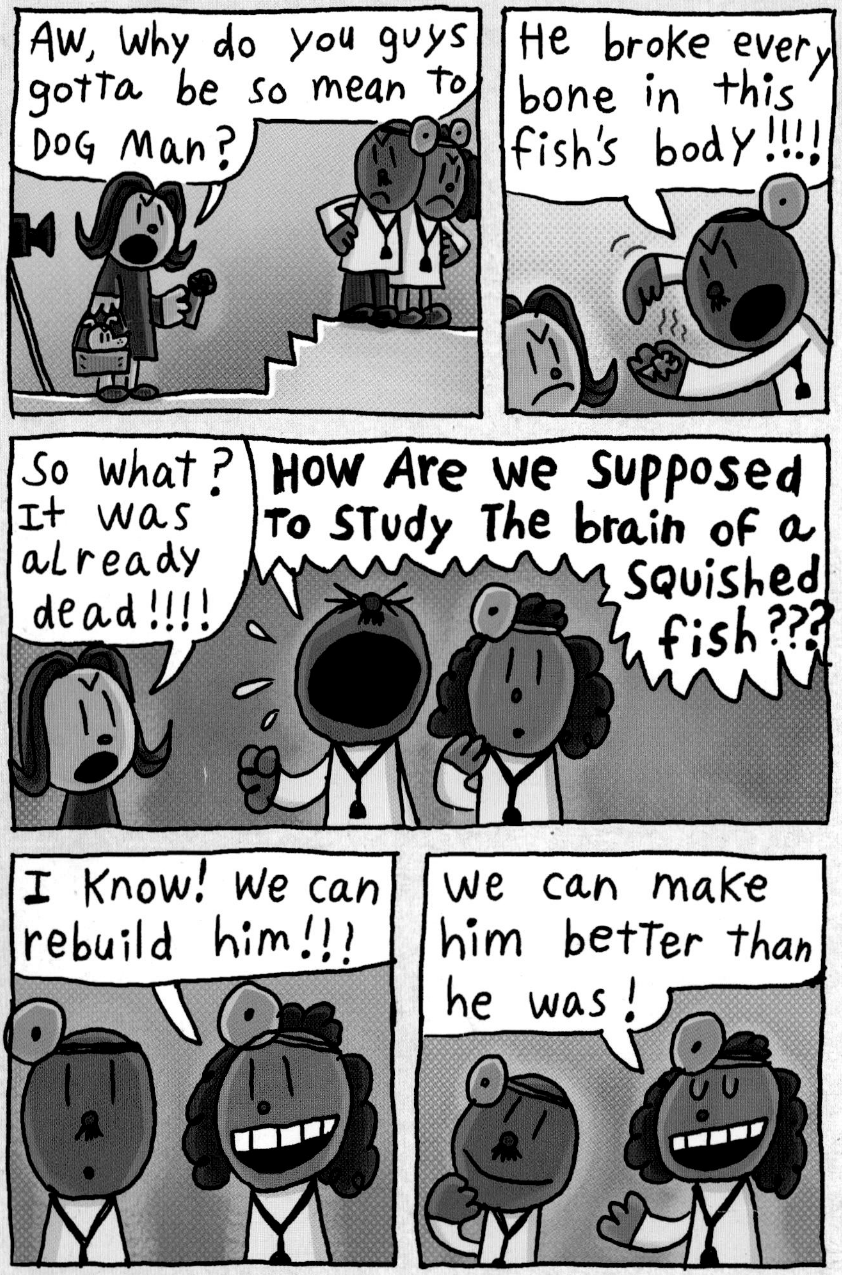
AW, Why do you guys gotta be so mean to DOG Man?
He broke every bone in this fish's body!!!!
So what? It was already dead!!!!
HOW Are we Supposed To STudy The brain of a SQUished fish???
I Know! We can rebuild him!!!
We can make him better than he was!

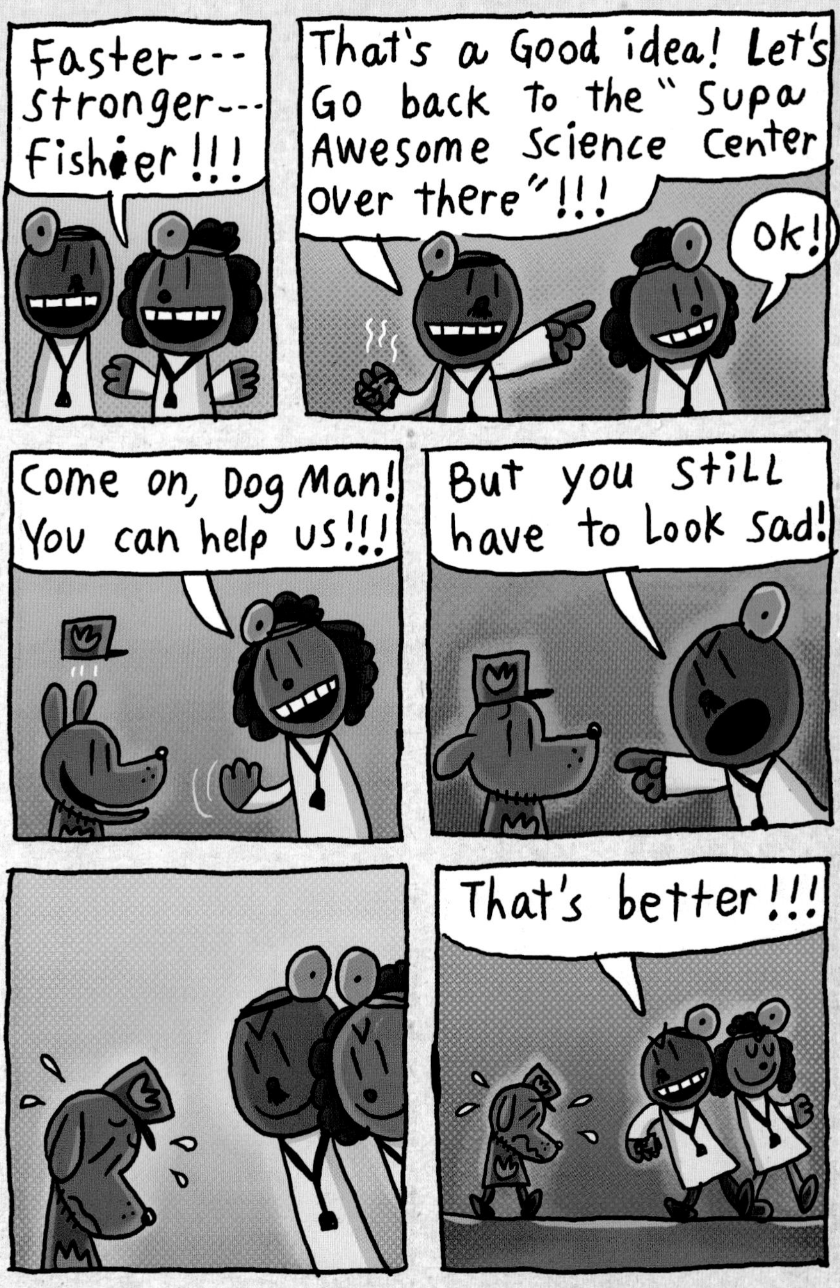
Faster--- Stronger--- Fishier!!!
That's a Good idea! Let's Go back to the "Supa Awesome Science Center over there"!!!
Ok!
Come on, Dog Man! You can help us!!!
But you STILL have to Look sad!
That's better!!!

THE SUPA AWESOME SCIENCE CENTER OVER THERE

Soon, the scientists had a big operation.

They replaced all of Flippy's broken bones...

...with bionics!

Flippy was now more machine than fish.

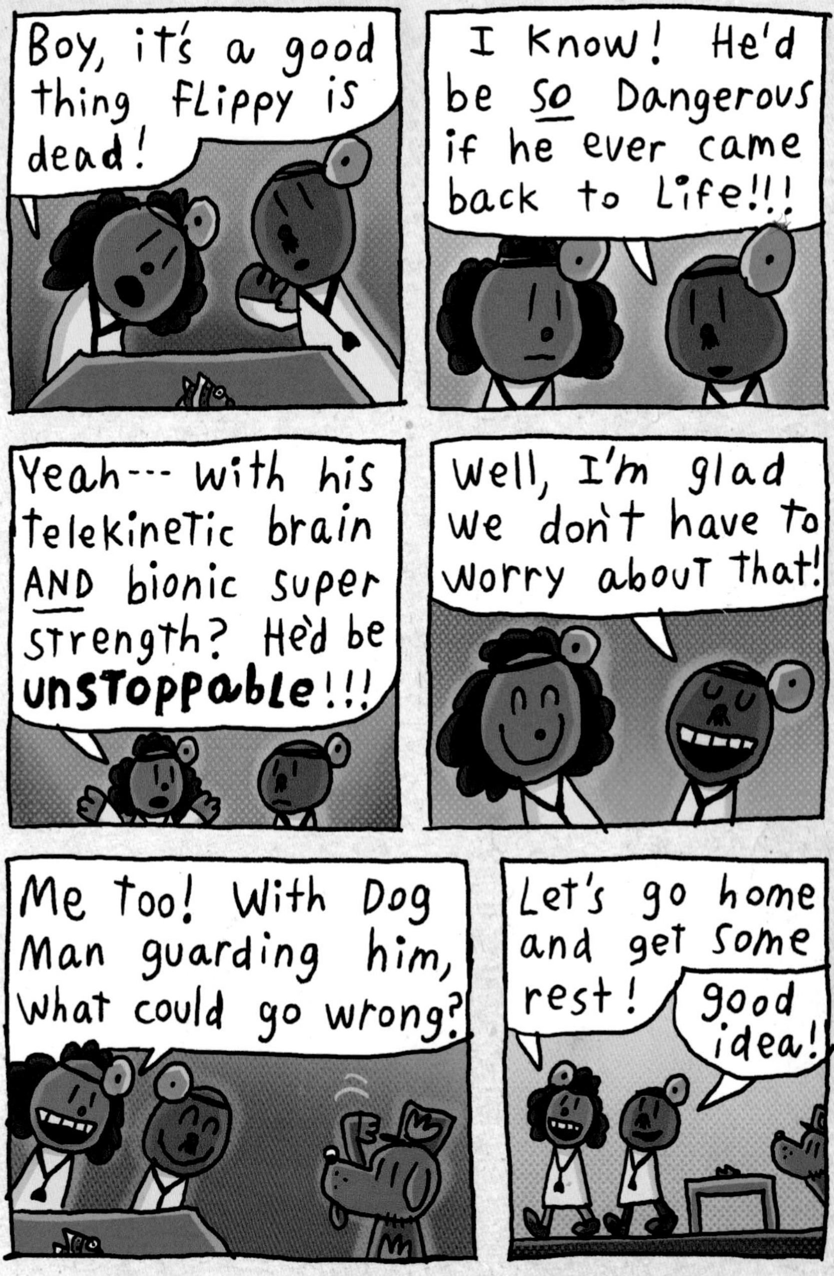

Boy, it's a good thing Flippy is dead!
I know! He'd be SO Dangerous if he ever came back to Life!!!
Yeah--- with his telekinetic brain AND bionic super strength? He'd be UNSTOPPABLE!!!
Well, I'm glad we don't have to worry about that!
Me too! With Dog Man guarding him, What could go wrong?
Let's go home and get some rest!
good idea!

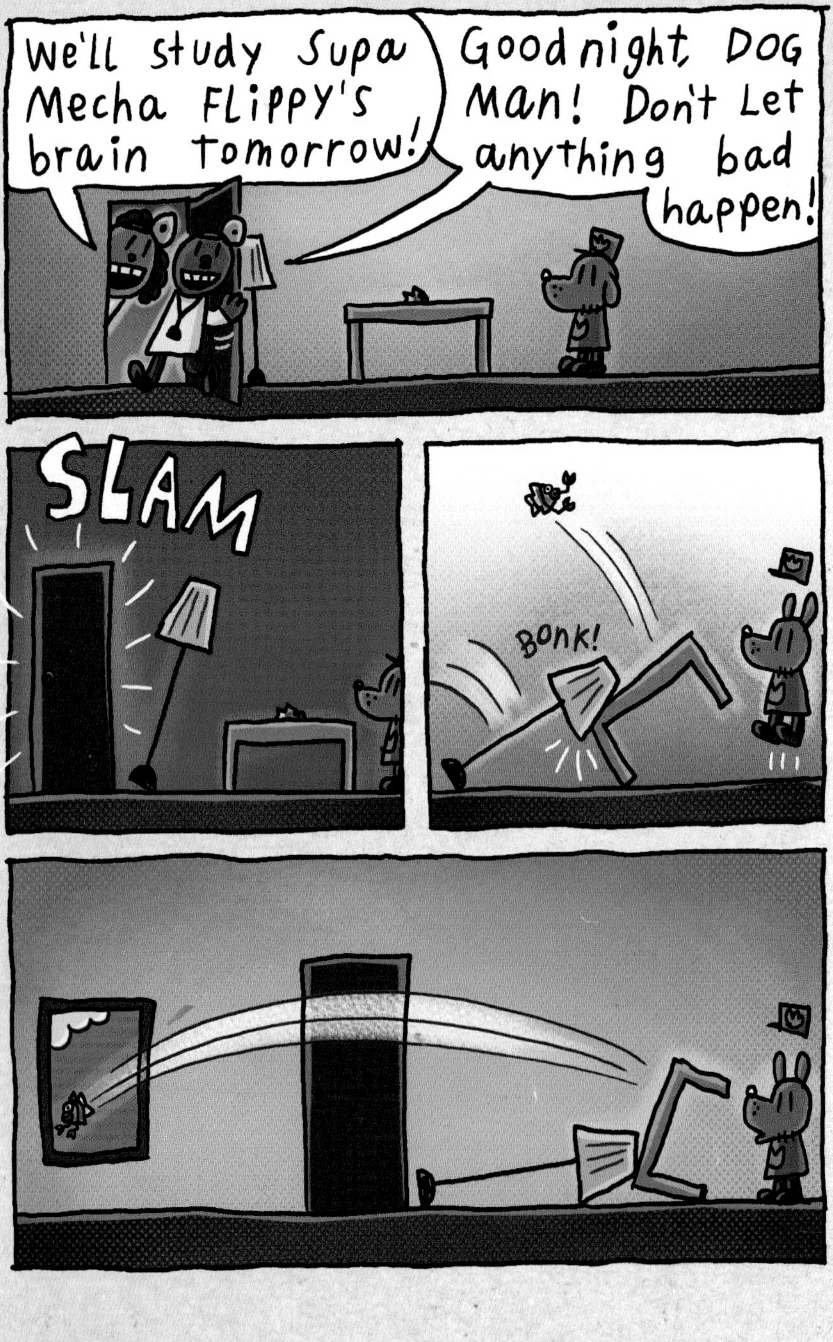
We'll study Supa Mecha Flippy's brain tomorrow!
Goodnight, Dog Man! Don't let anything bad happen!
SLAM
BONK!

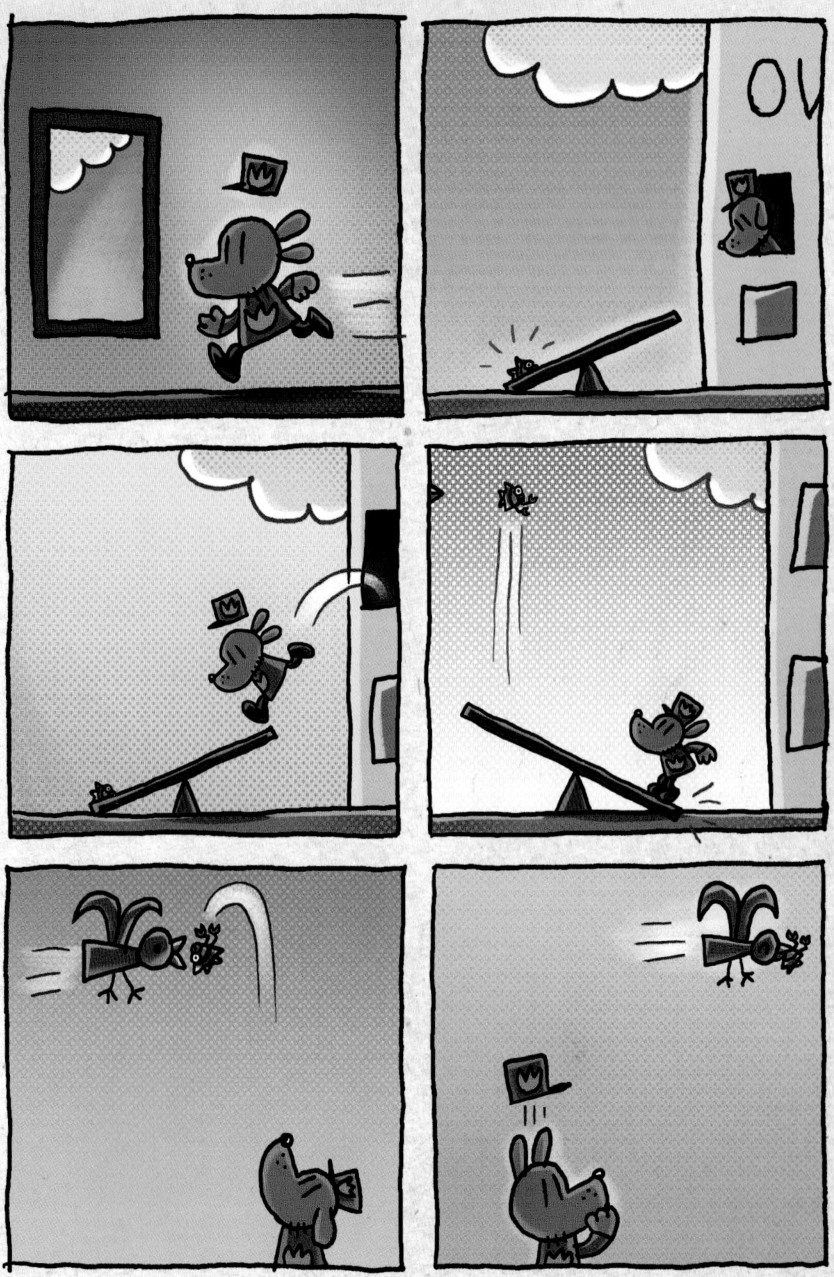
OV

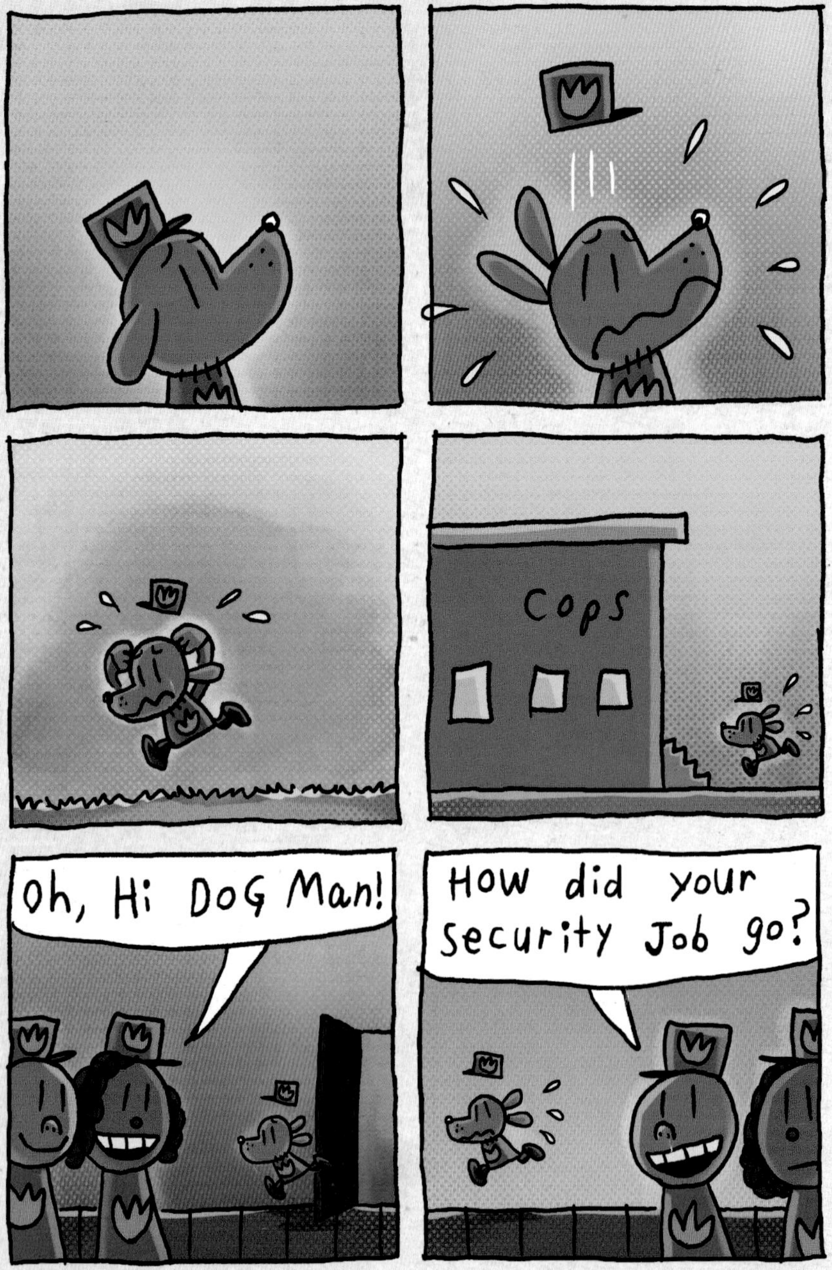
Cops
Oh, Hi DOG Man!
How did your security Job go?

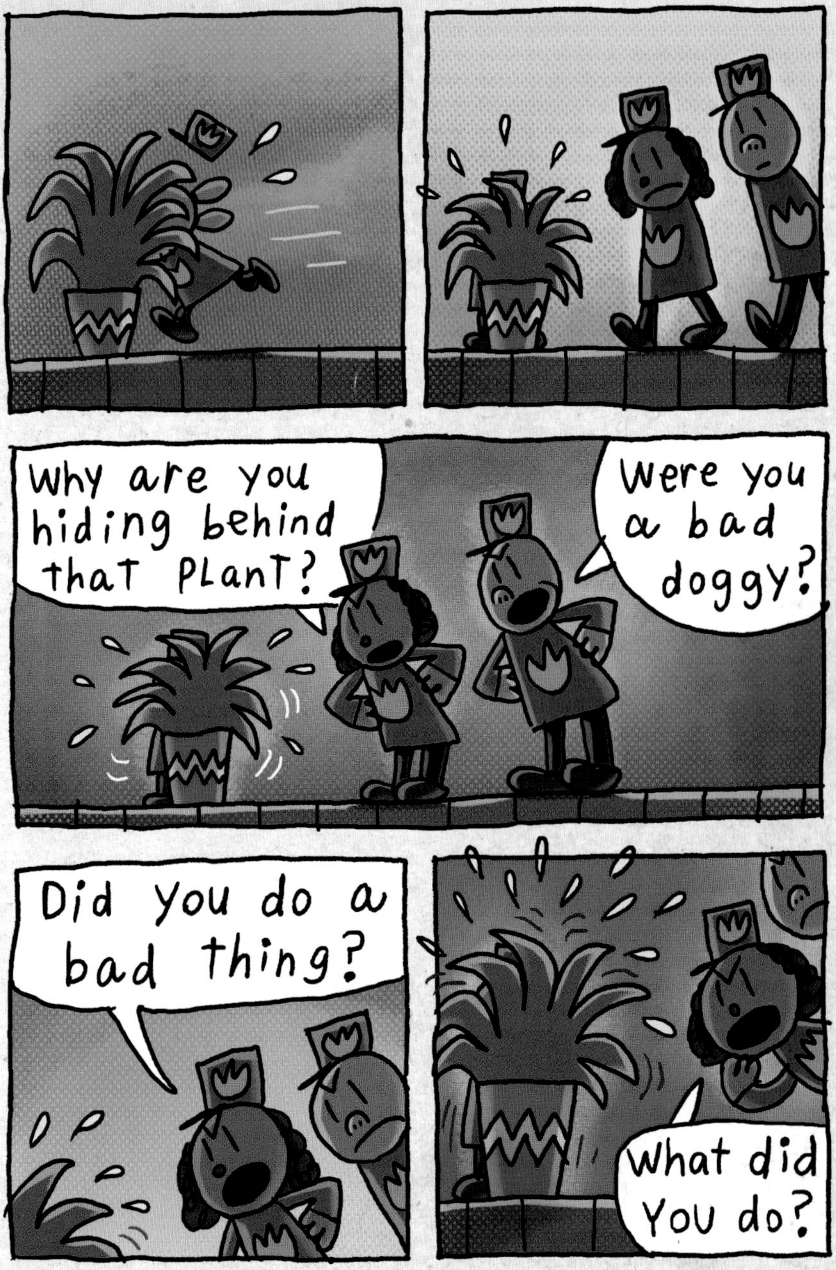
Why are you hiding behind that PLanT?
Were you a bad doggy?
Did you do a bad thing?
What did You do?

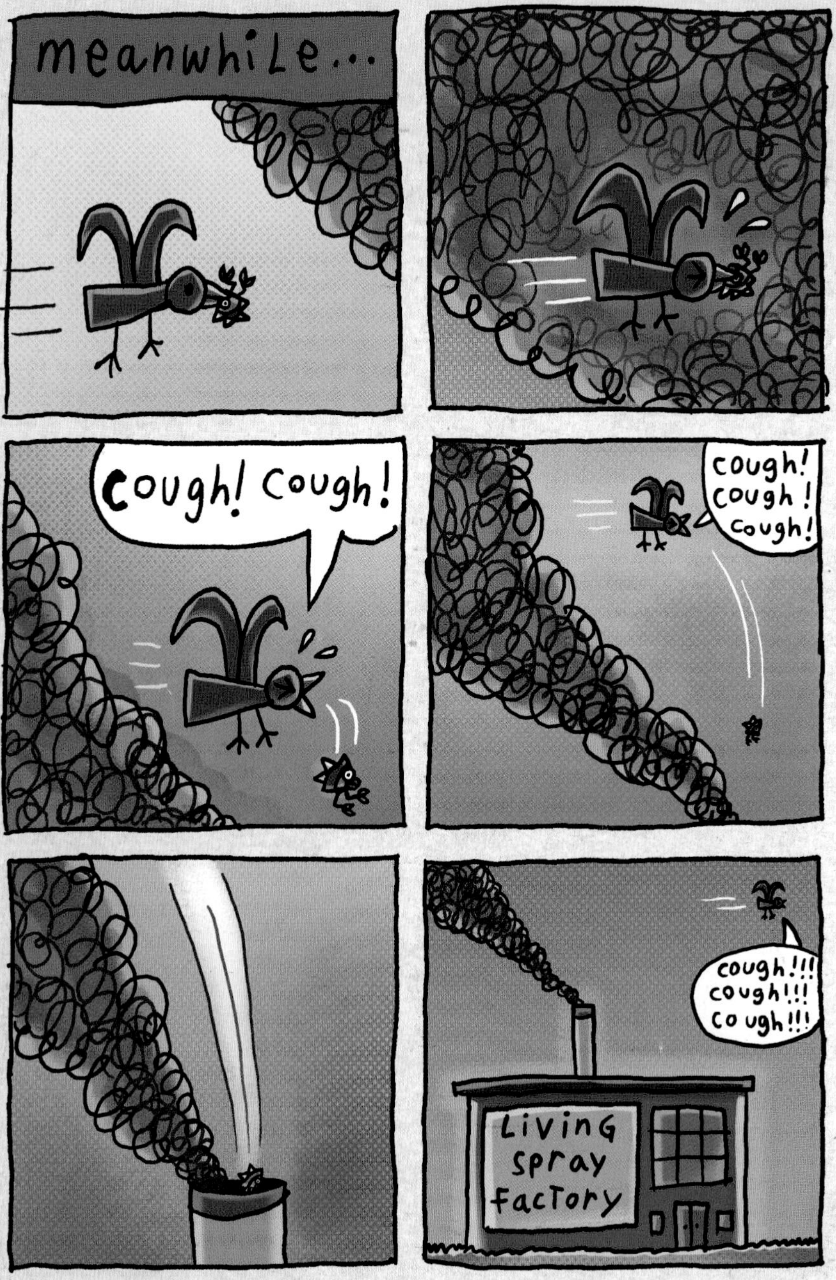
meanwhiLe...
Cough! cough!
cough!
cough!
cough!
cough!!!
cough!!!
cough!!!
Living
spray
factory

Chapter the Fourth

No More Kitten Around!

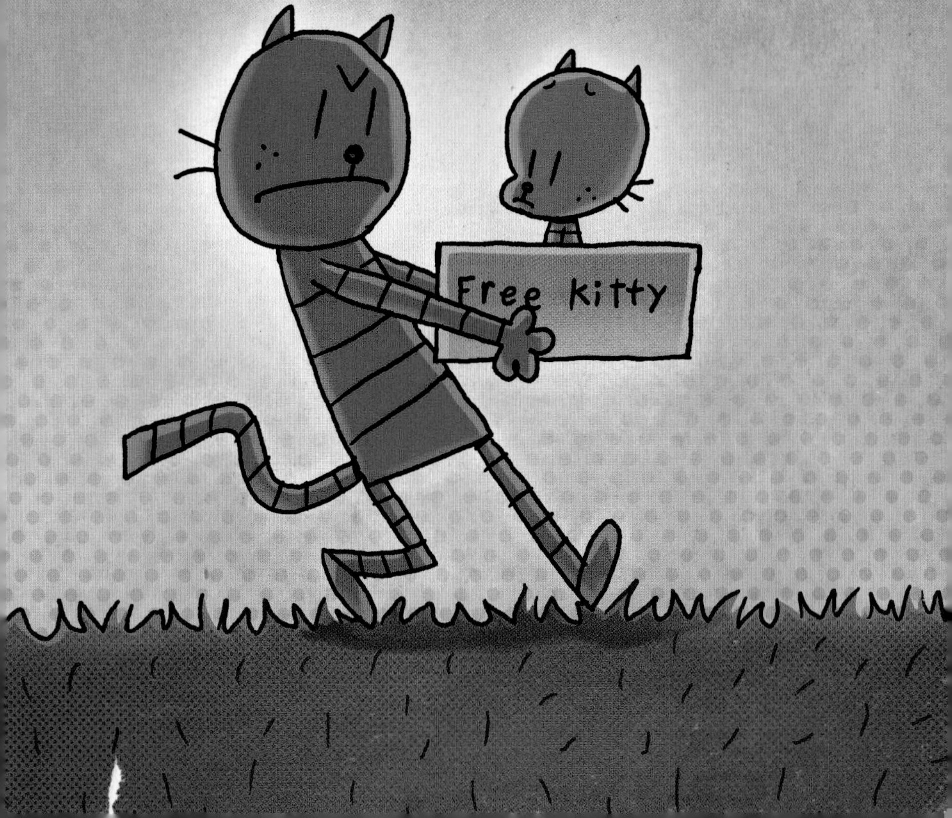
Free kitty

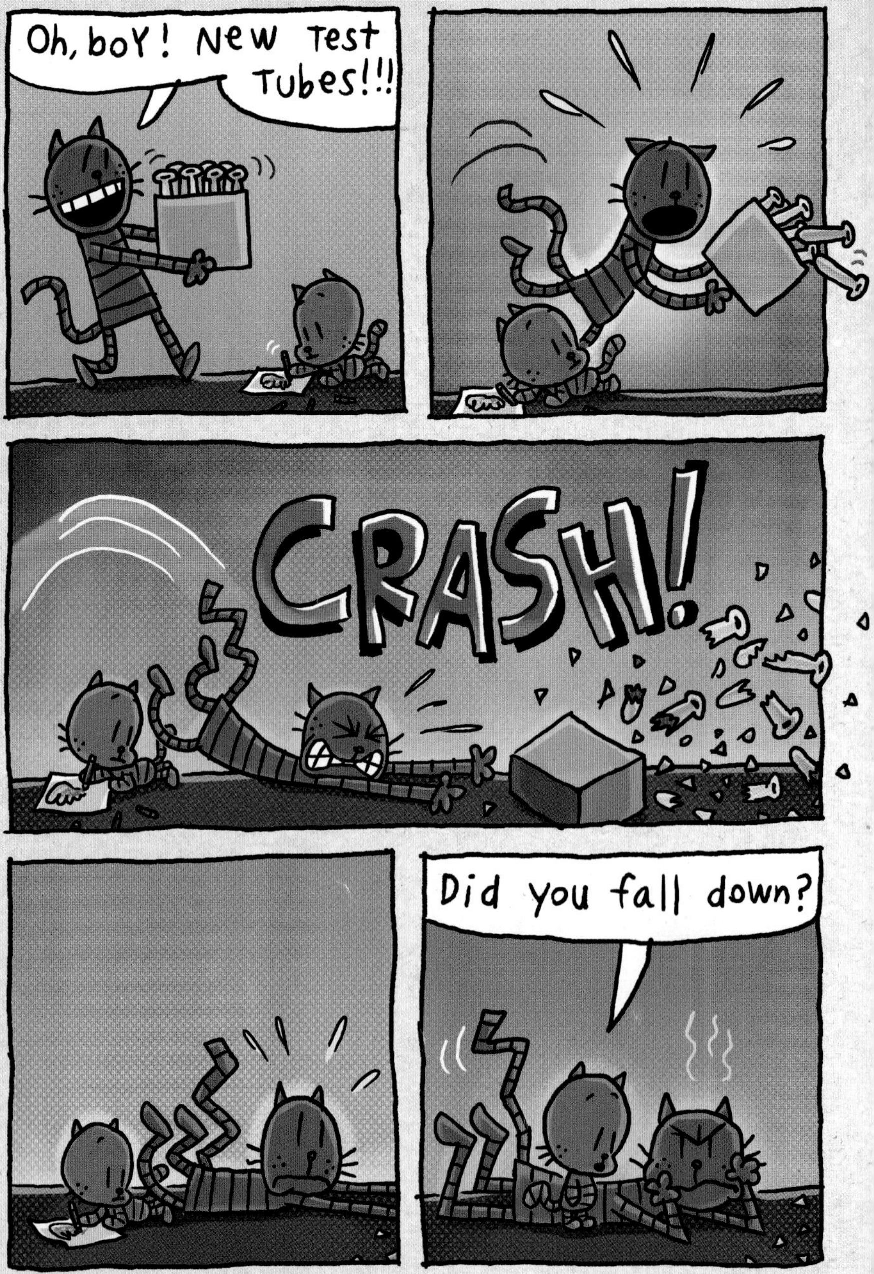
Oh, boY! New Test Tubes!!!
CRASH!
Did you fall down?

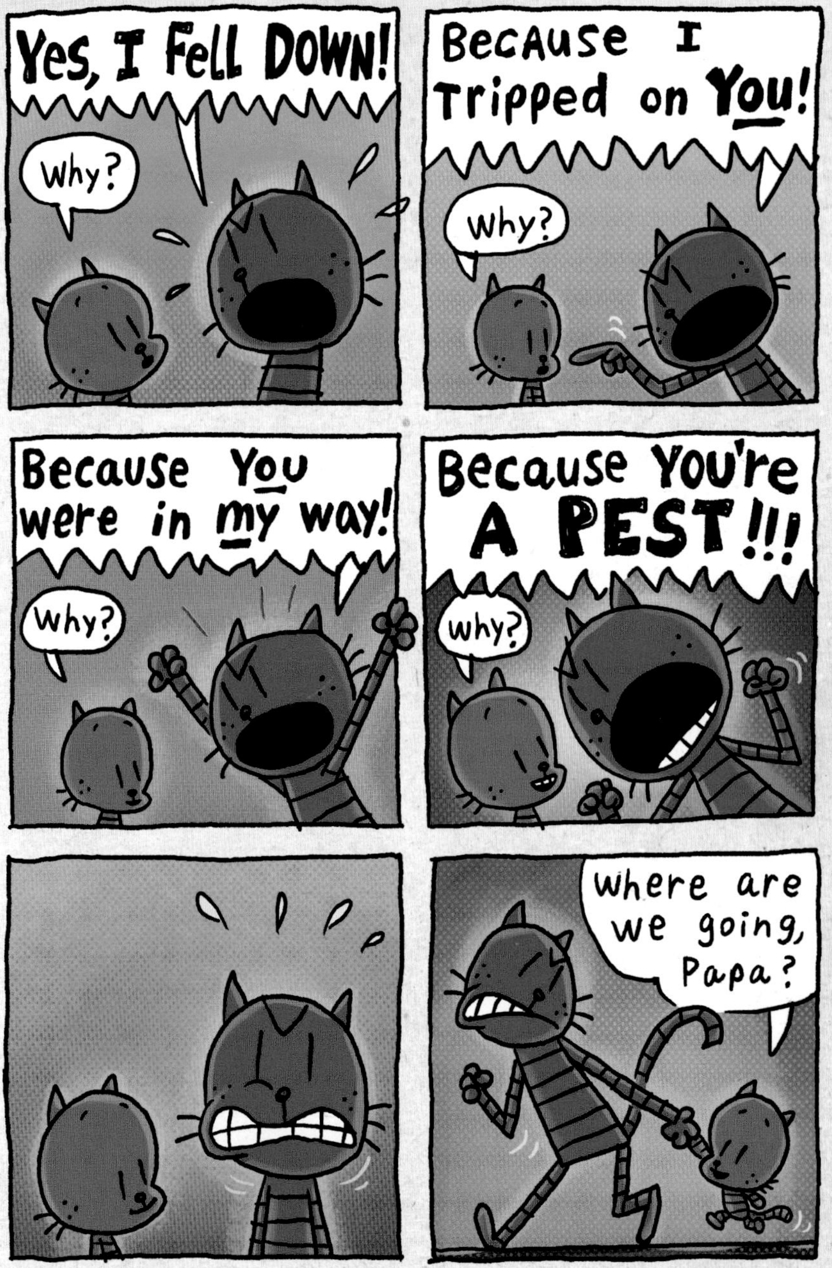

Yes, I Fell DOWN!
Why?
Because I Tripped on You!
Why?
Because You were in my way!
Why?
Because You're A PEST!!!
Why?
Where are we going, Papa?

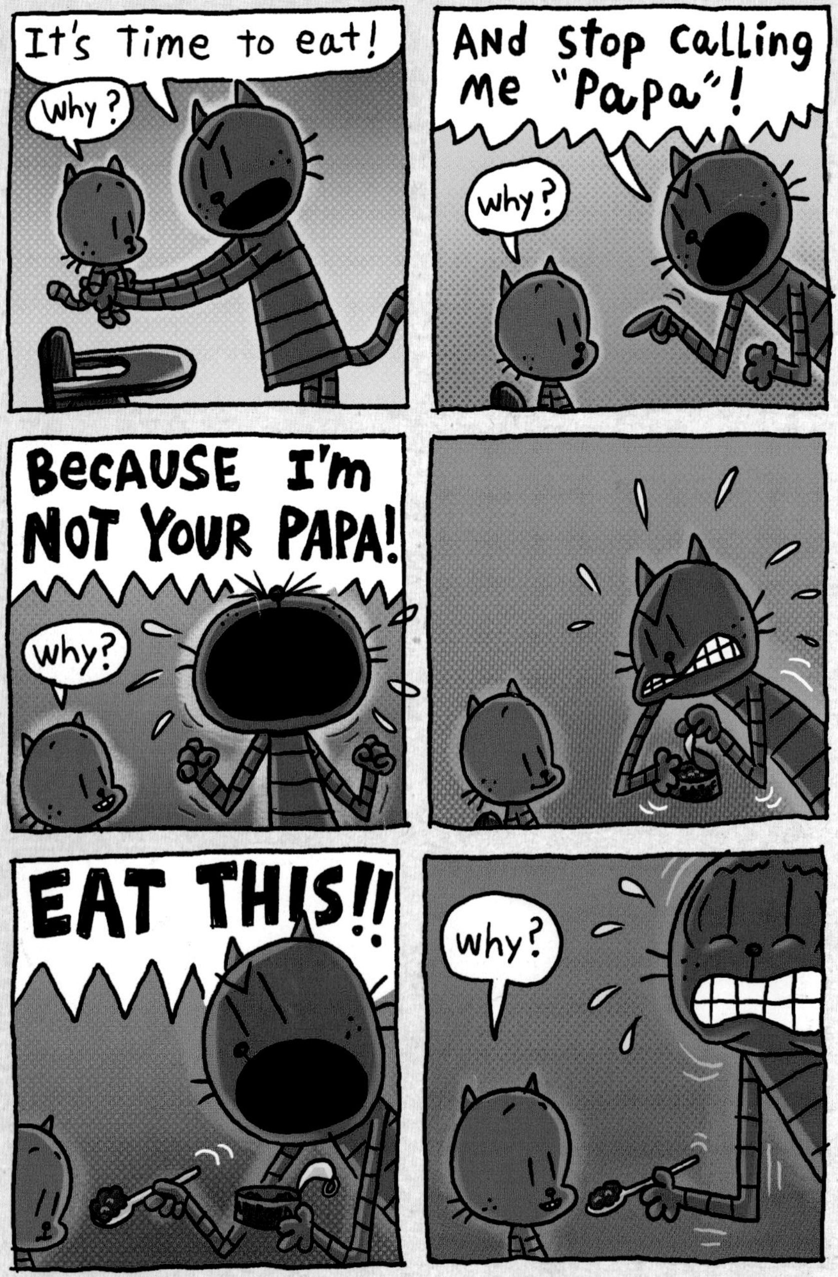
It's Time to eat!
Why?
AND Stop calling me "Papa"!
Why?
BECAUSE I'm NOT YOUR PAPA!
Why?
EAT THIS!!
Why?

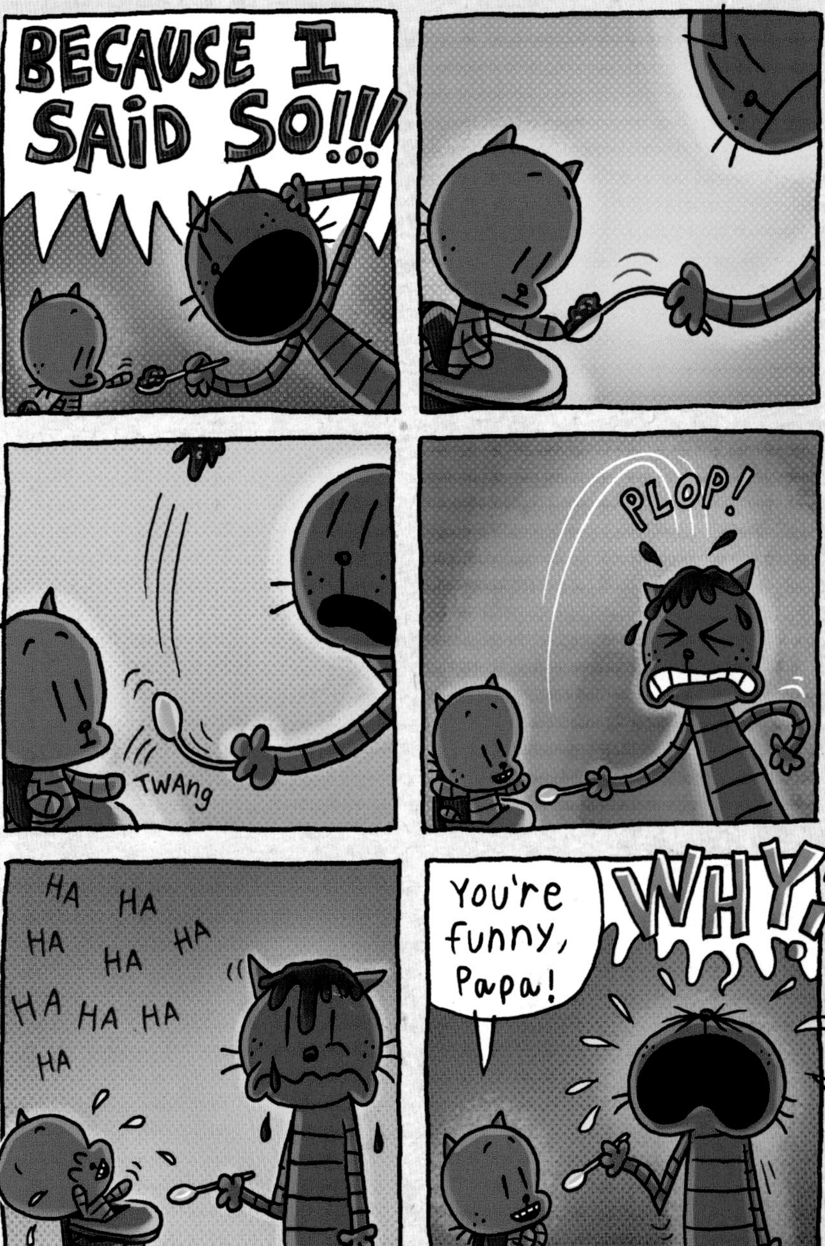
BECAUSE I SAID SO!!!
TWAng
PLOP!
HA HA HA HA HA HA HA HA HA HA
You're funny, Papa!
WHY?

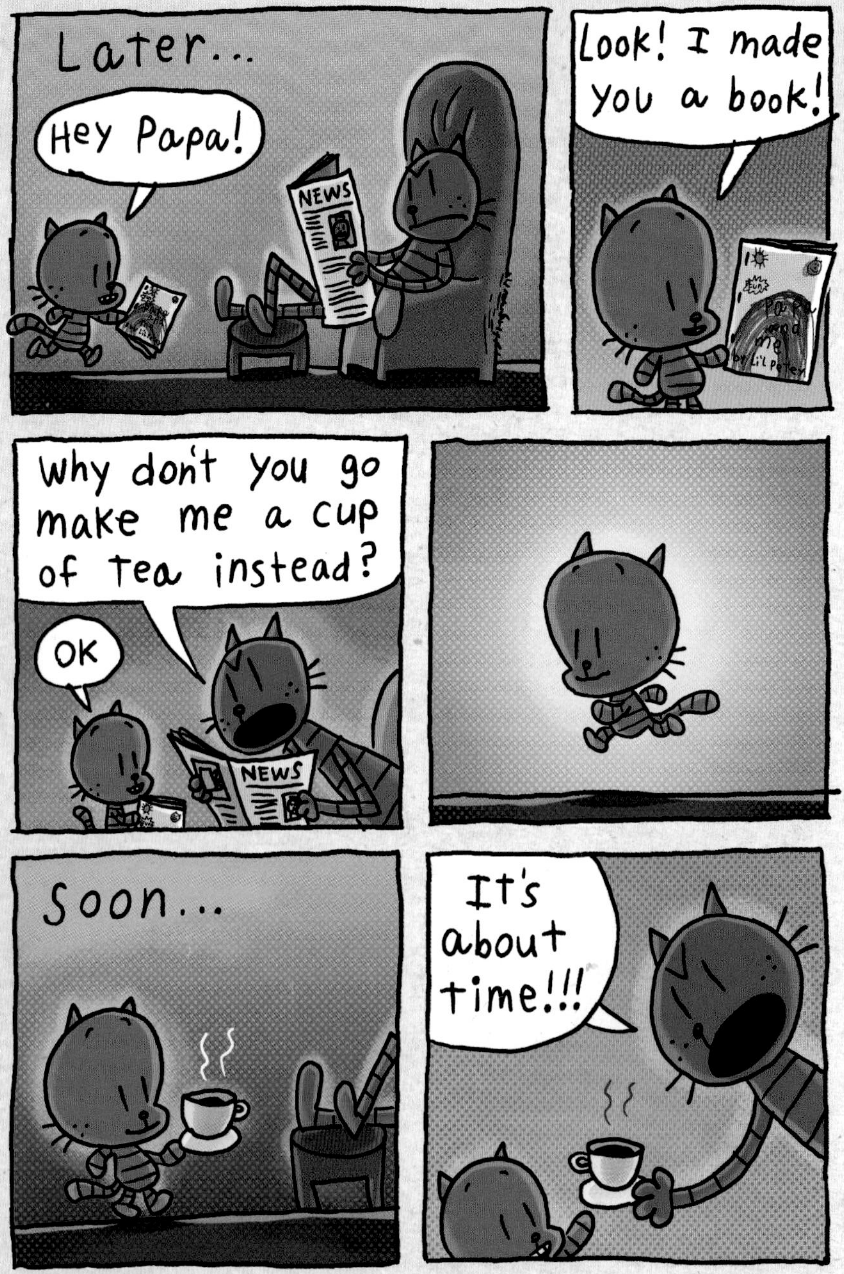
Later...
Hey Papa!
NEWS
Look! I made you a book!
Papa and me
by Li'l Petey
Why don't you go make me a cup of tea instead?
OK
NEWS
Soon...
It's about time!!!

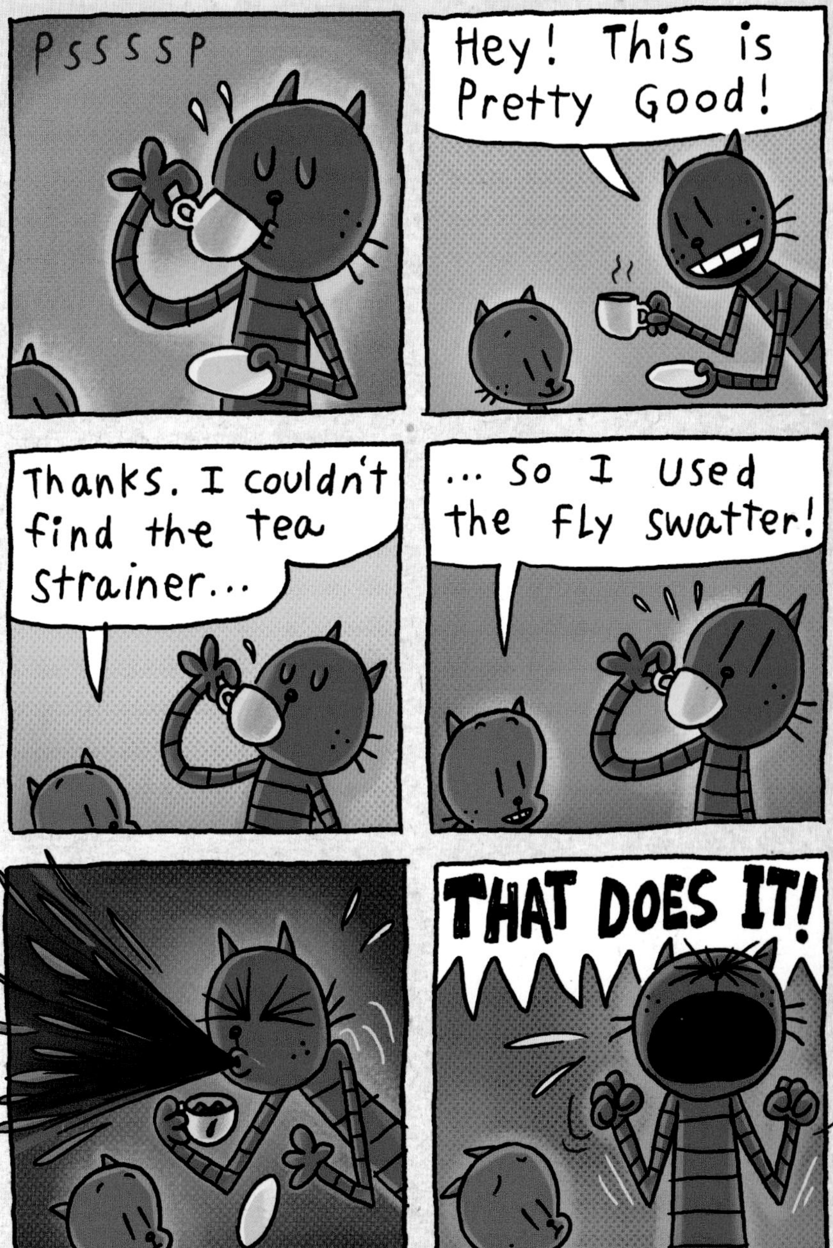
PSSSSP
Hey! This is Pretty Good!
Thanks. I couldn't find the tea strainer...
... So I used the fly swatter!
THAT DOES IT!

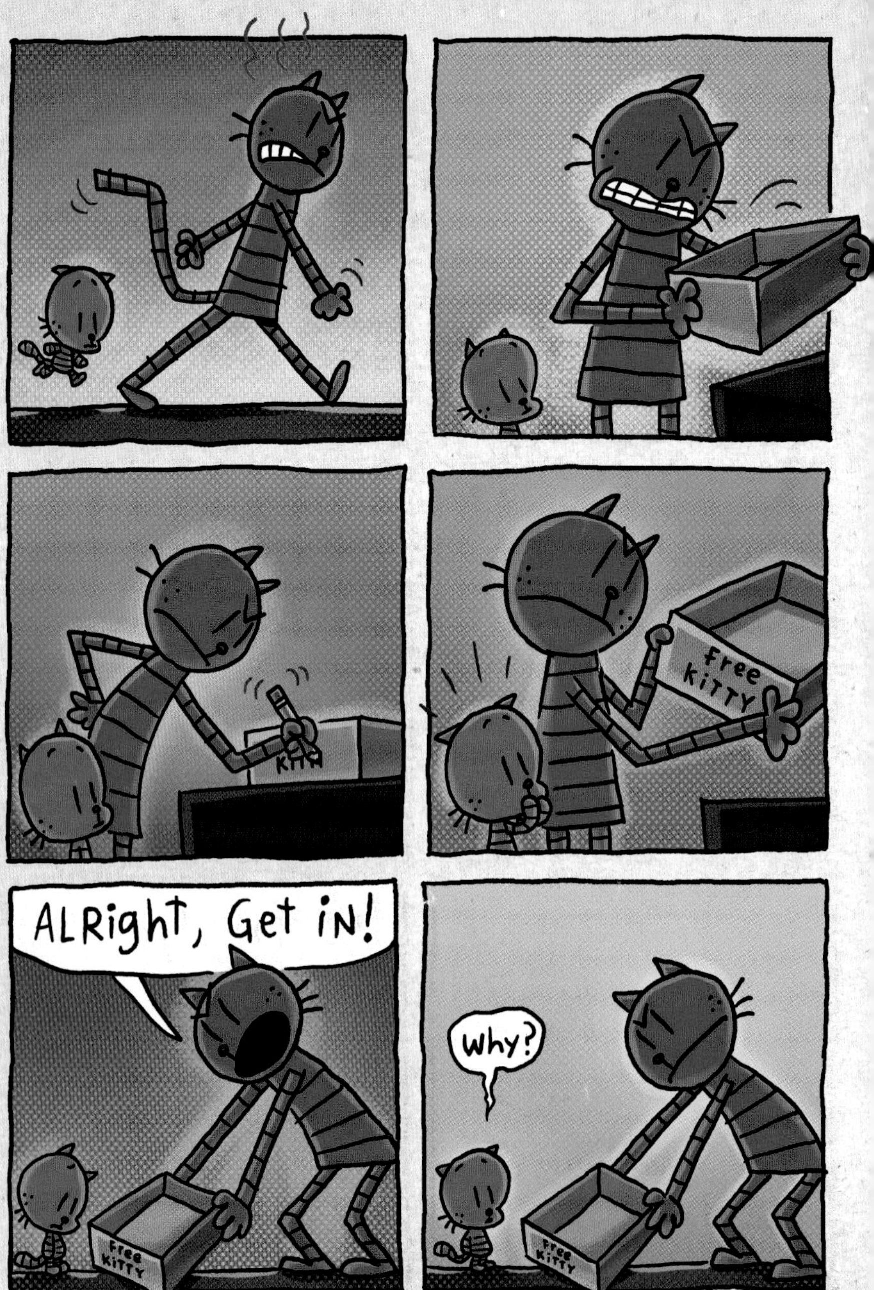
KITTY
Free KITTY
ALRight, Get iN!
Free KITTY
Why?
Free KITTY

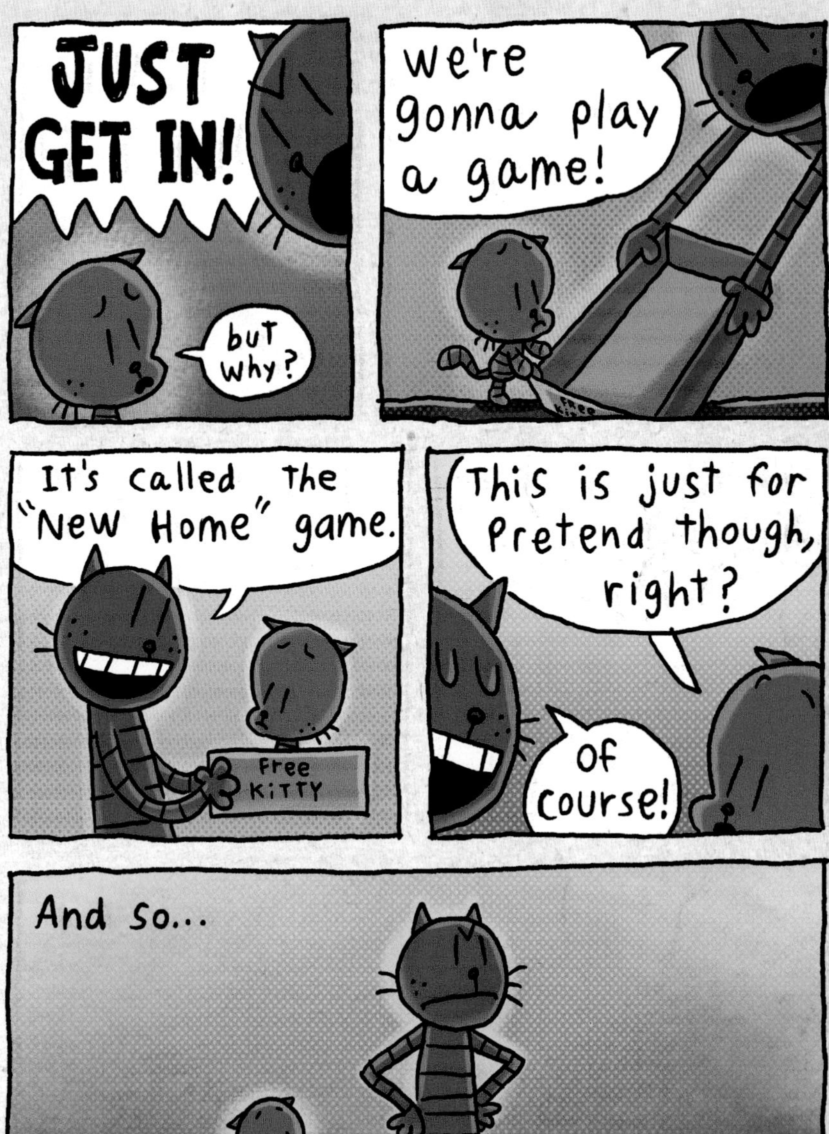
JUST GET IN!
but why?
we're gonna play a game!
It's called the "New Home" game.
Free KiTTY
This is just for pretend though, right?
Of course!
And so...
Free KiTTY

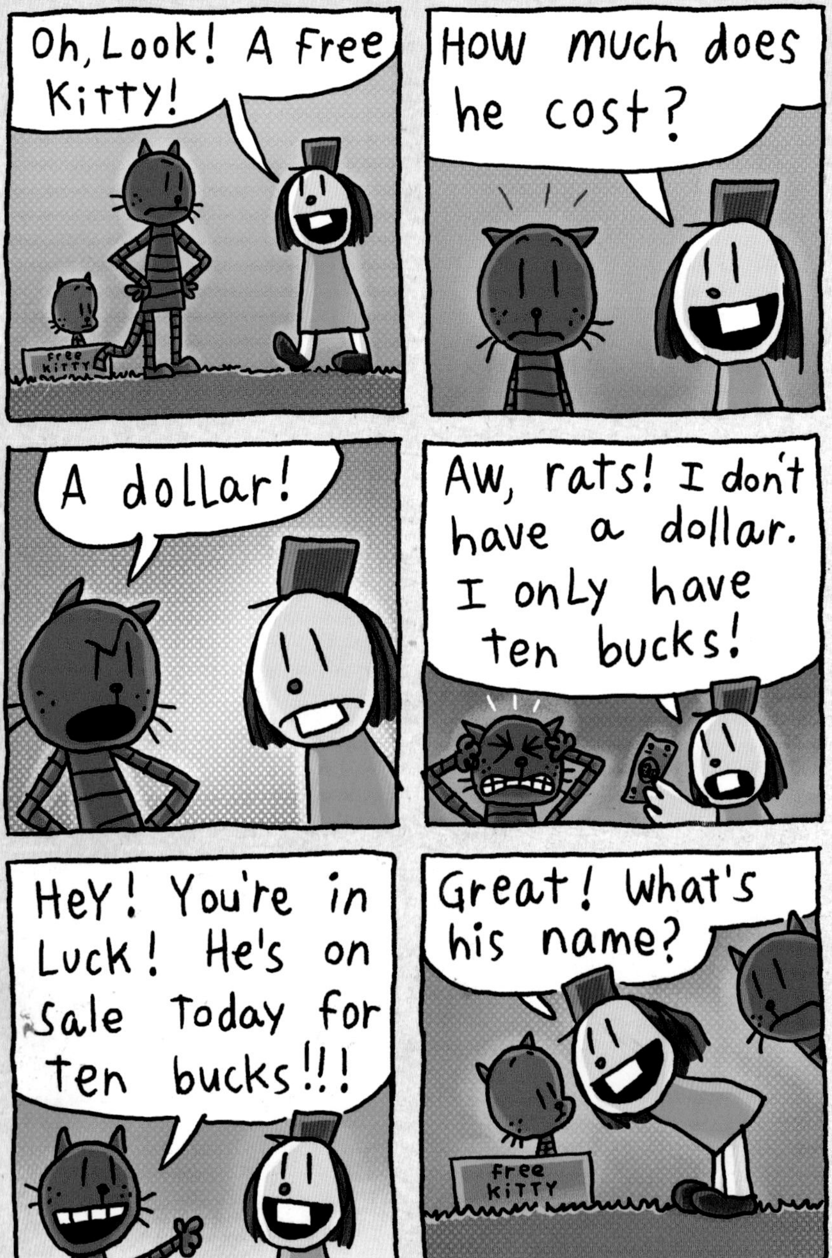
Oh, Look! A Free Kitty!
Free Kitty
How much does he cost?
A dollar!
Aw, rats! I don't have a dollar. I only have ten bucks!
Hey! You're in Luck! He's on Sale Today for ten bucks!!!
Great! What's his name?
Free Kitty

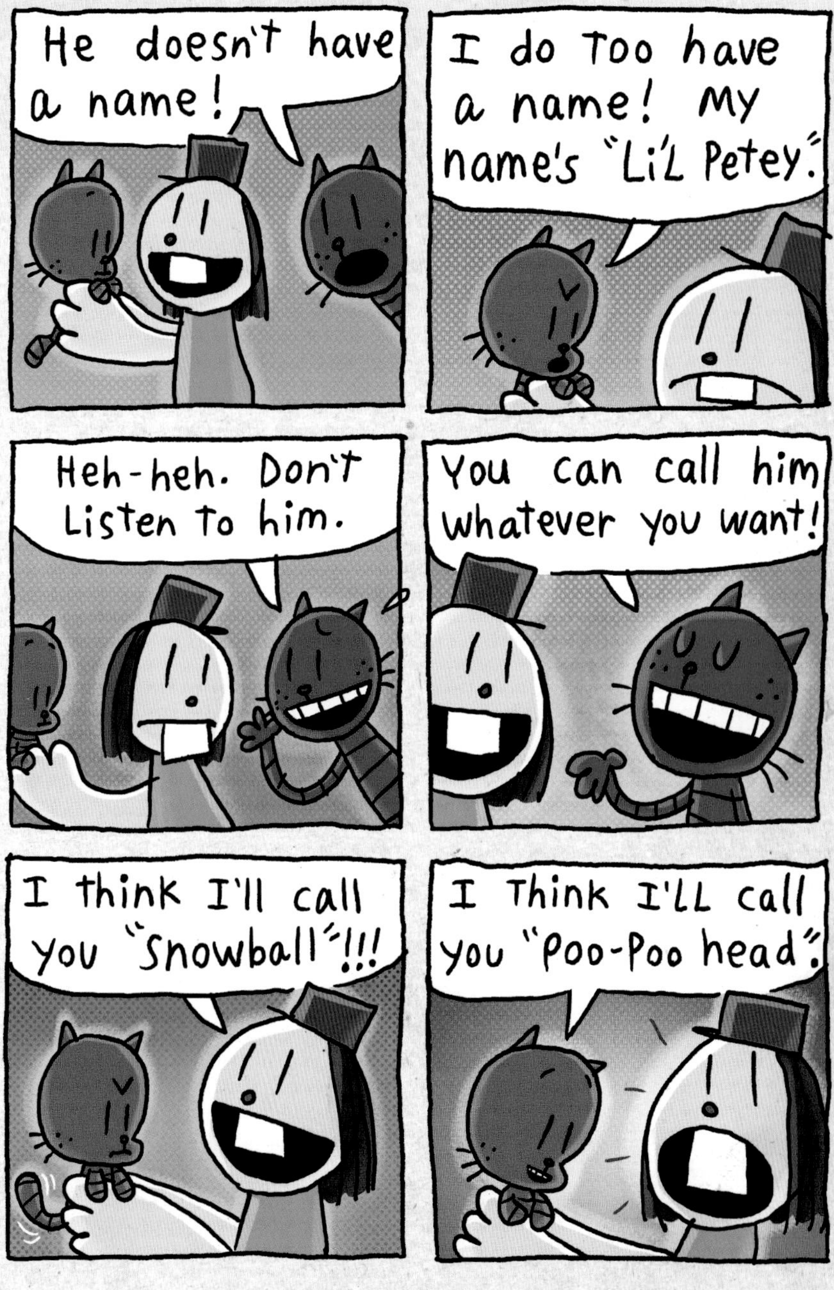
He doesn't have a name!
I do Too have a name! My name's "Li'L Petey."
Heh-heh. Don't Listen to him.
You can call him whatever you want!
I think I'll call you "Snowball"!!!
I Think I'LL call you "Poo-Poo head".

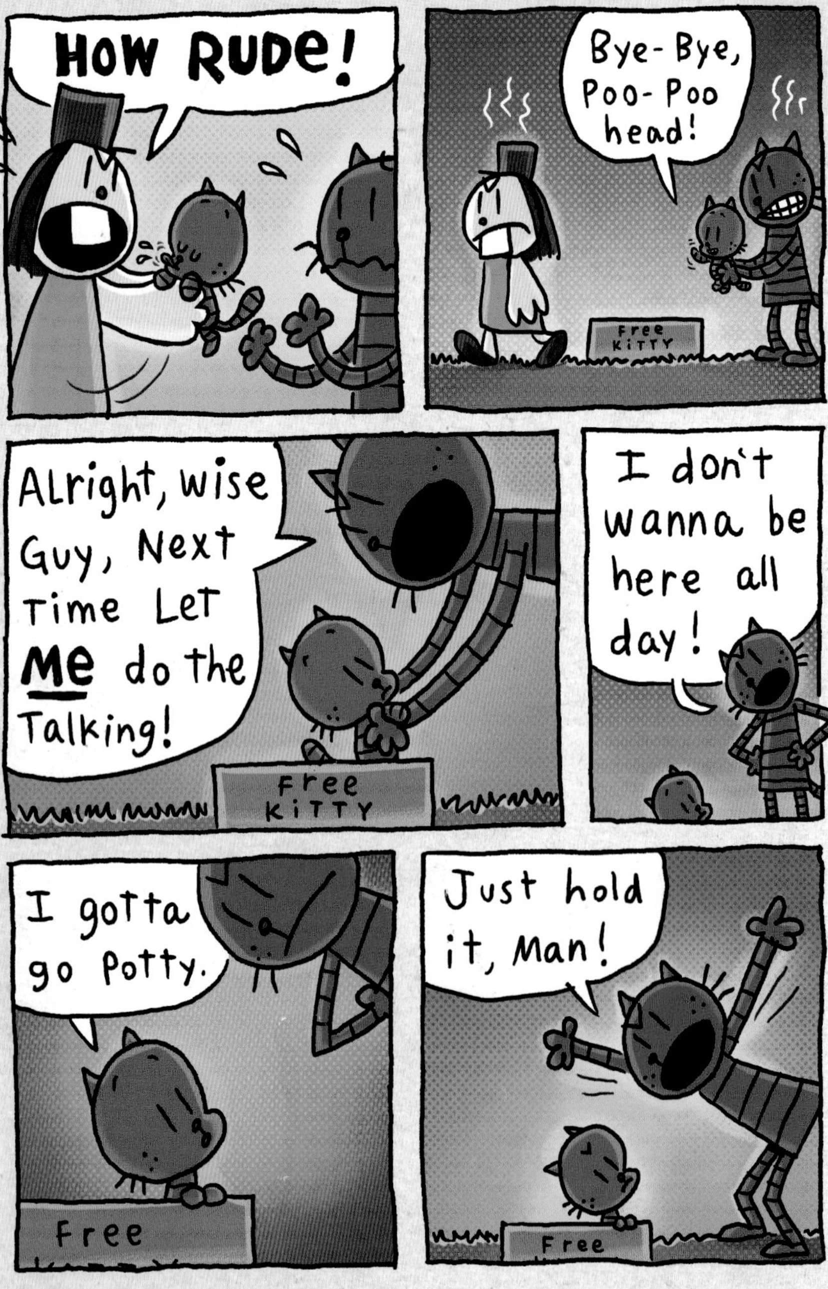
HOW RUDE!
Bye-Bye, Poo-Poo head!
Free KITTY
Alright, wise Guy, Next Time Let ME do the Talking!
Free KITTY
I don't wanna be here all day!
I gotta go Potty.
Free
Just hold it, Man!
Free

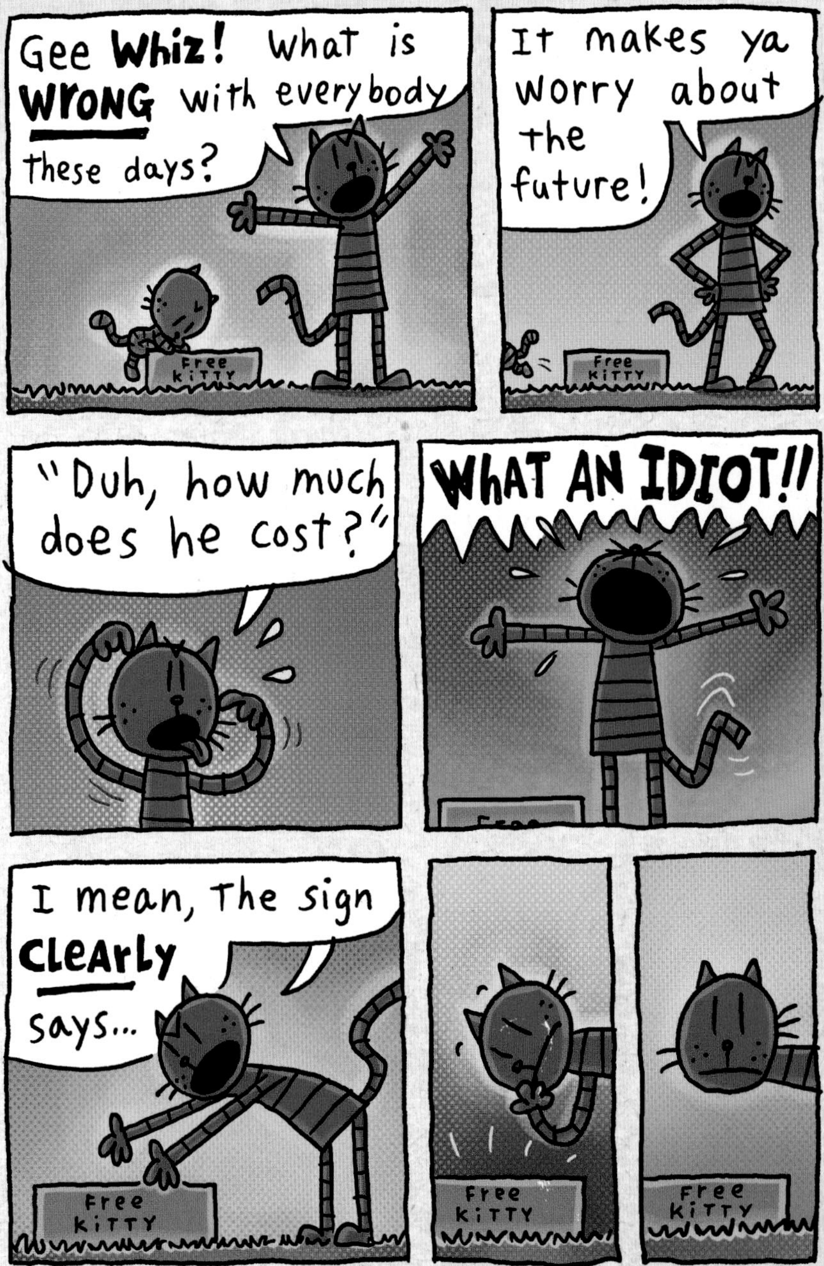
Gee Whiz! What is WRONG with everybody these days?
Free kitty
It makes ya worry about the future!
Free kitty
"Duh, how much does he cost?"
WHAT AN IDIOT!!
I mean, the sign CLEARLY says...
Free kitty
Free kitty
Free kitty

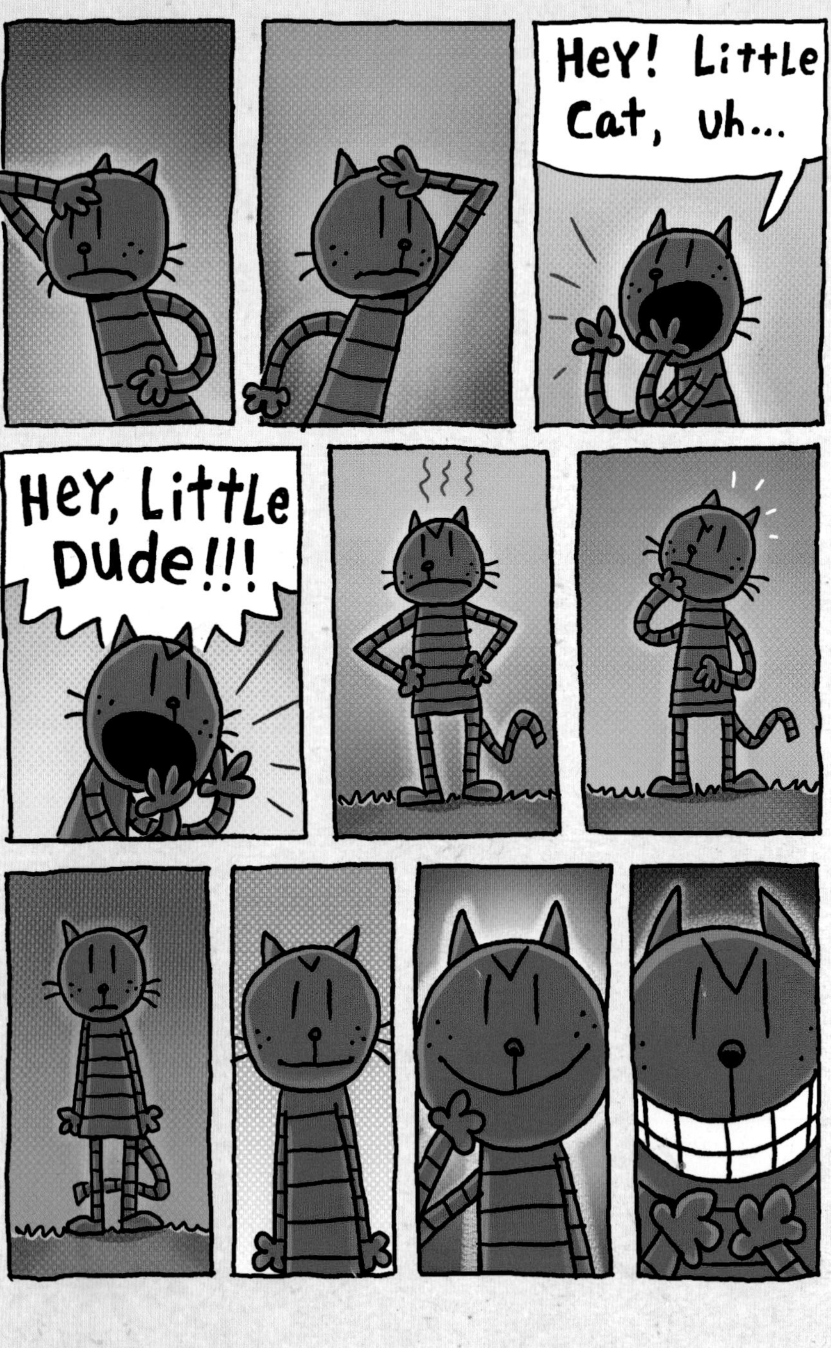
HEY! Little Cat, uh...
HEY, LitTLe DUde!!!

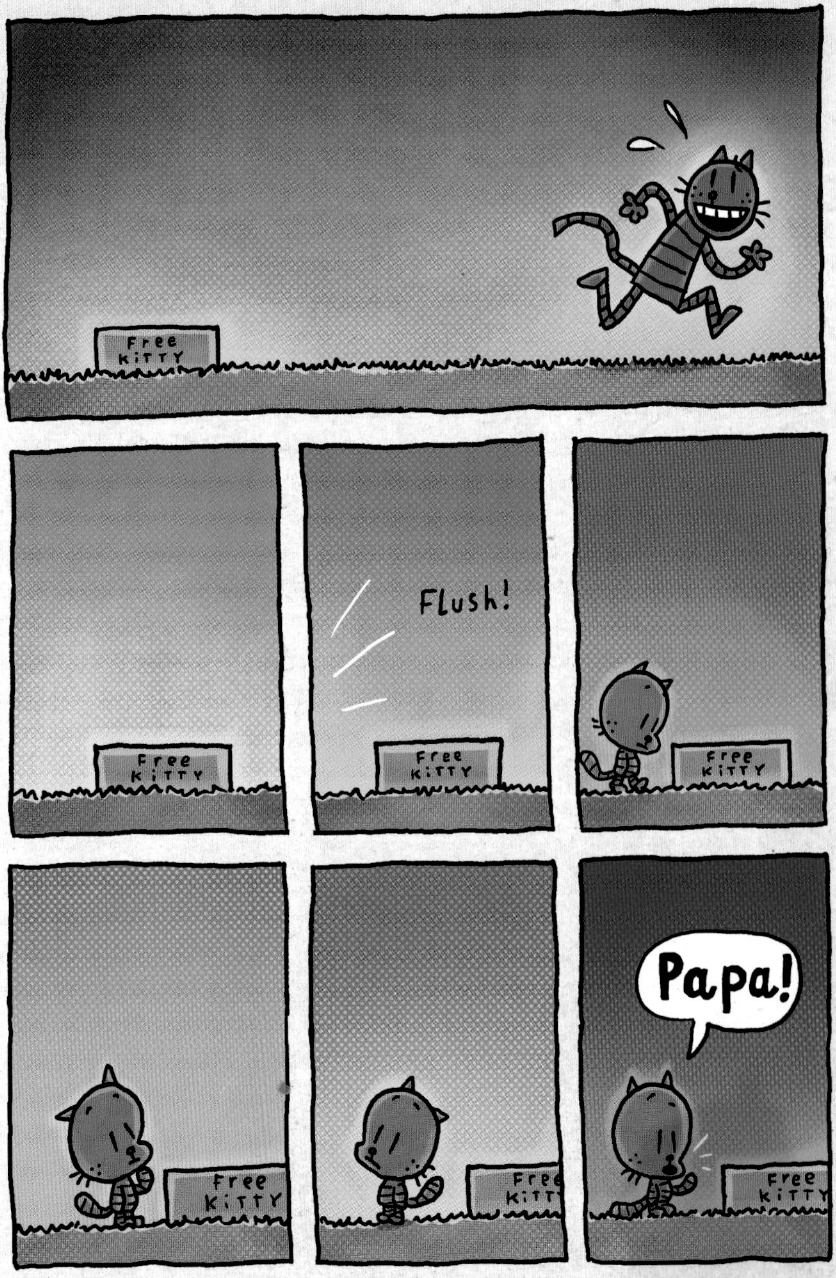

Free Kitty
Free Kitty
Flush!
Free Kitty
Free Kitty
Free Kitty
Free Kitty
Papa!
Free Kitty

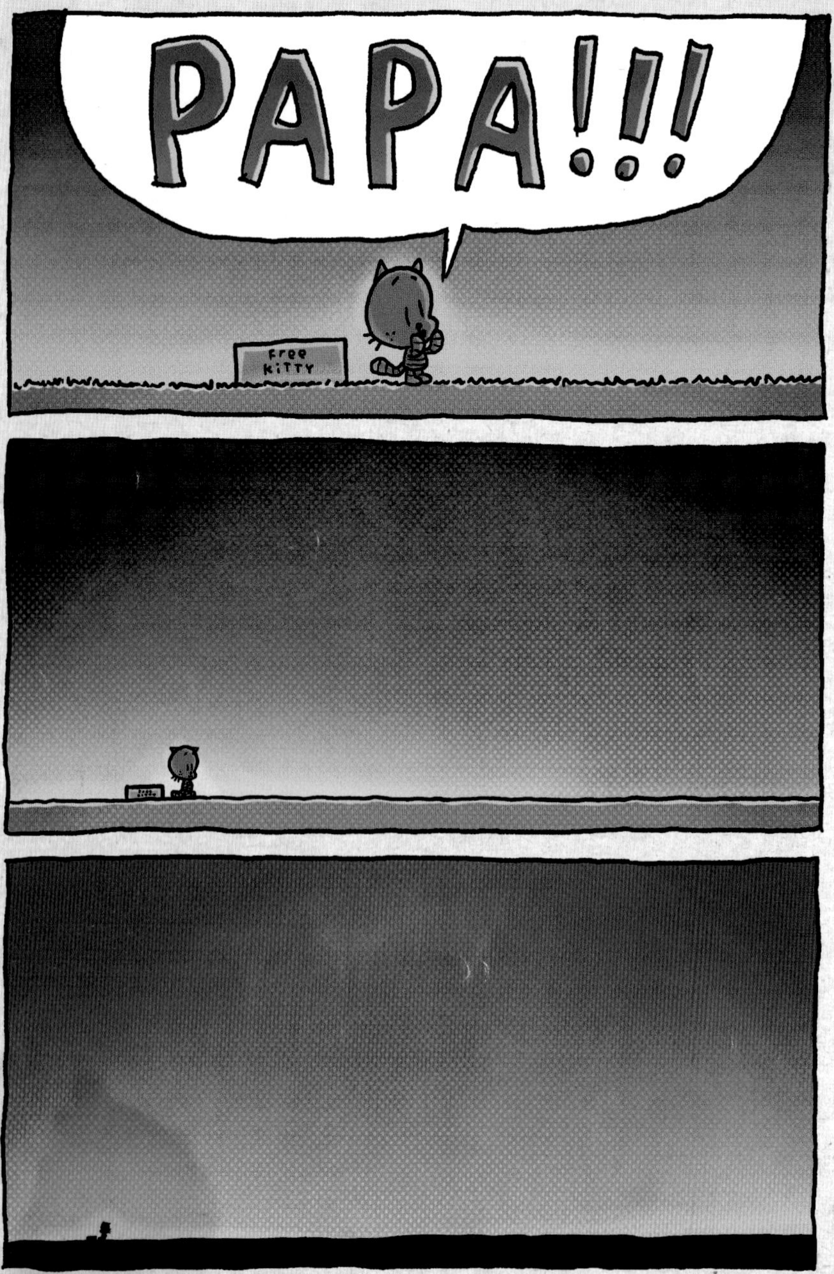
PAPA!!!
Free
kitty

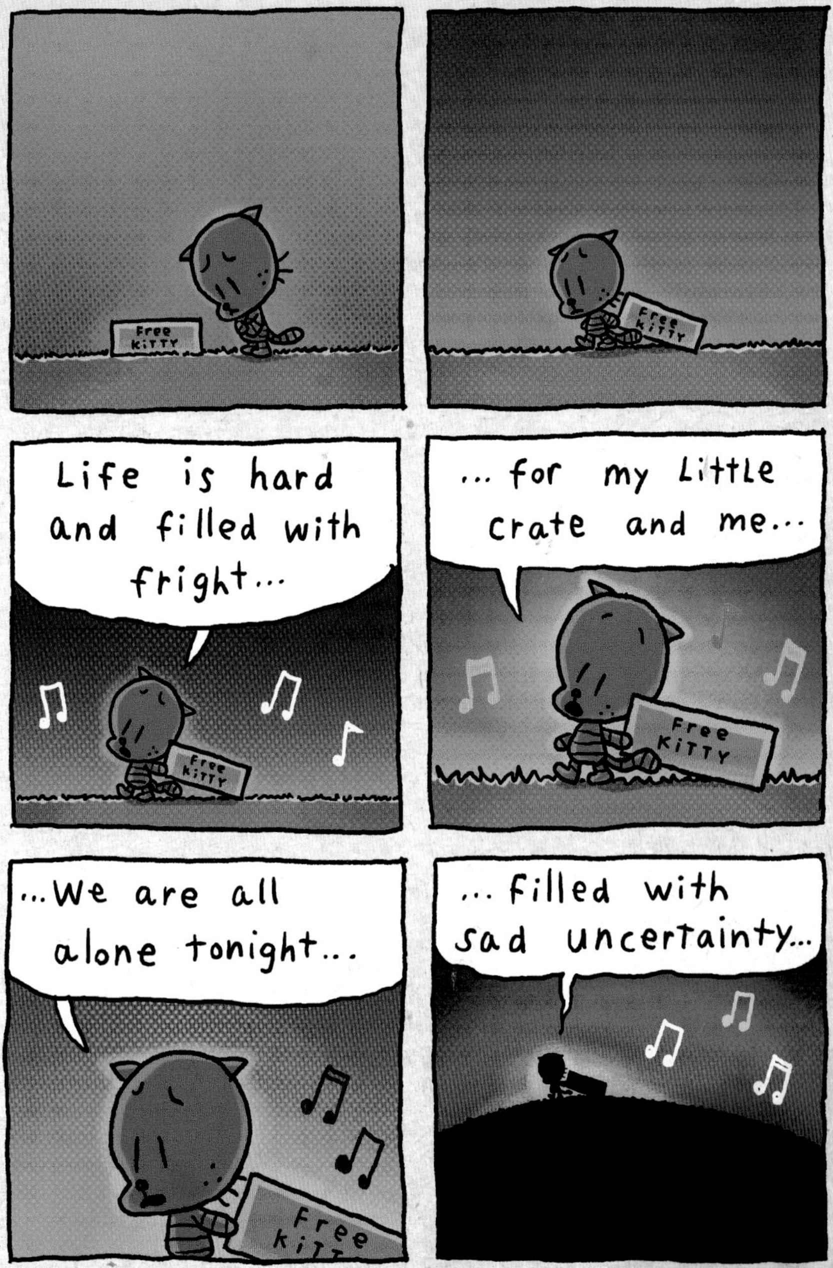

Free KiTTY
Free KiTTY
Life is hard and filled with fright...
Free KiTTY
... for my Little crate and me...
Free KiTTY
...We are all alone tonight...
... filled with sad uncertainty...

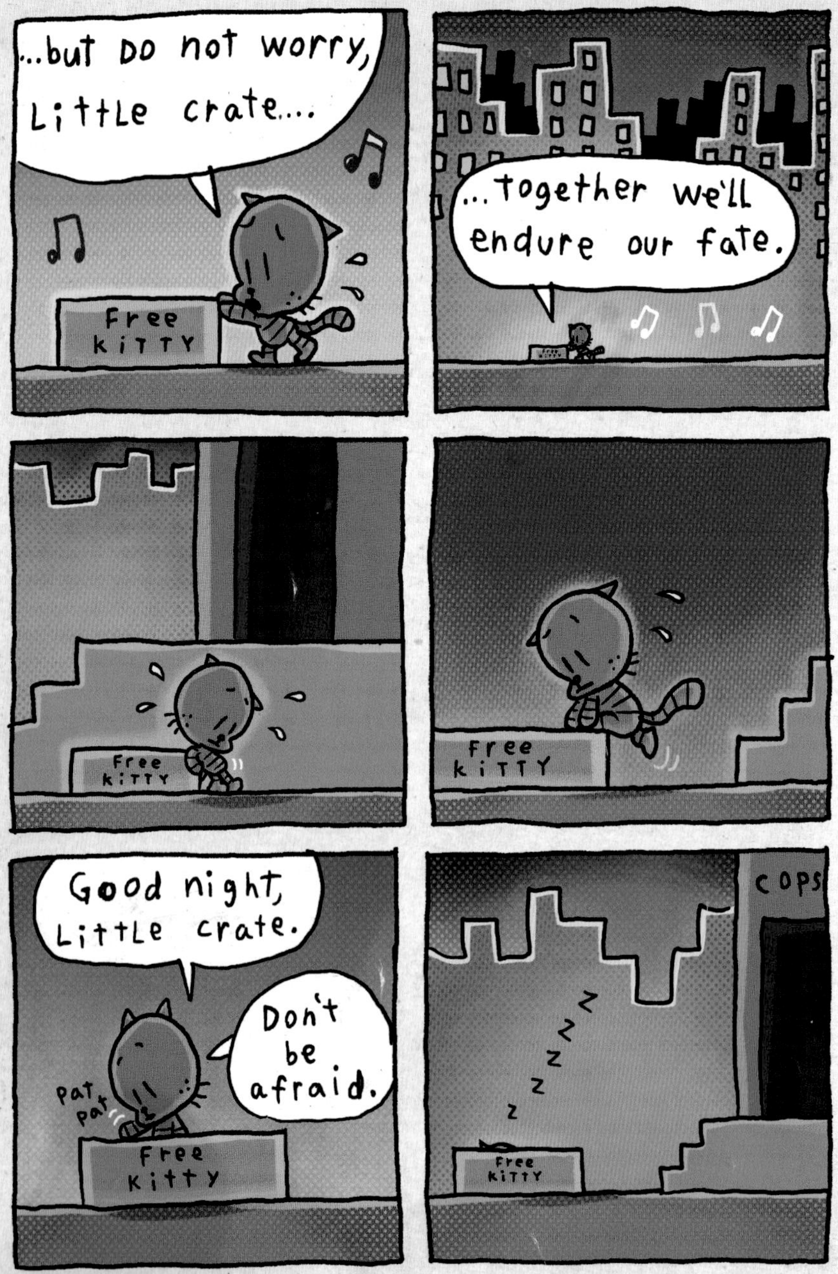
...but DO not worry, Little crate....
Free KiTTY
...together we'll endure our fate.
Free KiTTY
Free KiTTY
Free KiTTY
Good night, Little crate.
Don't be afraid.
pat pat
Free Kitty
Z Z Z Z Z
Free KiTTY
COPS

Chapter the Fifth

CRATE EXPECTATIONS

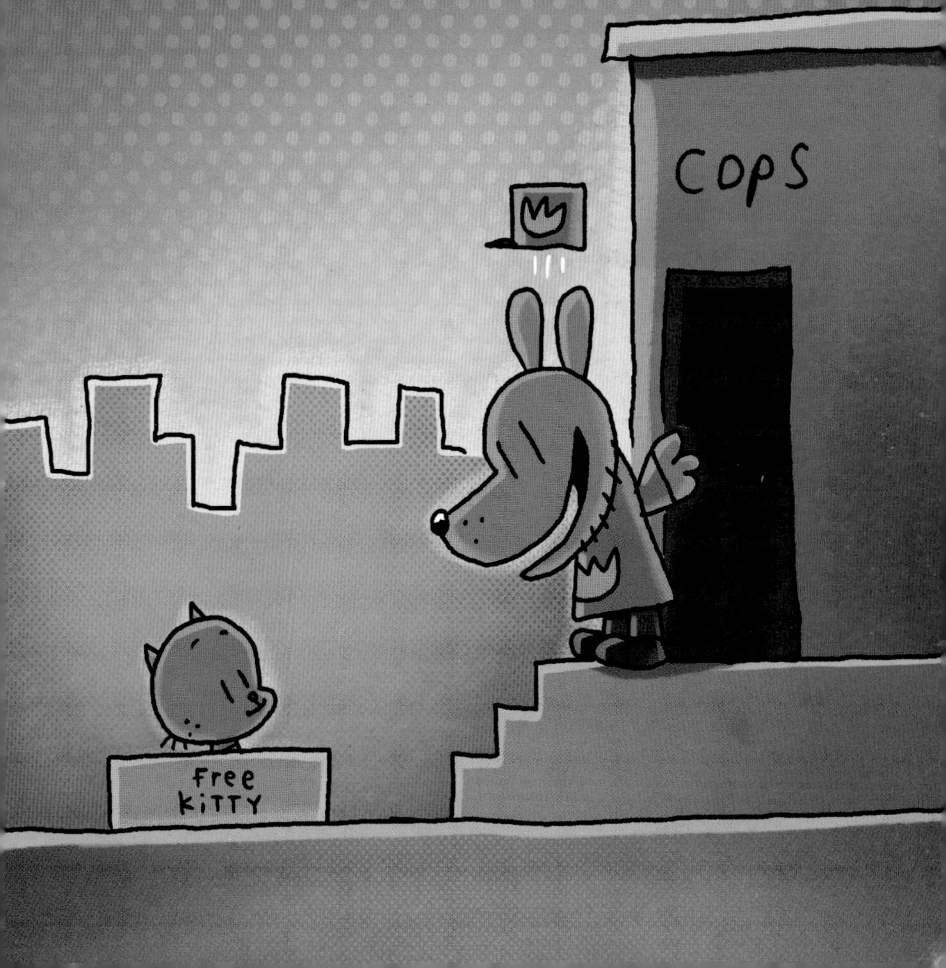

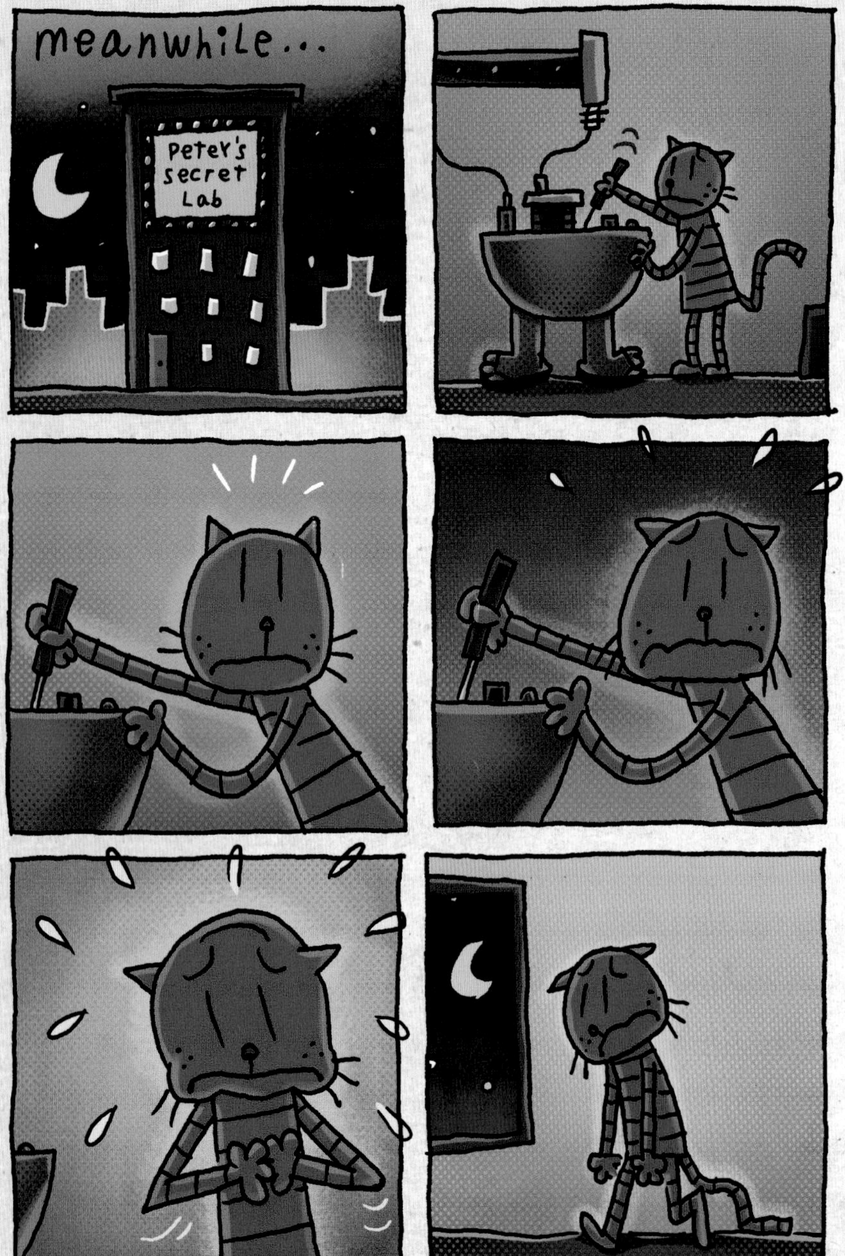
meanwhile...
Peter's secret Lab

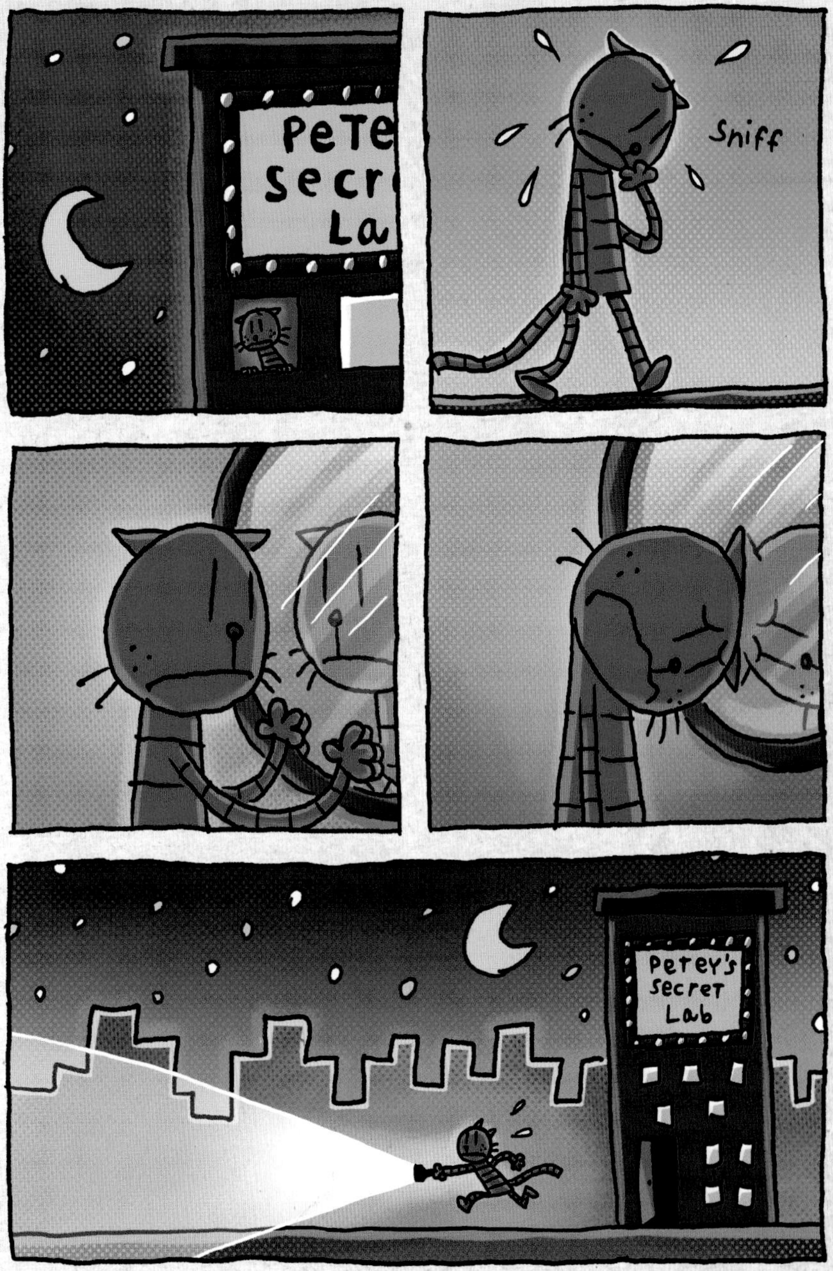
PeTe
Secr
La
Sniff
PeTeY's
Secret
Lab

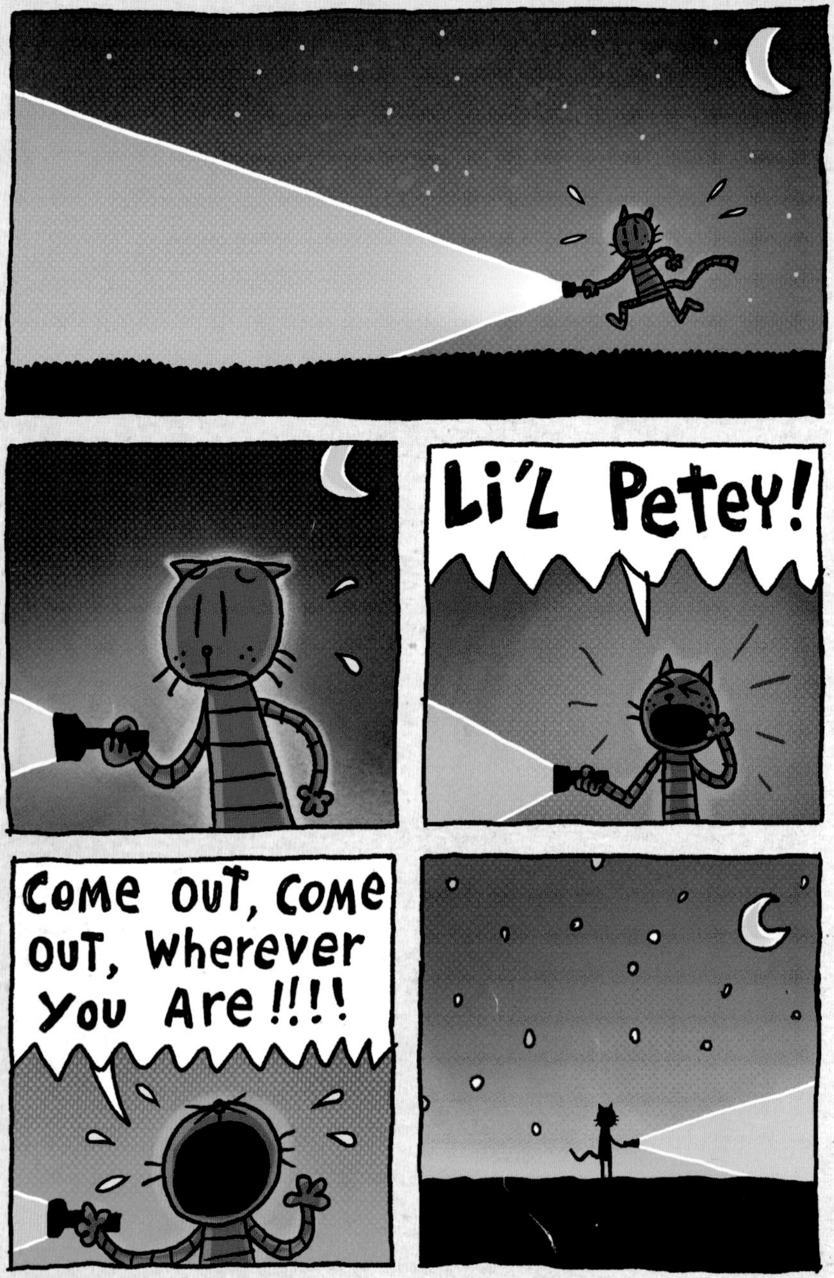
Li'L Petey!
Come out, come out, wherever you Are!!!!

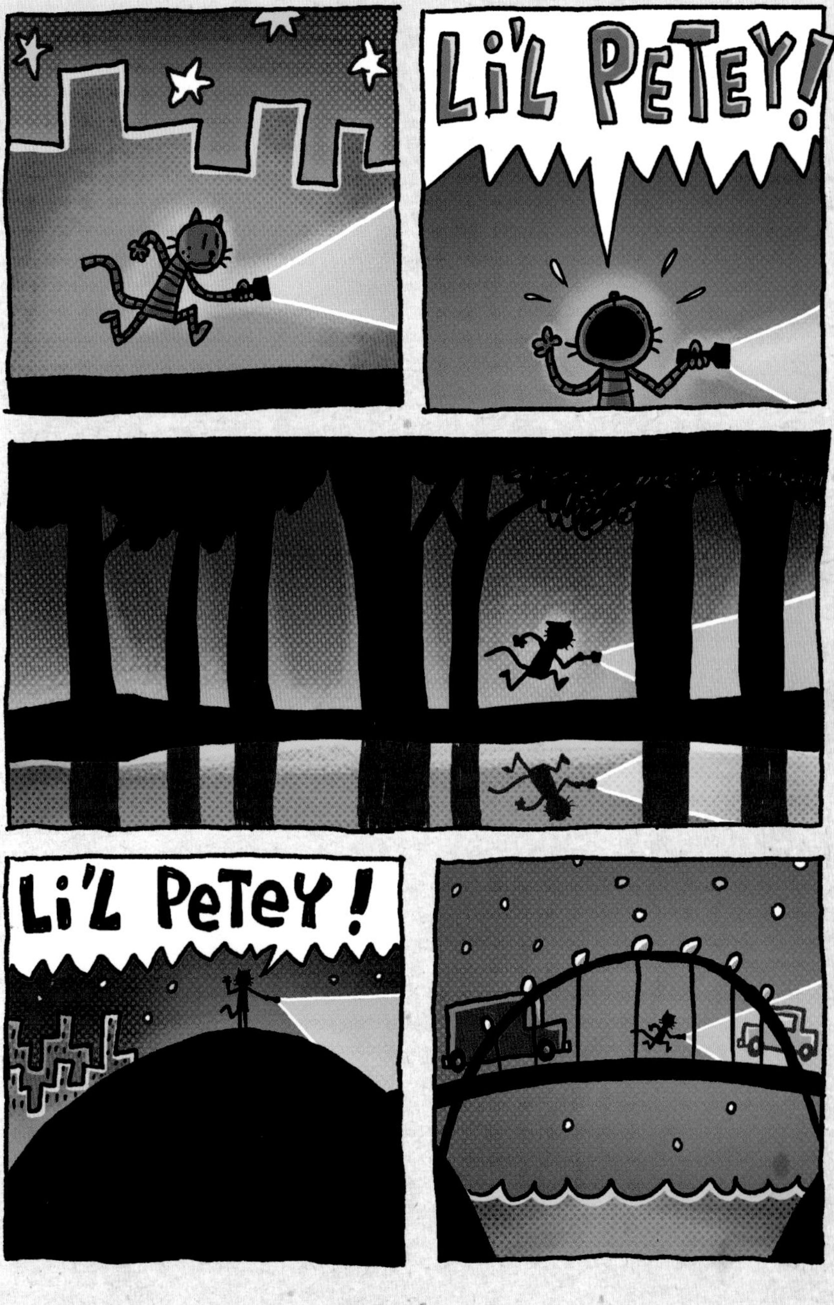
LI'L PETEY!
LI'L PETEY!

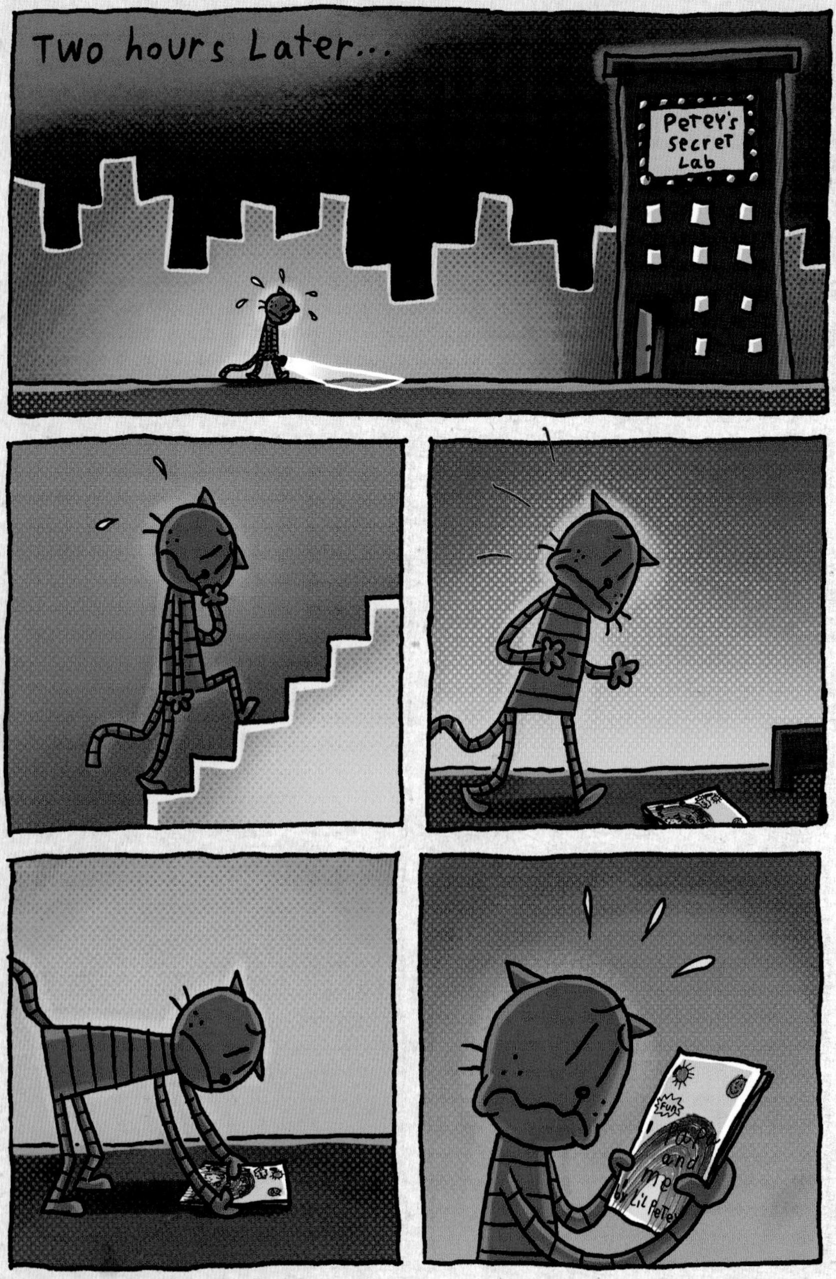
Two hours Later...
Petey's Secret Lab
Fun
Papa and me by Li'l Petey

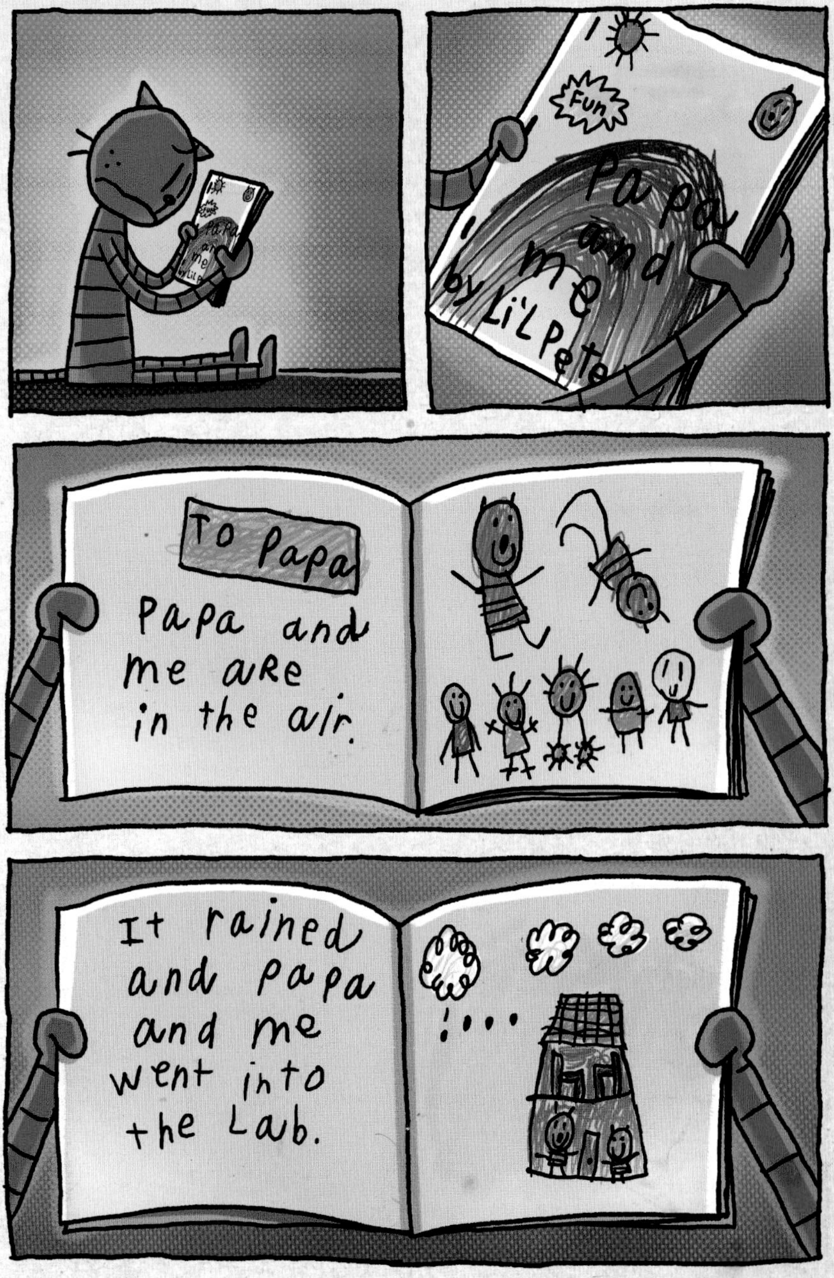

Fun
Papa and me by Li'L Pete
To Papa
Papa and me are in the air.
It rained and papa and me went into the Lab.

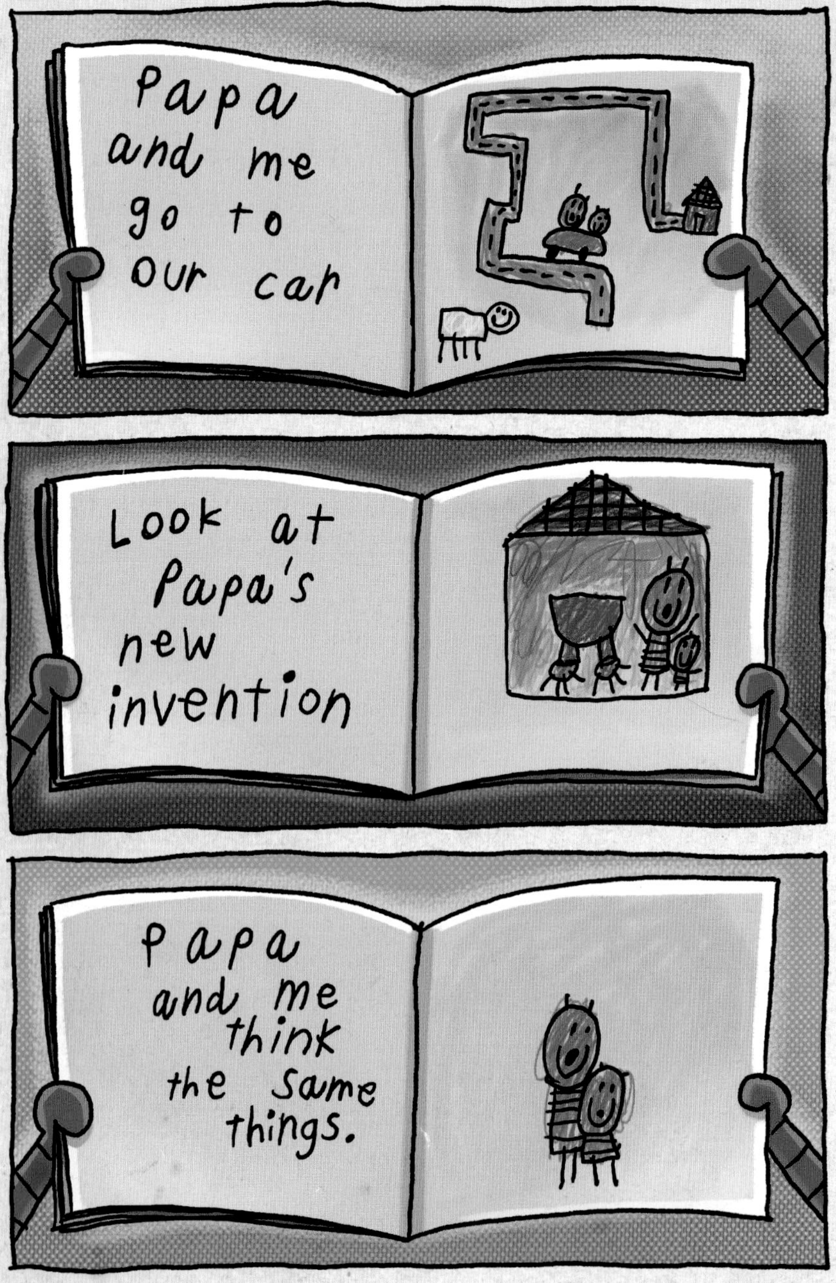
Papa and me go to our car
Look at Papa's new invention
Papa and me think the same things.

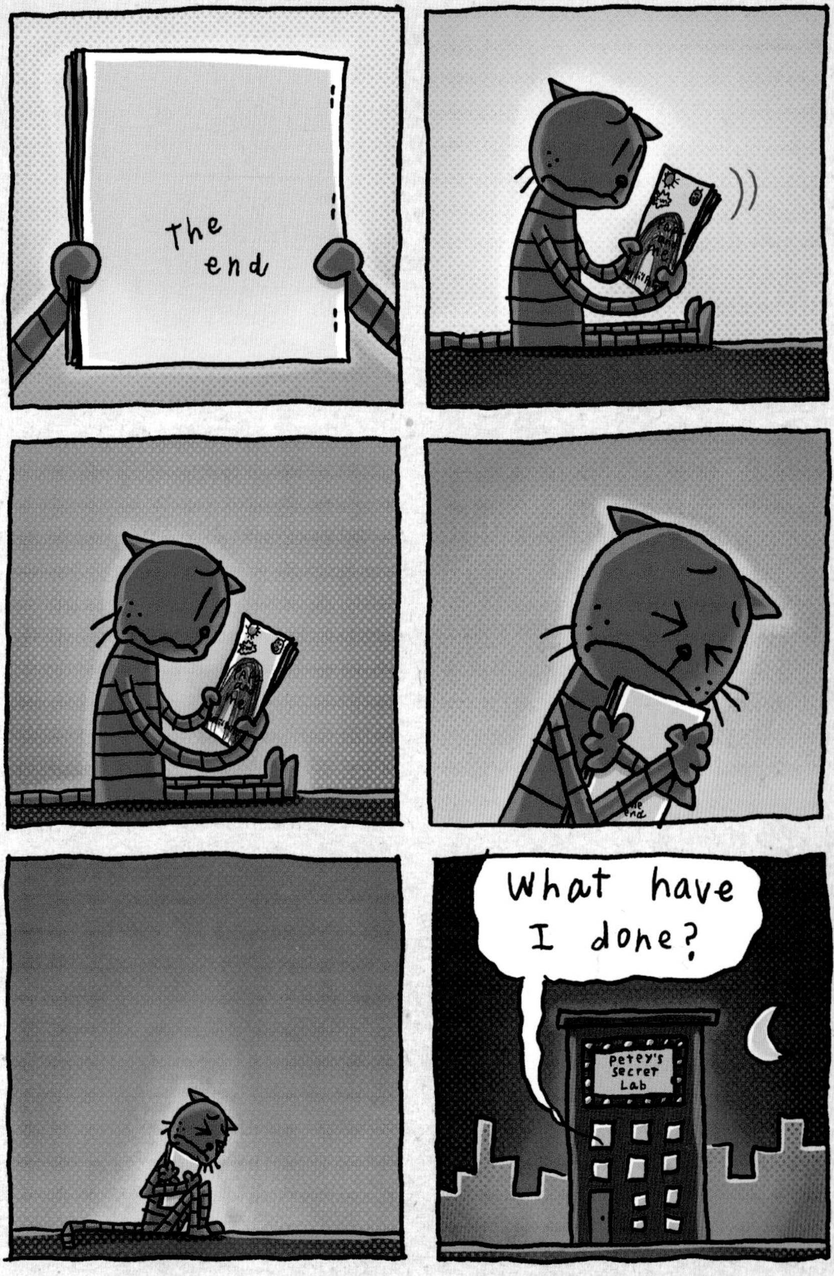
The
end
What have
I done?
Petey's
Secret
Lab

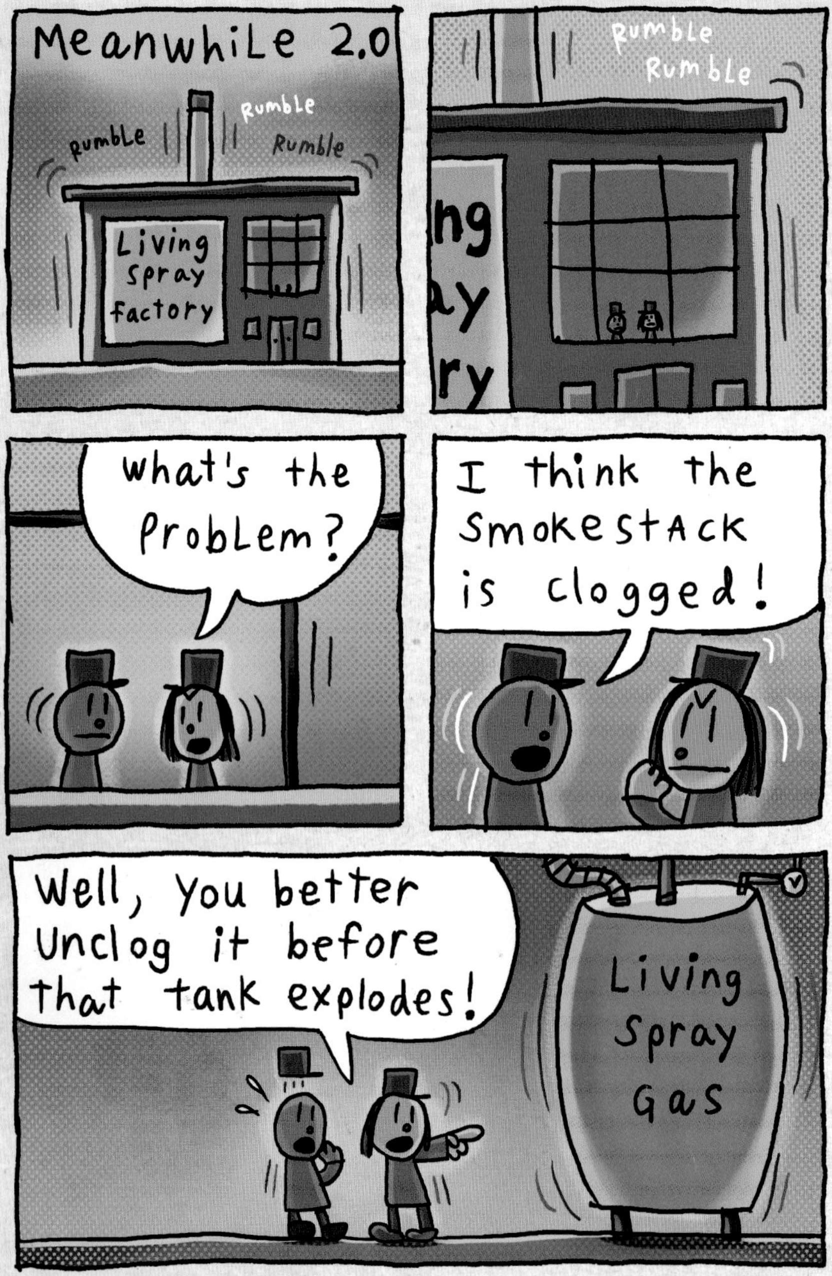
Meanwhile 2.0
Rumble
Rumble
Rumble
Living Spray Factory
Rumble
Rumble
What's the problem?
I think the smokestack is clogged!
Well, you better unclog it before that tank explodes!
Living Spray Gas

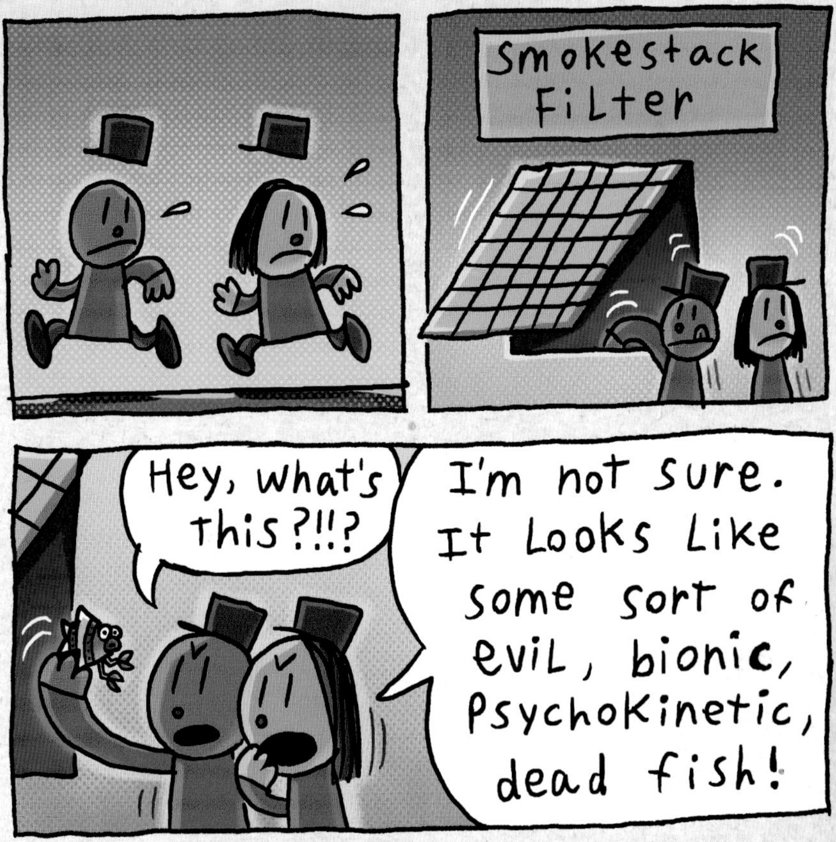
Smokestack Filter
Hey, what's this?!!?
I'm not sure. It looks like some sort of evil, bionic, psychokinetic, dead fish!
But how did it get stuck in our smoke-stack?
And who could be responsible for such a thing?

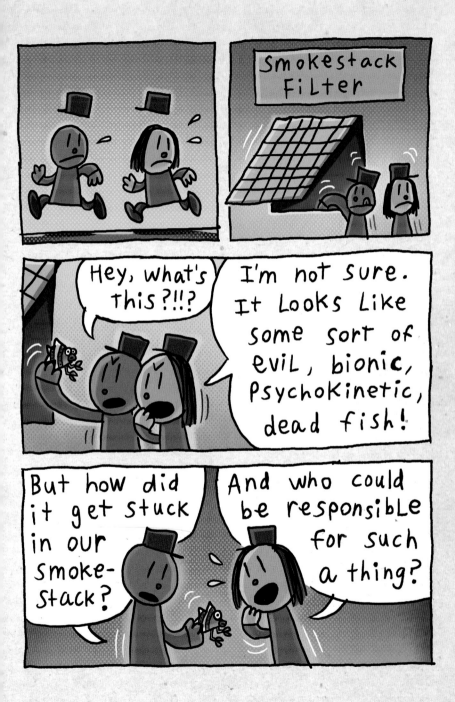

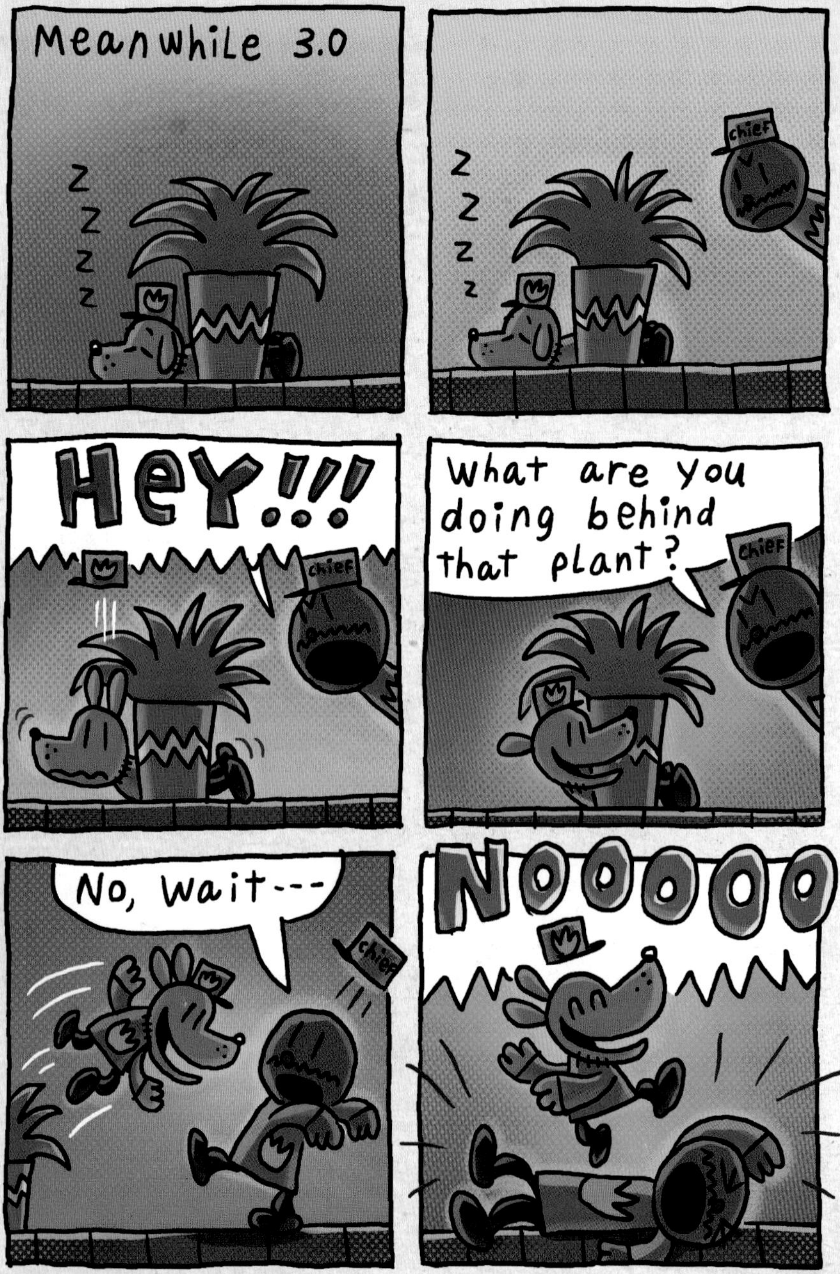
Meanwhile 3.0
Z Z Z Z
Z Z Z Z
chief
HEY!!!
chief
What are you doing behind that plant?
chief
No, wait---
chief
NOOOOO

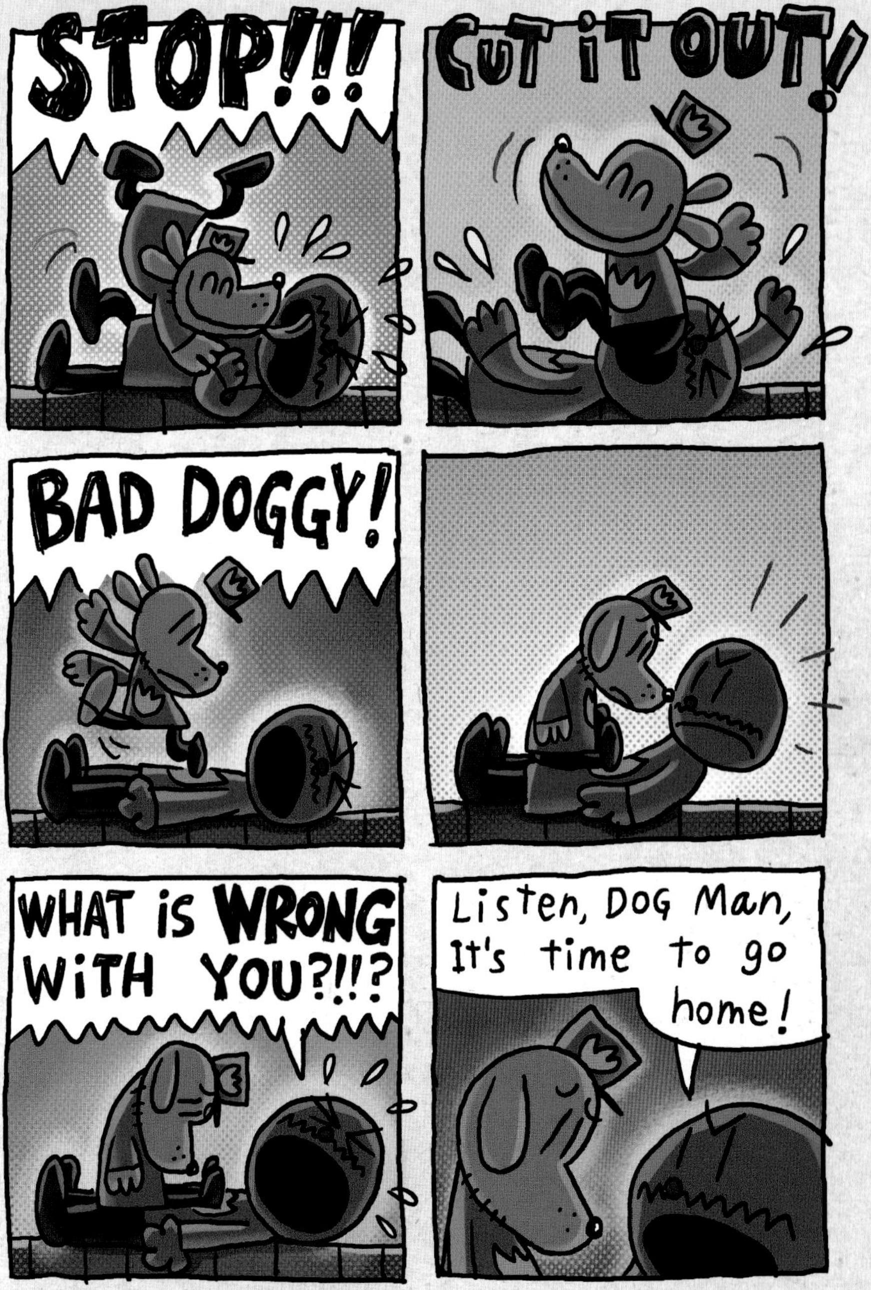
STOP!!!
CUT IT OUT!
BAD DOGGY!
WHAT is WRONG WiTH YOU?!!?
Listen, DOG Man, It's time to go home!

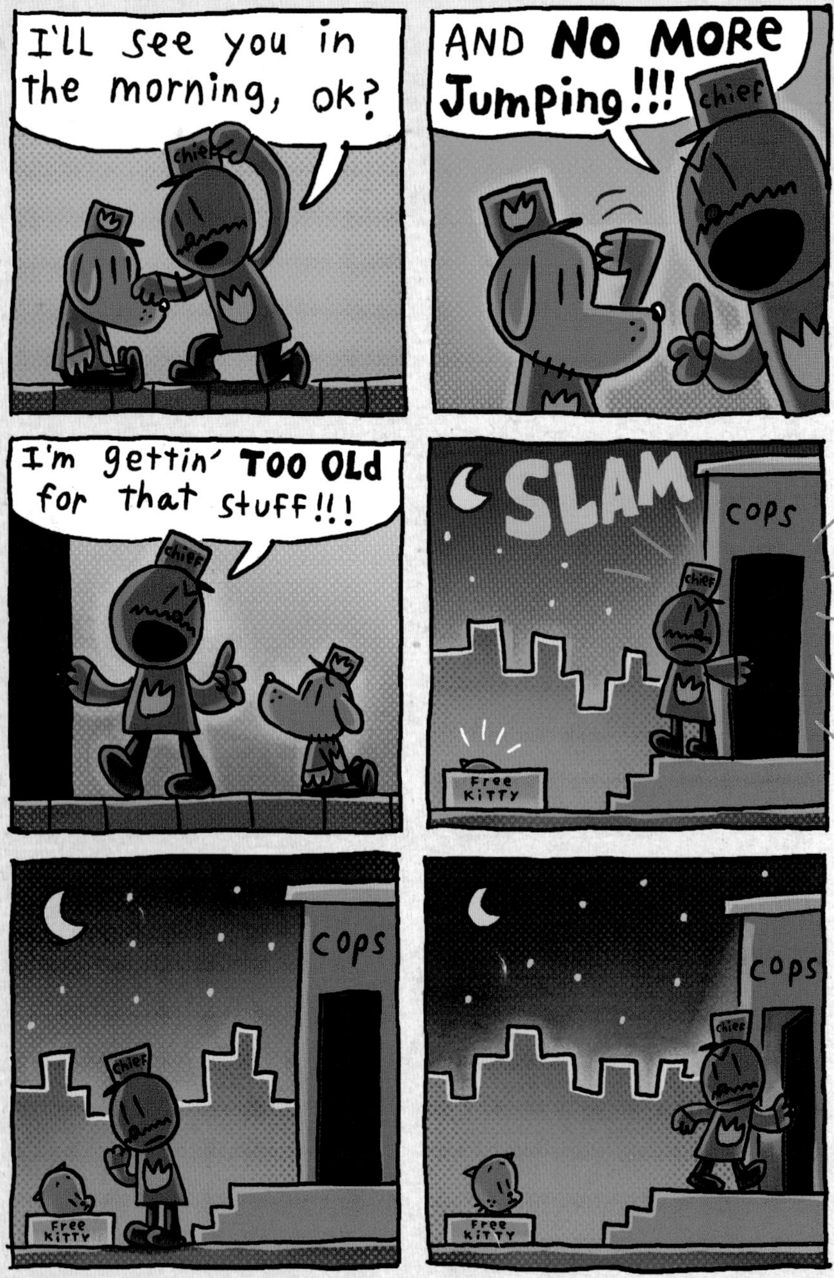

I'LL see you in the morning, ok?
chief
AND NO MORE Jumping!!!
chief
I'm gettin' TOO OLd for that stuff!!!
chief
SLAM
cops
chief
Free KiTTY
cops
chief
Free KiTTY
cops
chief
Free KiTTY

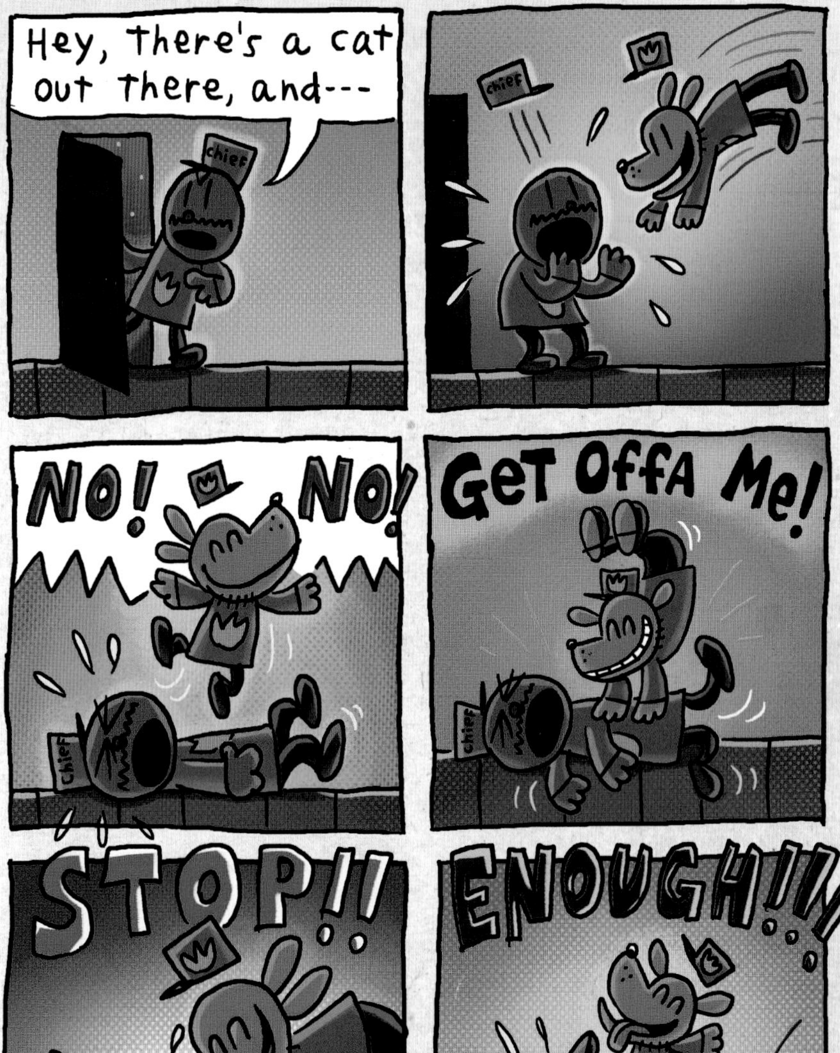
Hey, there's a cat out there, and---
chief
NO! NO!
Get Offa Me!
STOP!!
ENOUGH!!!

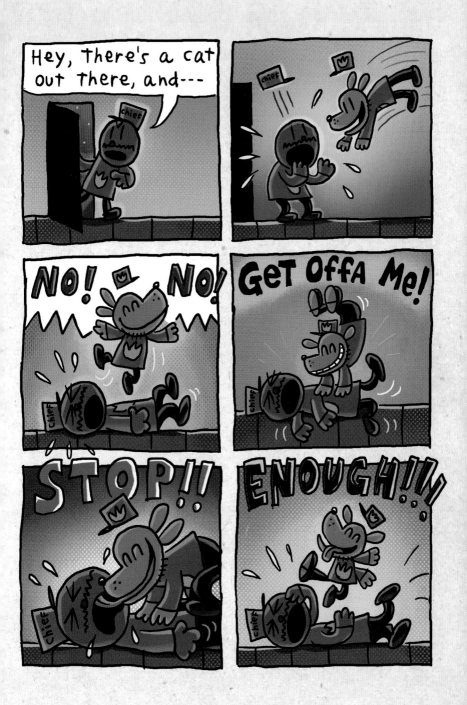

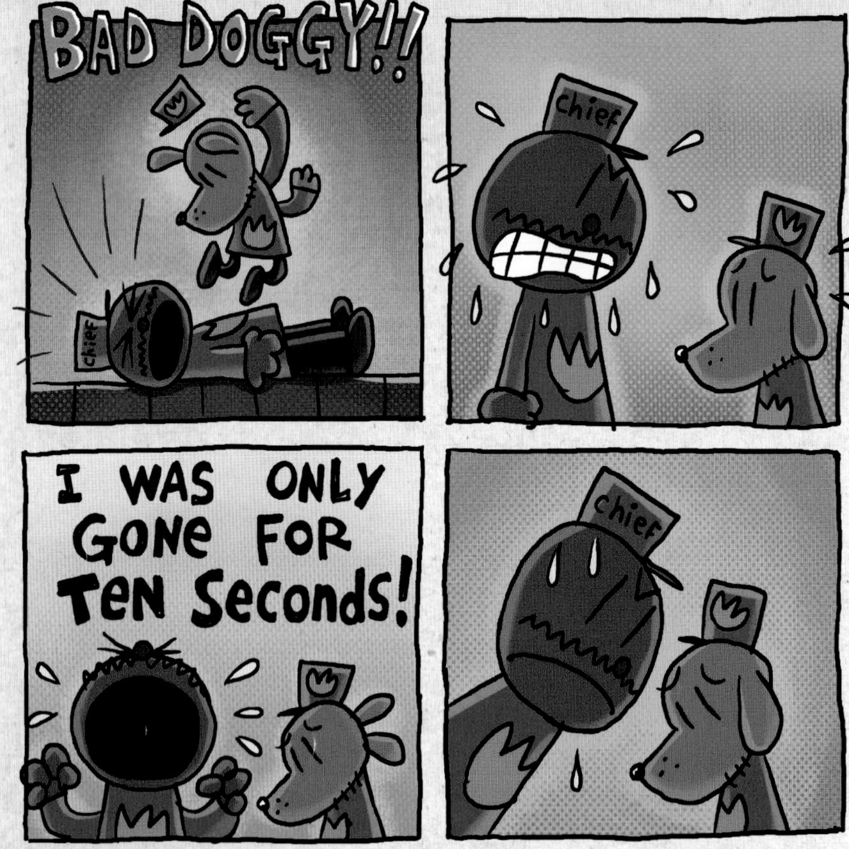

BAD DOGGY!!
chief
chief
I WAS ONLY GONE FOR TEN SECONDS!
chief
DOG Man, there's a cat outside.
chief
You need to get rid of him!
chief

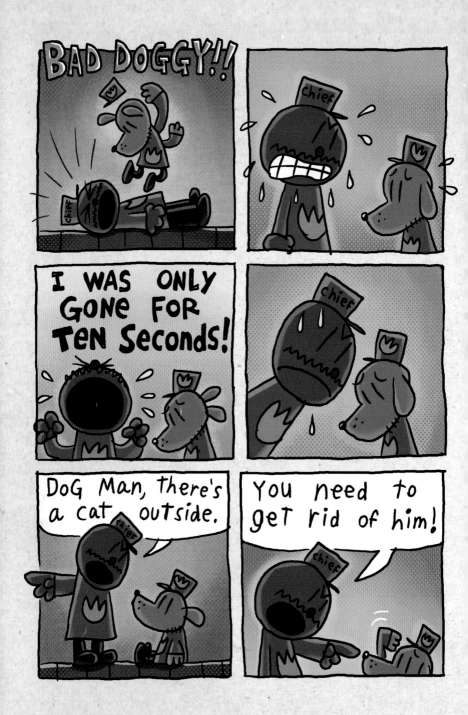

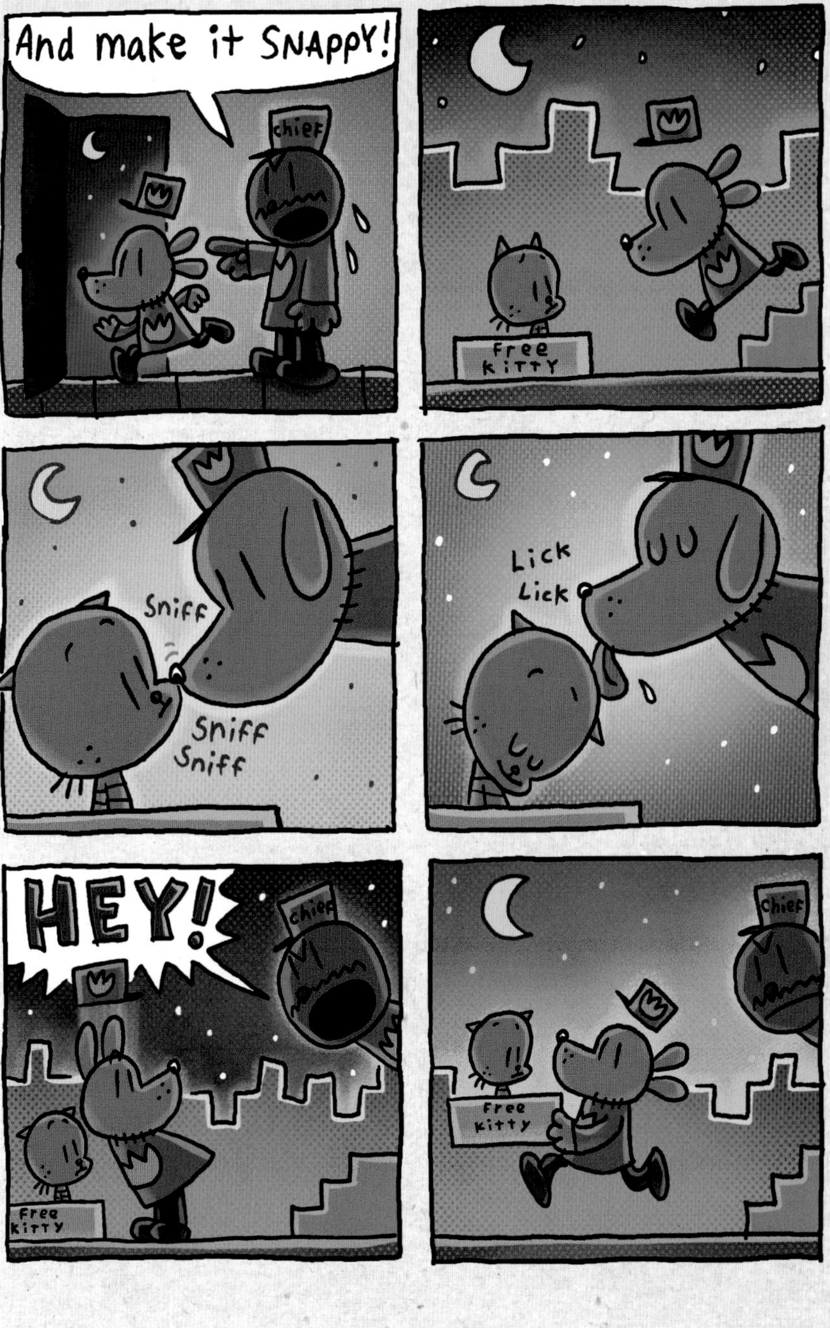
And make it SNAPPY!
chief
Free
Kitty
Sniff
Sniff
Sniff
Lick
Lick
HEY!
chief
Free
Kitty
Chief
Free
Kitty

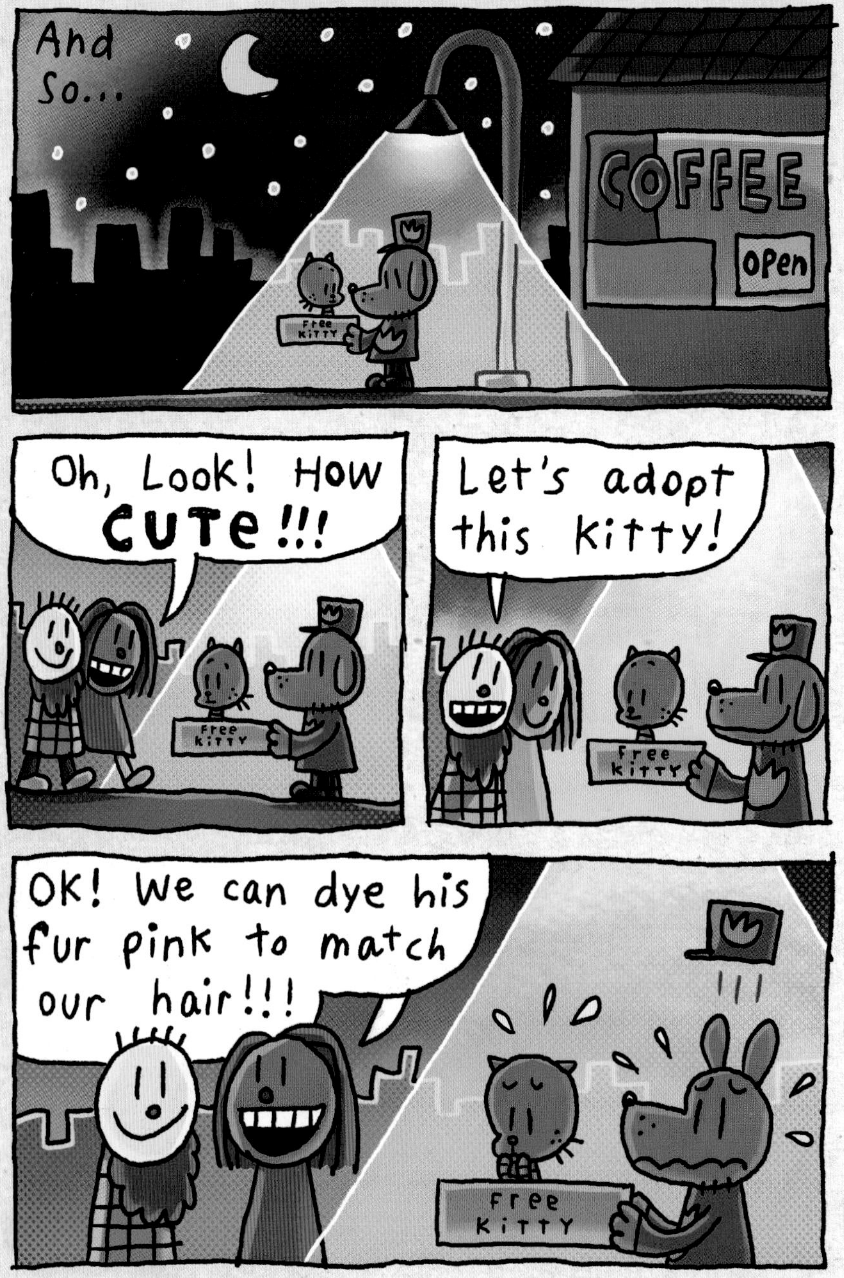
And So...
COFFEE
Open
Free KITTY
Oh, Look! How CUTE!!!
Free KITTY
Let's adopt this kitty!
Free KITTY
OK! We can dye his fur pink to match our hair!!!
Free KITTY

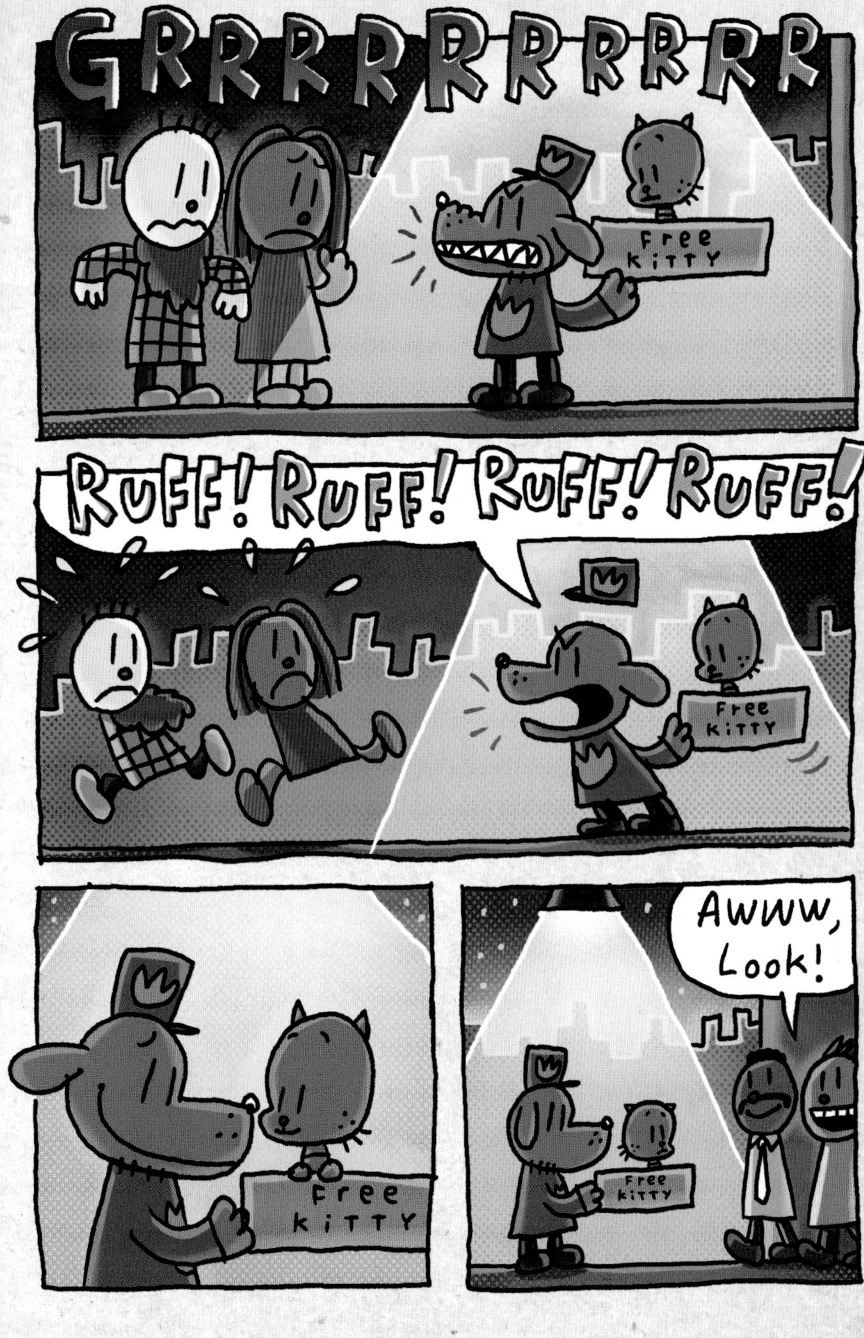
GRRRRRRRRRRR
Free kitty
RUFF! RUFF! RUFF! RUFF!
Free kitty
Free kitty
AWWW, Look!
Free kitty

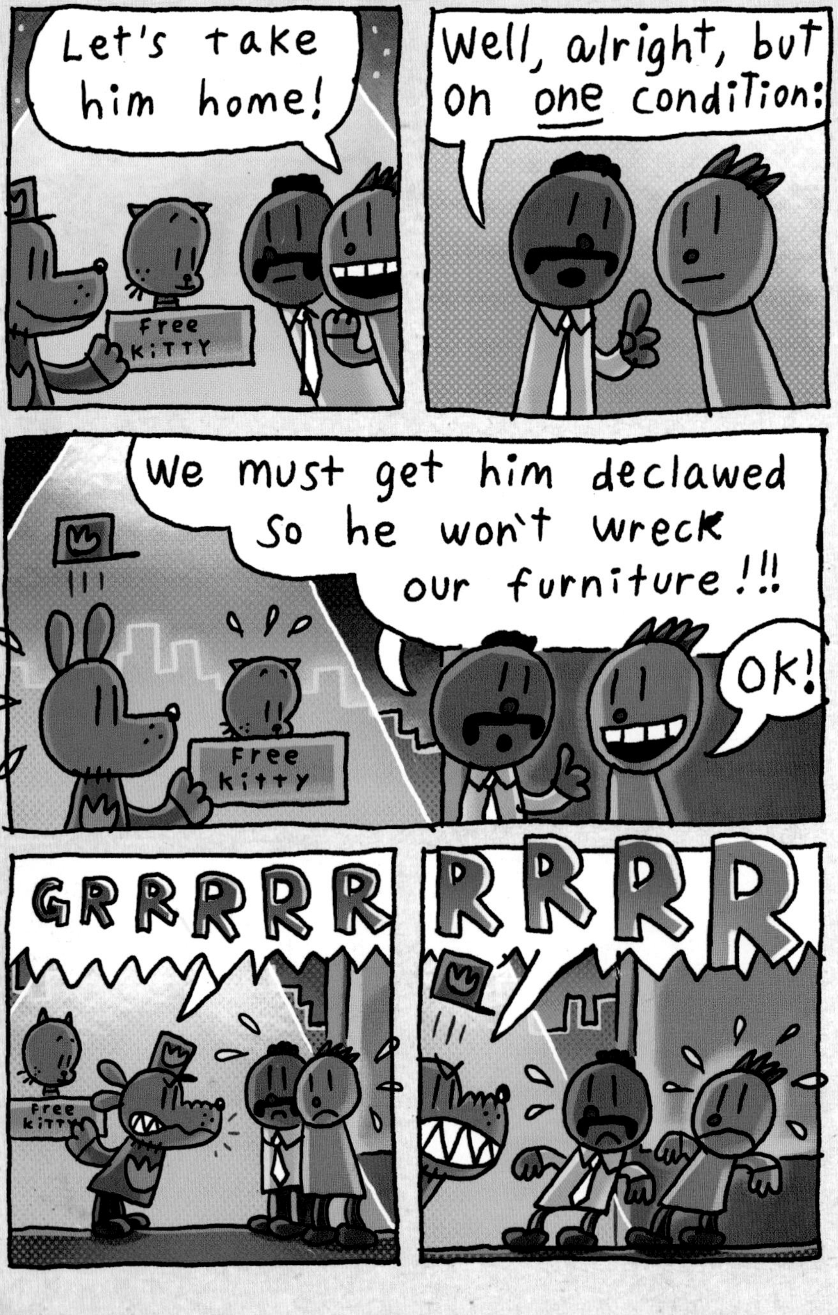
Let's take him home!
Free KiTTY
Well, alright, but on one condition:
We must get him declawed so he won't wreck our furniture!!!
Free kitty
OK!
GRRRRR
Free KiTTY
RRRR

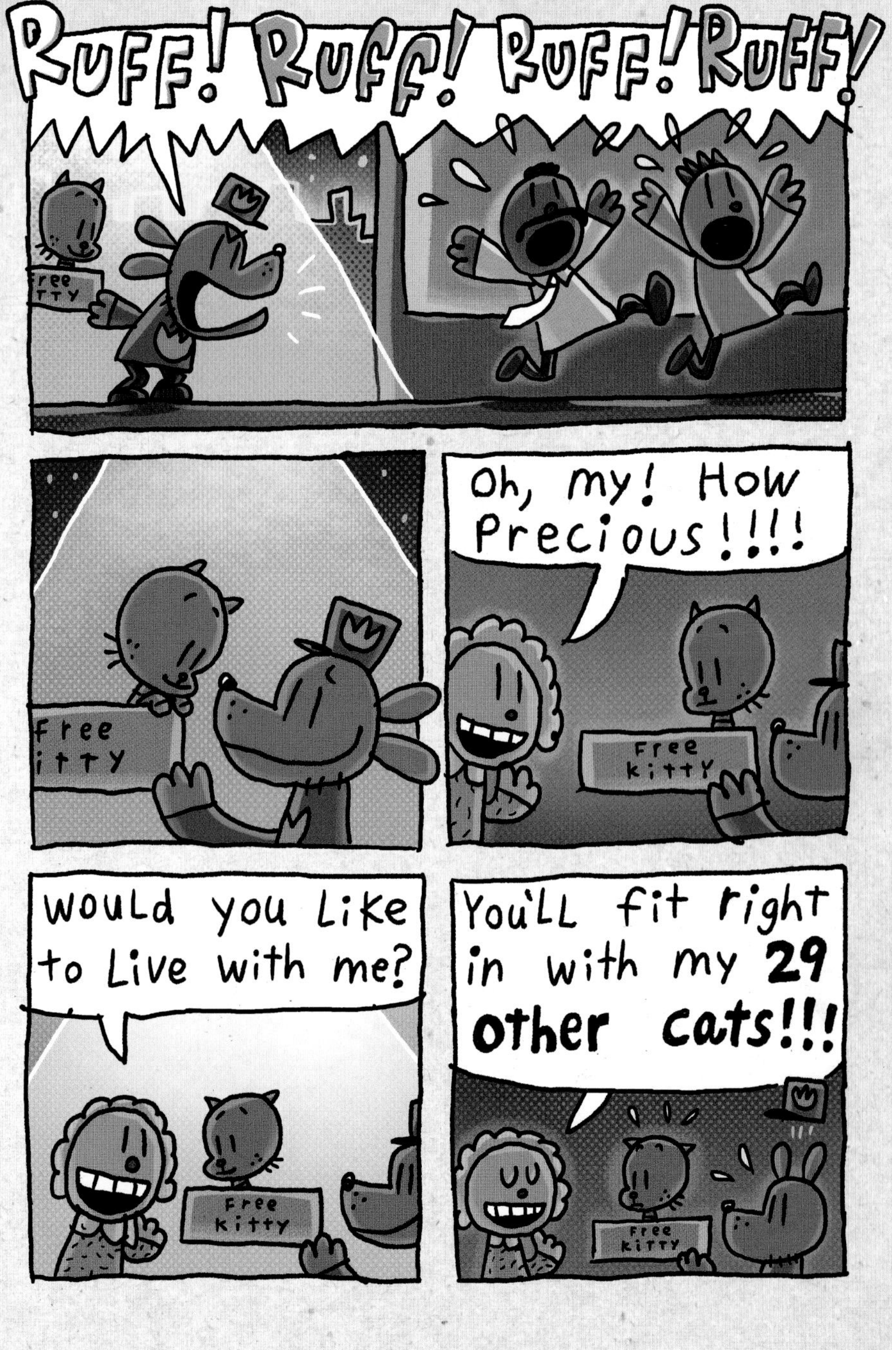
RUFF! RUFF! RUFF! RUFF!
Free Kitty
Free kitty
Oh, my! How Precious!!!!
Free kitty
Would you Like to Live with me?
Free kitty
You'LL fit right in with my **29 other cats!!!**
Free kitty

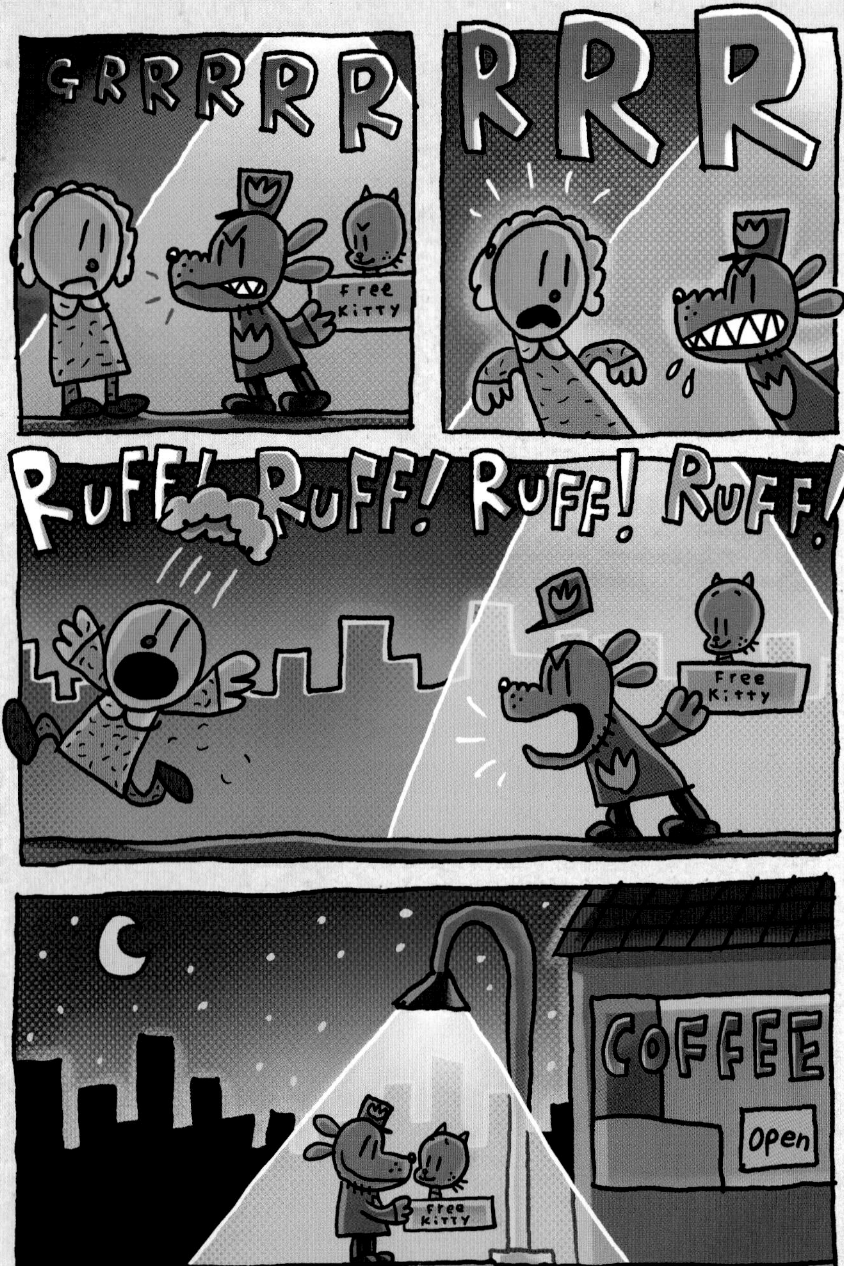
GRRRRRR
RRR
Free Kitty
RUFF! RUFF! RUFF! RUFF!
Free Kitty
COFFEE
Open
Free Kitty

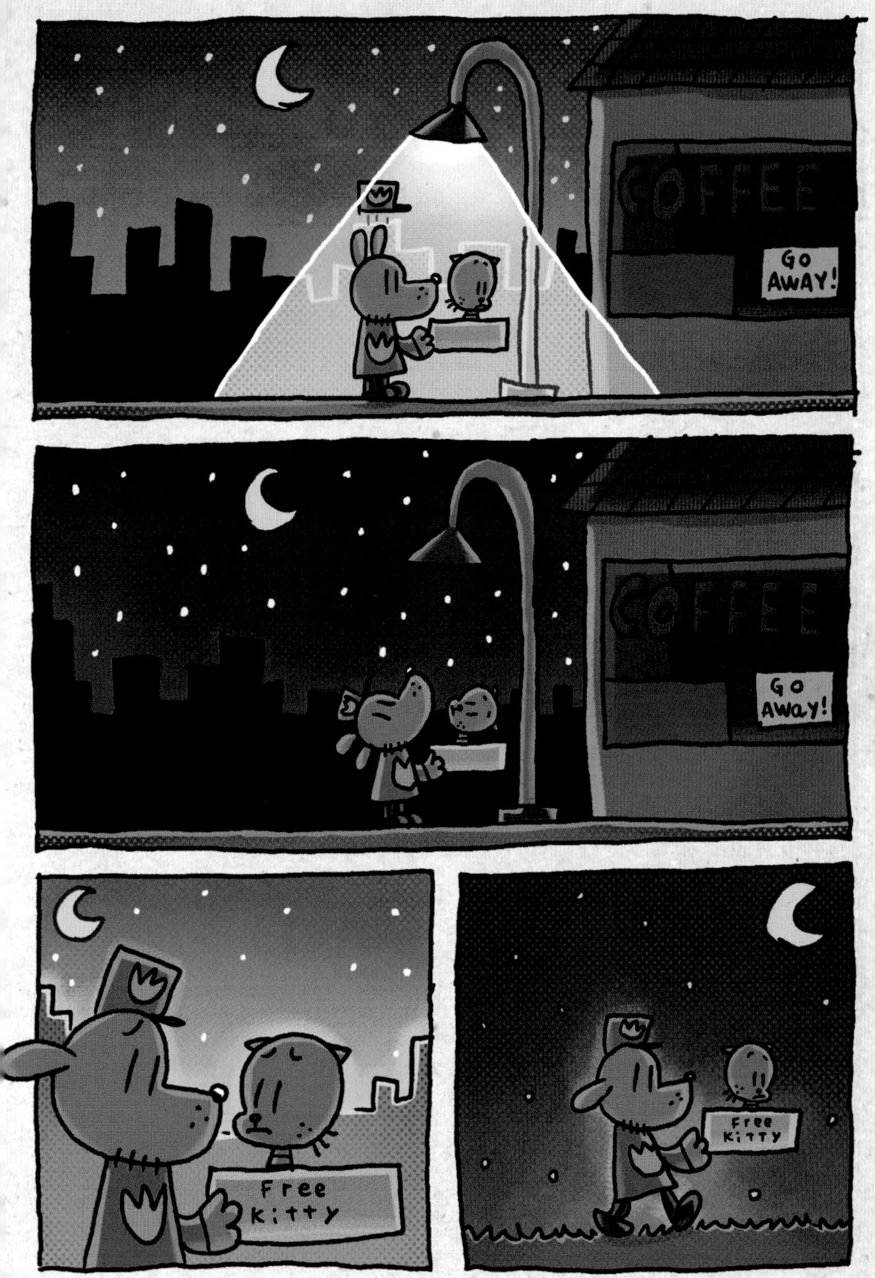
COFFEE
GO AWAY!
COFFEE
GO AWAY!
Free kitty
Free kitty

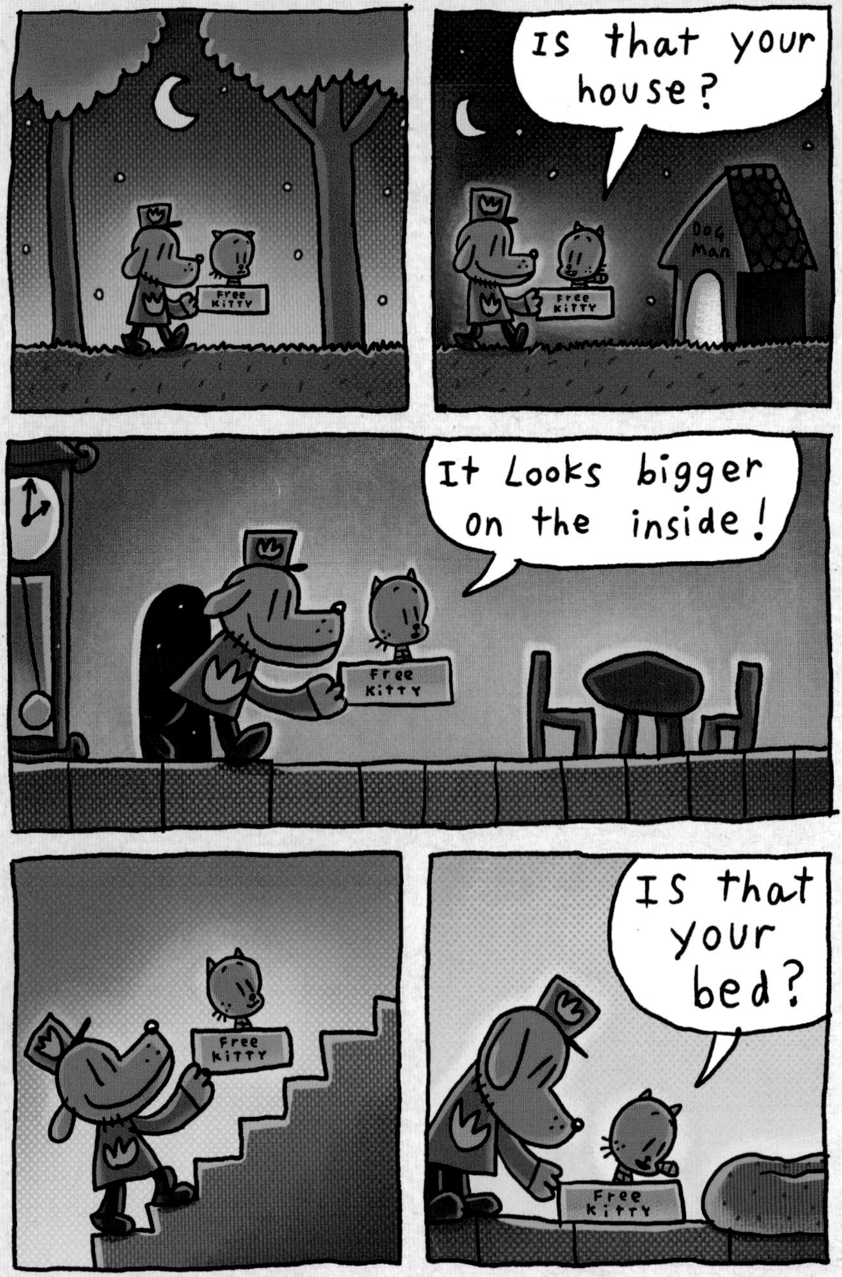
FREE KITTY
Is that your house?
FREE KITTY
DOG MAN
It Looks bigger on the inside!
Free Kitty
Free Kitty
Is that your bed?
Free Kitty

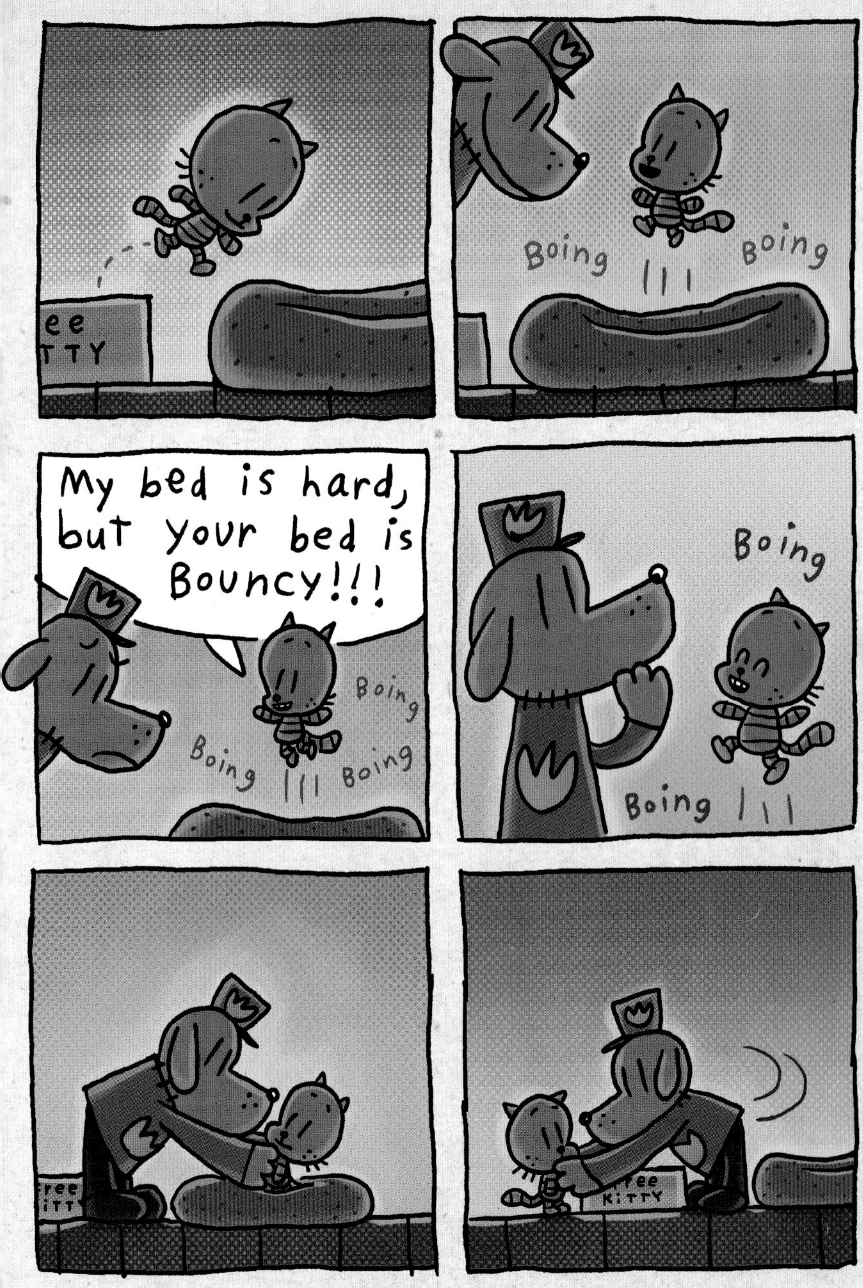
ee
TTY
Boing
Boing
My bed is hard, but your bed is Bouncy!!!
Boing
Boing
Boing
Boing
Boing
ree
ITTY
ree
KITTY

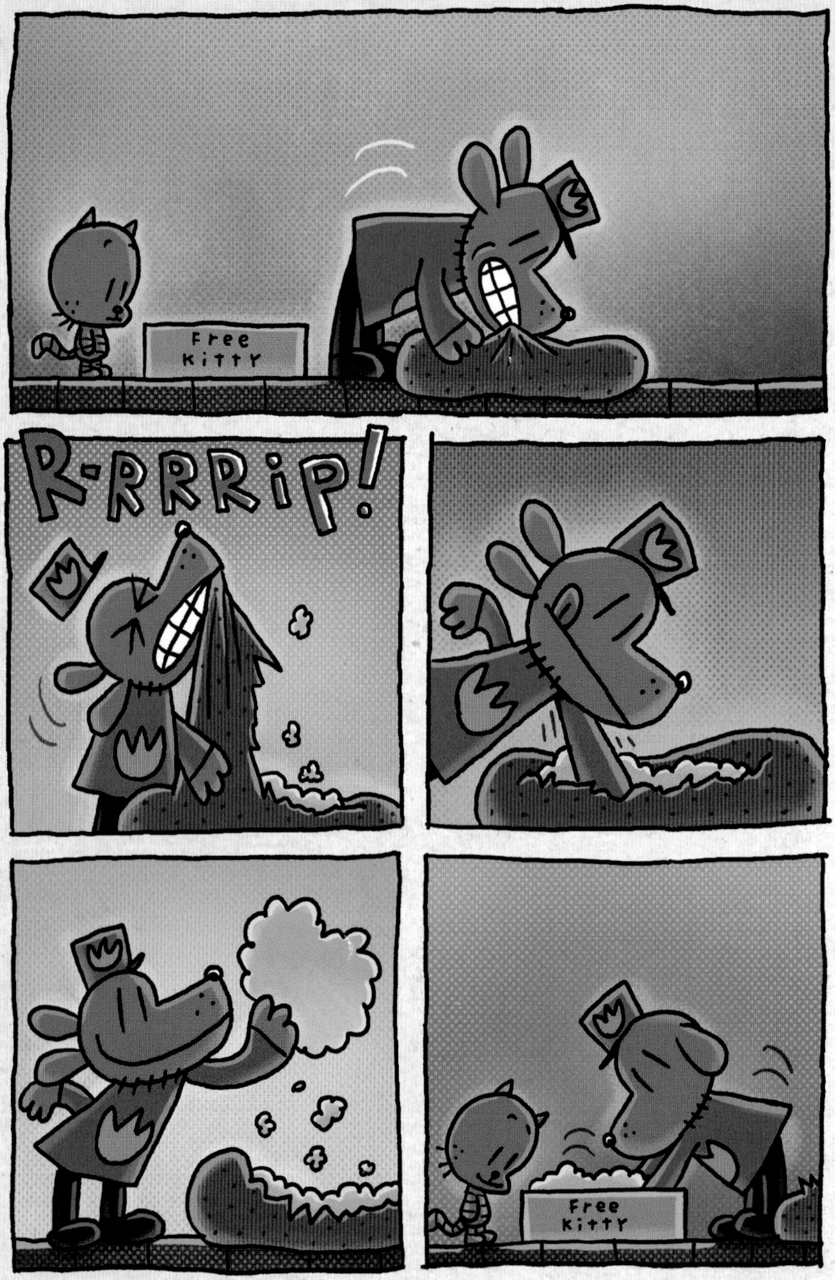
Free
Kitty
R-RRRIP!
Free
Kitty

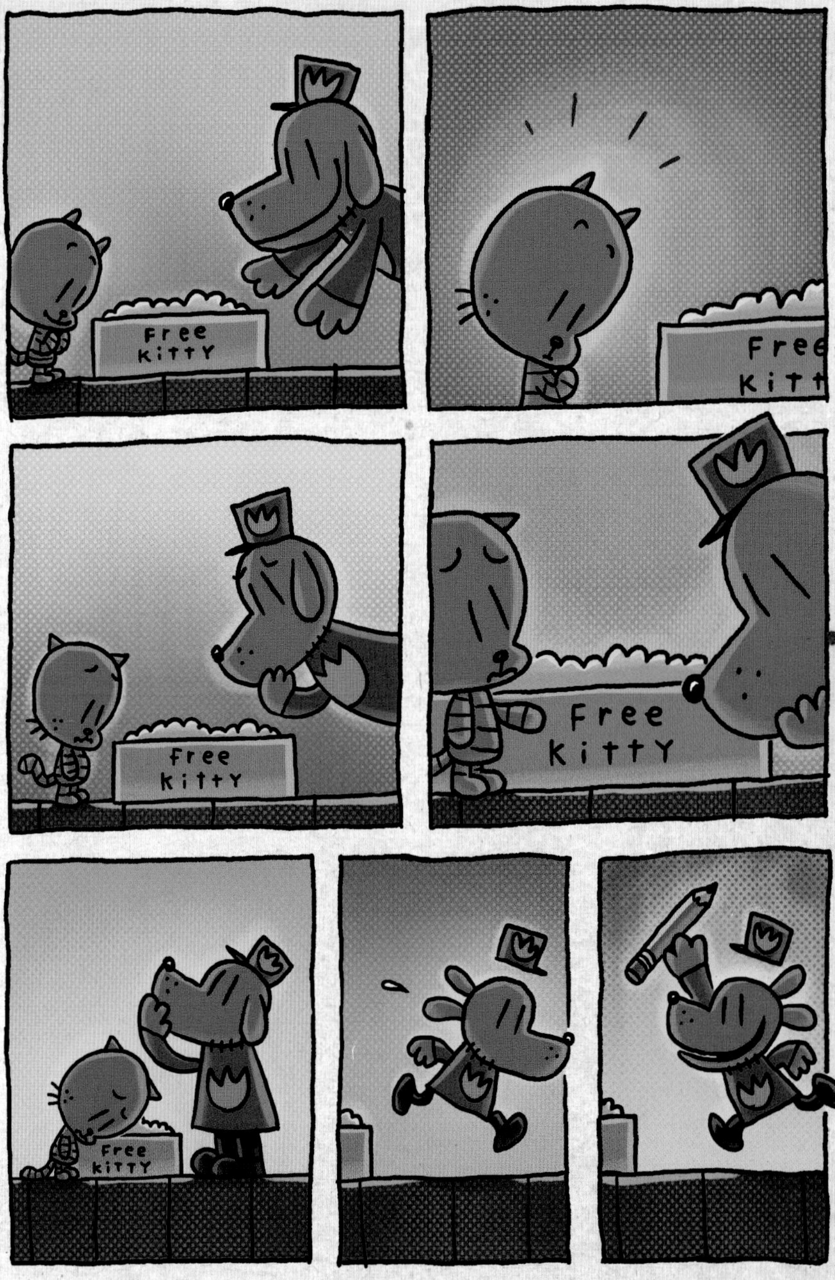

Free
kitty
Free
kitt
Free
kitty
Free
kitty
Free
kitty

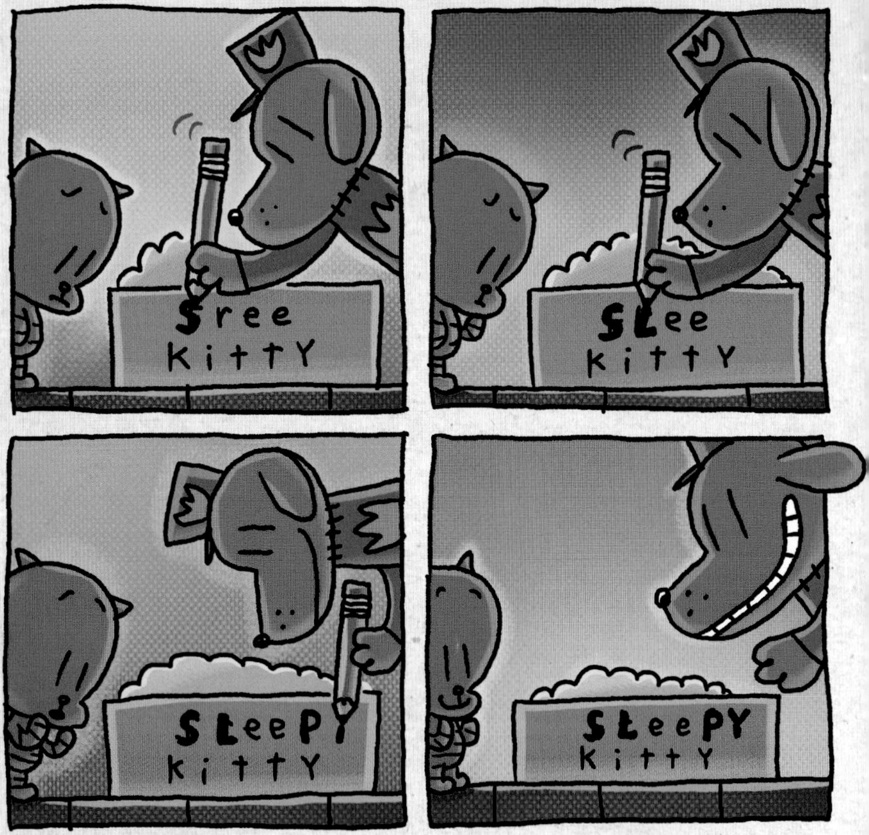
Sree Kitty
Slee kitty
Sleepy kitty
Sleepy kitty

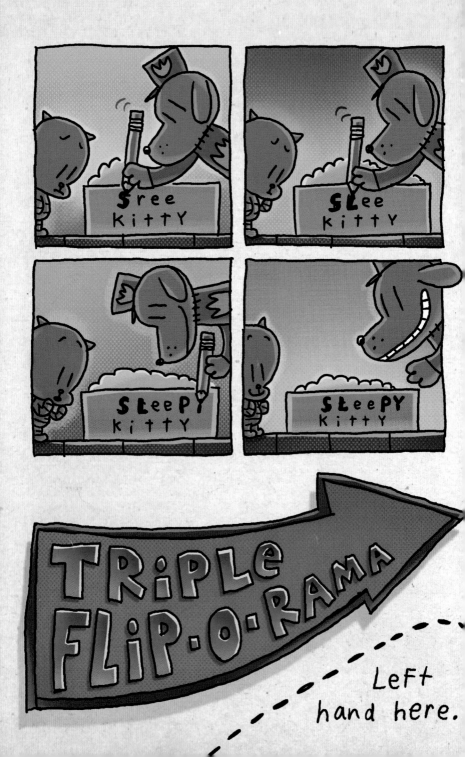

TRIPLE FLIP-O-RAMA

Left hand here.

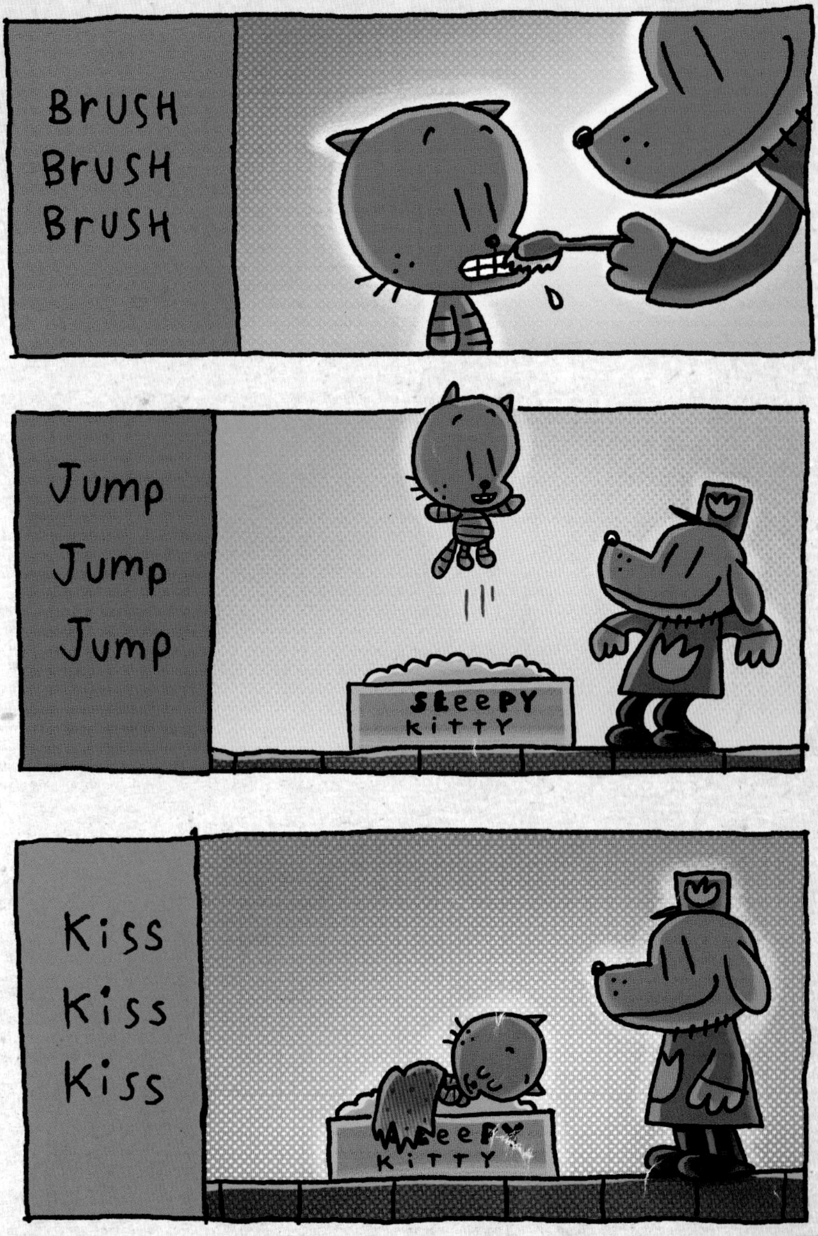
Brush
Brush
Brush
Jump
Jump
Jump
SLEEPY
KITTY
Kiss
Kiss
Kiss

Right Thumb here.

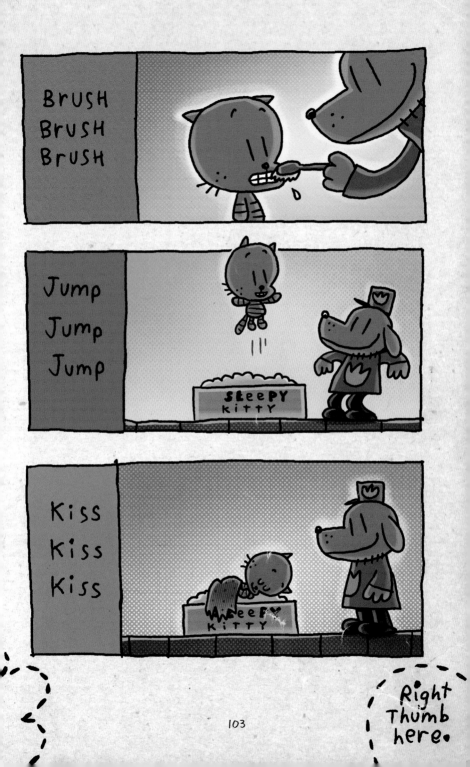

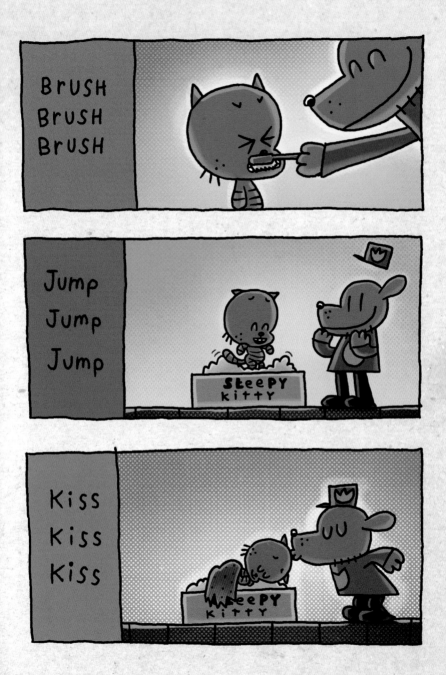

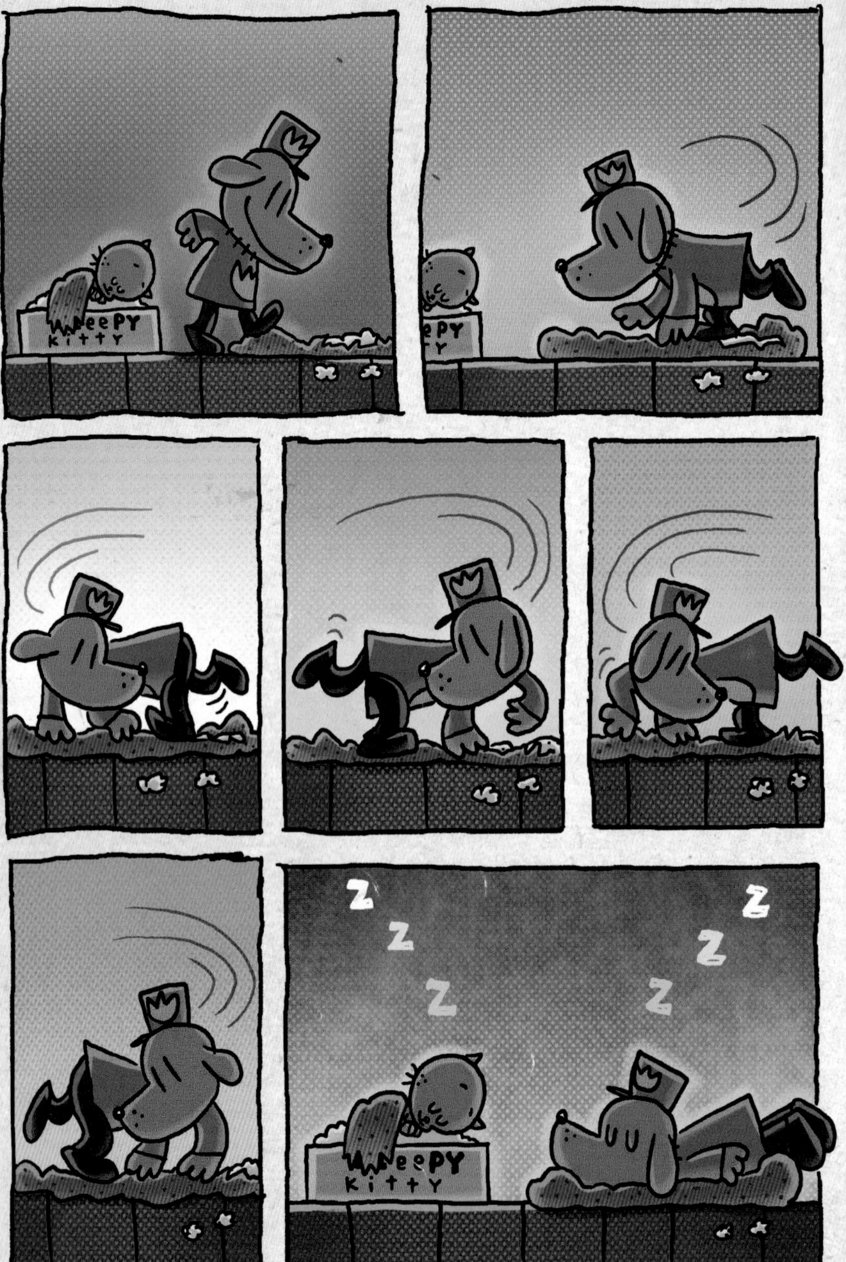
eePY
kitty
eePY
kitty
Z Z Z
Z Z Z

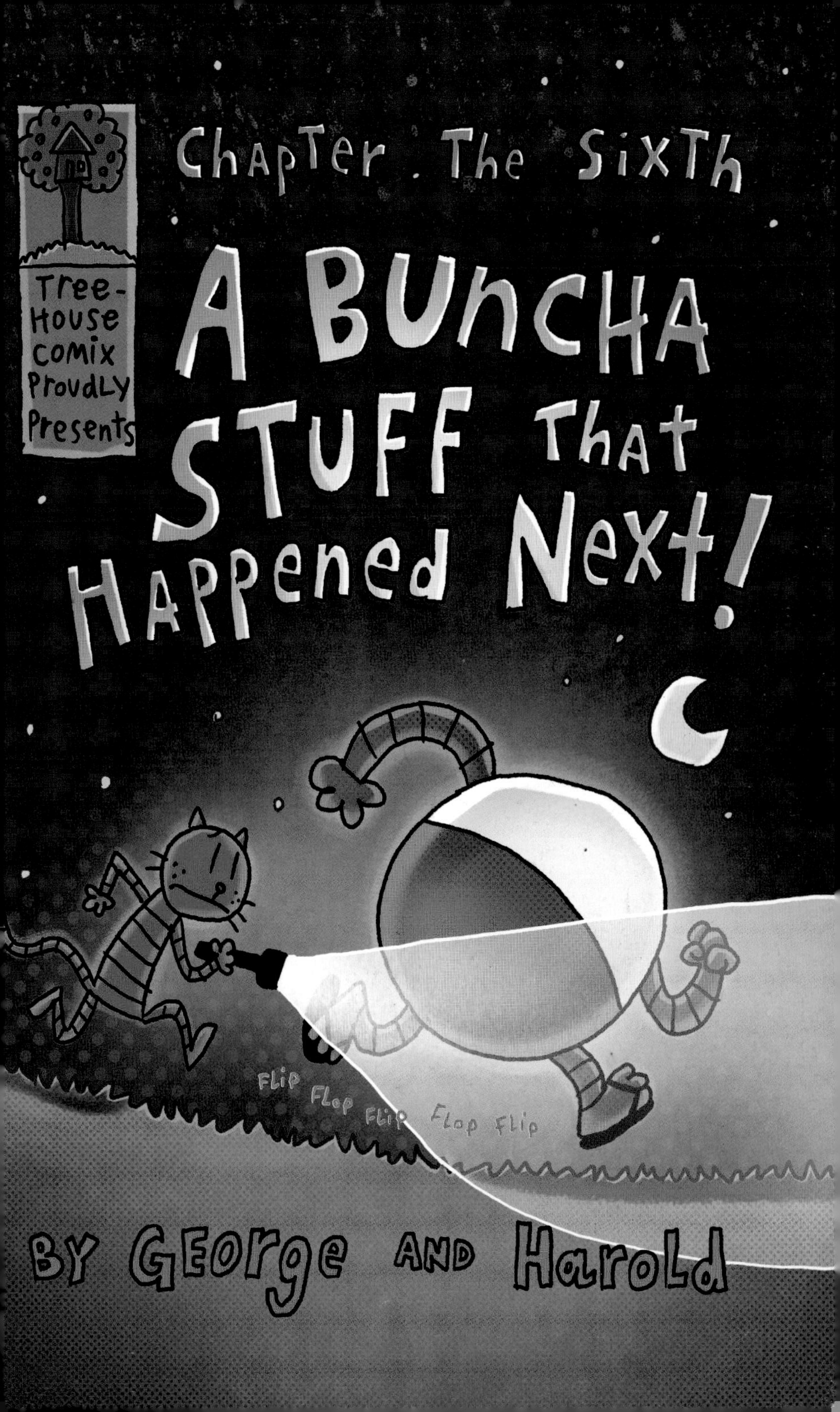
Tree-House Comix Proudly Presents
Chapter the Sixth
A Buncha Stuff That Happened Next!
Flip Flop Flip Flop Flip
By George and Harold

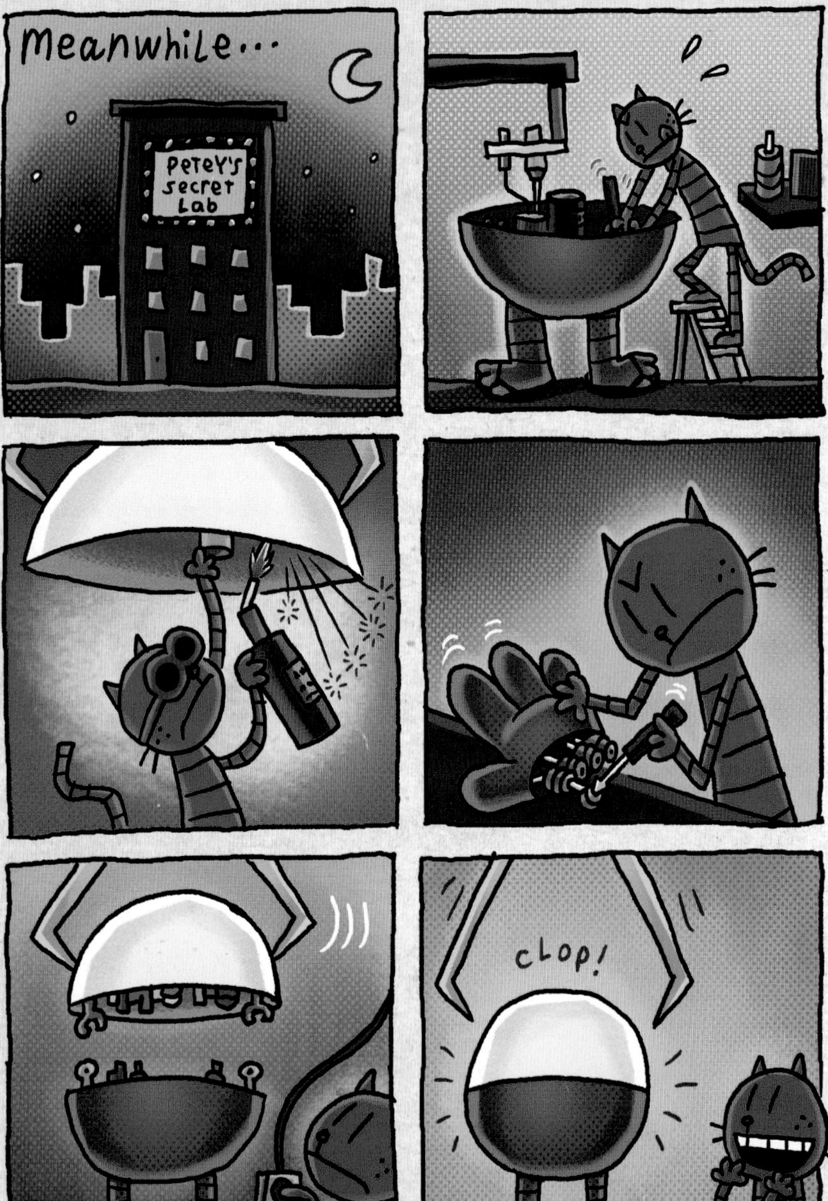
Meanwhile...
Petey's Secret Lab
CLOP!

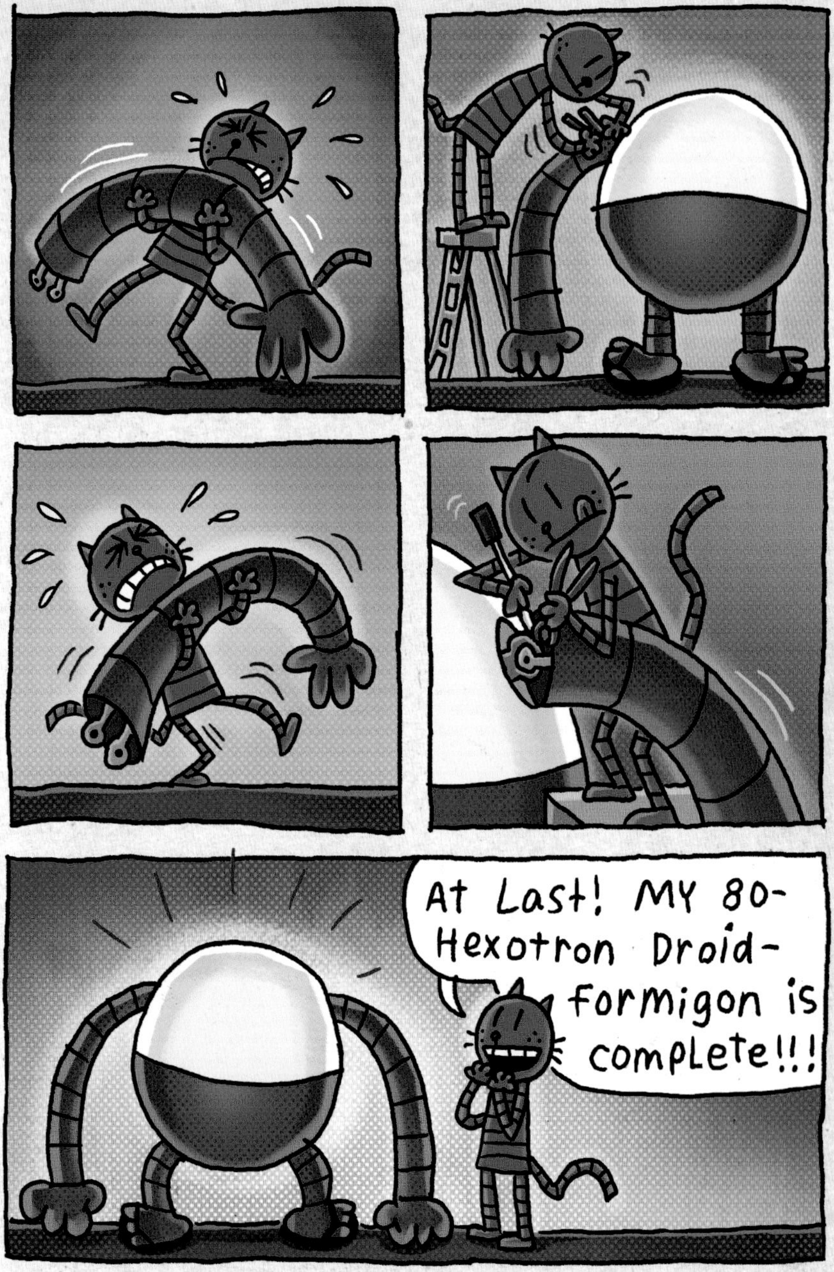
At Last! MY 80-Hexotron Droid-Formigon is compLete!!!

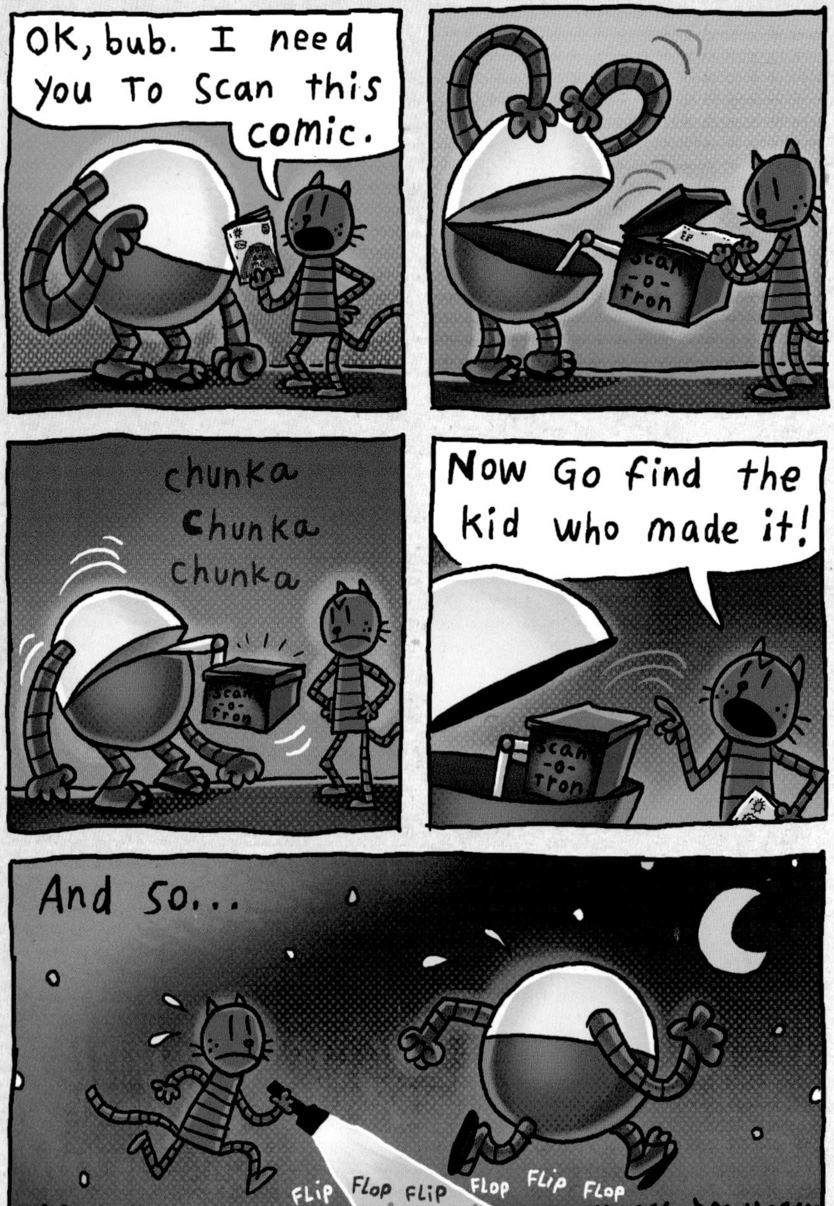
OK, bub. I need you To Scan this comic.
Scan -o- Tron
chunka Chunka chunka
Scan -o- Tron
Now Go find the kid who made it!
Scan -o- Tron
And so...
FLiP FLop FLiP FLop FLiP FLop

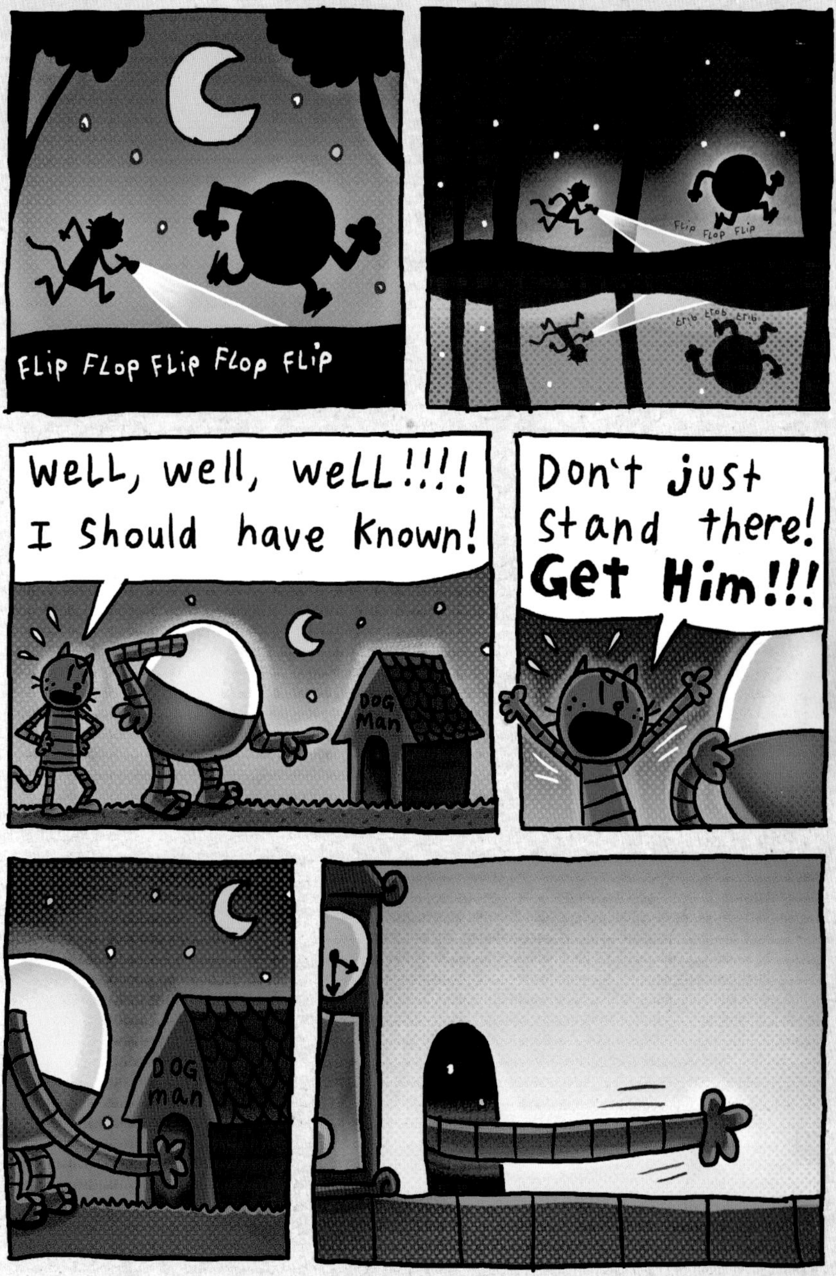

FLIP FLOP FLIP FLOP FLIP
FLIP FLOP FLIP
WELL, well, WELL!!!! I Should have Known!
DOG Man
Don't just stand there! Get Him!!!
DOG man

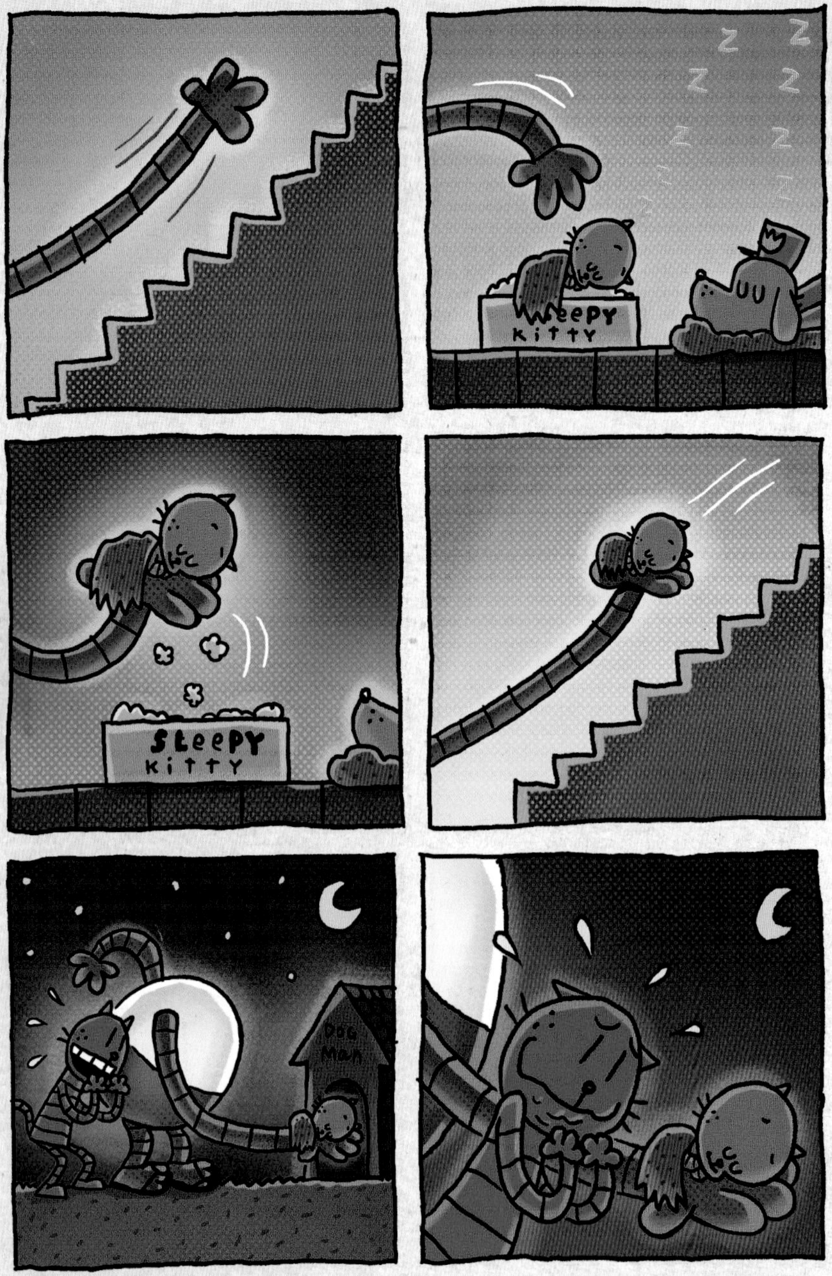
Z Z Z Z Z Z
eepy
Kitty
Sleepy
Kitty
DOG
MAN

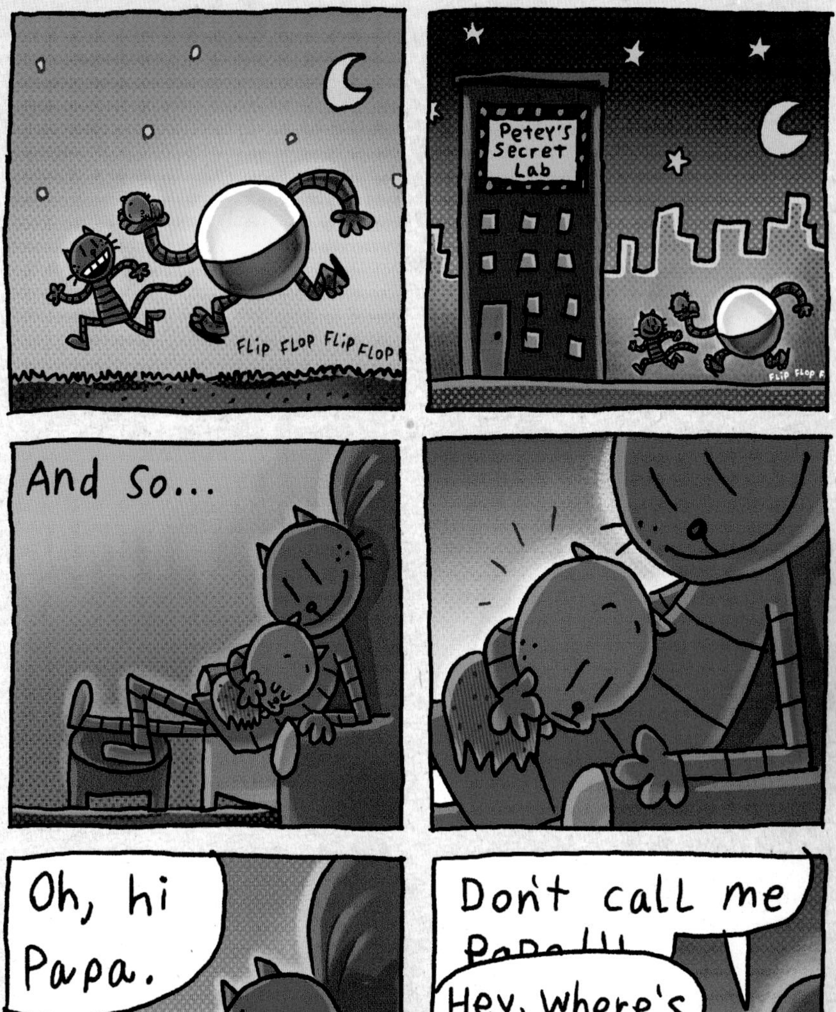
FLIP FLOP FLIP FLOP
Petey's Secret Lab
And so...
Oh, hi Papa.
Don't call me
Hey, where's Dog Man?

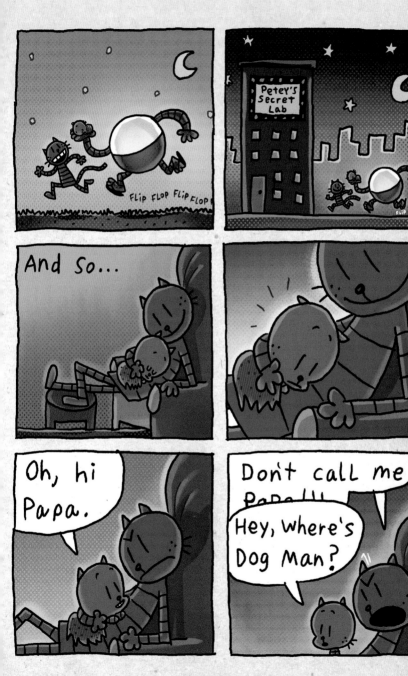

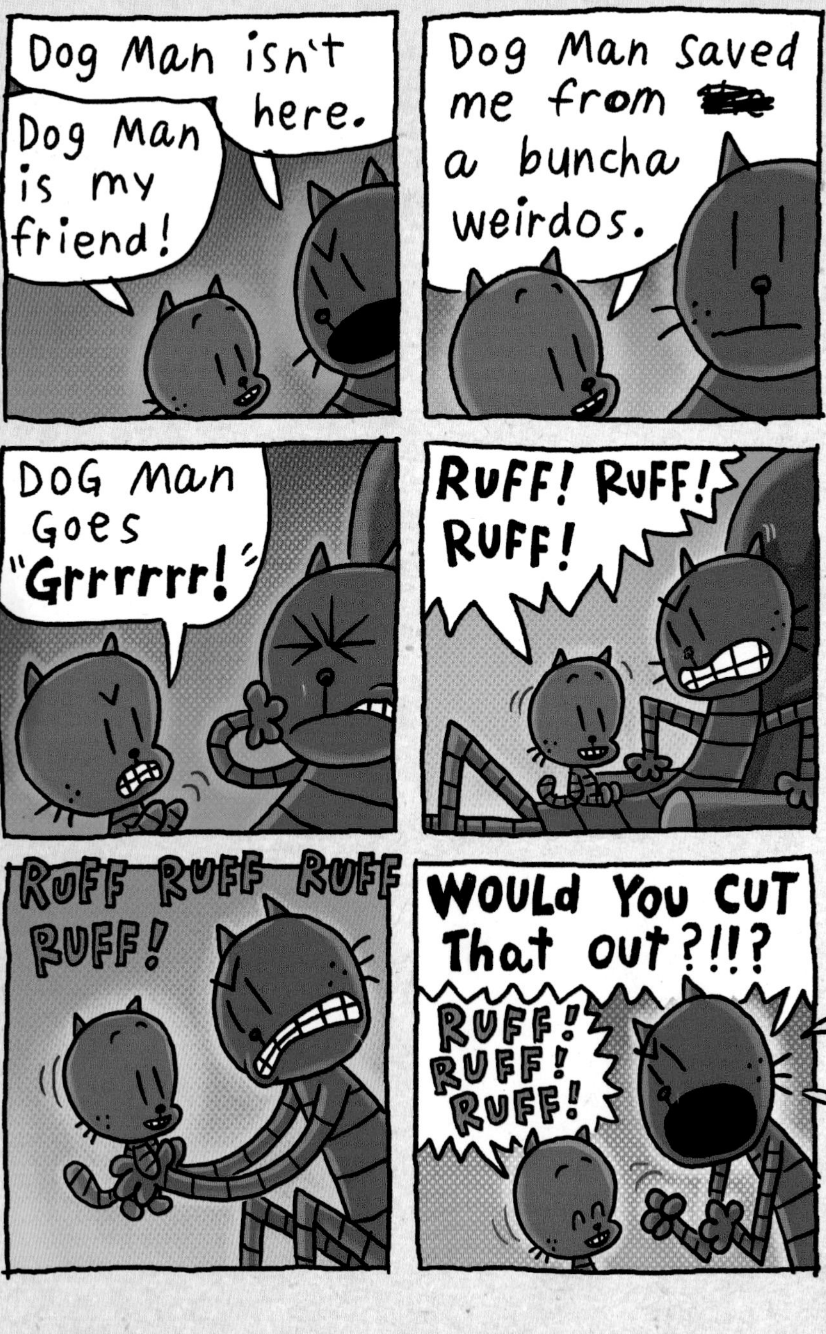
Dog Man isn't here.
Dog Man is my friend!
Dog Man saved me from a buncha weirdos.
DOG Man Goes "Grrrrrr!"
RUFF! RUFF! RUFF!
RUFF RUFF RUFF RUFF!
WOULd You CUT That out?!!?
RUFF! RUFF! RUFF!

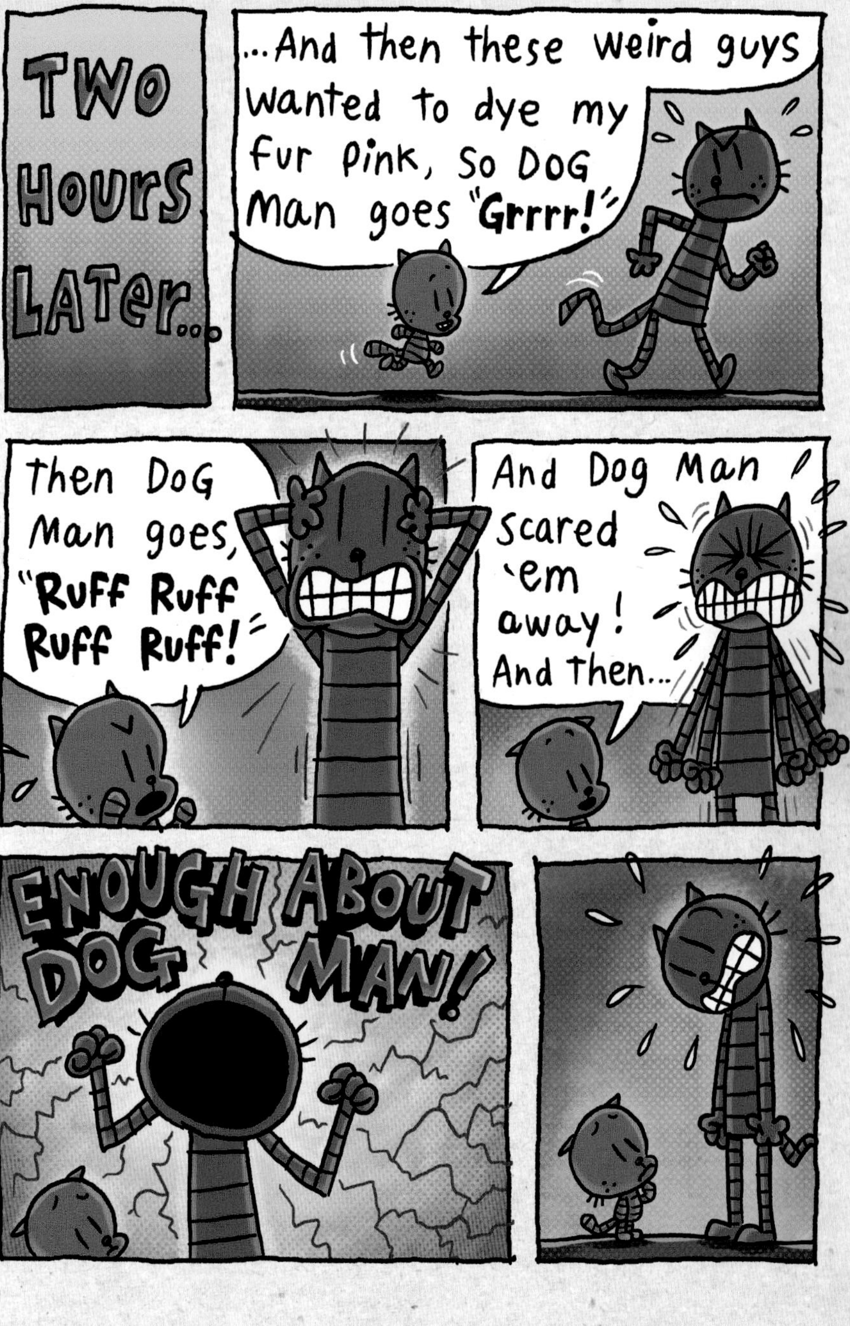
TWO HOURS LATER...
...And then these weird guys wanted to dye my fur pink, so DOG Man goes "Grrrr!"
Then DoG Man goes, "RUFF Ruff Ruff Ruff!"
And Dog Man scared 'em away! And Then...
ENOUGH ABOUT DOG MAN!

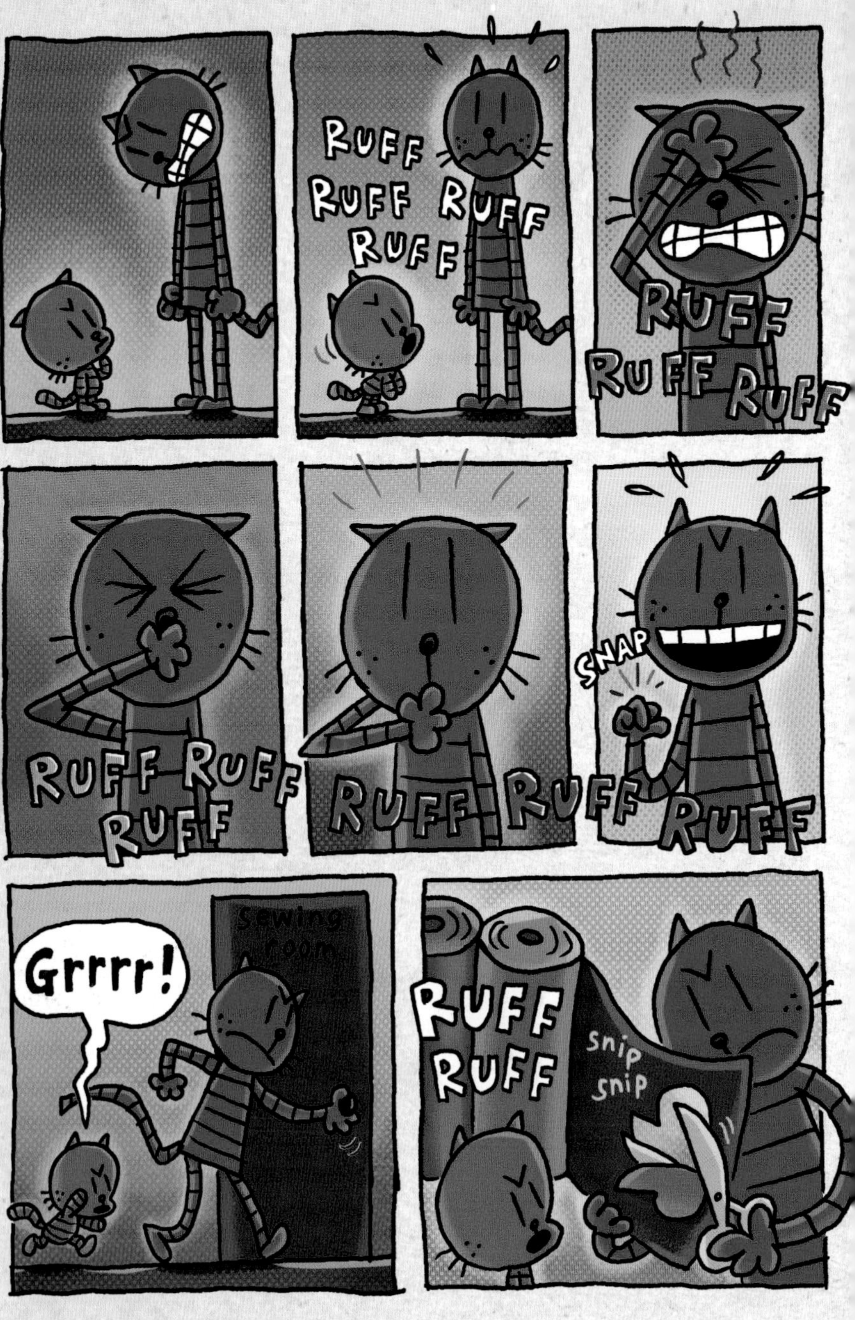
RUFF
RUFF RUFF
RUFF
RUFF
RUFF RUFF
RUFF RUFF
RUFF
RUFF RUFF
SNAP
RUFF
Grrrr!
Sewing room
RUFF
RUFF
snip
snip

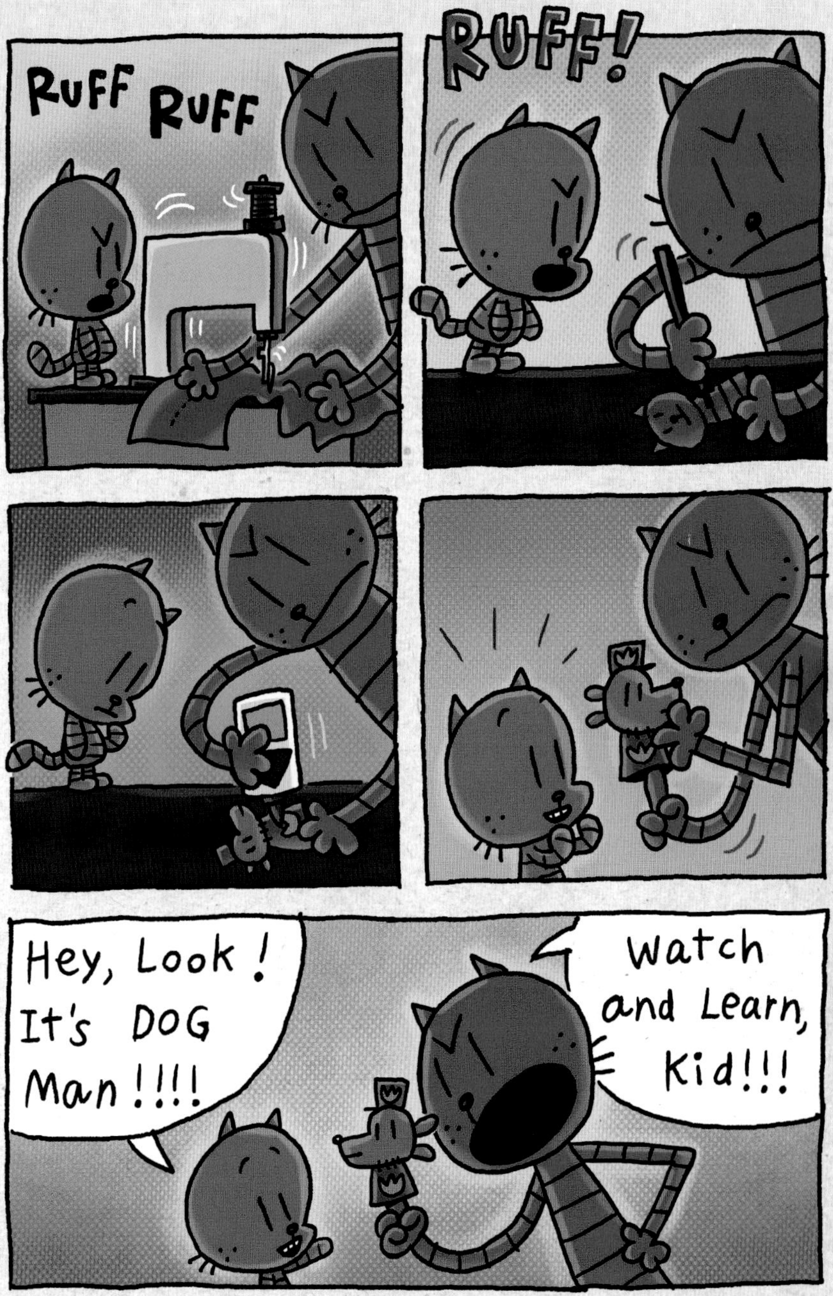
RUFF RUFF
RUFF!
Hey, Look! It's DOG Man!!!!
Watch and Learn, Kid!!!

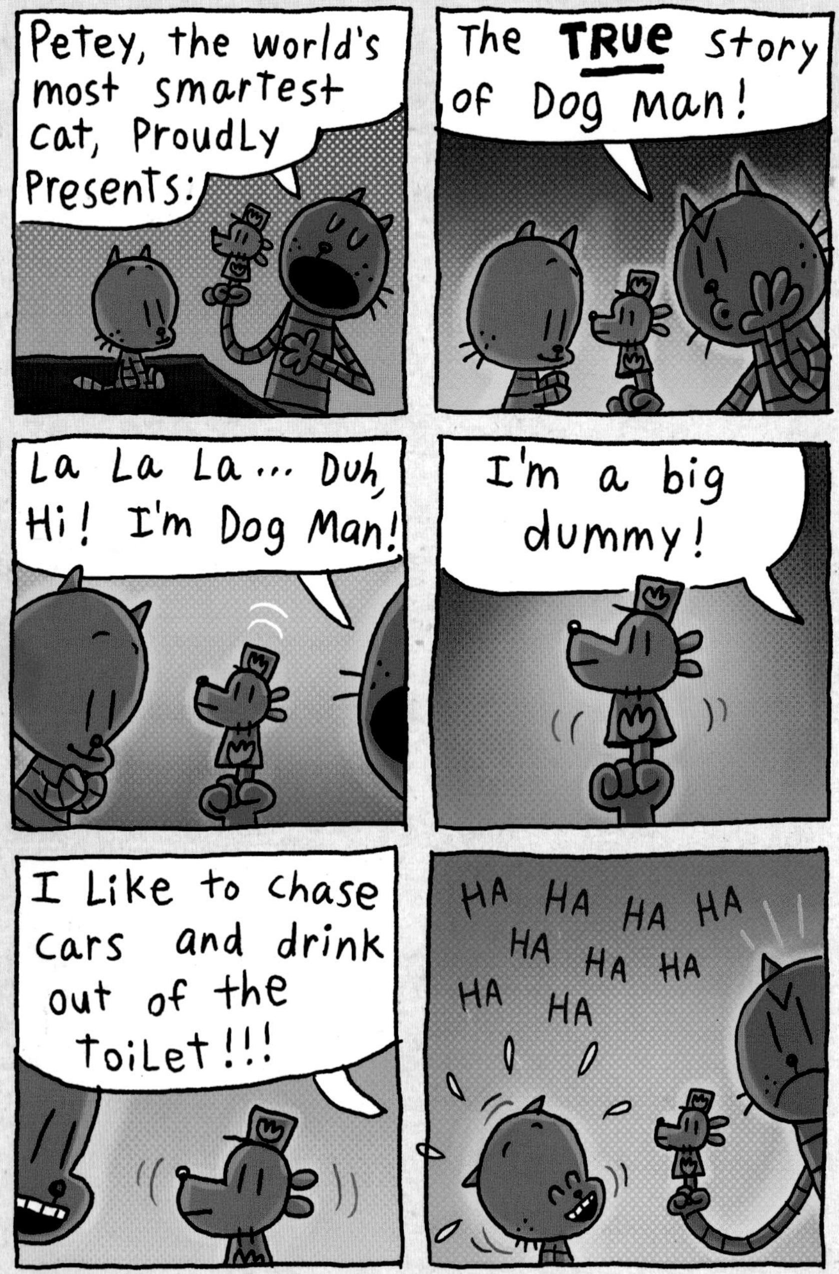
Petey, the world's most smartest cat, ProudLy Presents:
The TRUE story of Dog Man!
La La La... Duh, Hi! I'm Dog Man!
I'm a big dummy!
I Like to chase cars and drink out of the toiLet!!!
HA HA HA HA HA HA HA HA HA

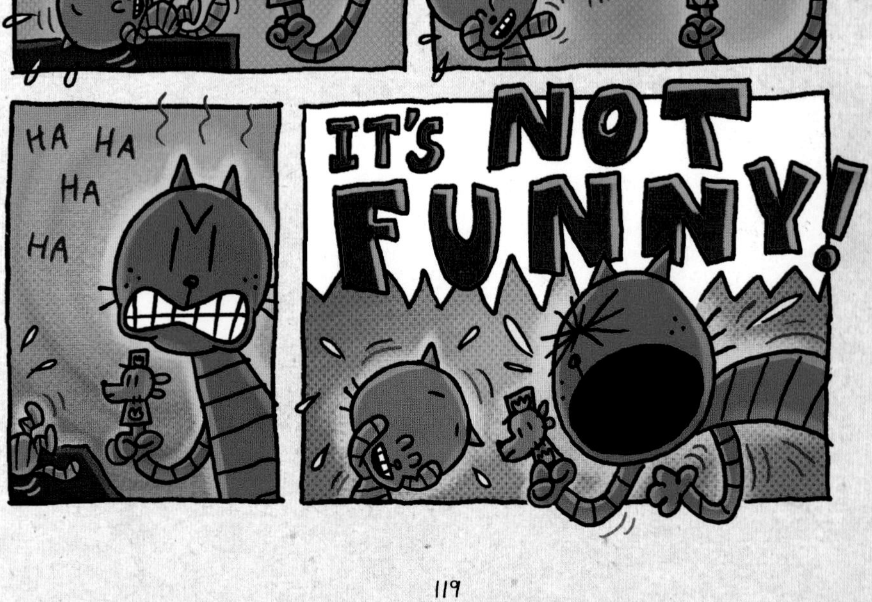
It's NOT FUNNY!
HA HA HA HA HA
Duh, I gotta go sniff other dogs' butts, and...
HA HA HA
... and roll around in duck poop... and... and...
HA HA HA HA HA
... and go take "stupid lessons" so I can be ...
HA HA HA HA HA HA
HA HA HA HA
IT'S NOT FUNNY!

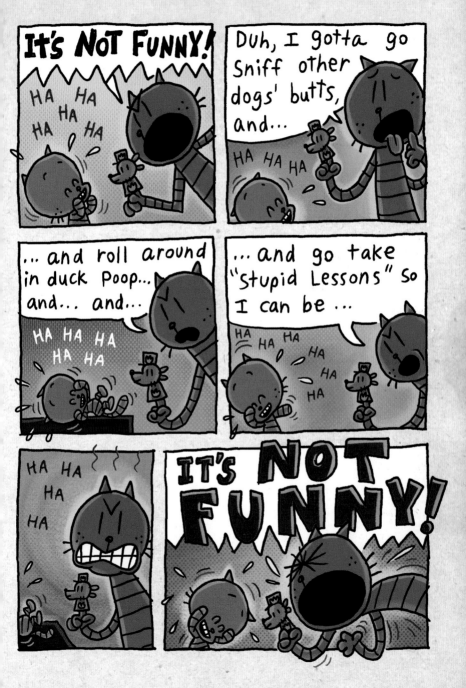

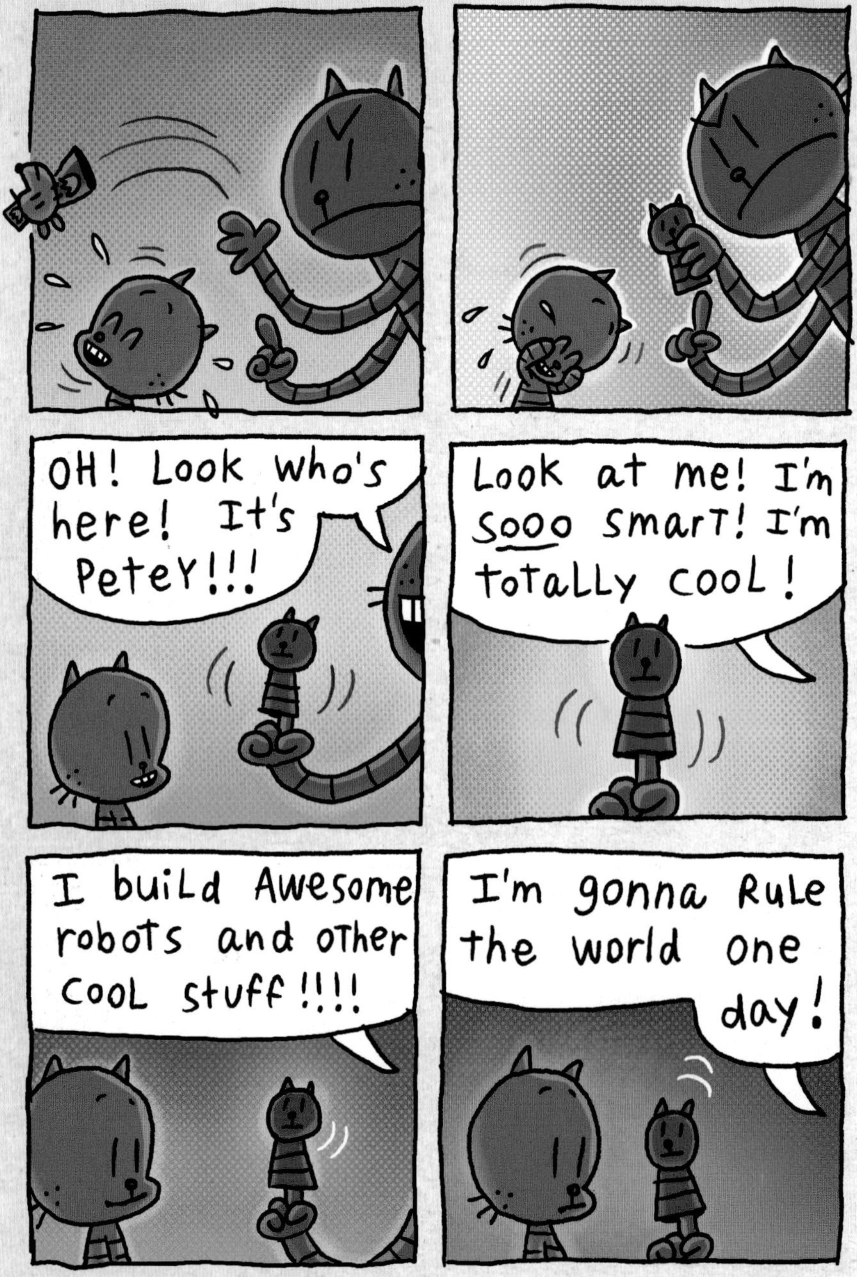
OH! Look who's here! It's Petey!!!
Look at me! I'm sooo smart! I'm totally cool!
I build awesome robots and other cool stuff!!!!
I'm gonna rule the world one day!

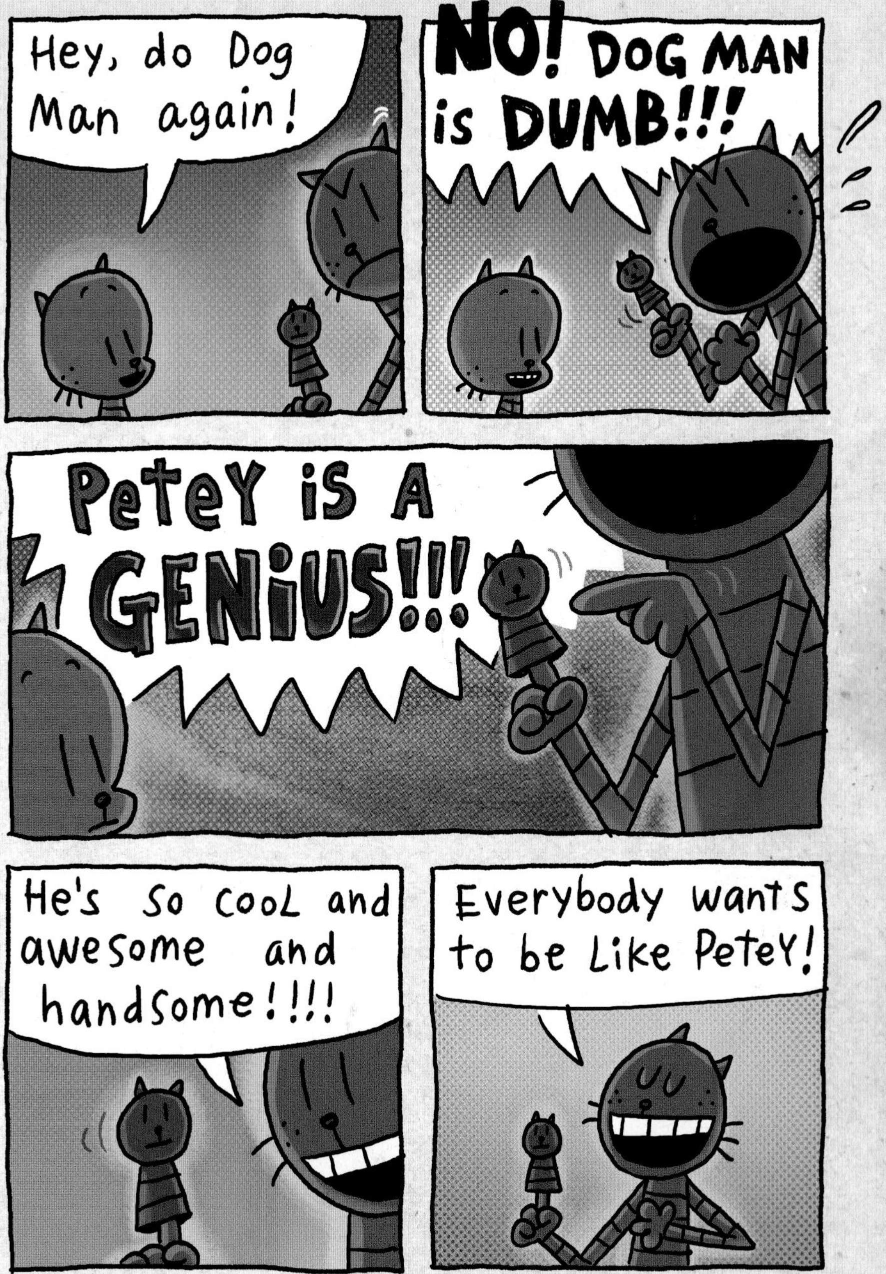
Hey, do Dog Man again!
NO! DOG MAN is DUMB!!!
PeteY iS A GENiUS!!!
He's So CooL and awesome and handSome!!!!
Everybody wantS to be Like PeteY!

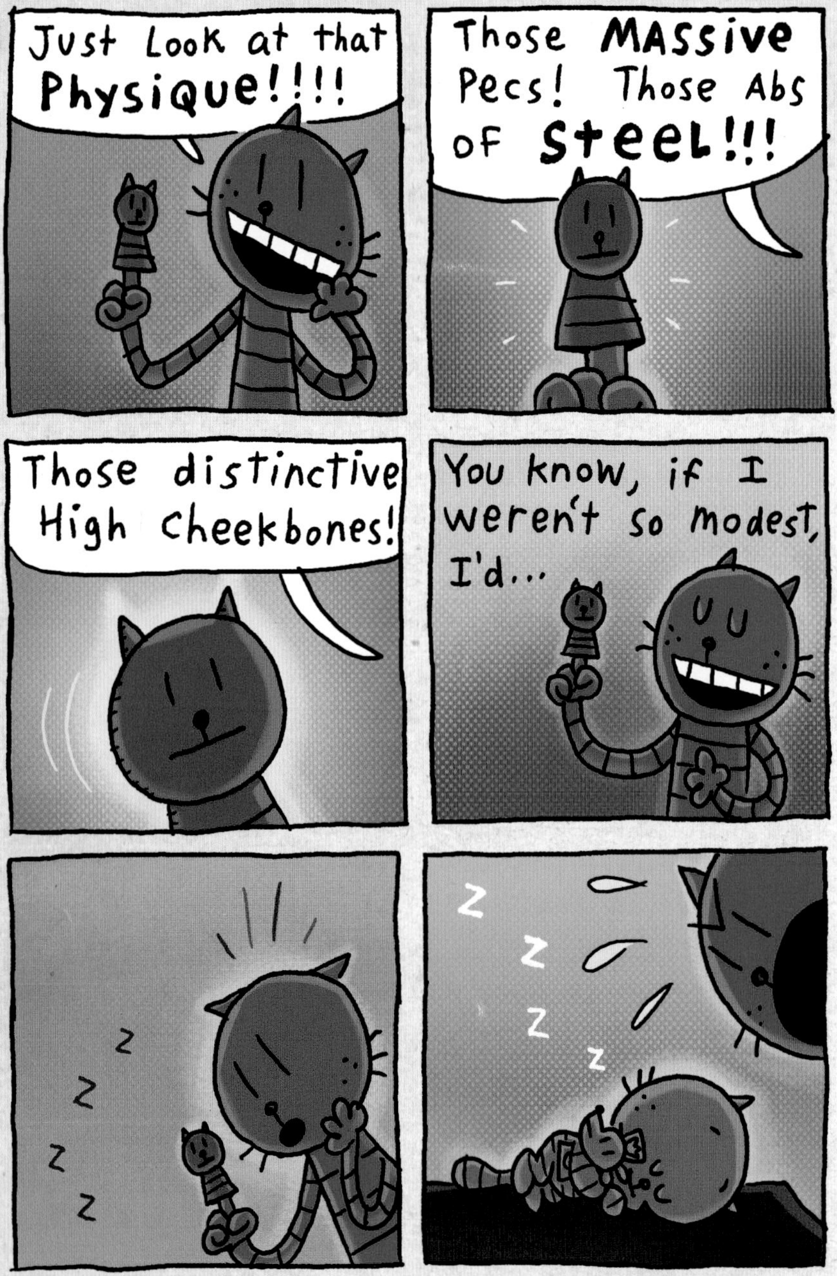
Just Look at that Physique!!!!
Those MASSive Pecs! Those Abs of Steel!!!
Those distinctive High cheekbones!
You know, if I weren't so modest, I'd...
Z Z Z Z
Z Z Z Z

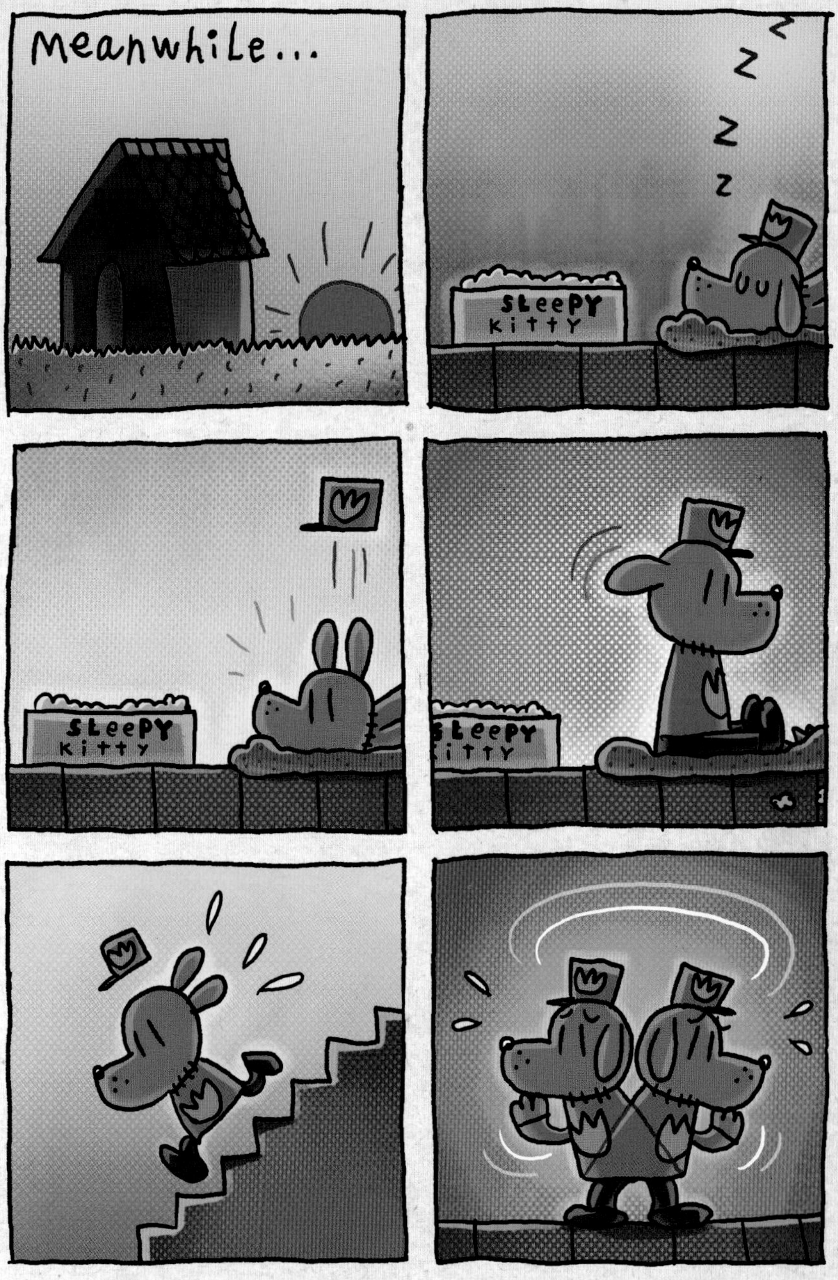
Meanwhile...
Z
Z
Z
Z
SLEEPY KITTY
SLEEPY KITTY
SLEEPY KITTY

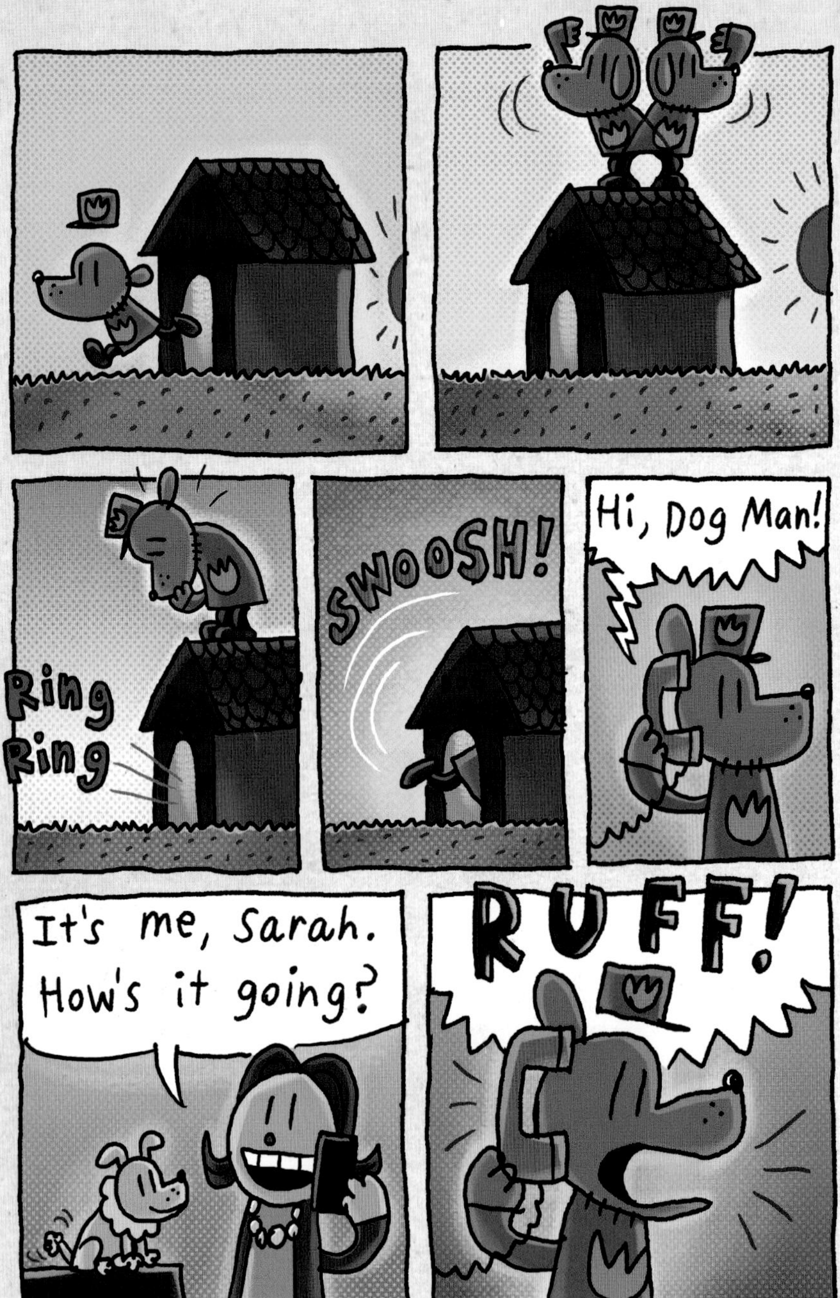

Ring
Ring
SWOOSH!
Hi, Dog Man!
It's me, Sarah. How's it going?
RUFF!

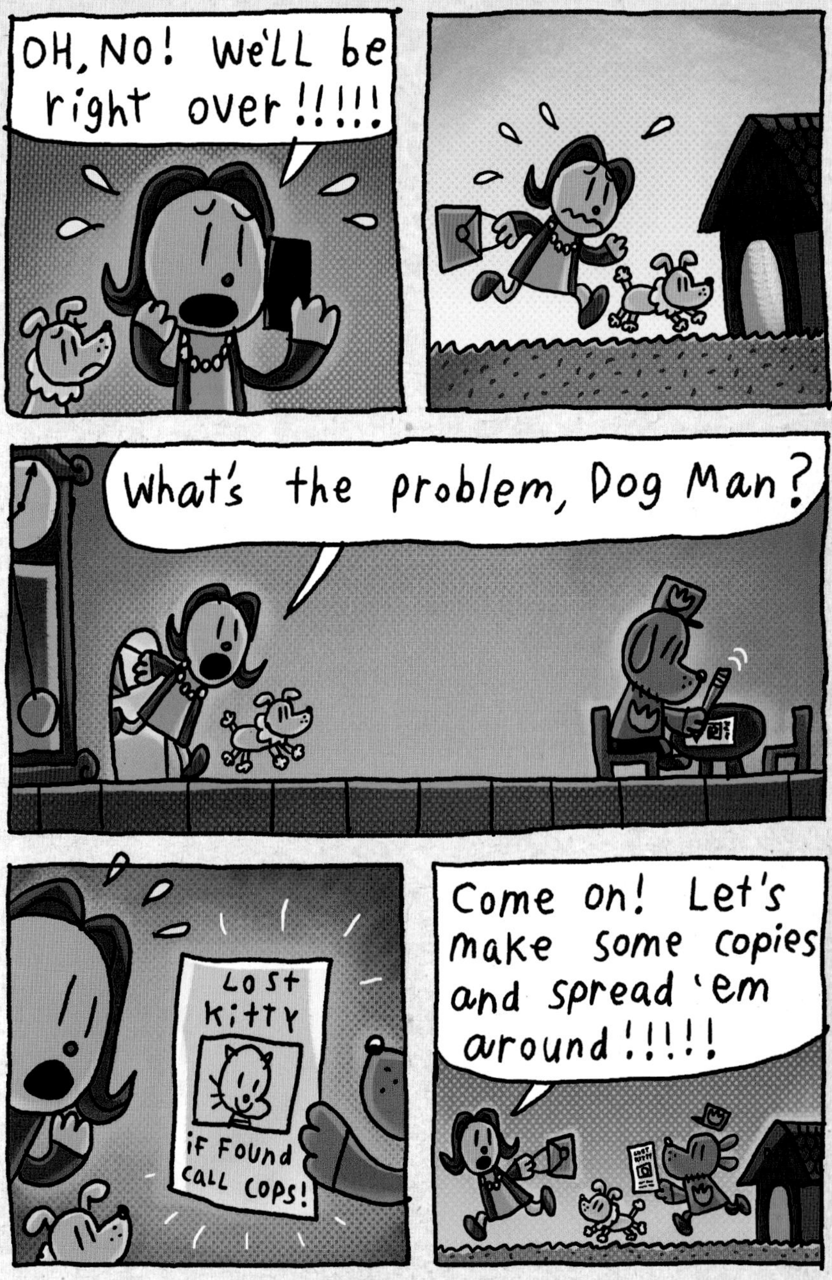
OH, NO! WE'LL be right over!!!!!
What's the problem, Dog Man?
LOST KITTY
IF FOUND CALL COPS!
Come on! Let's make some copies and spread 'em around!!!!!

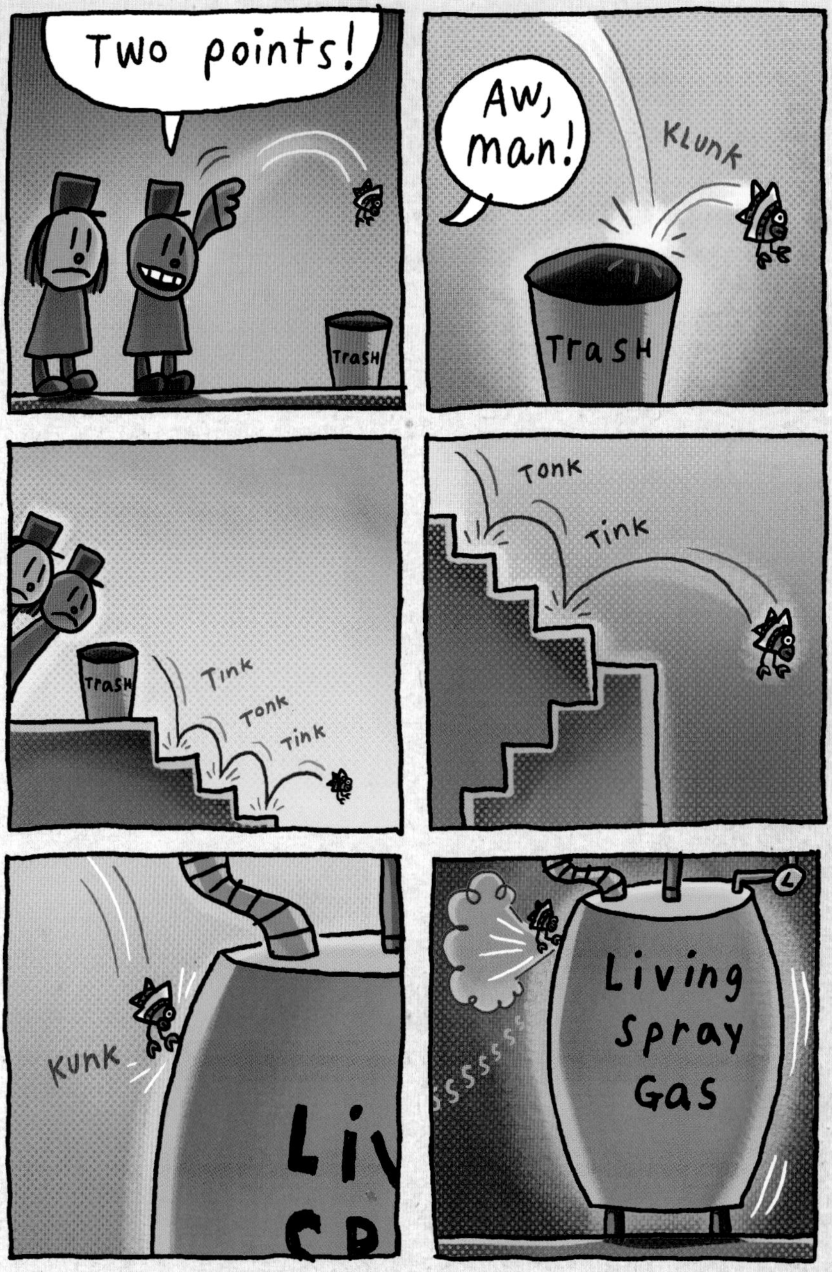
Two points!
TRASH
Aw, man!
KLUNK
TRASH
TRASH
TINK
TONK
TINK
TONK
TINK
KUNK
Li
Living Spray Gas
SSSSSSSSS

128

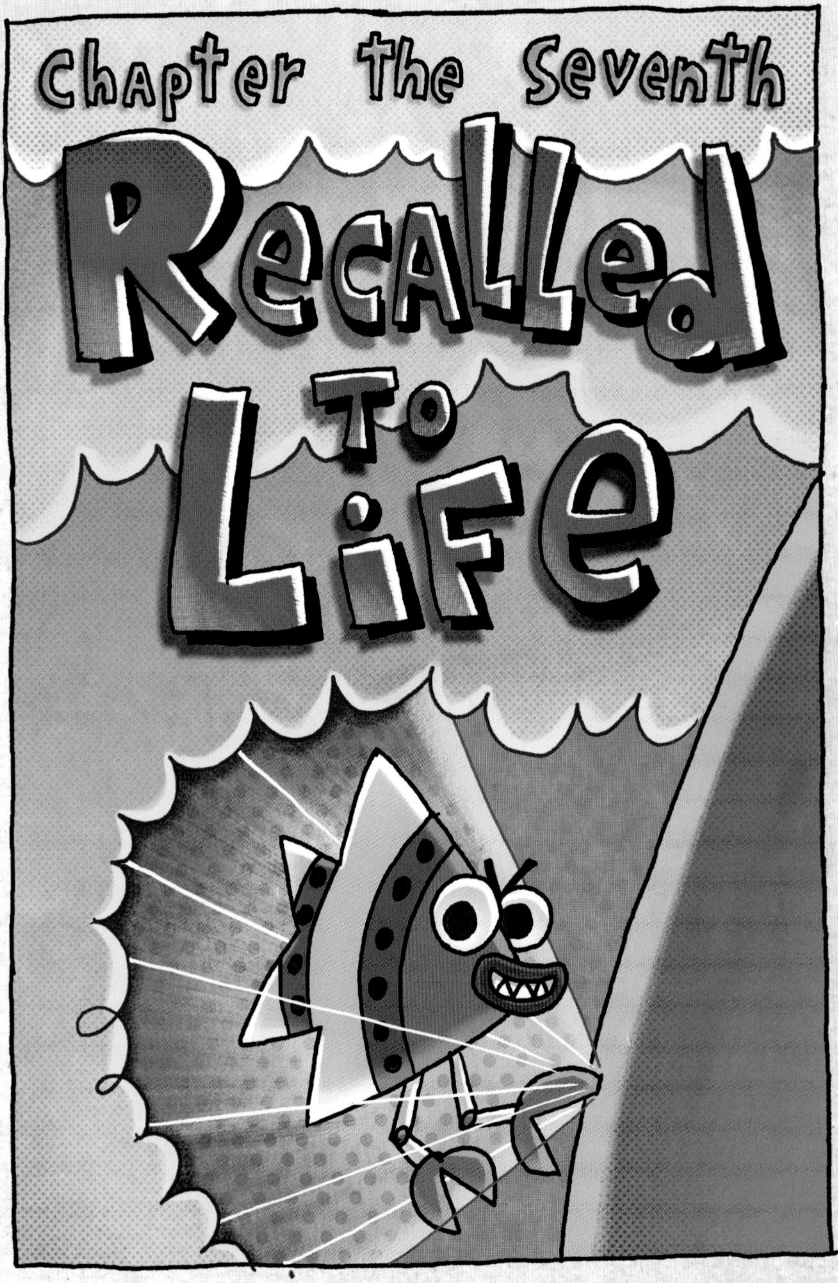
Chapter the Seventh
Recalled To Life

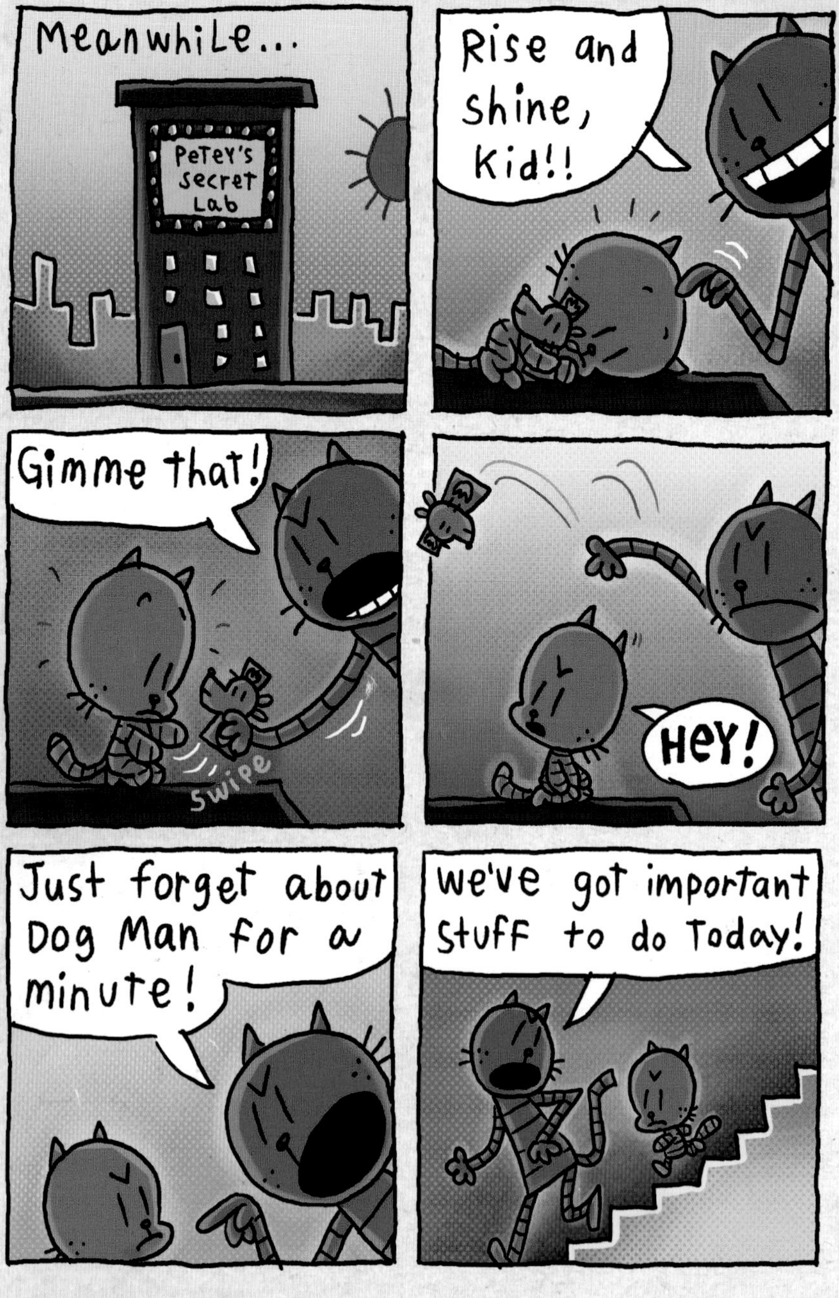
Meanwhile...
Petey's Secret Lab
Rise and shine, Kid!!
Gimme that!
Swipe
HEY!
Just forget about Dog Man for a minute!
We've got important stuff to do Today!

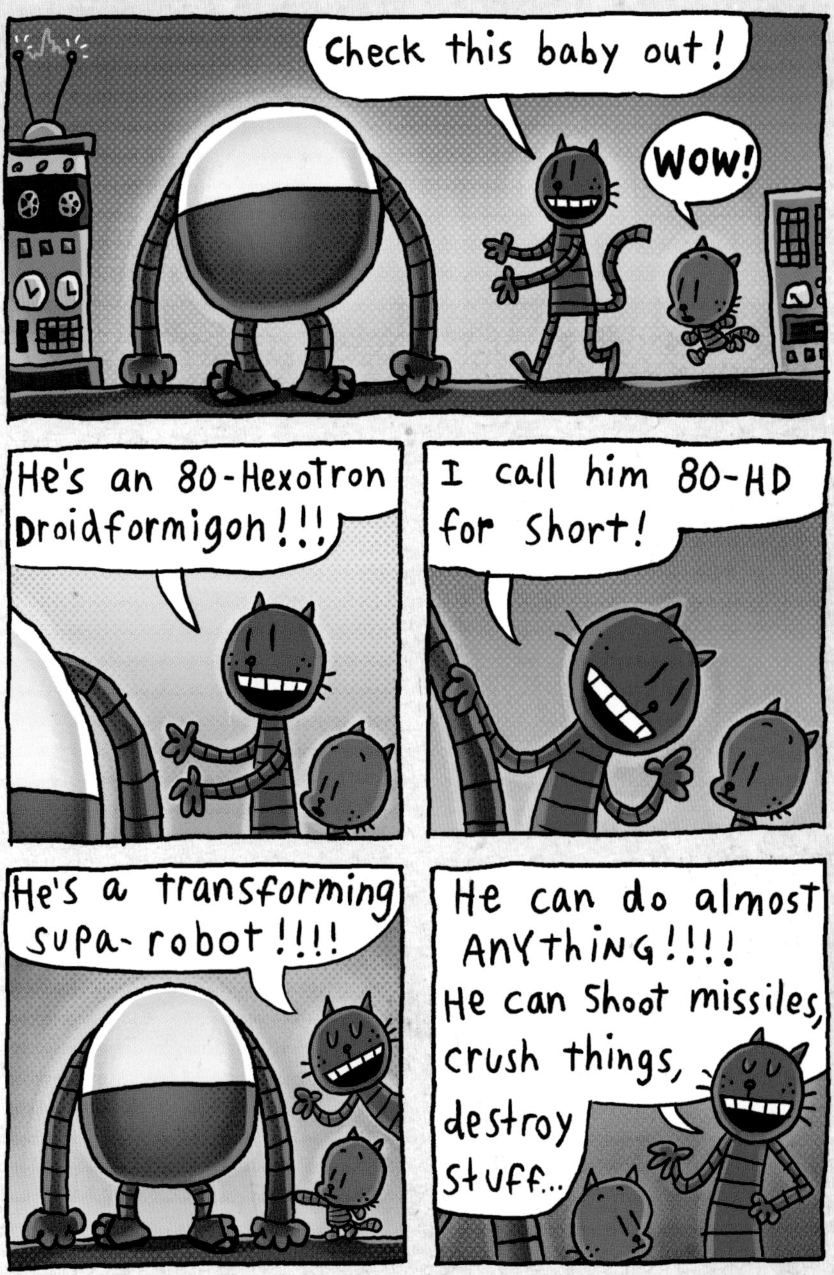
Check this baby out!
WOW!
He's an 80-Hexotron Droidformigon!!!
I call him 80-HD for Short!
He's a transforming supa-robot!!!!
He can do almost ANYTHING!!!!
He can Shoot missiles, crush things, destroy stuff...

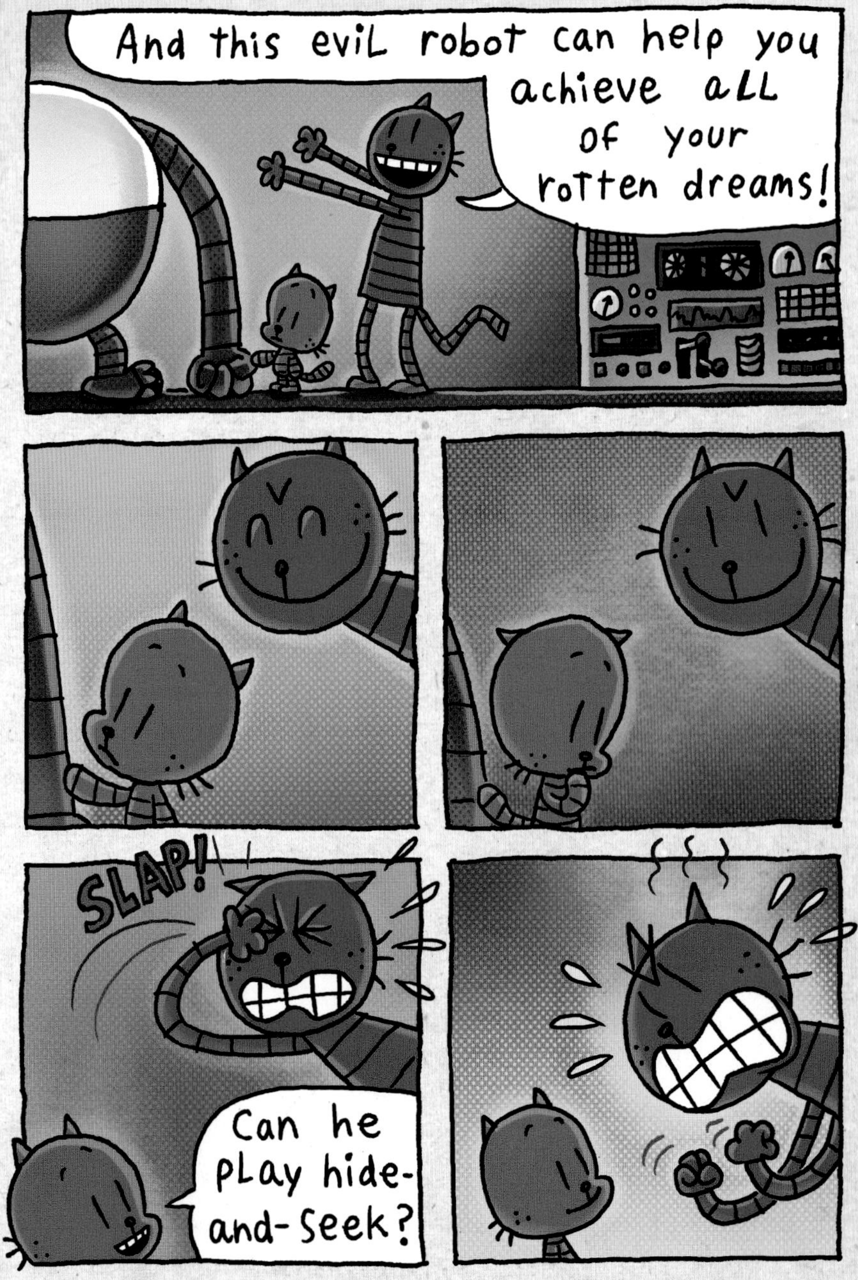
And this eviL robot can help you achieve aLL of your rotten dreams!
SLAP!
Can he pLay hide-and-seek?

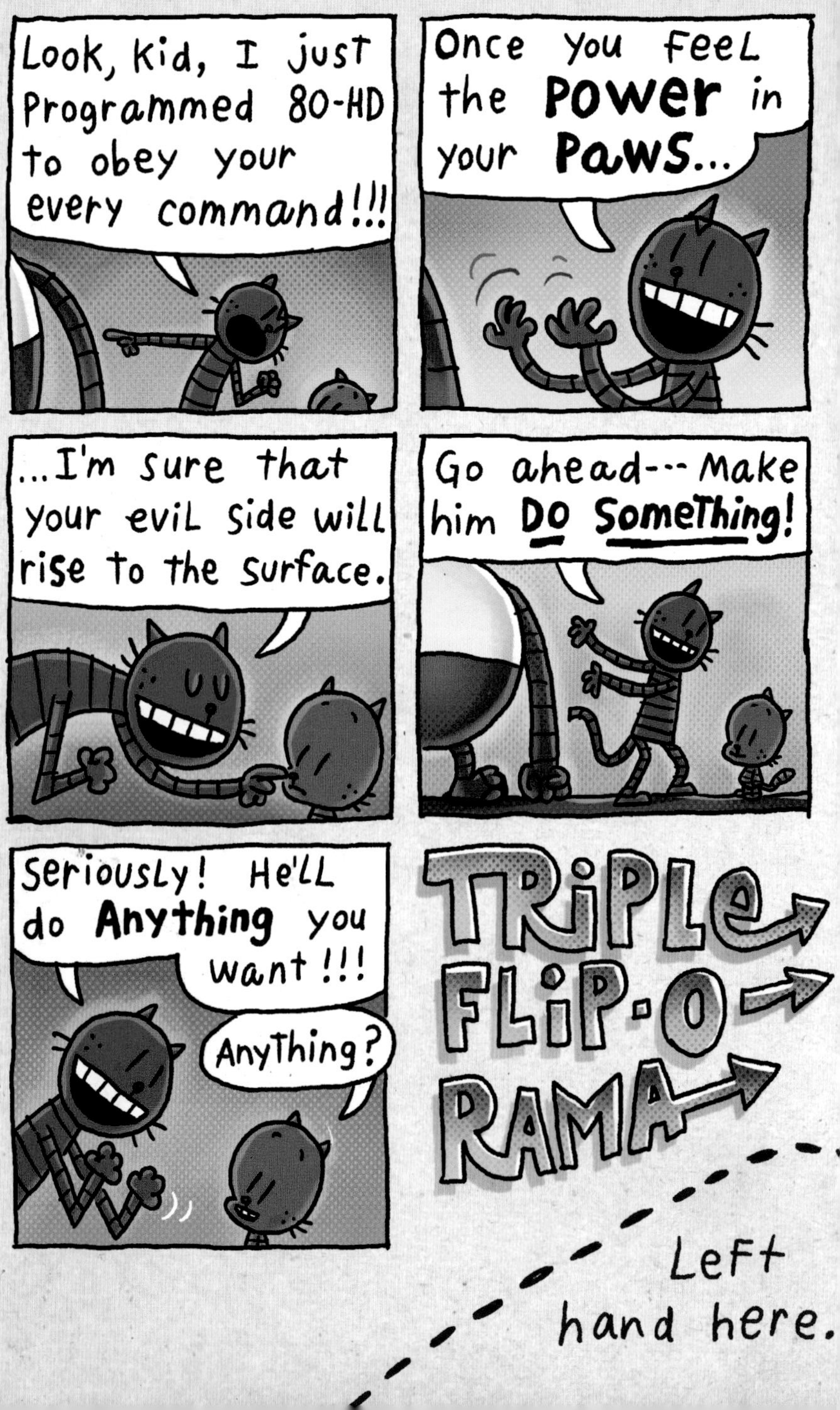
Look, Kid, I just Programmed 80-HD to obey your every command!!!
Once you FeeL the POWER in your PAWS...
...I'm sure that your eviL Side wiLL rise to the surface.
Go ahead--- Make him DO SomeThing!
SeriousLy! He'LL do Anything you want!!!
AnyThing?
TRiPLe FLiP-O RAMA
LeFt hand here.

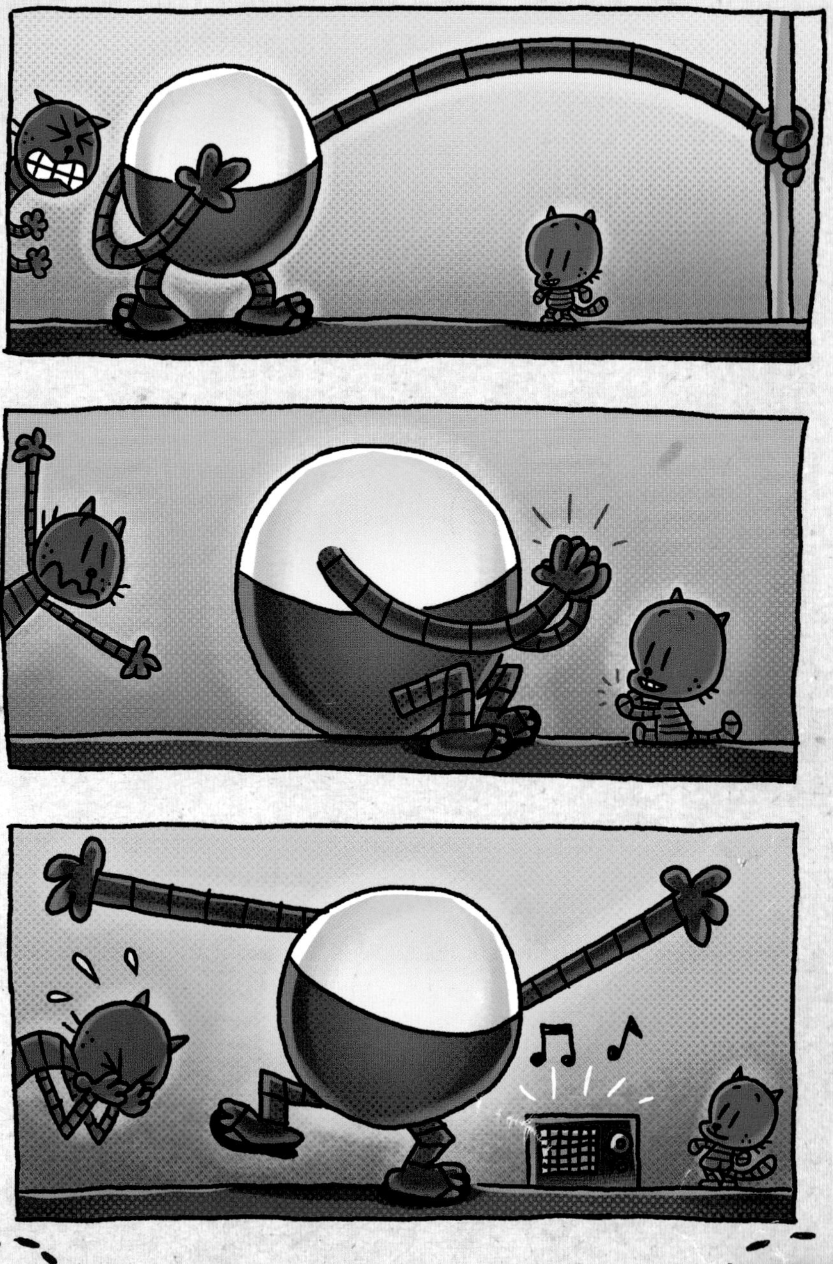

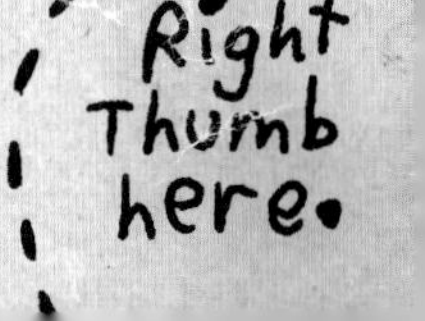
Right Thumb here.

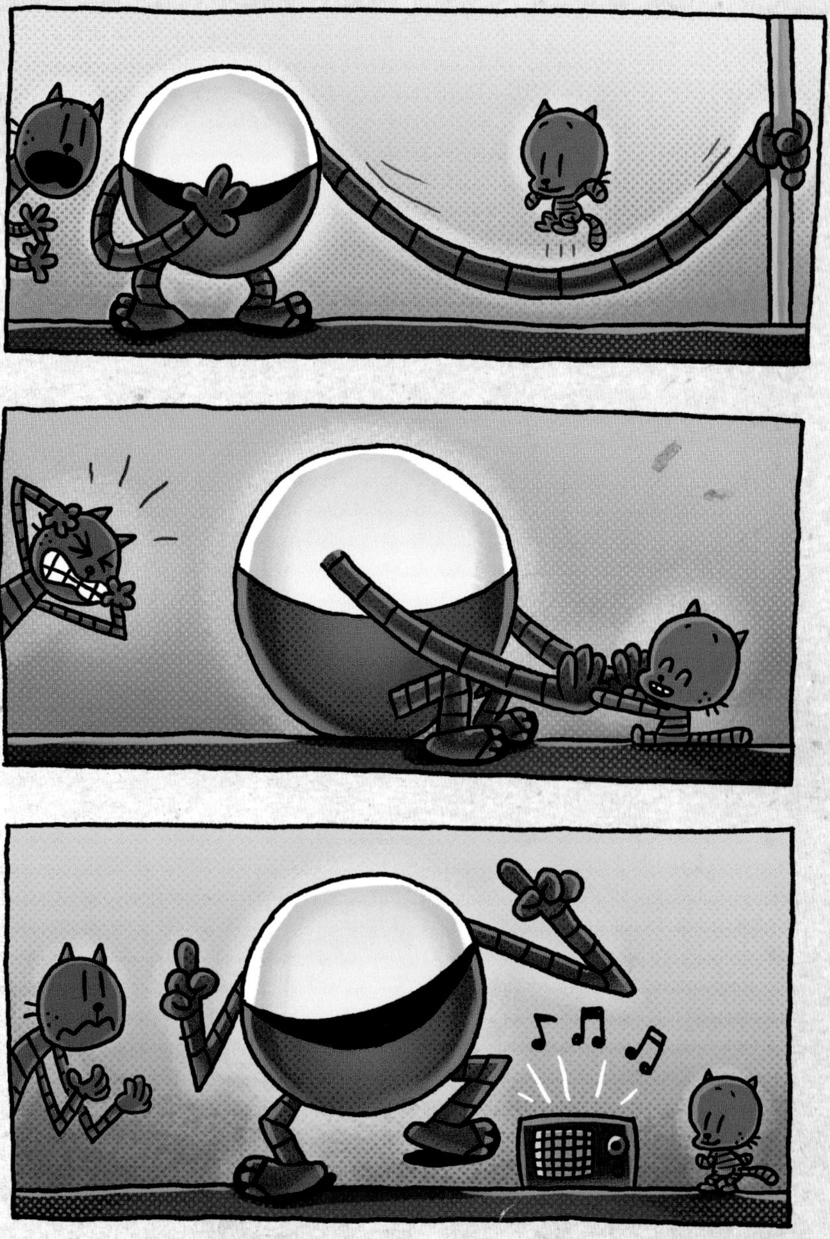

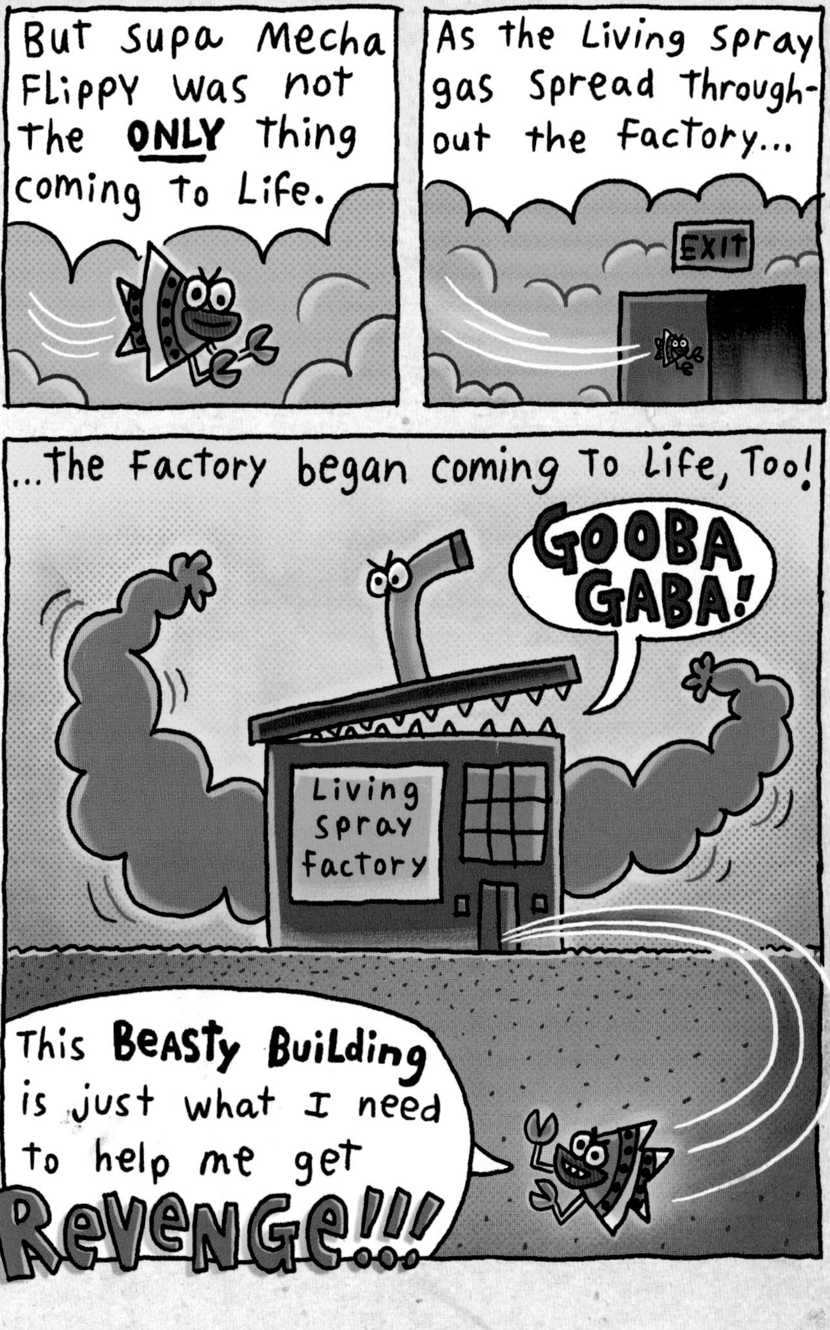
But Supa Mecha Flippy was not the **ONLY** thing coming to Life.
As the Living Spray gas Spread through-out the Factory...
EXIT
...the Factory began coming to Life, Too!
GOOBA GABA!
Living Spray Factory
This **BEASTY BUILDING** is just what I need to help me get
REVENGE!!!

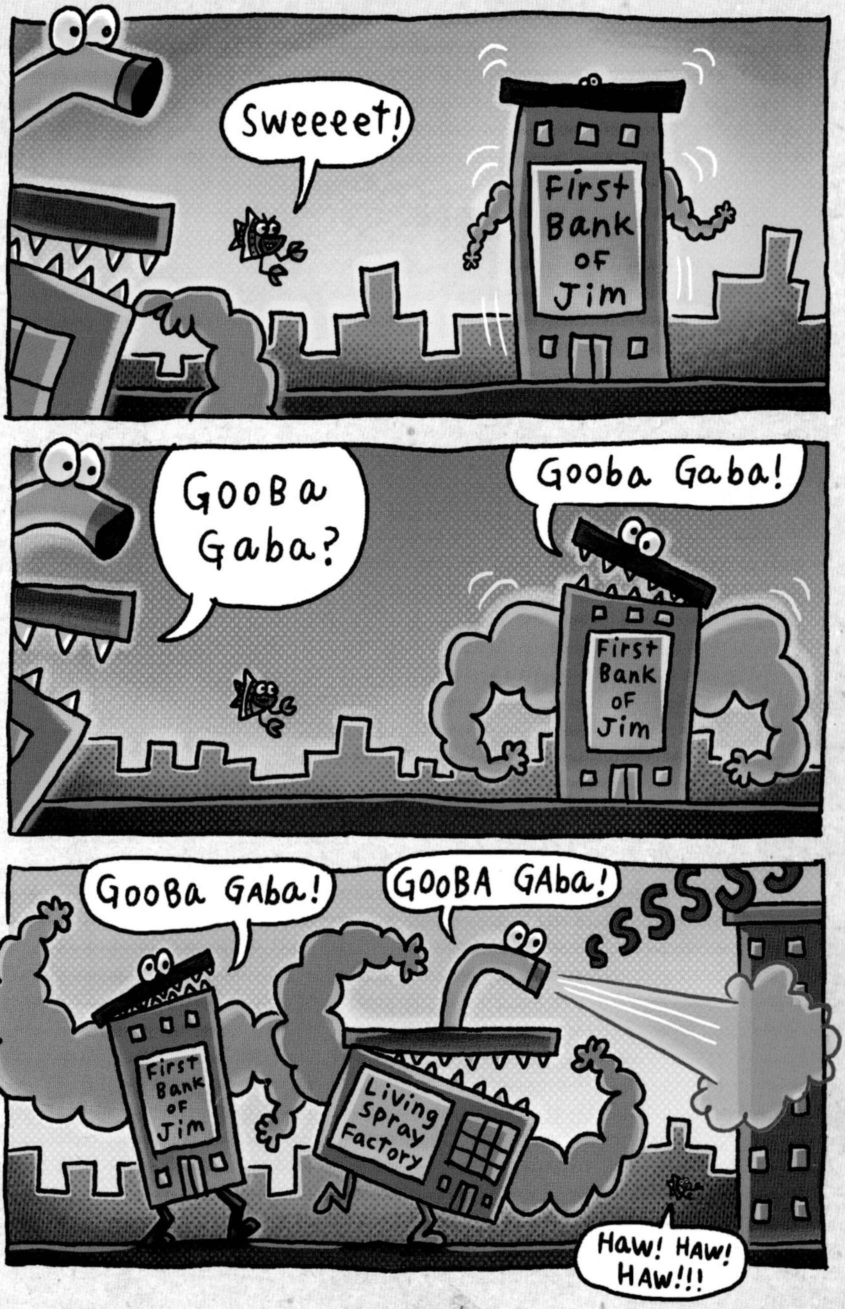
Sweeeet!
First Bank of Jim
GooBa Gaba?
Gooba Gaba!
First Bank of Jim
GooBa GAba!
GOOBA GAba!
SSSSSS
First Bank of Jim
Living Spray Factory
HAW! HAW! HAW!!!

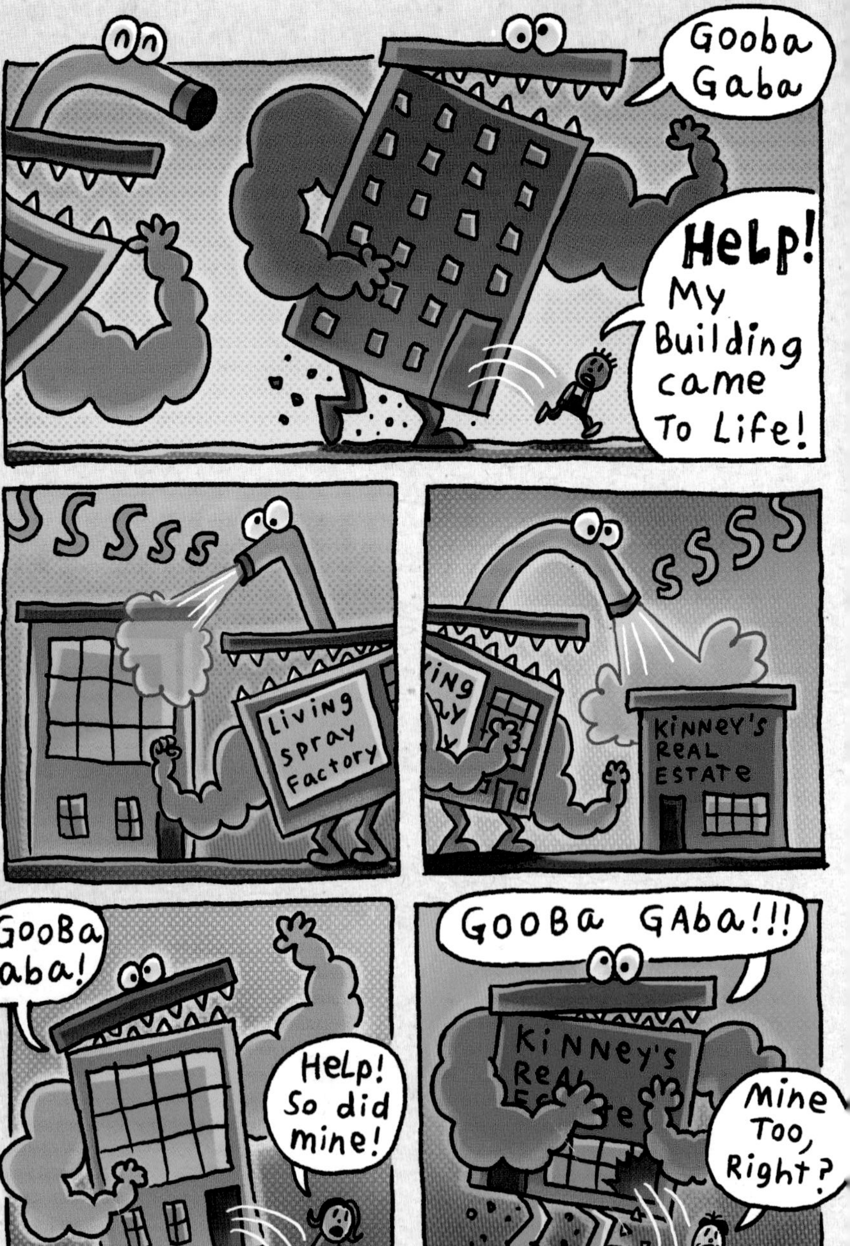
Gooba Gaba
HELP! My Building came To Life!
Living spray Factory
KiNNEY'S REAL ESTATE
GooBa Gaba!
HeLp! So did mine!
GOOBa GAba!!!
KiNNey's
Mine Too, Right?

143

144

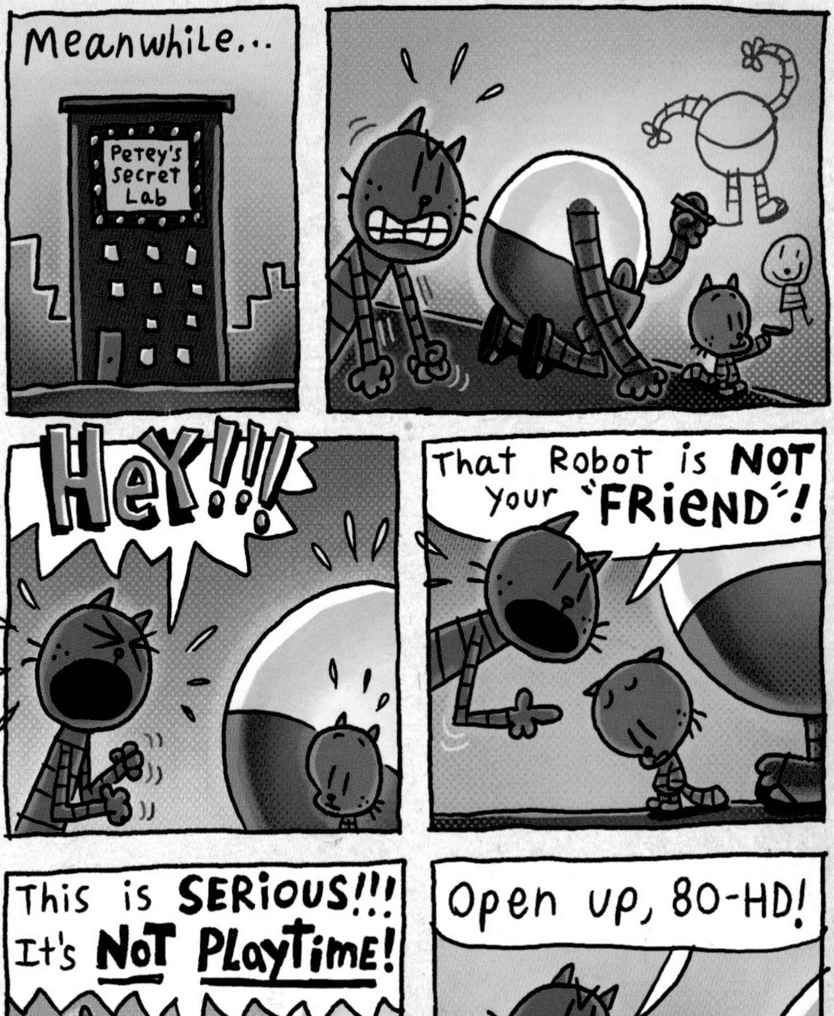
Meanwhile...
Petey's Secret Lab
HEY!!!
That Robot is NOT your "FRIEND"!
This is SERIOUS!!! It's NOT PLAYTIME!
Open up, 80-HD!

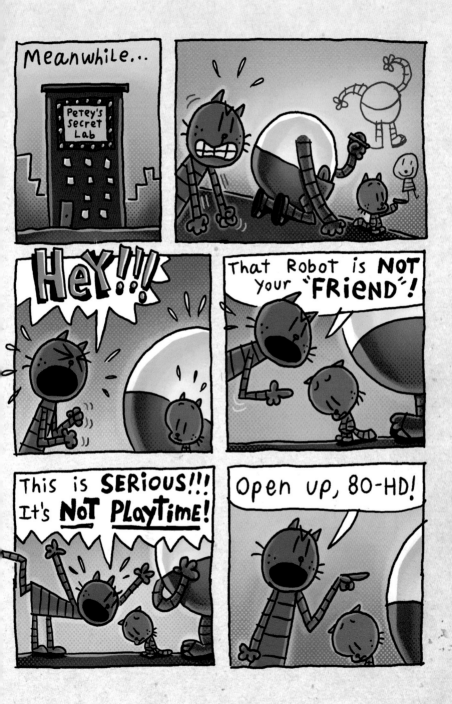

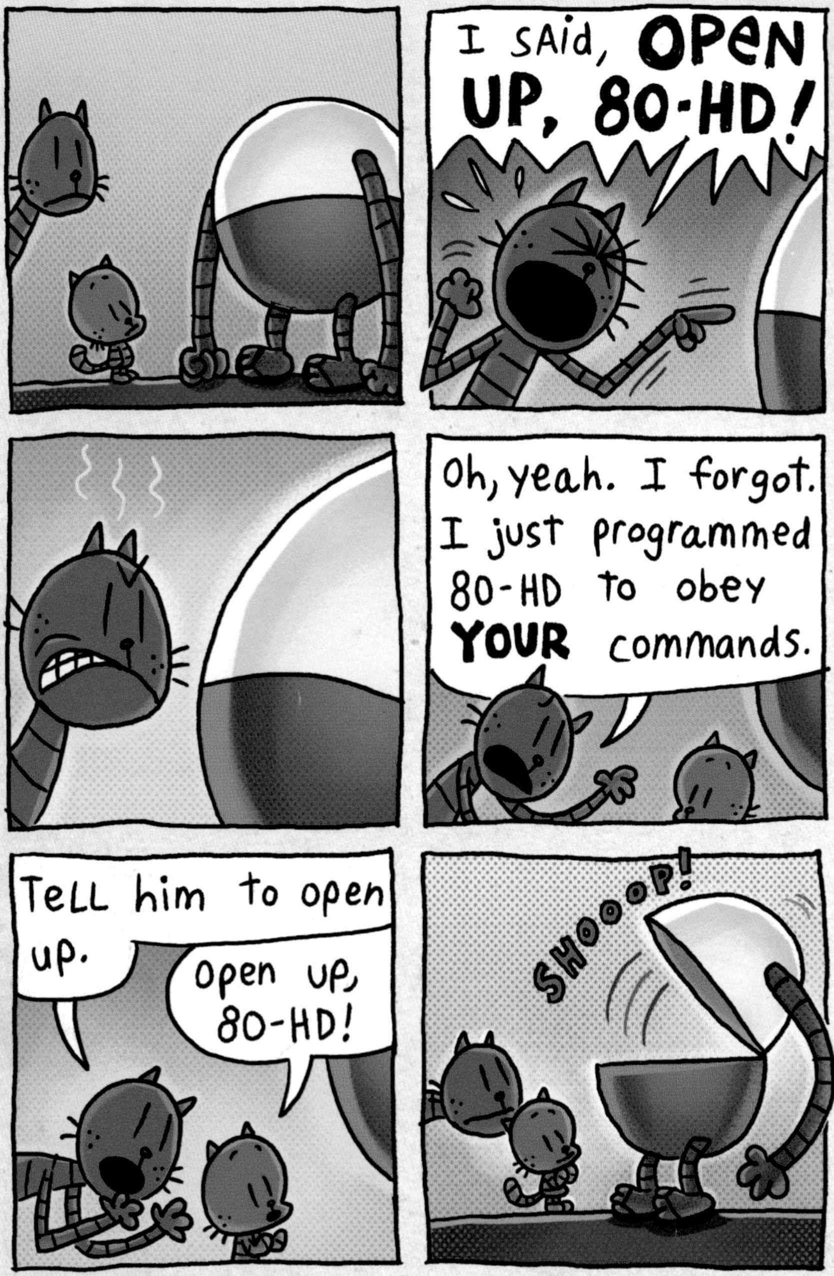
I SAid, OPEN UP, 80-HD!
Oh, yeah. I forgot. I just programmed 80-HD to obey YOUR commands.
TeLL him to open up.
Open up, 80-HD!
SHOOOP!

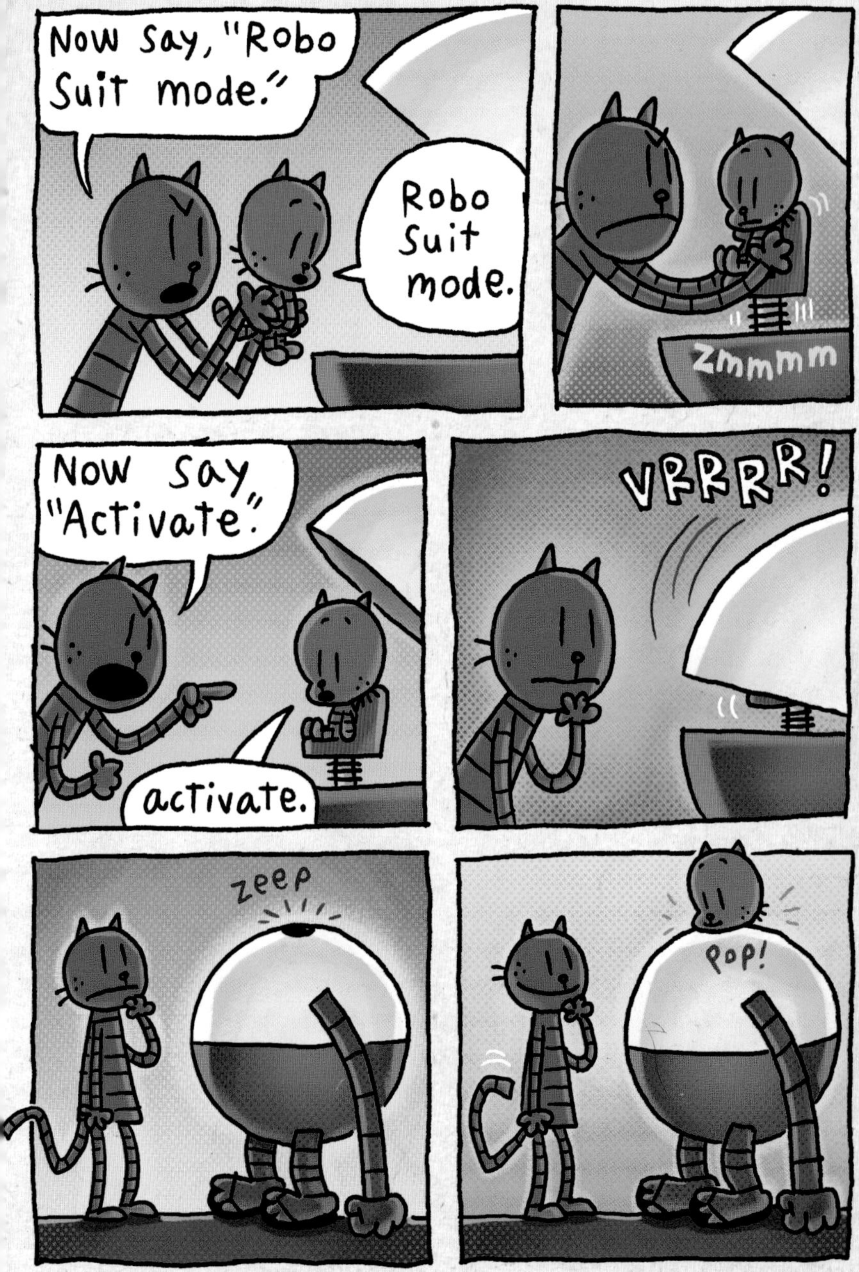
Now say, "Robo Suit mode."
Robo Suit mode.
Zmmmm
Now say "Activate."
activate.
VRRRR!
zeep
POP!

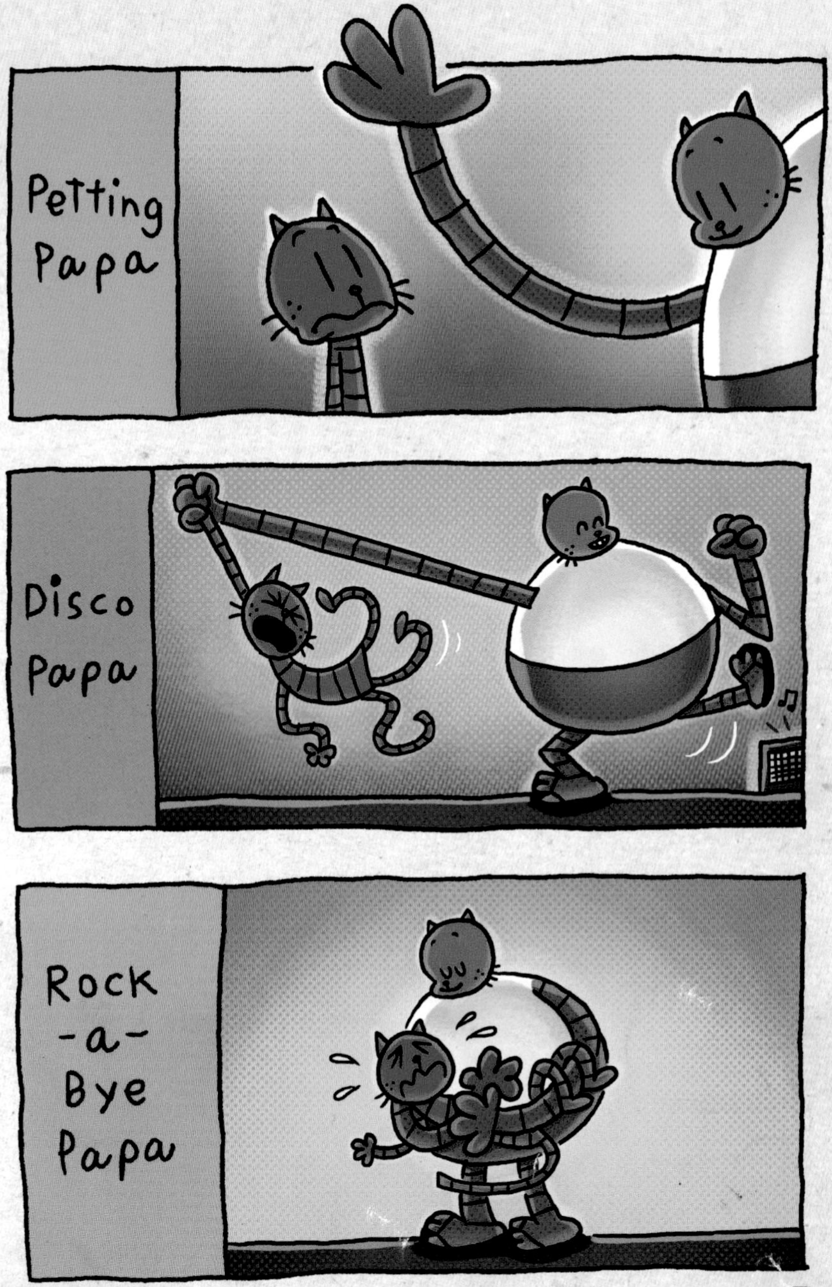
Petting Papa
Disco Papa
Rock-a-Bye Papa

Right Thumb here.

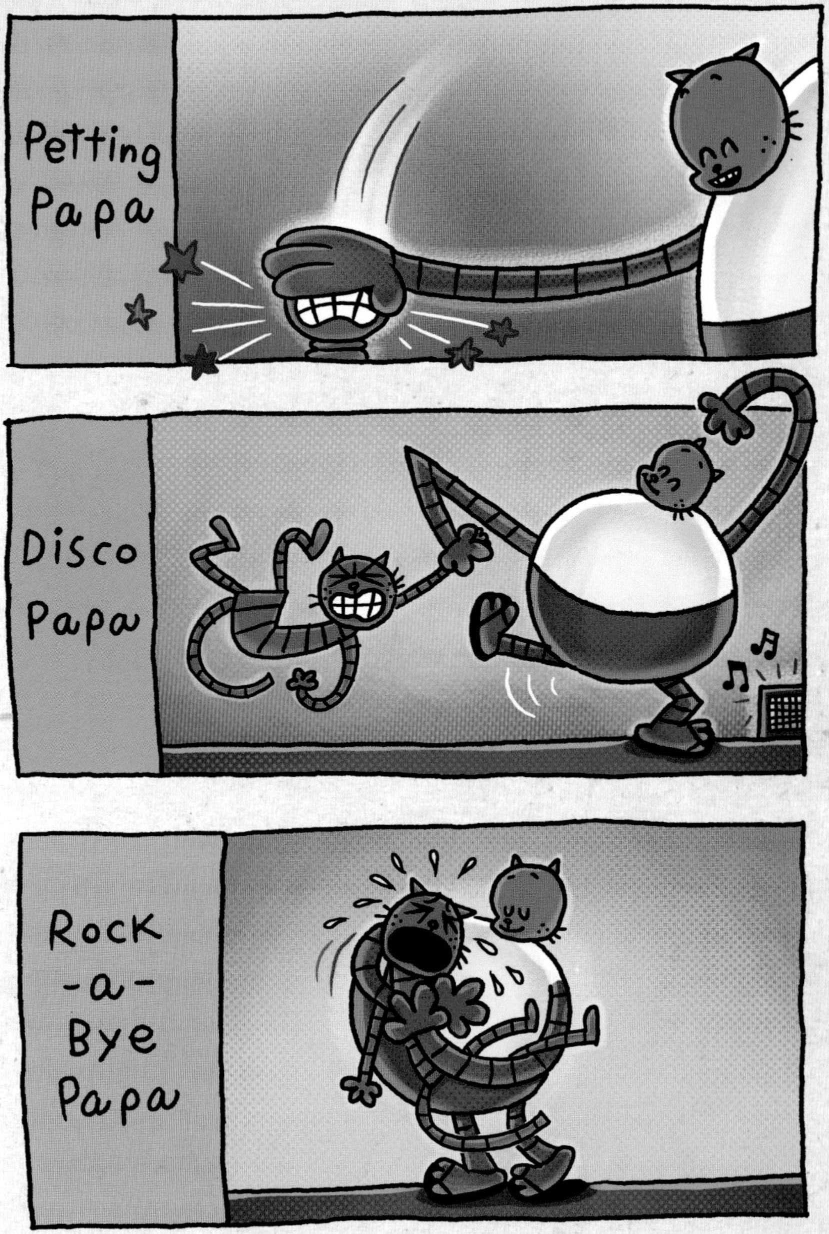
Petting Papa
Disco Papa
Rock -a- Bye Papa

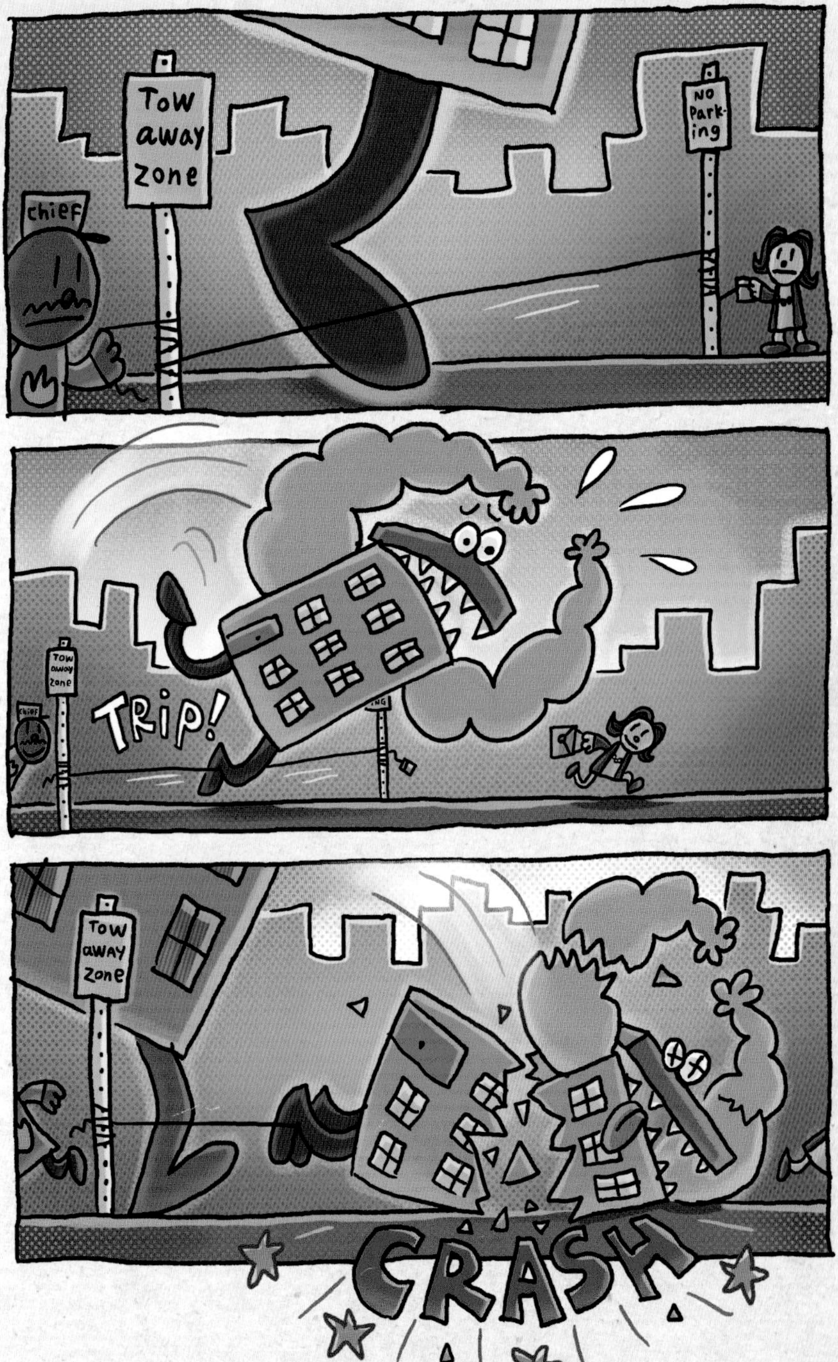

Tow away zone
chief
No Park-ing
Tow away zone
chief
TRIP!
Tow away zone
CRASH

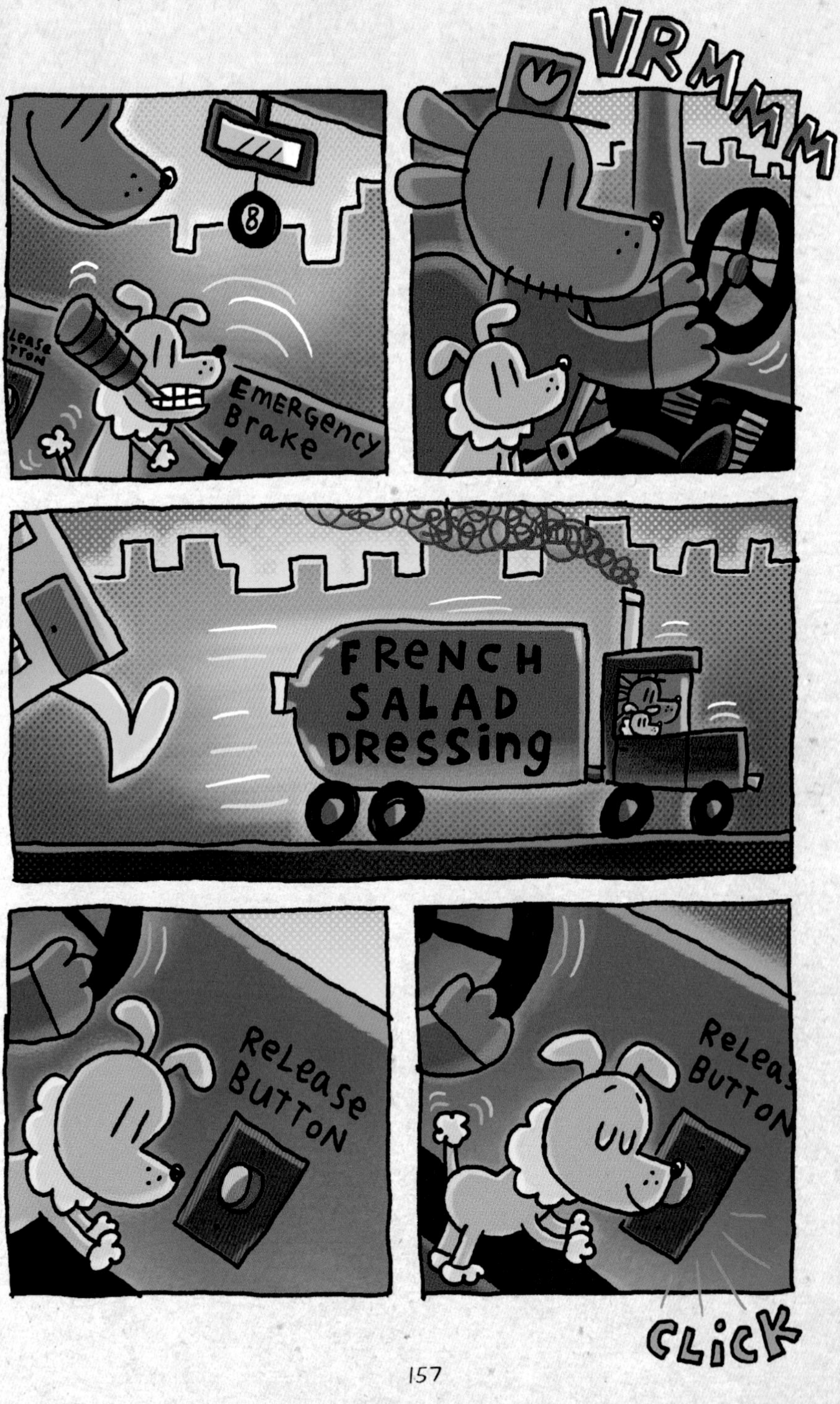
EMERGENCY BRAKE
VRMMMM
FRENCH SALAD DRESSING
RELEASE BUTTON
CLICK

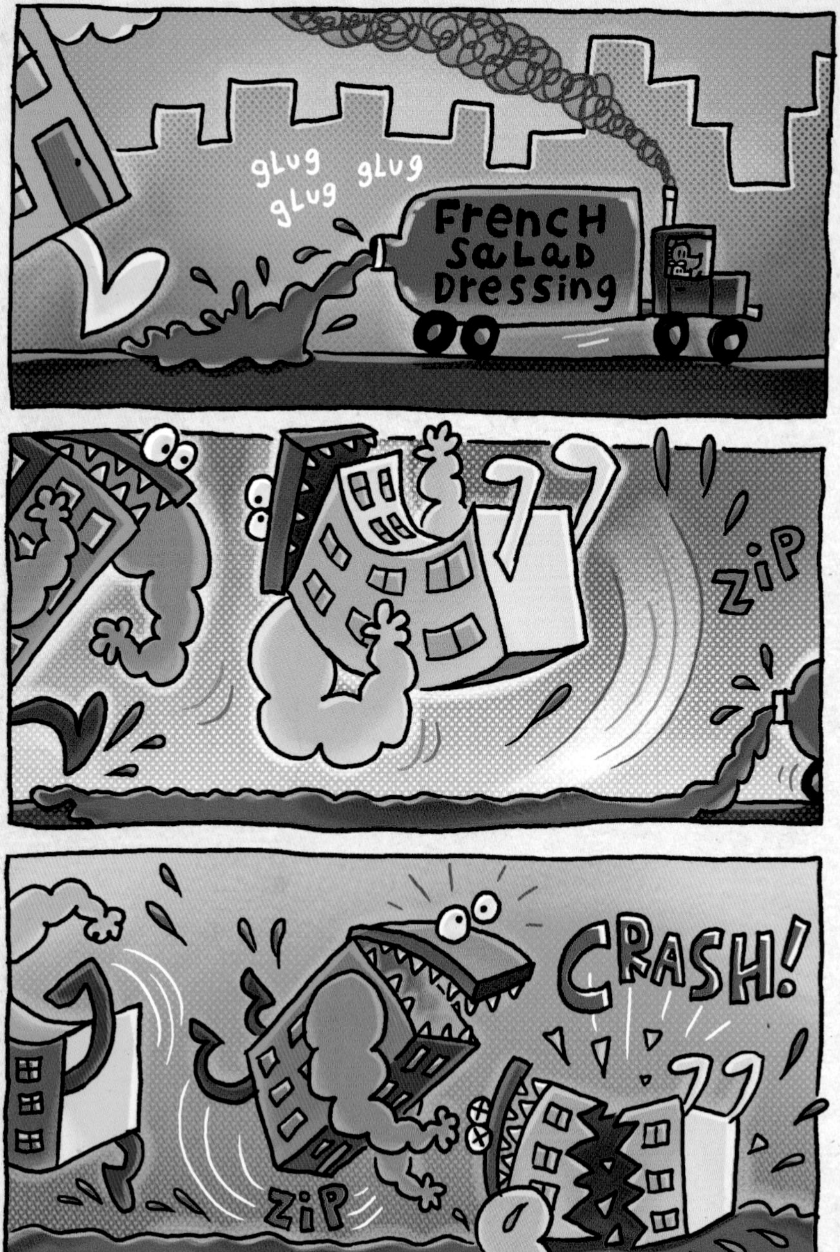
glug
glug
glug
French Salad Dressing
ZIP
ZIP
CRASH!

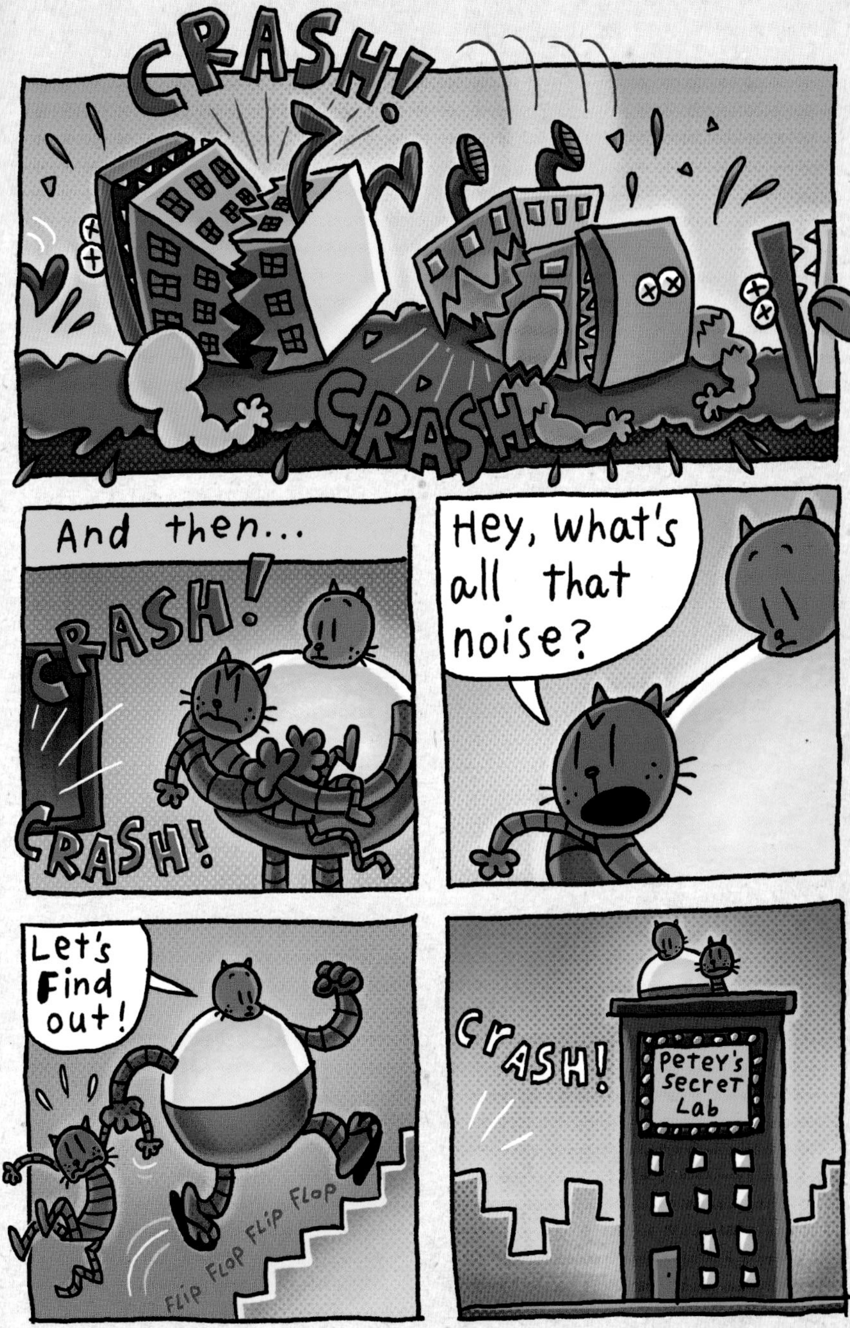
CRASH!
CRASH
And then...
CRASH!
CRASH!
Hey, what's all that noise?
Let's Find out!
FLIP FLOP FLIP FLOP
CRASH!
Petey's Secret Lab

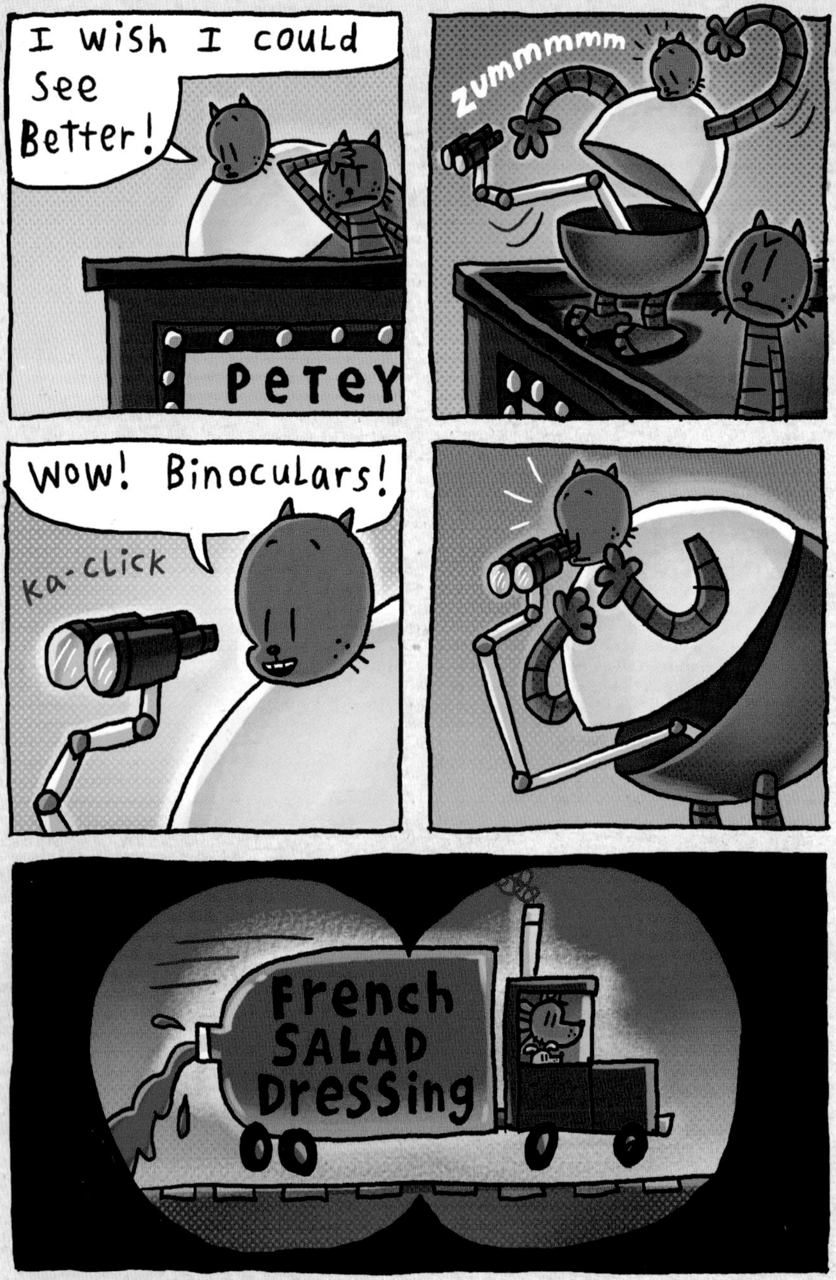
I WISH I COULD See Better!
PeTeY
ZUMMMMMM
WOW! Binoculars!
Ka-CLICK
French SALAD DreSSing

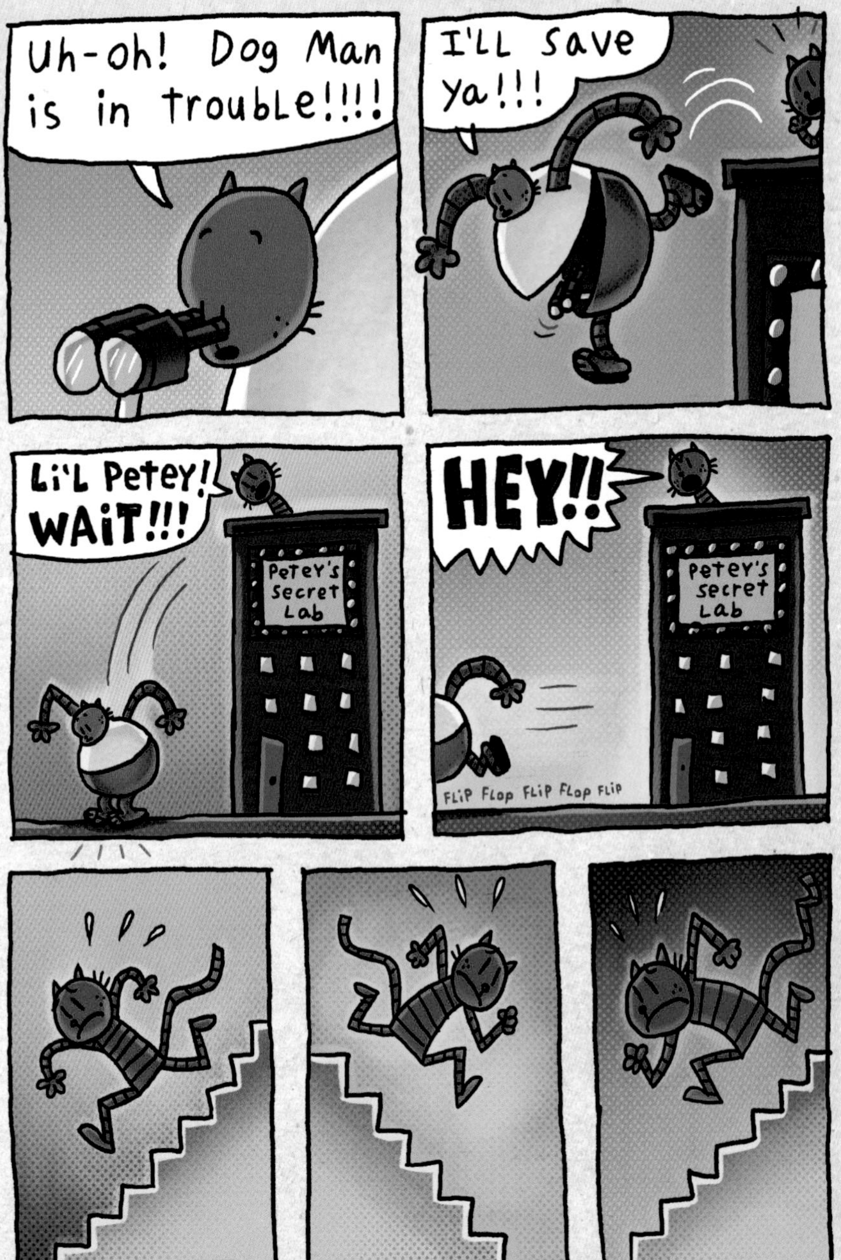

Uh-Oh! Dog Man is in trouble!!!!
I'LL Save ya!!!
Li'L Petey! WAIT!!!
Petey's Secret Lab
HEY!!
Petey's Secret Lab
FLiP FLop FLiP FLop FLiP

162

Chapter the Eighth

THE French Dressing Revolution

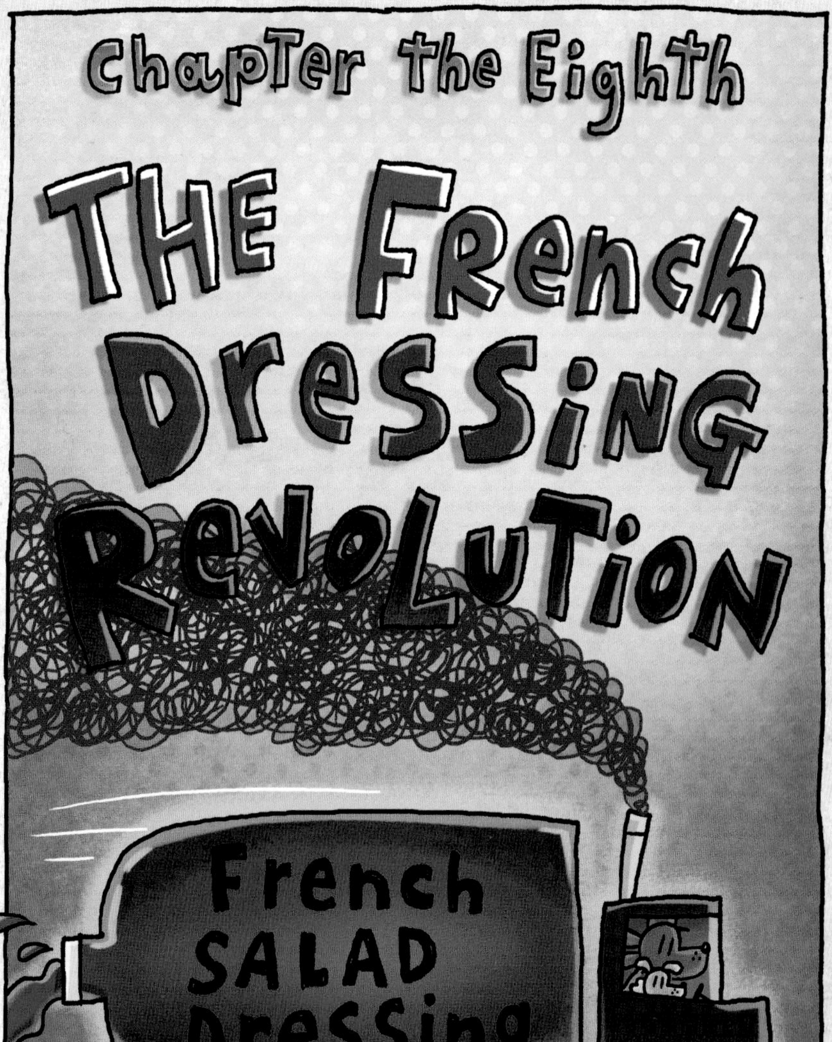
French
SALAD
Dressing

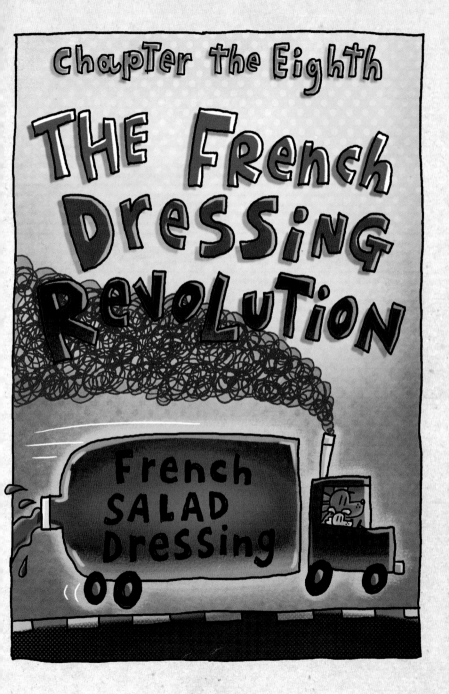

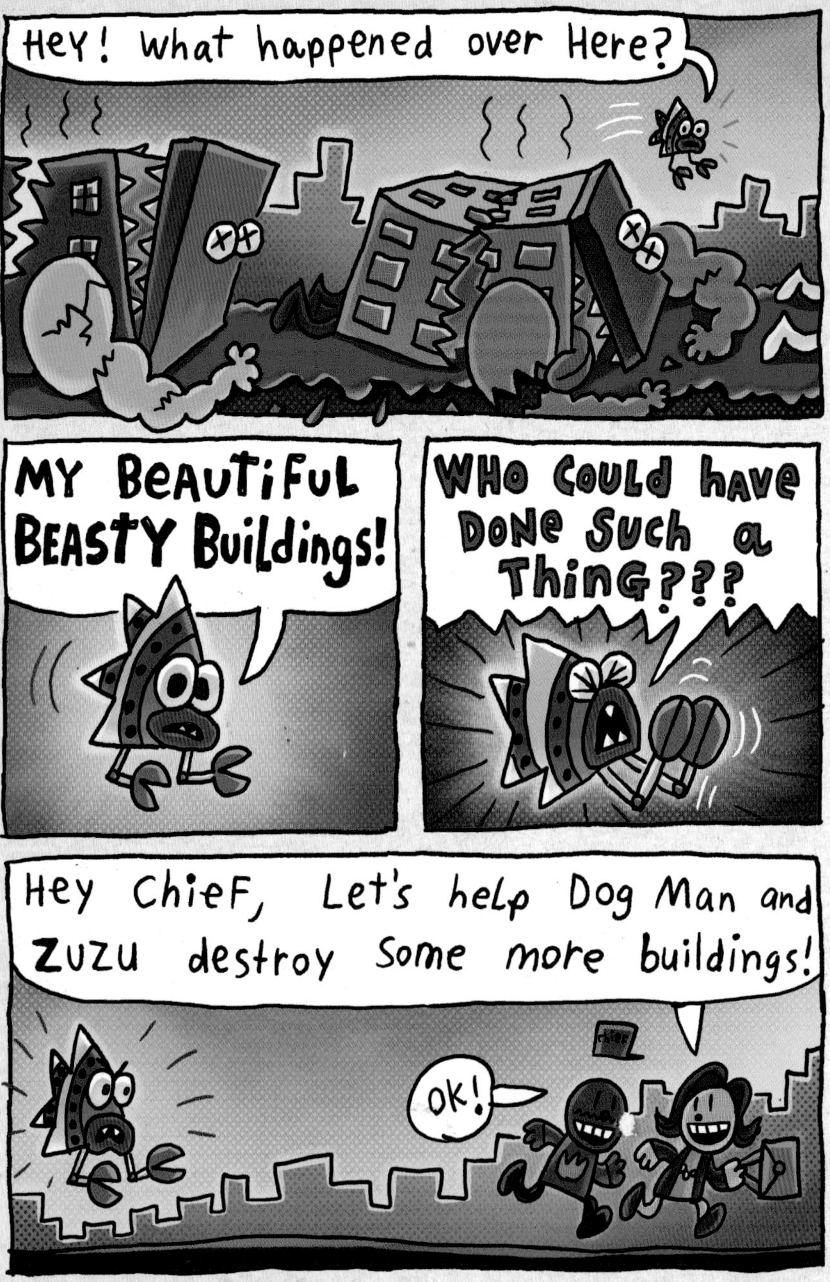
HEY! What happened over Here?
MY BEAUTIFUL BEASTY Buildings!
WHO COULD HAVE DONE SUCH a THING???
Hey Chief, Let's help Dog Man and ZUZU destroy Some more buildings!
OK!
CHIEF

165

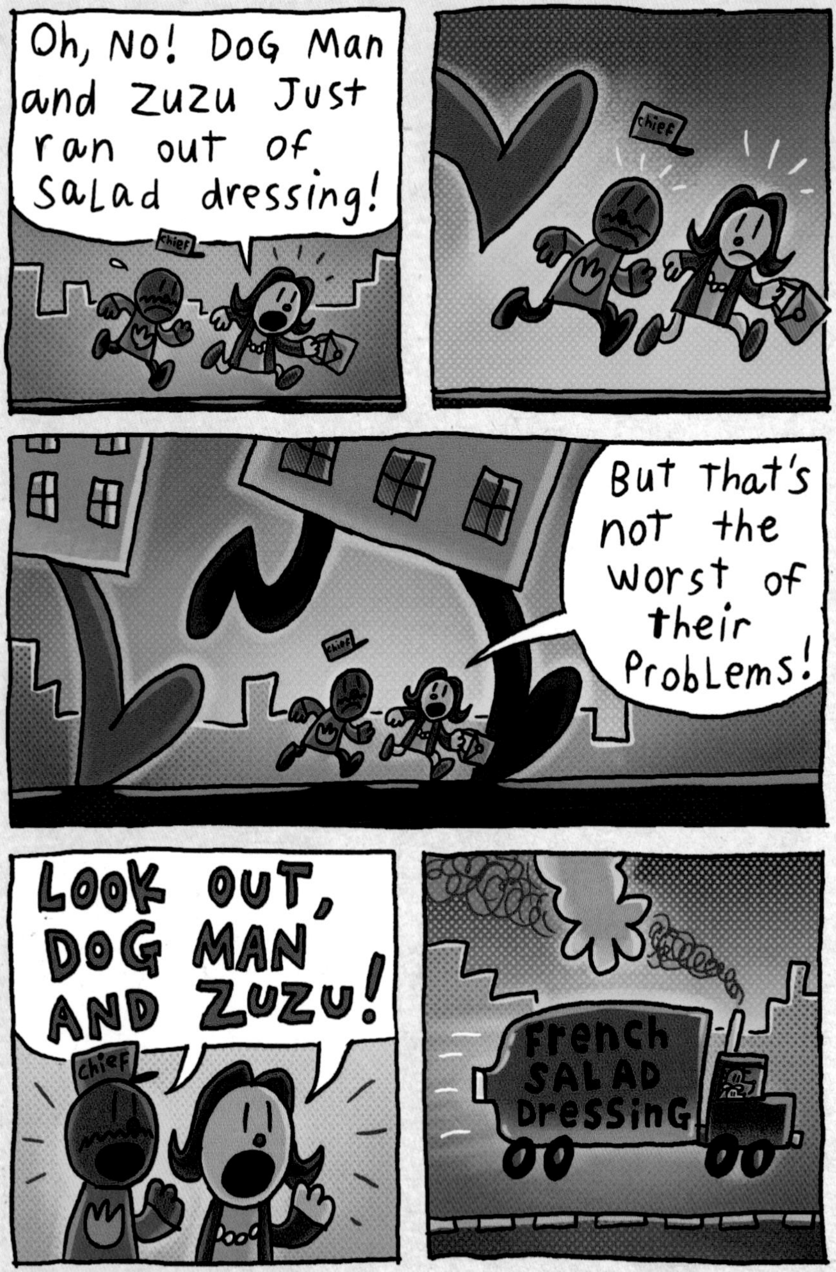
Oh, No! DOG Man and ZUZU Just ran out of SaLad dressing!
Chief
But That's not the worst of their ProbLems!
LOOK OUT, DOG MAN AND ZUZU!
French SALAD DreSSinG

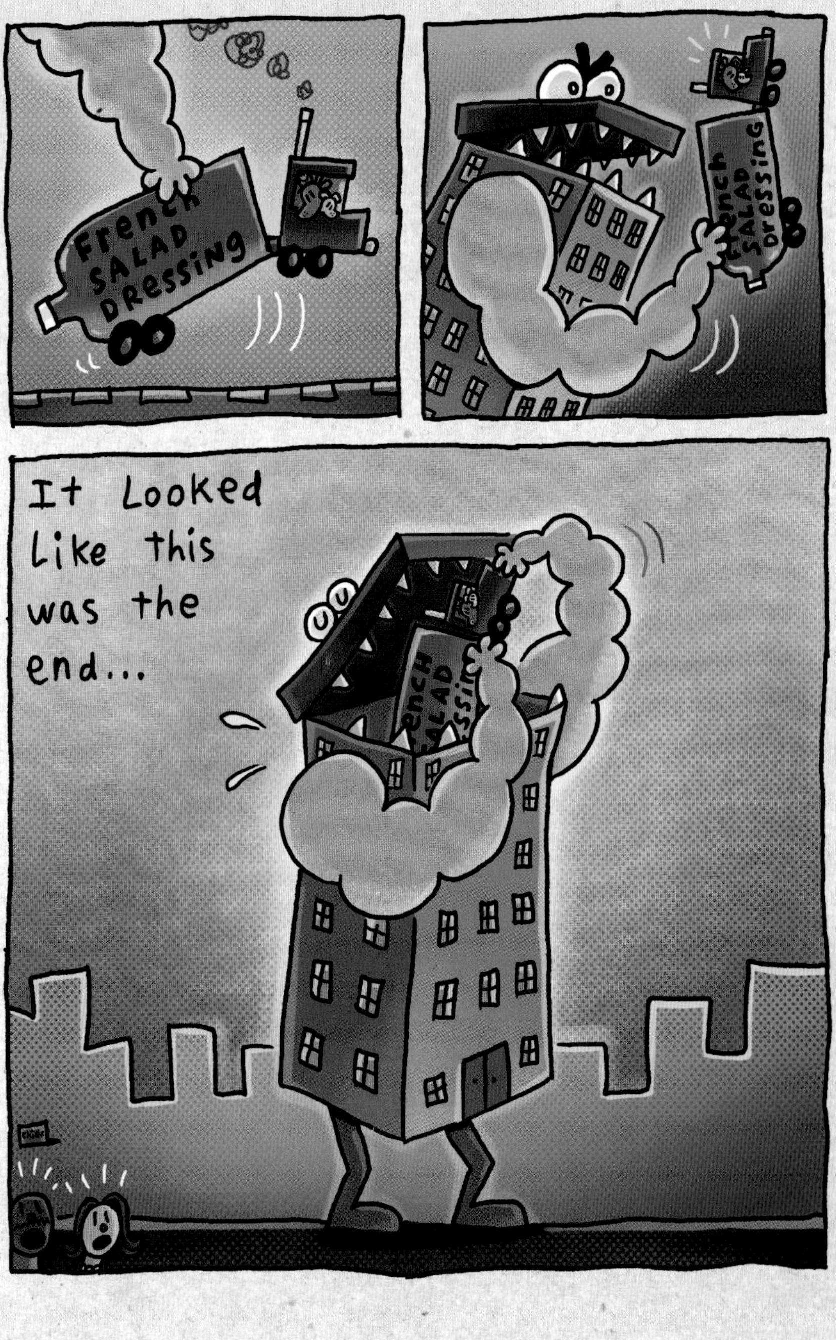
French SALAD DRESSING
French SALAD DRESSING
It Looked like this was the end...

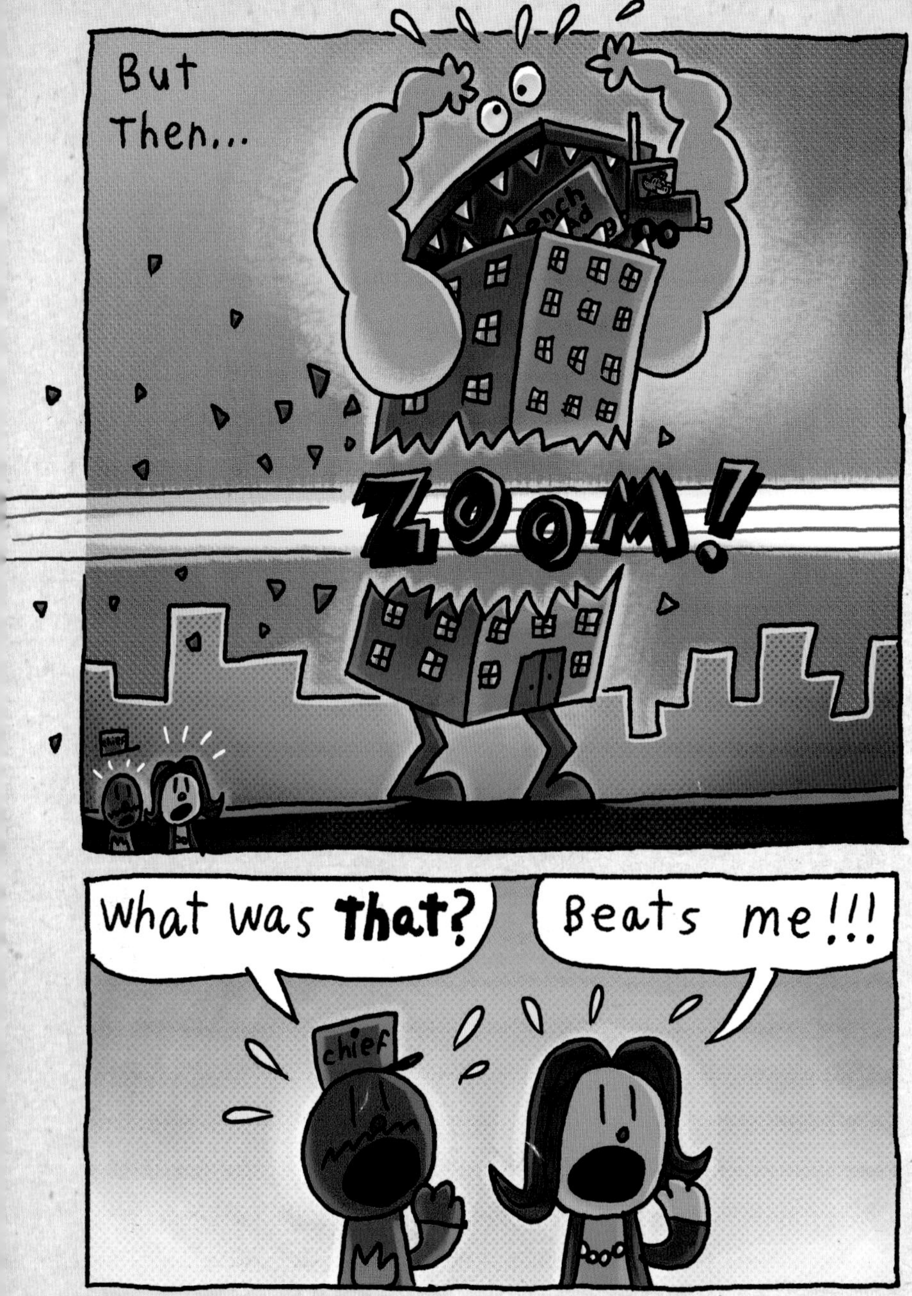
But Then...
ZOOM!
chief
What was That?
Beats me!!!

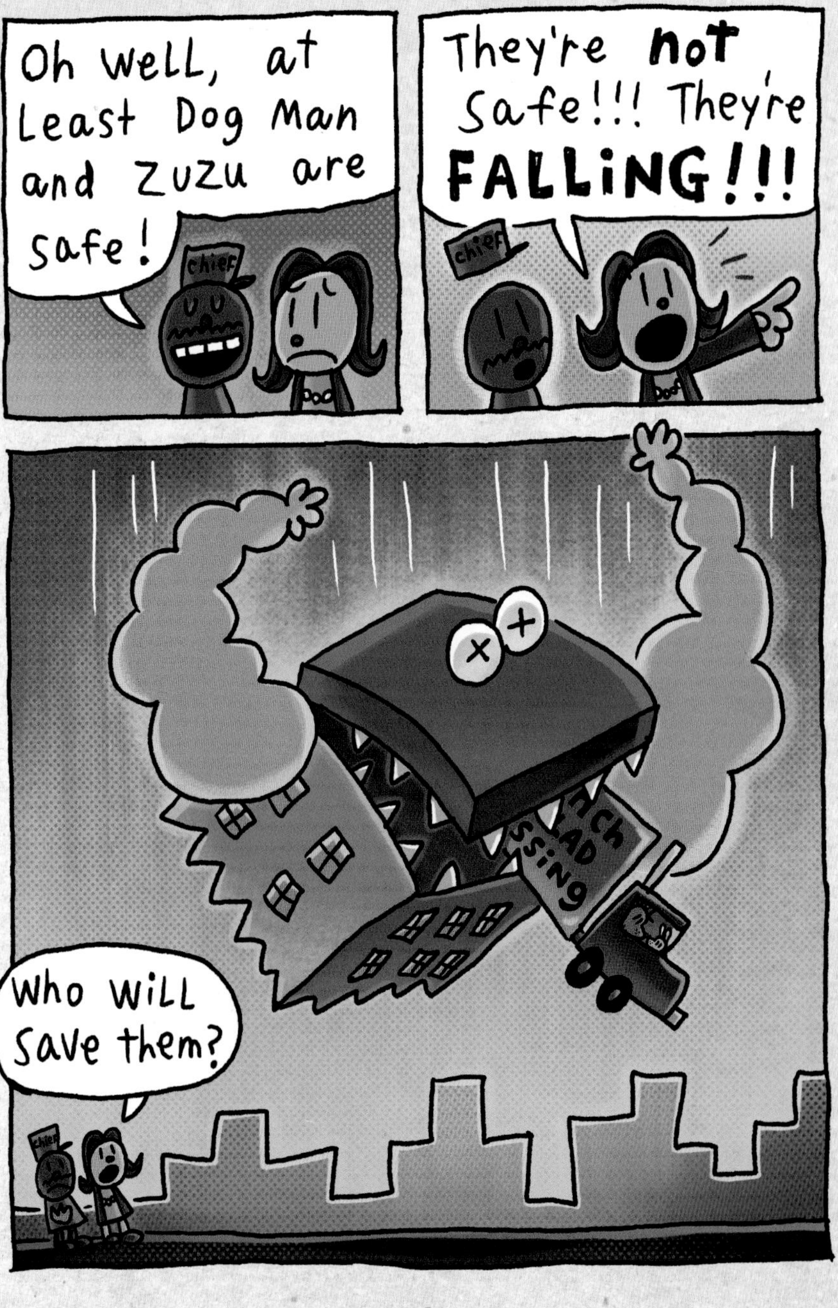
Oh WeLL, at Least Dog Man and ZUZU are safe!
chief
They're not Safe!!! They're FALLiNG!!!
chief
Who WiLL Save them?
chief

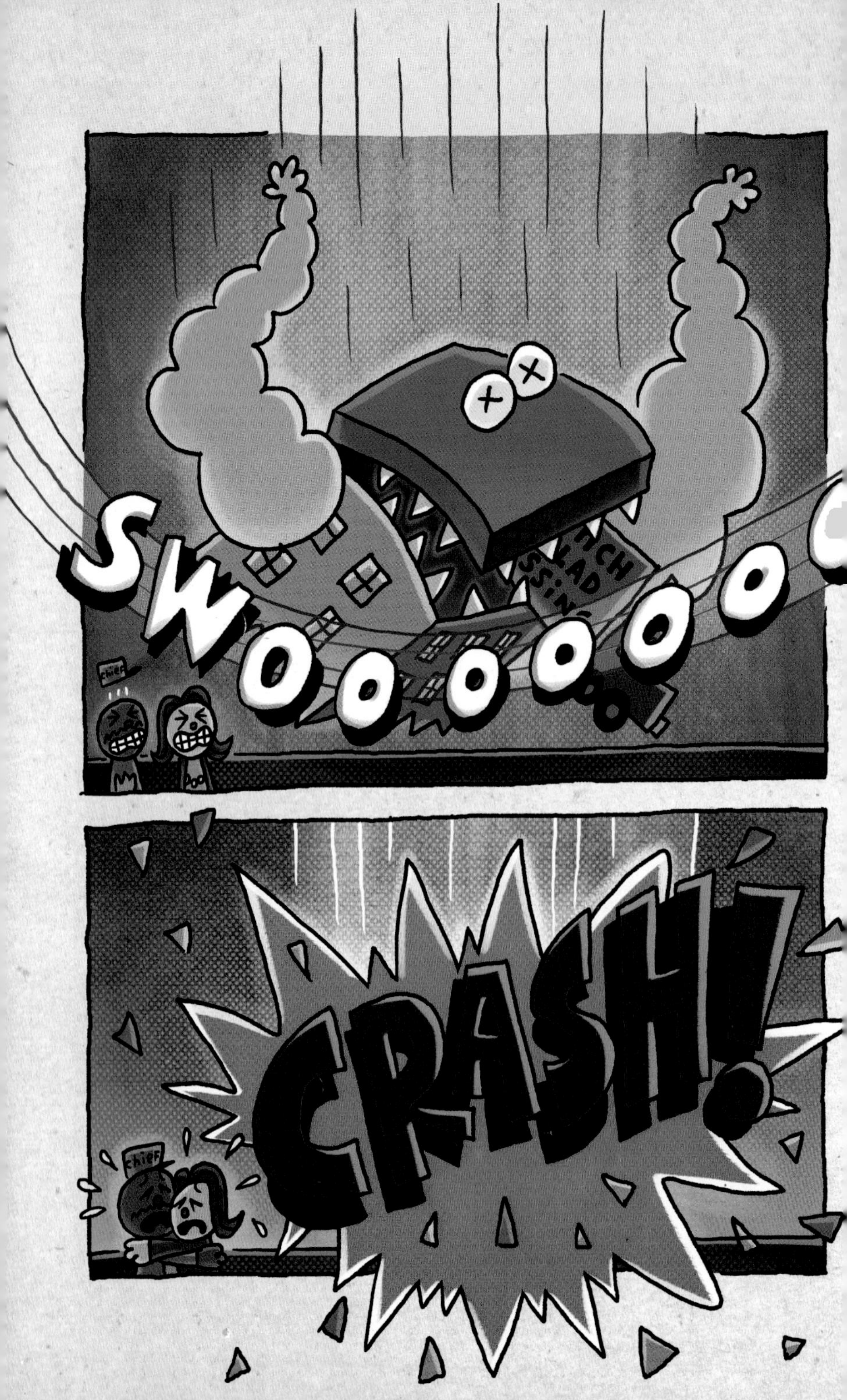

SWOOOOOO
chief
CRASH!
chief

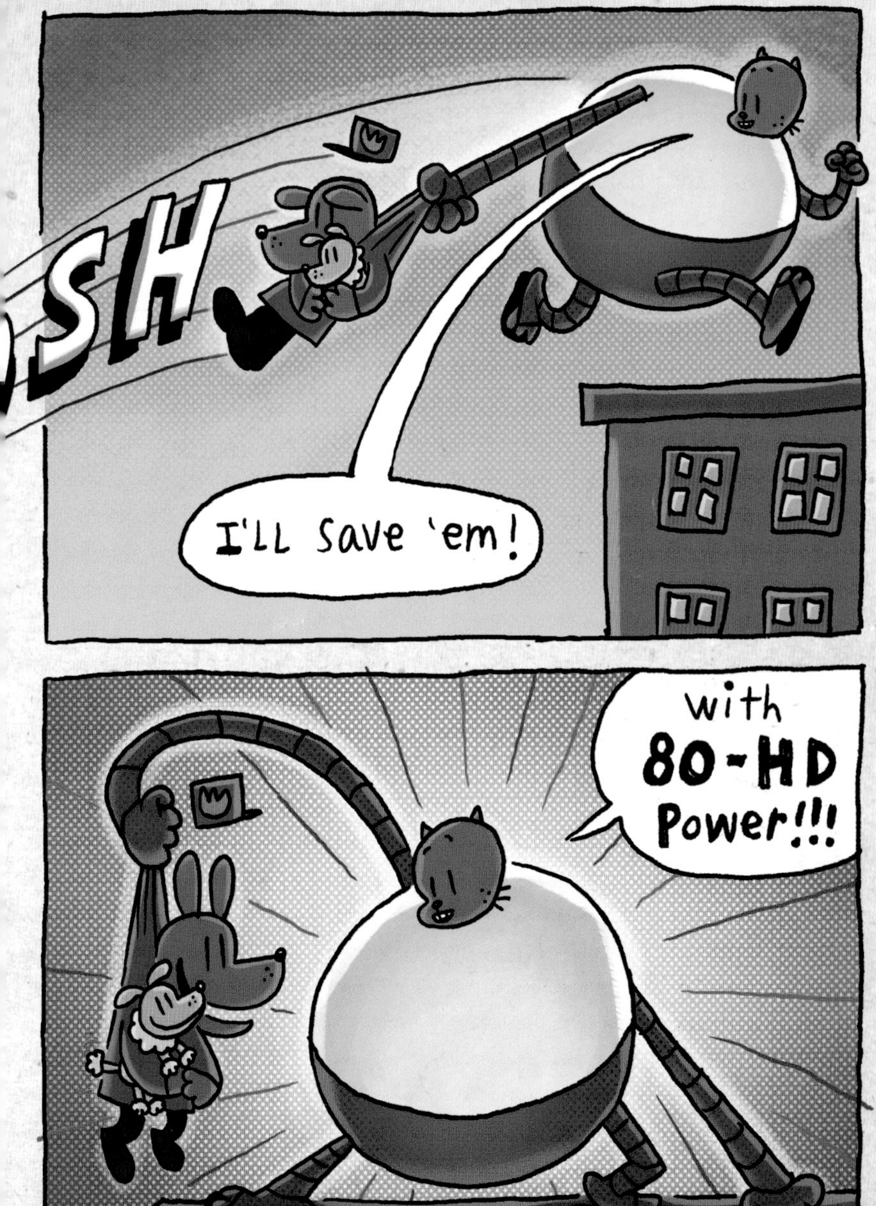
SH
I'LL Save 'em!
with 80-HD Power!!!

He takes a Lickin'
and keeps on Tickin'!!!

Right
Thumb
here.

He takes a Lickin'
and Keeps on Tickin'!!!

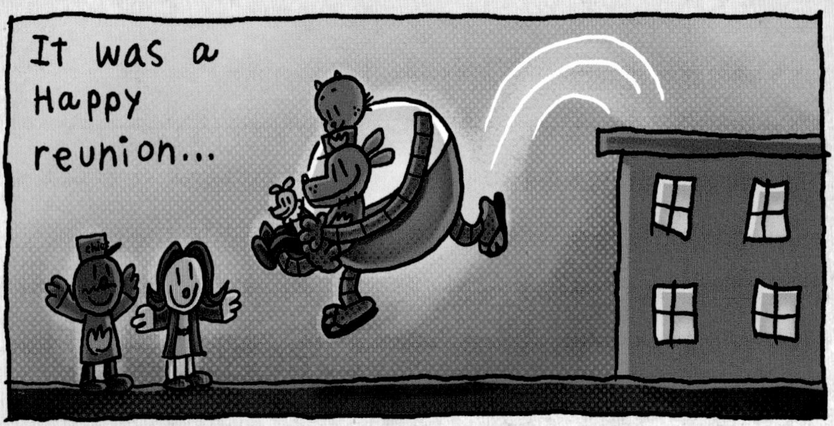
It was a Happy reunion...

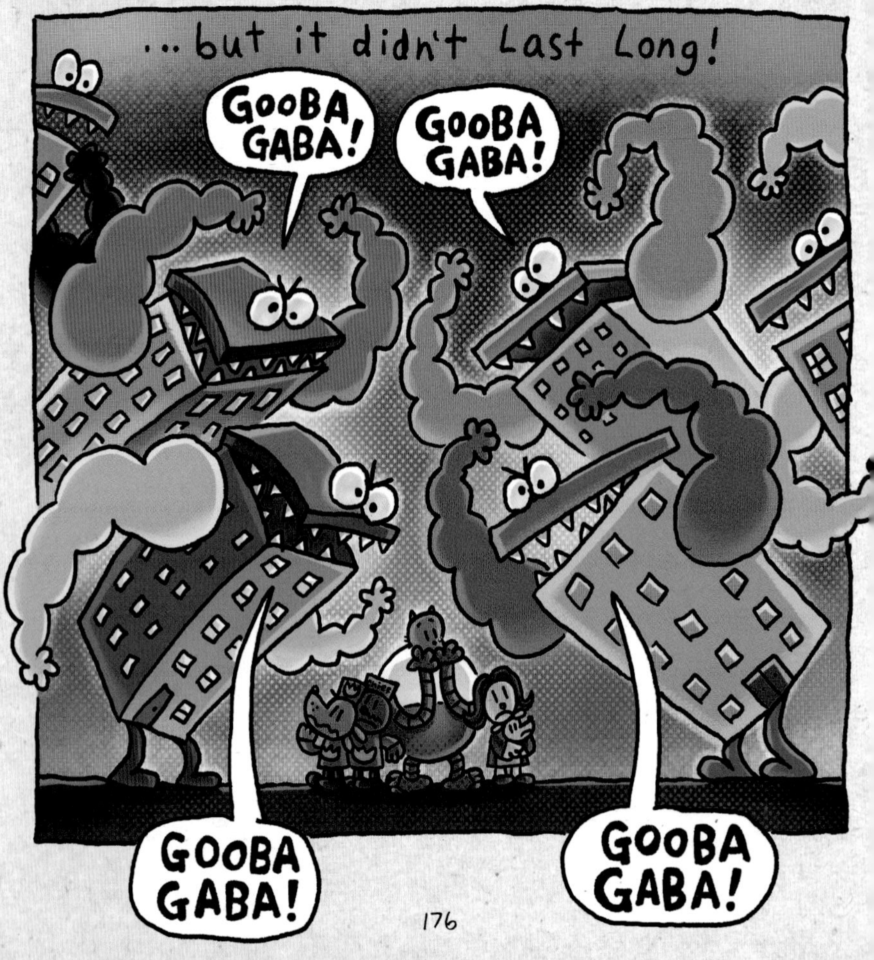
...but it didn't Last Long!
GOOBA GABA!
GOOBA GABA!
GOOBA GABA!
GOOBA GABA!

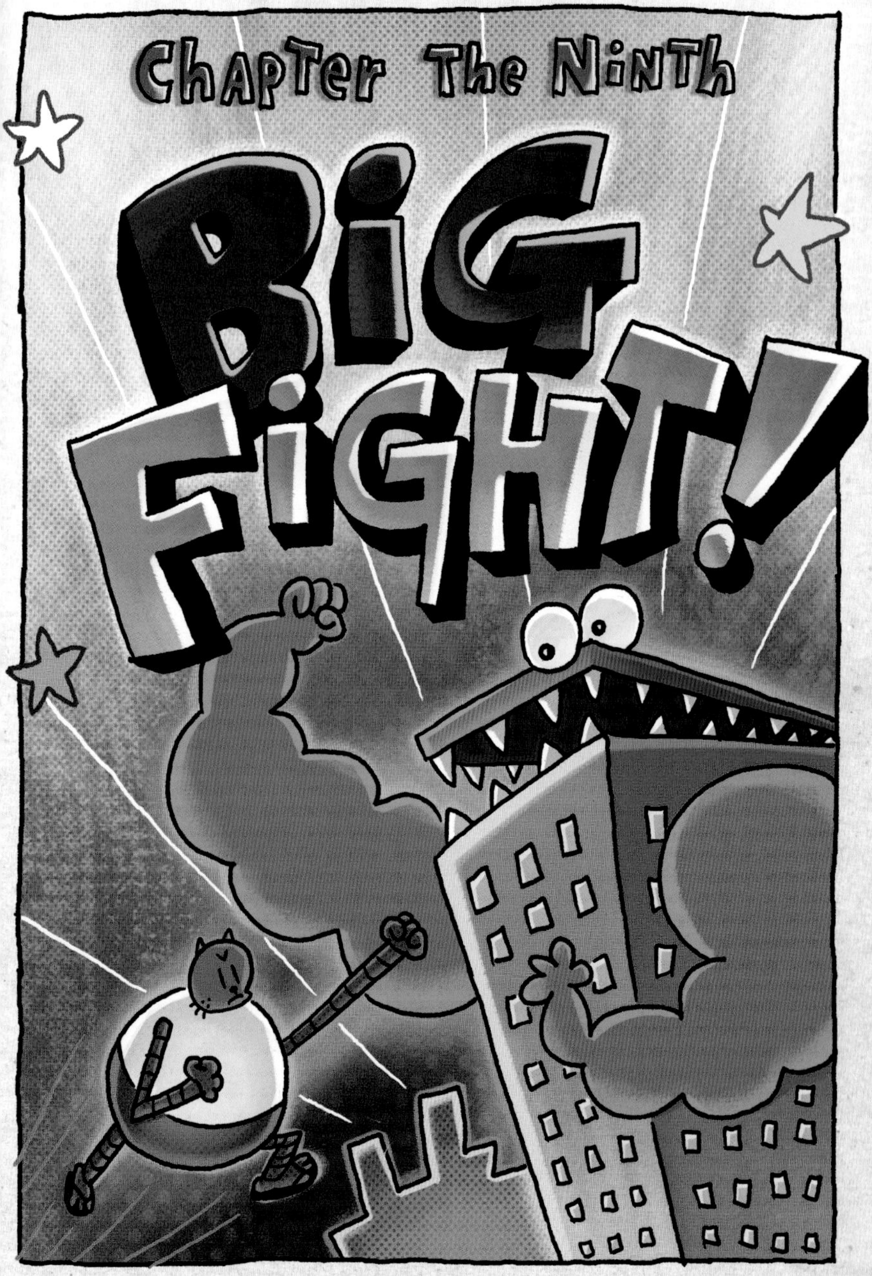
Chapter The Ninth
BIG FIGHT!

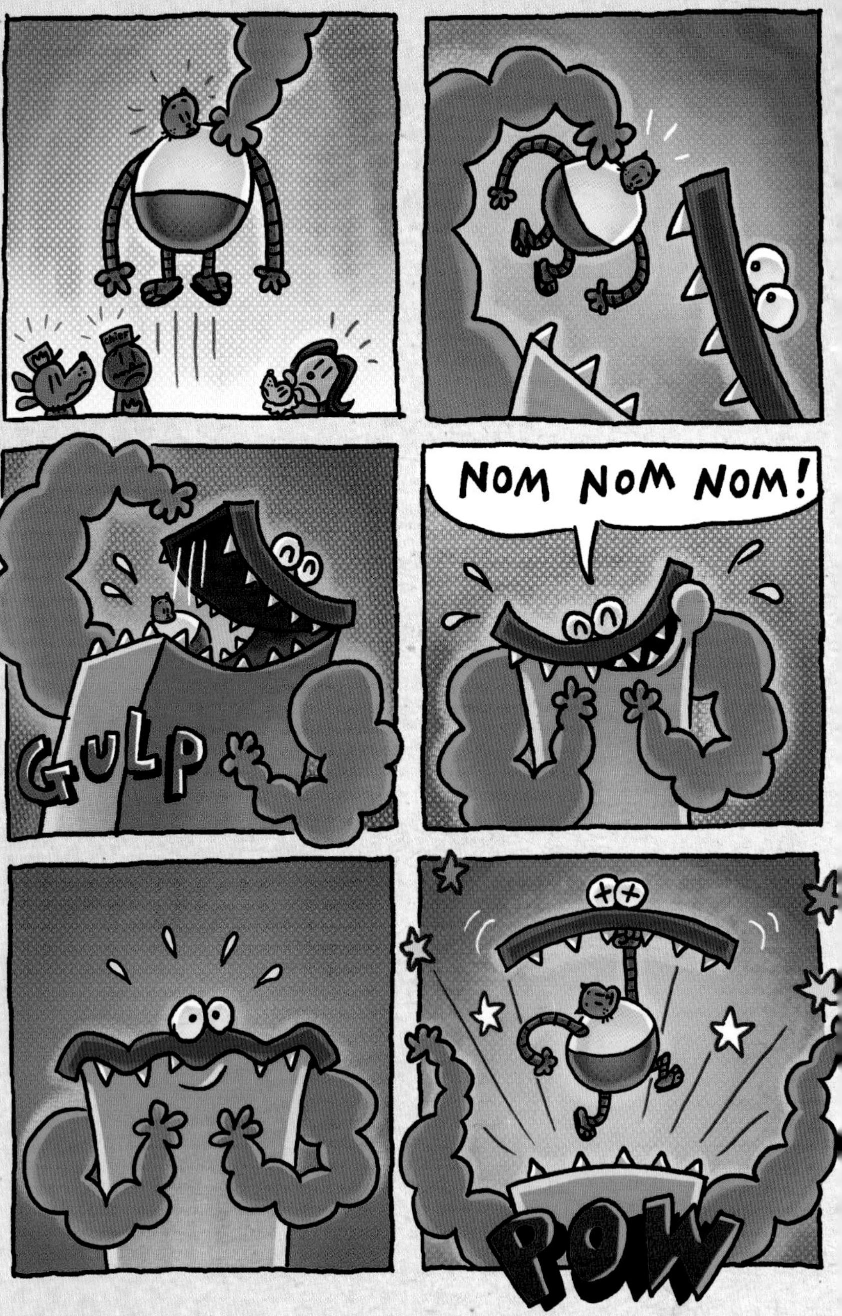
GULP
NOM NOM NOM!
POW

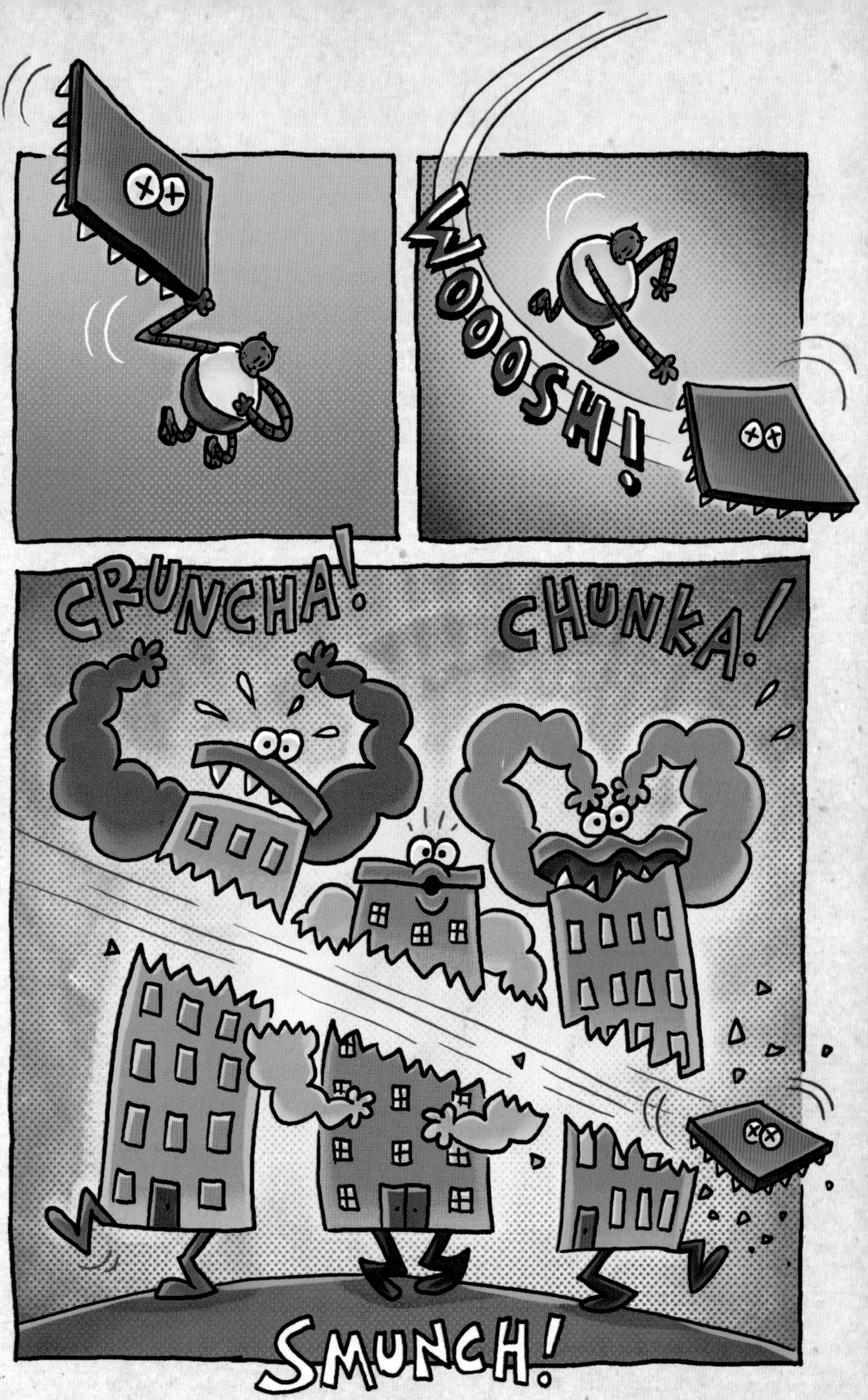
WOOOSH!
CRUNCHA!
CHUNKA!
SMUNCH!

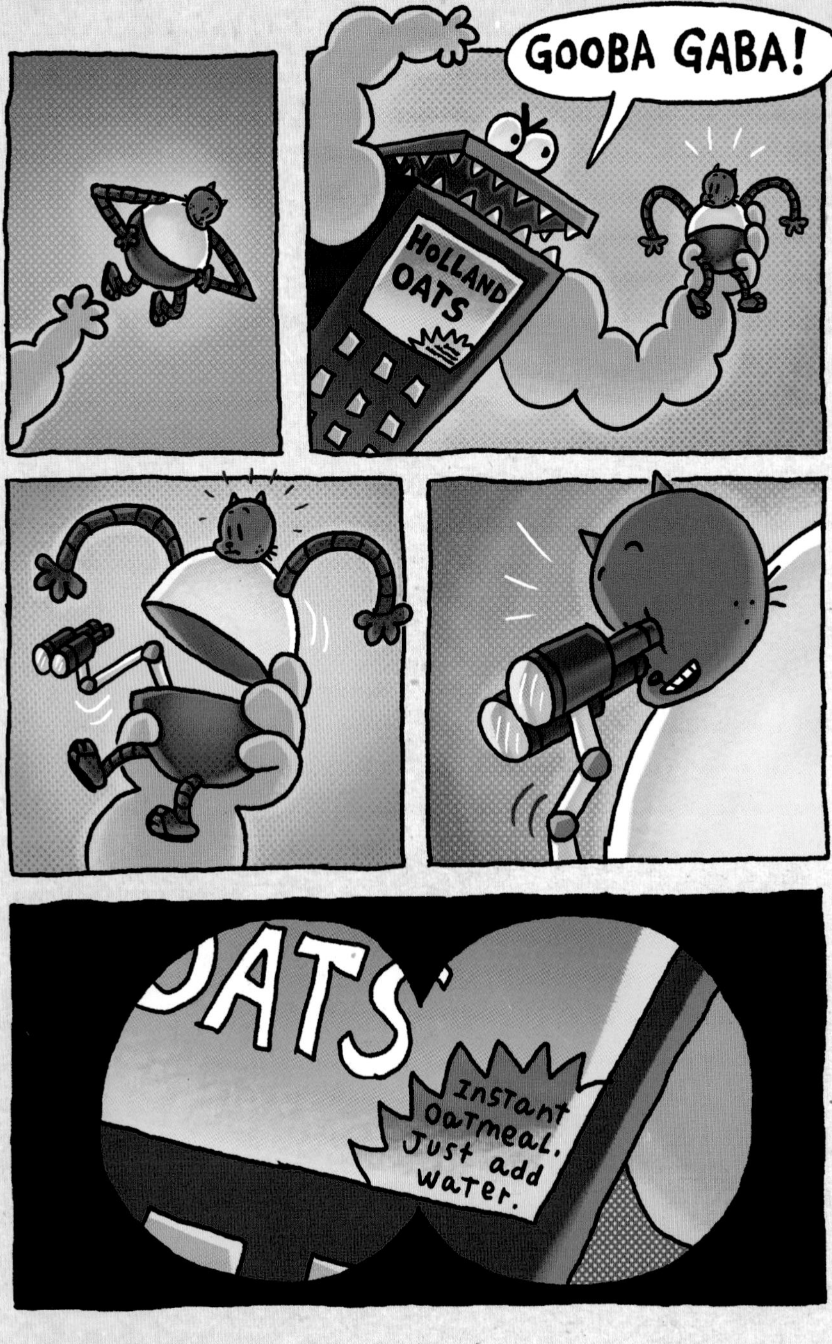
GOOBA GABA!
HOLLAND OATS
OATS
Instant Oatmeal. Just add water.

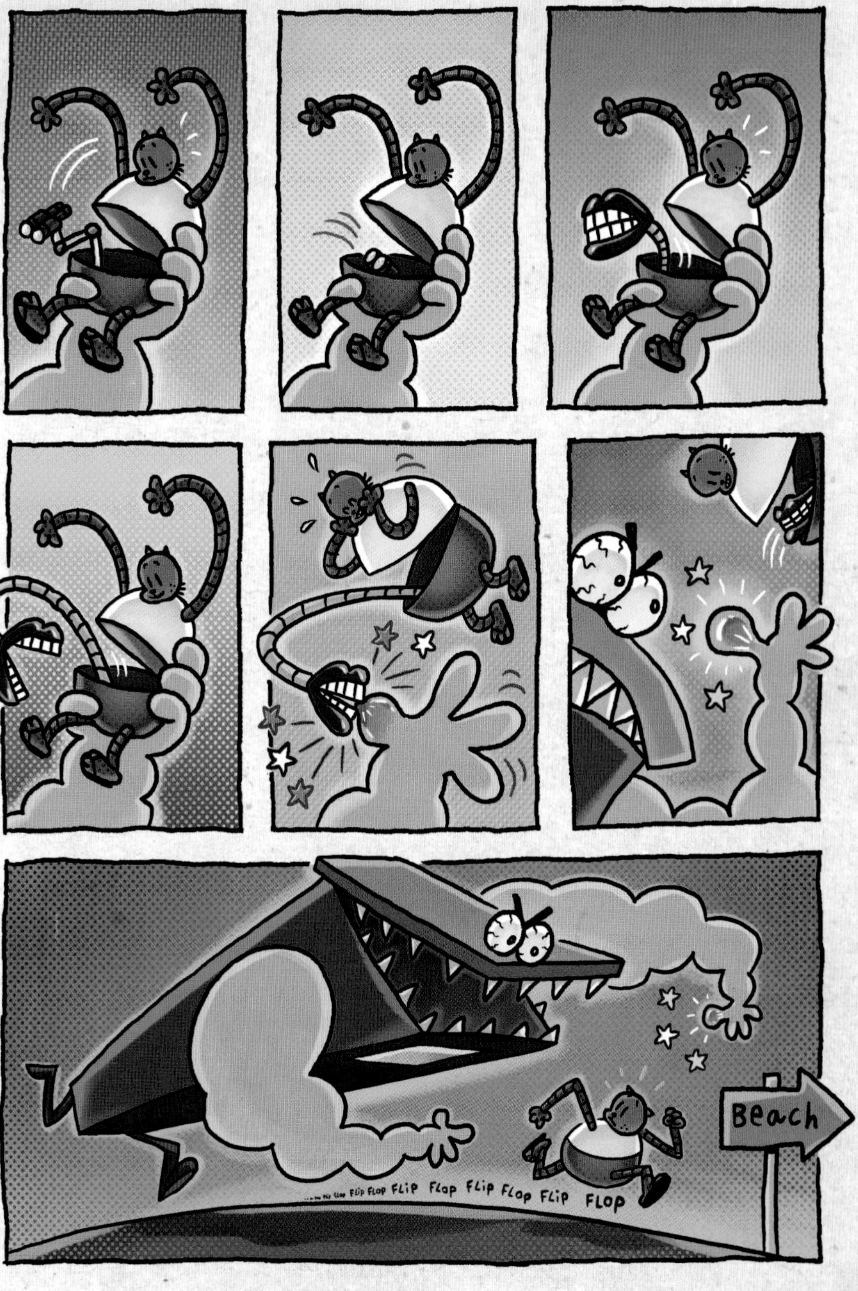
Beach
FLIP FLOP FLIP FLOP FLIP FLOP FLIP FLOP

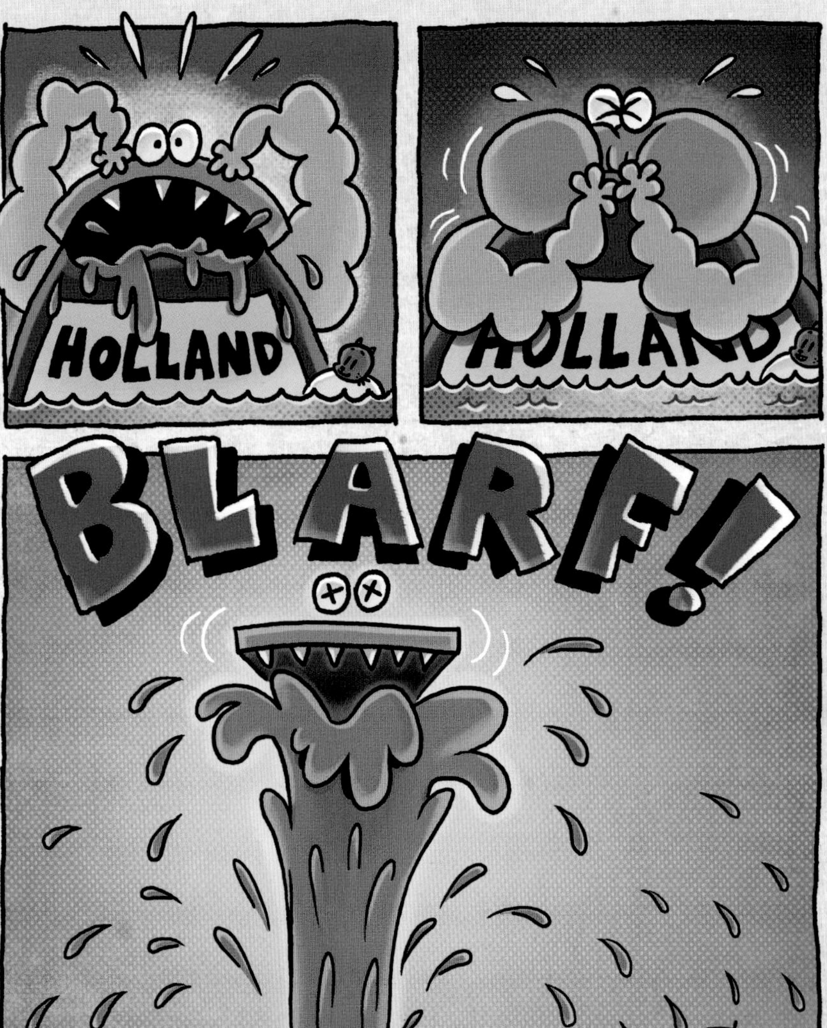
HOLLAND
HOLLAND
BLARF!
HOLLAND OATS

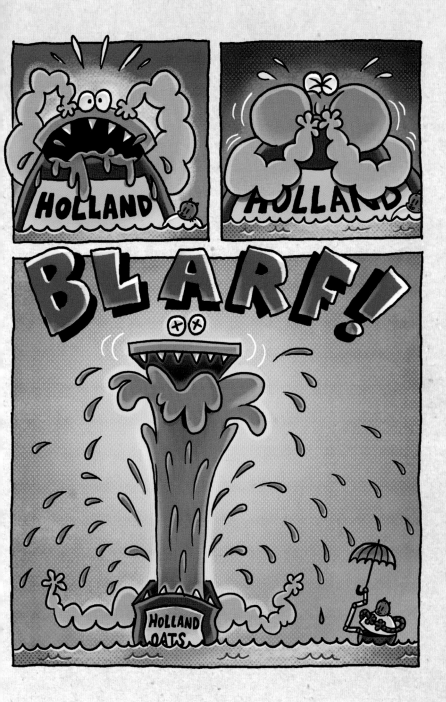

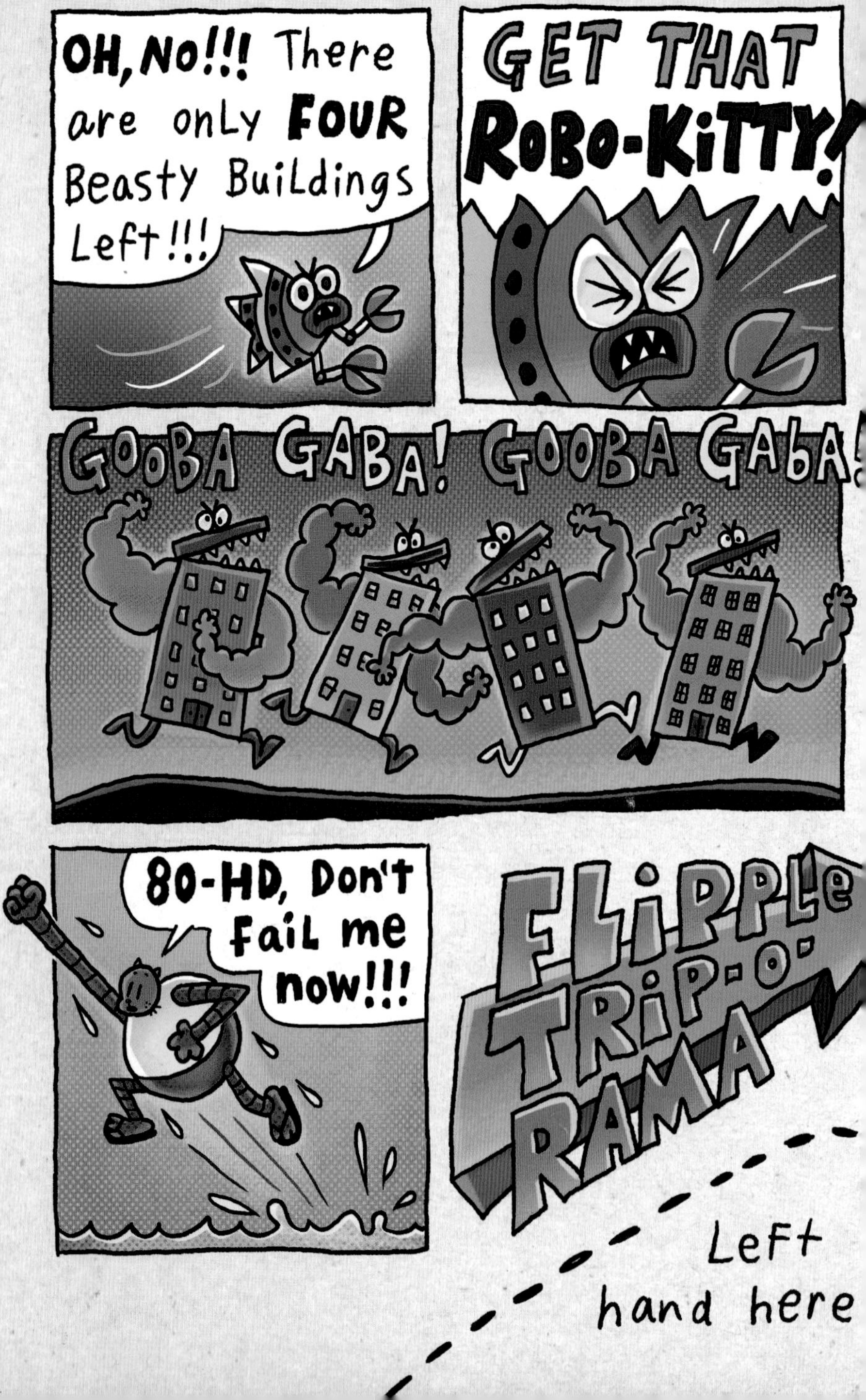

OH, NO!!! There are onLy FOUR Beasty BuiLdings Left!!!
GET THAT ROBO-KiTTY!
GOOBA GABA! GOOBA GABA!
80-HD, Don't FaiL me now!!!
FLiPPLe TRiP-O-RAMA
Left hand here

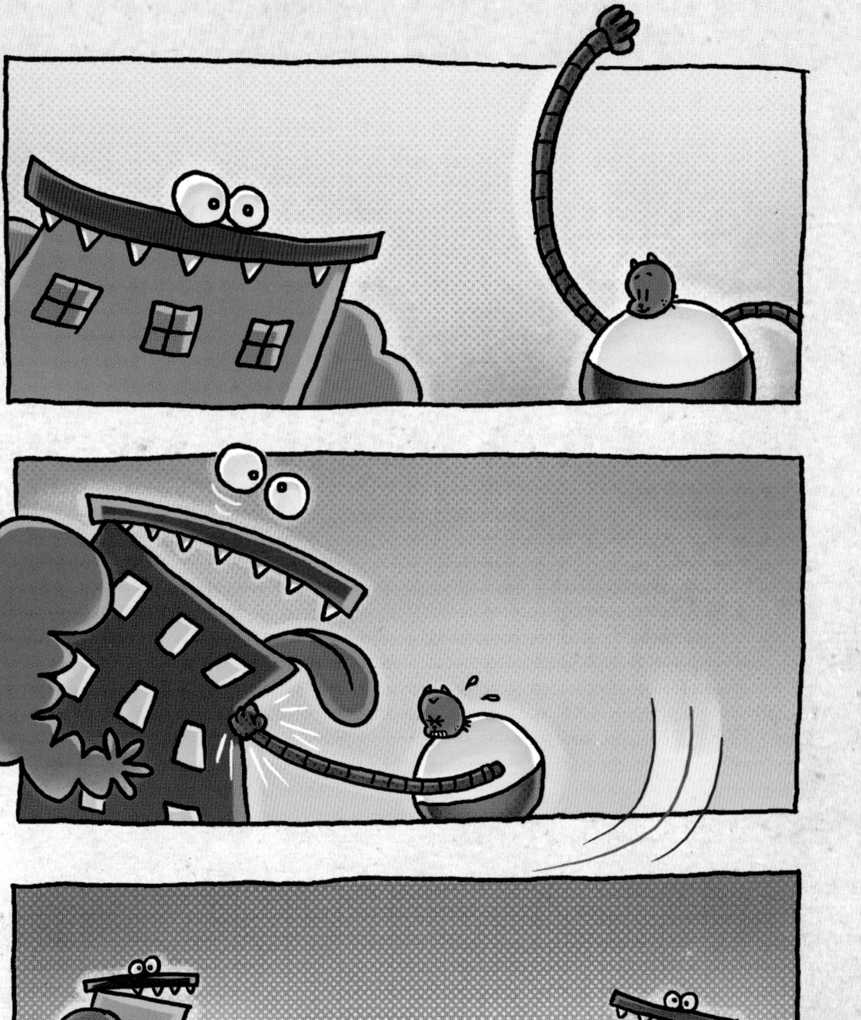

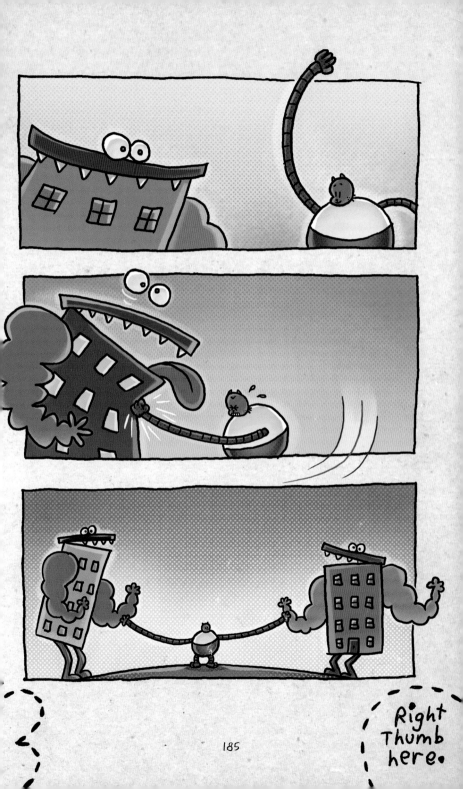

Right Thumb here.

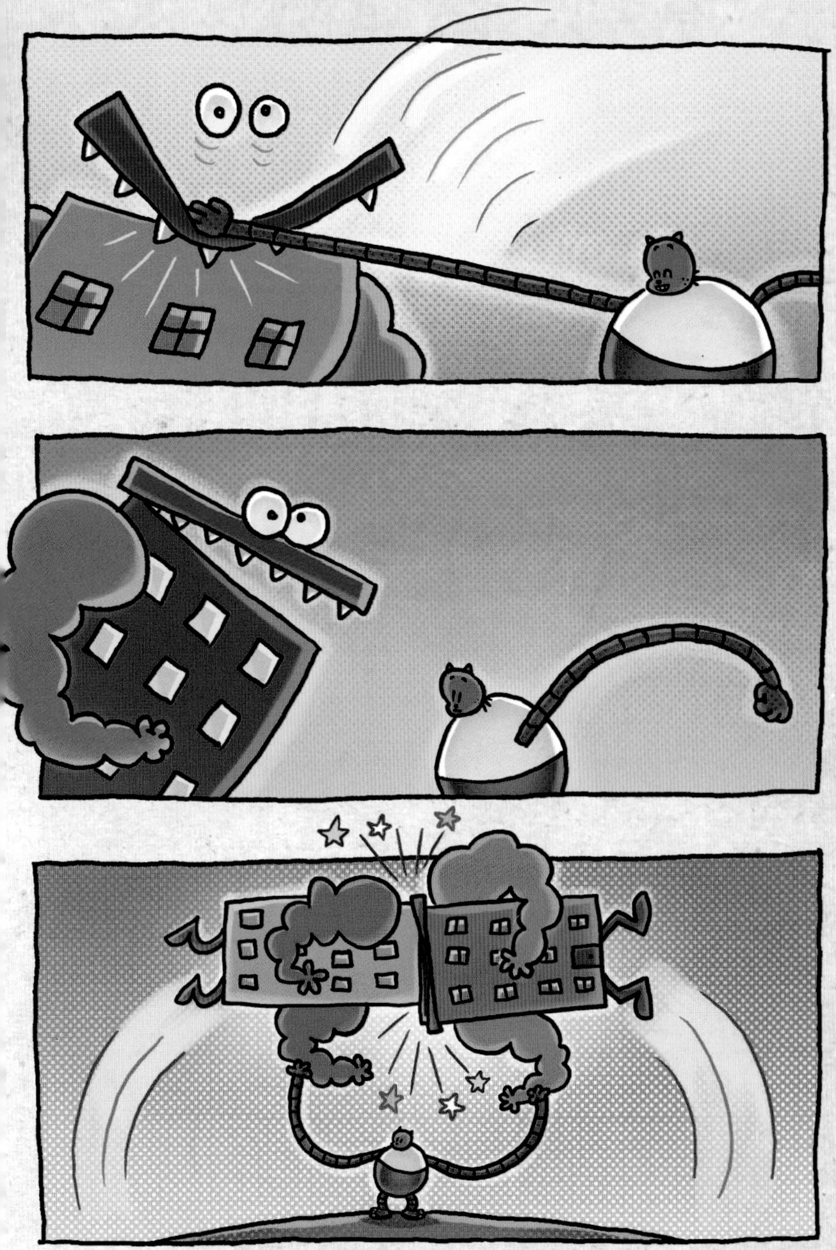

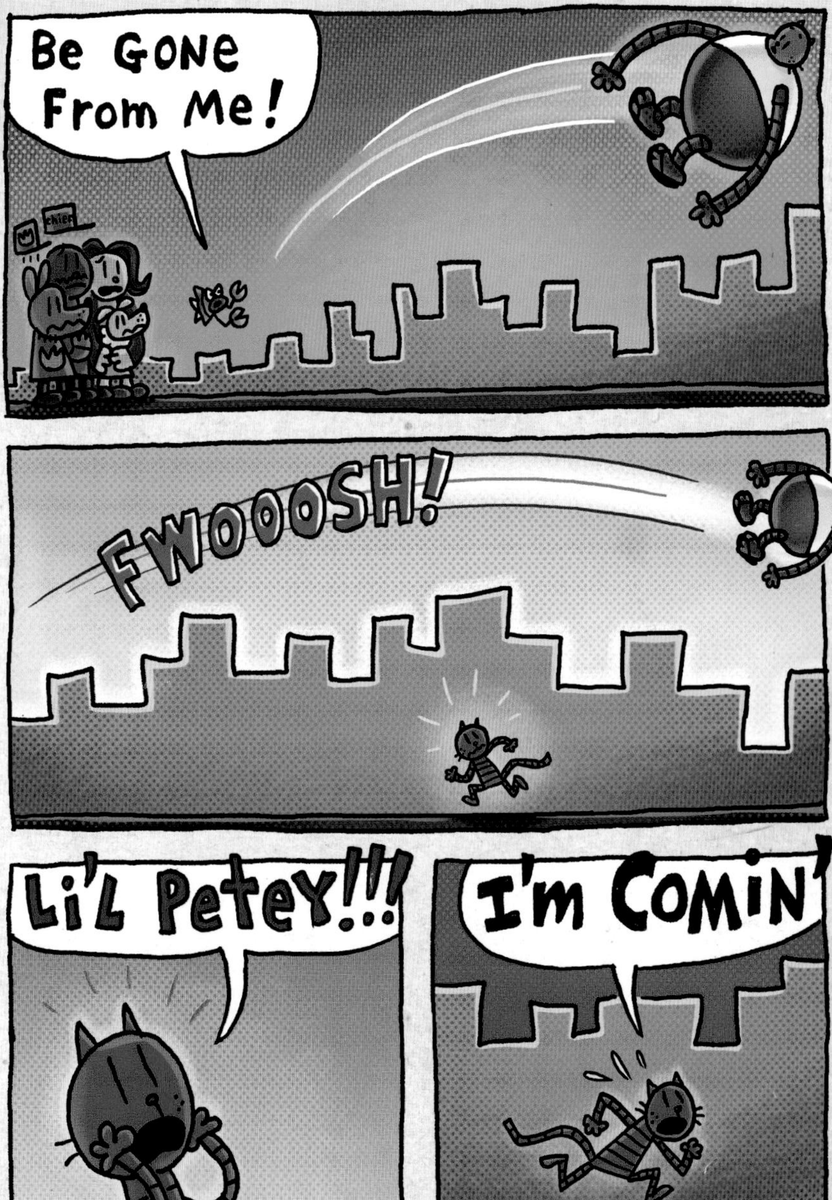
Be GONE From Me!
FWOOOSH!
Li'L Petey!!!
I'm COMIN'

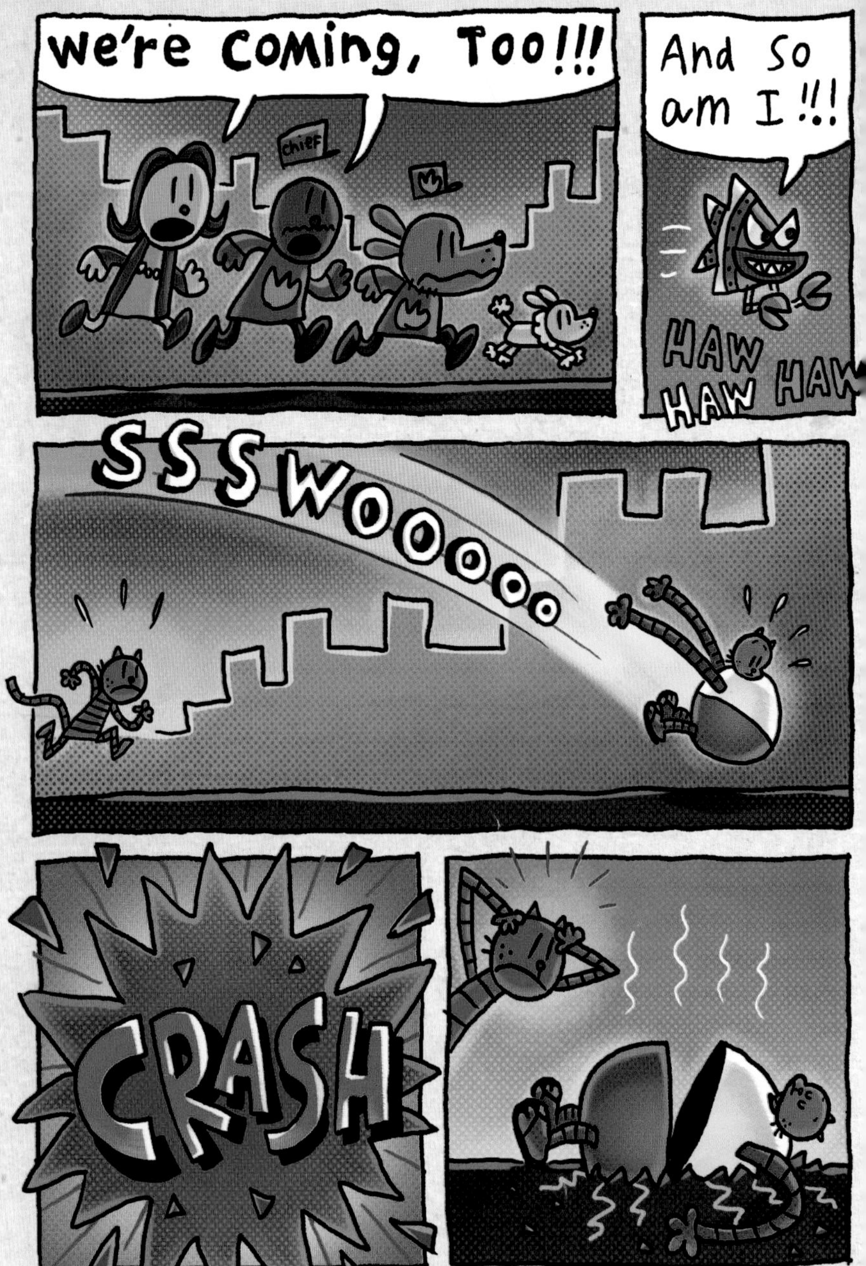
We're Coming, Too!!!
CHIEF
And So am I!!!
HAW HAW HAW HAW
SSSWOOOOOO
CRASH

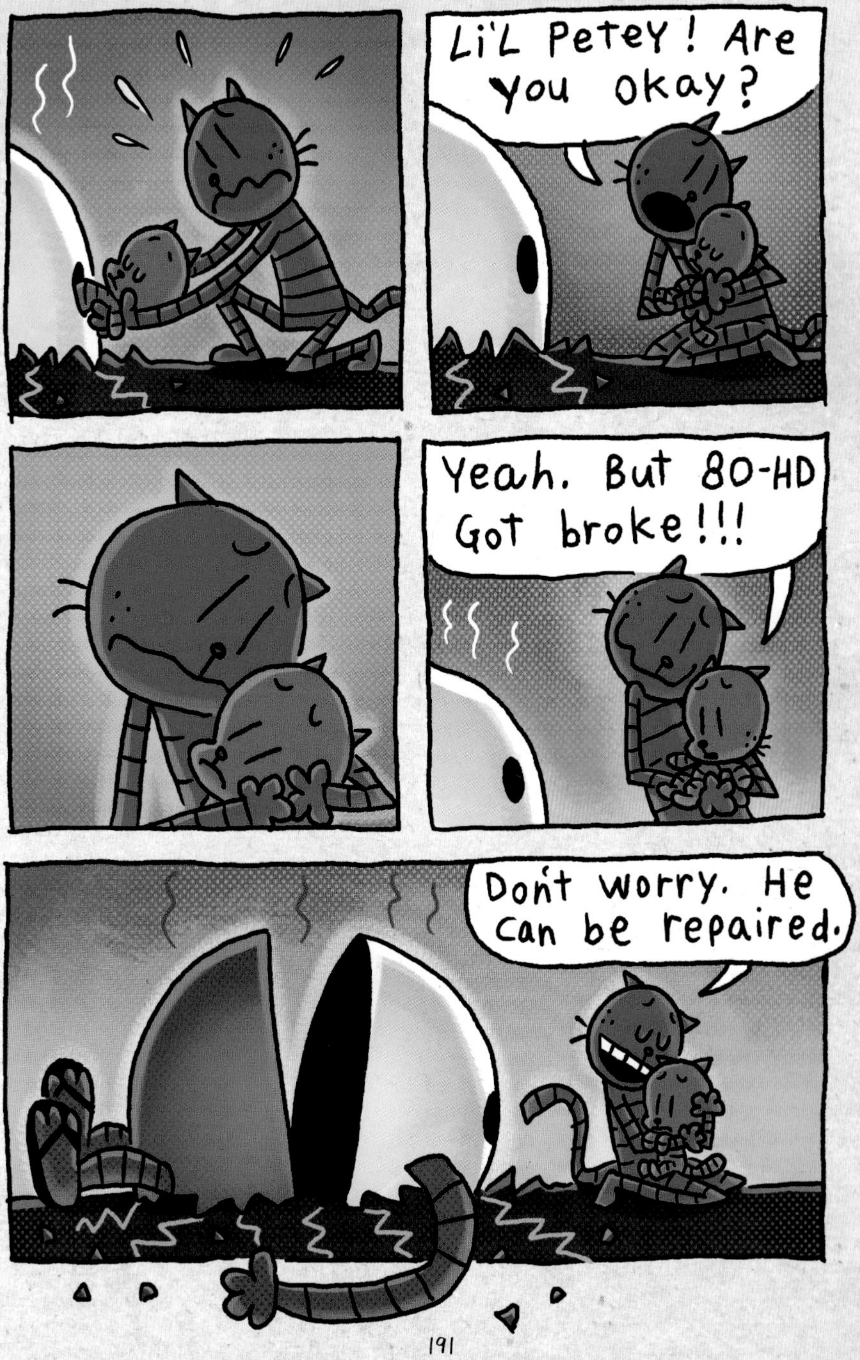
Li'L Petey! Are you okay?
Yeah. But 80-HD Got broke!!!
Don't worry. He can be repaired.

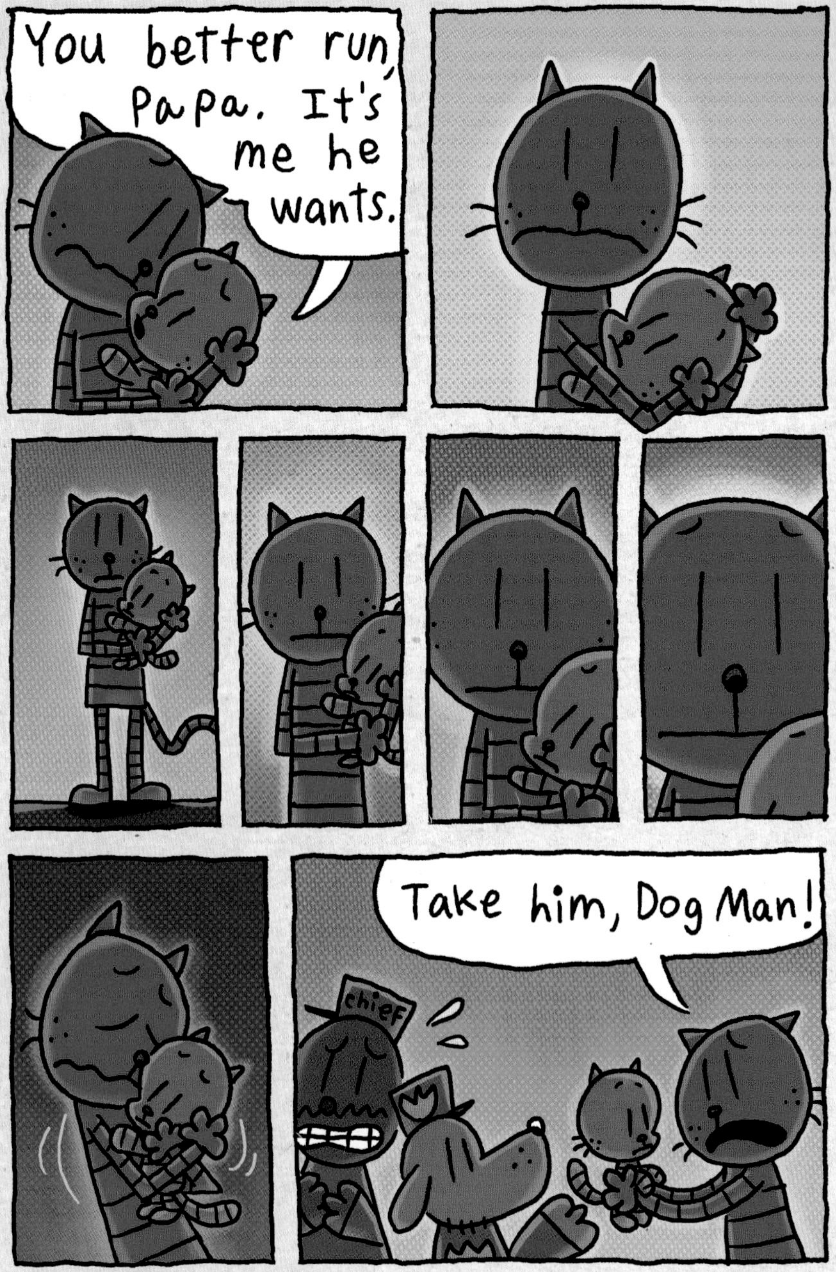
You better run, Papa. It's me he wants.
Take him, Dog Man!
chief

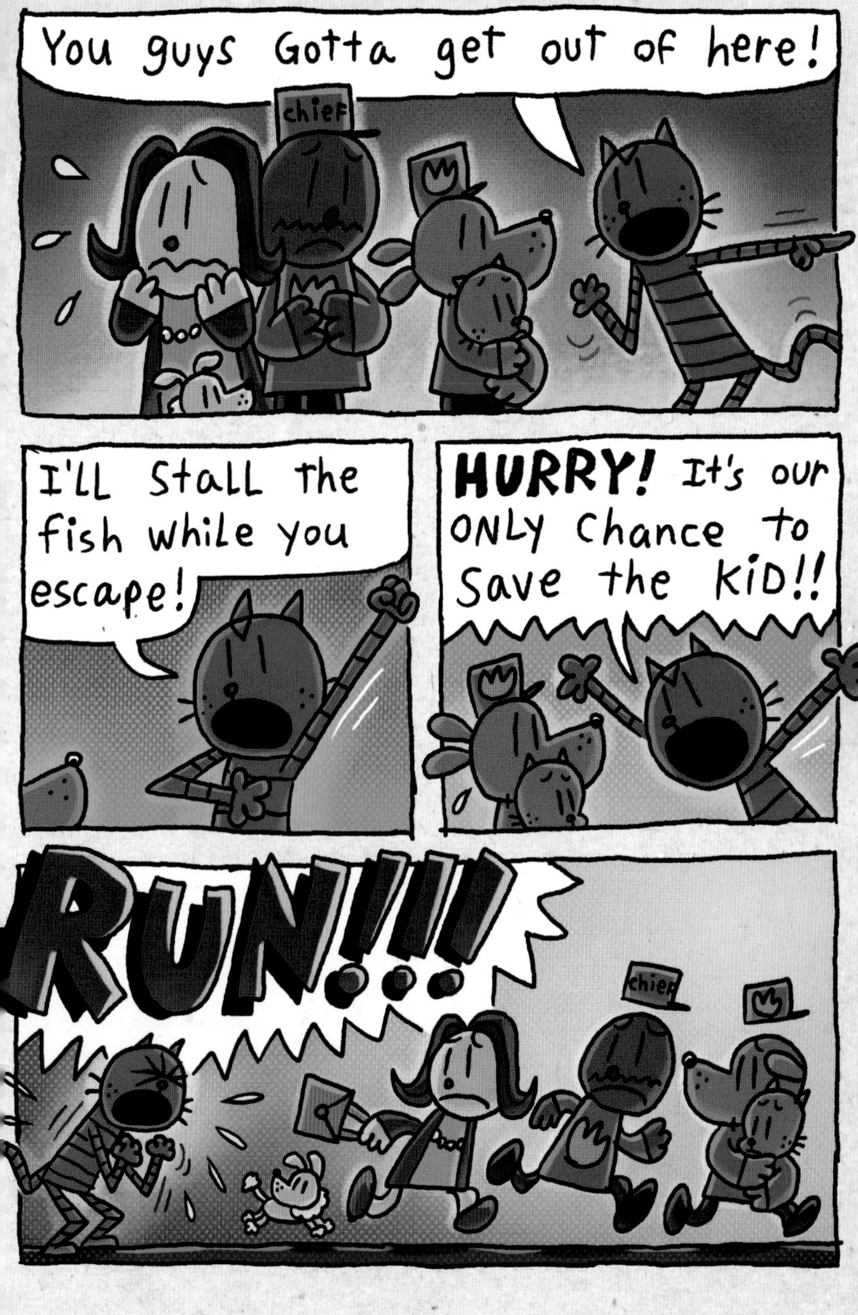

You guys Gotta get out of here!
chief
I'LL Stall the fish while you escape!
HURRY! It's our ONLY Chance to Save the KiD!!
RUN!!!!
chief

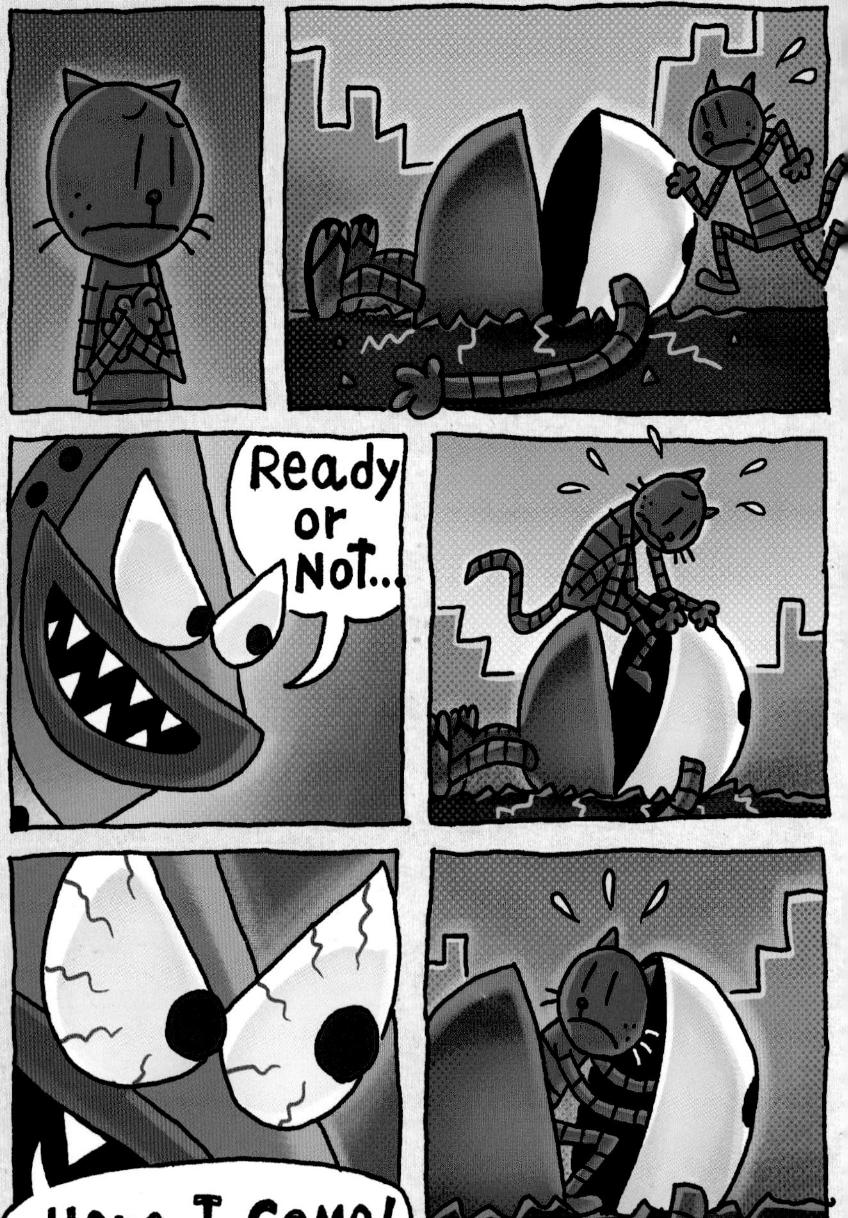
Ready or Not...
...Here I Come!

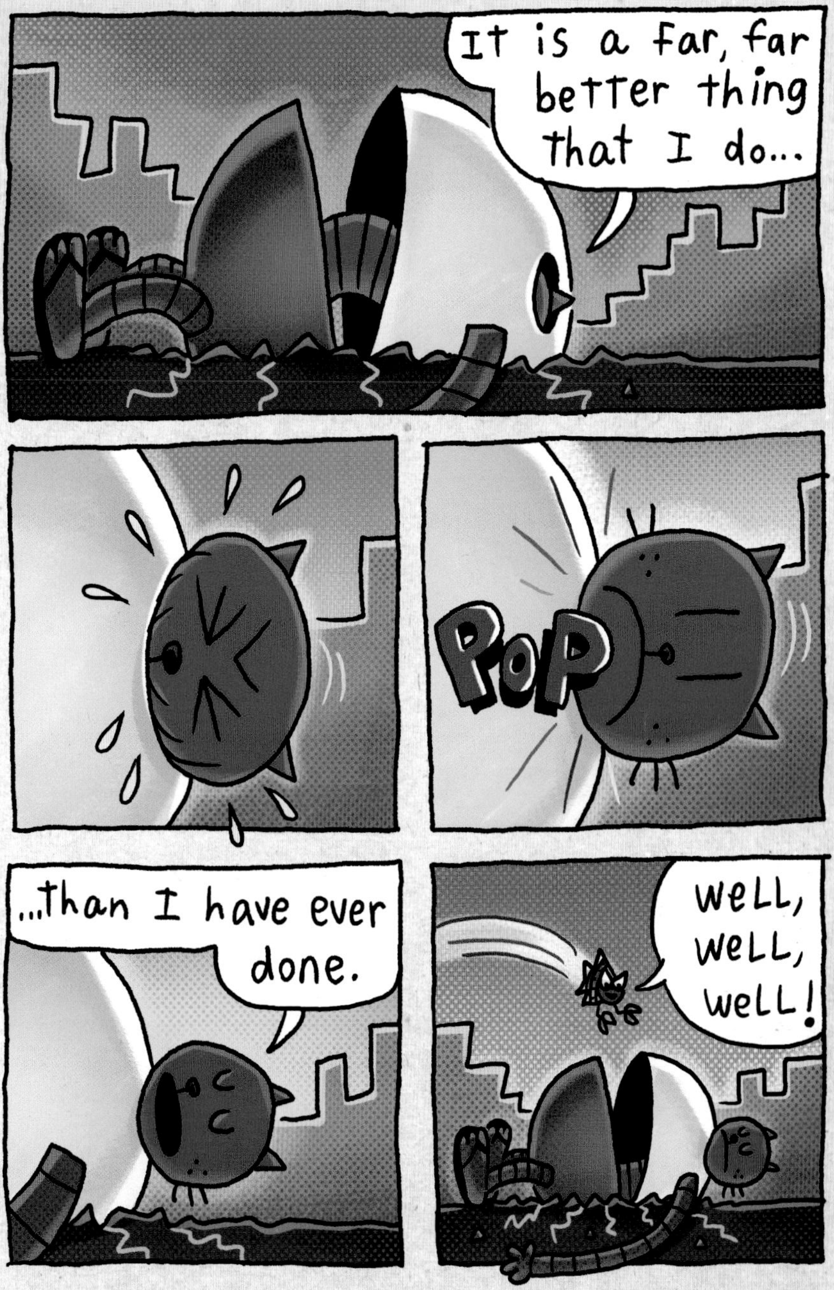
It is a far, far better thing that I do...
POP
...than I have ever done.
WELL, WELL, WELL!

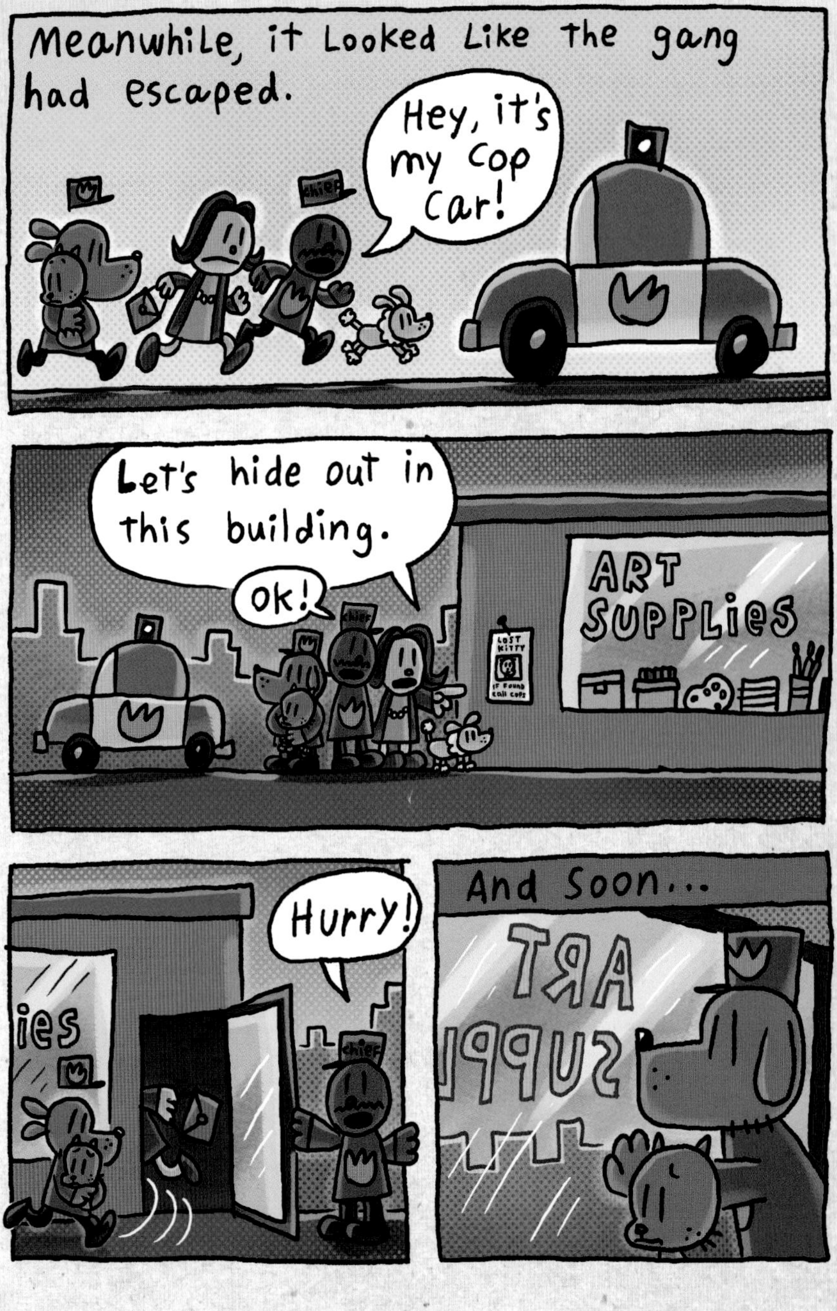
Meanwhile, it Looked Like the gang had escaped.
Hey, it's my cop car!
Let's hide out in this building.
Ok!
ART SUPPLIES
LOST KITTY
IF FOUND call cops
Hurry!
And Soon...

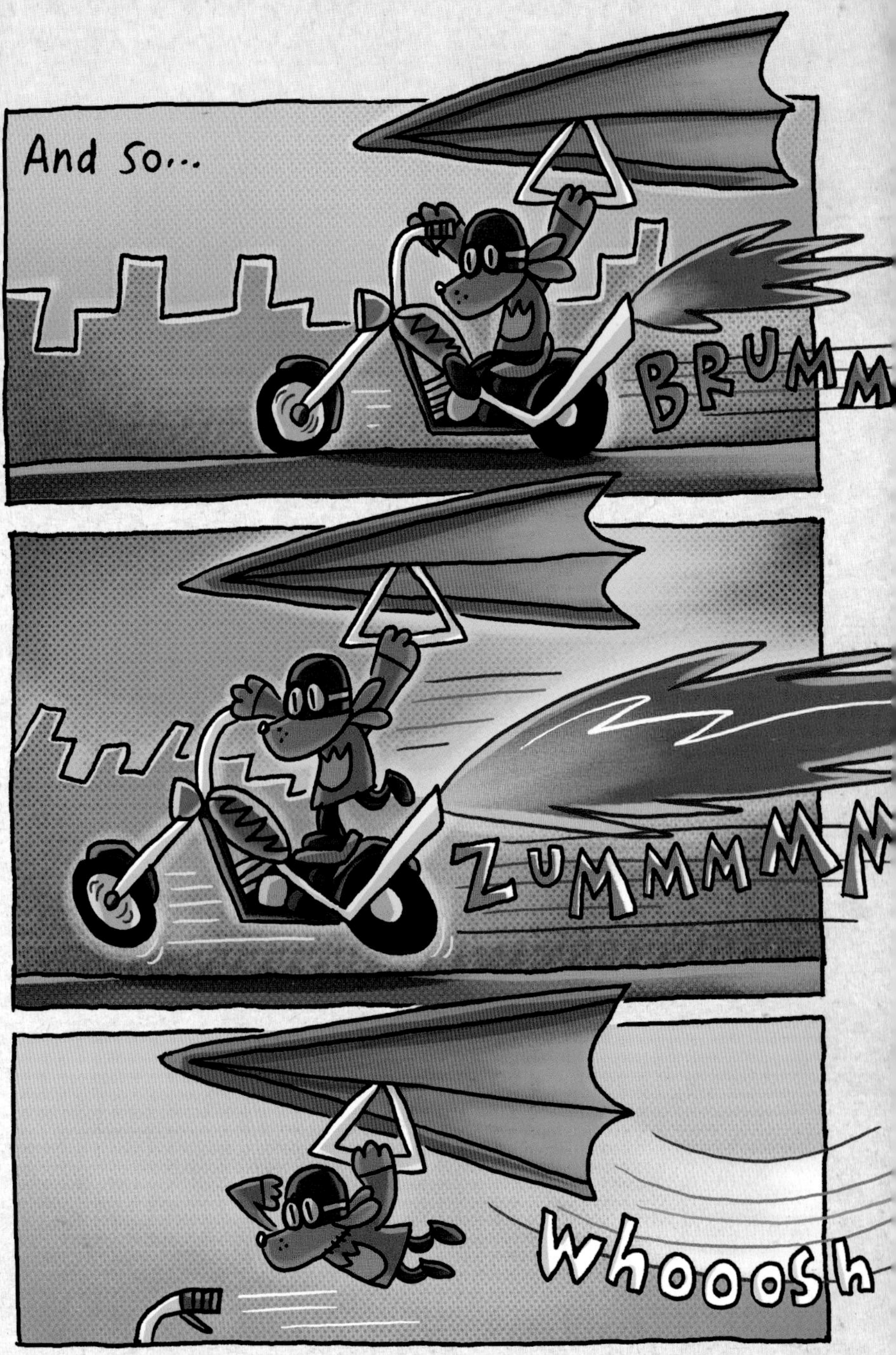
And so...
BRUMM
ZUMMMMMM
Whooosh

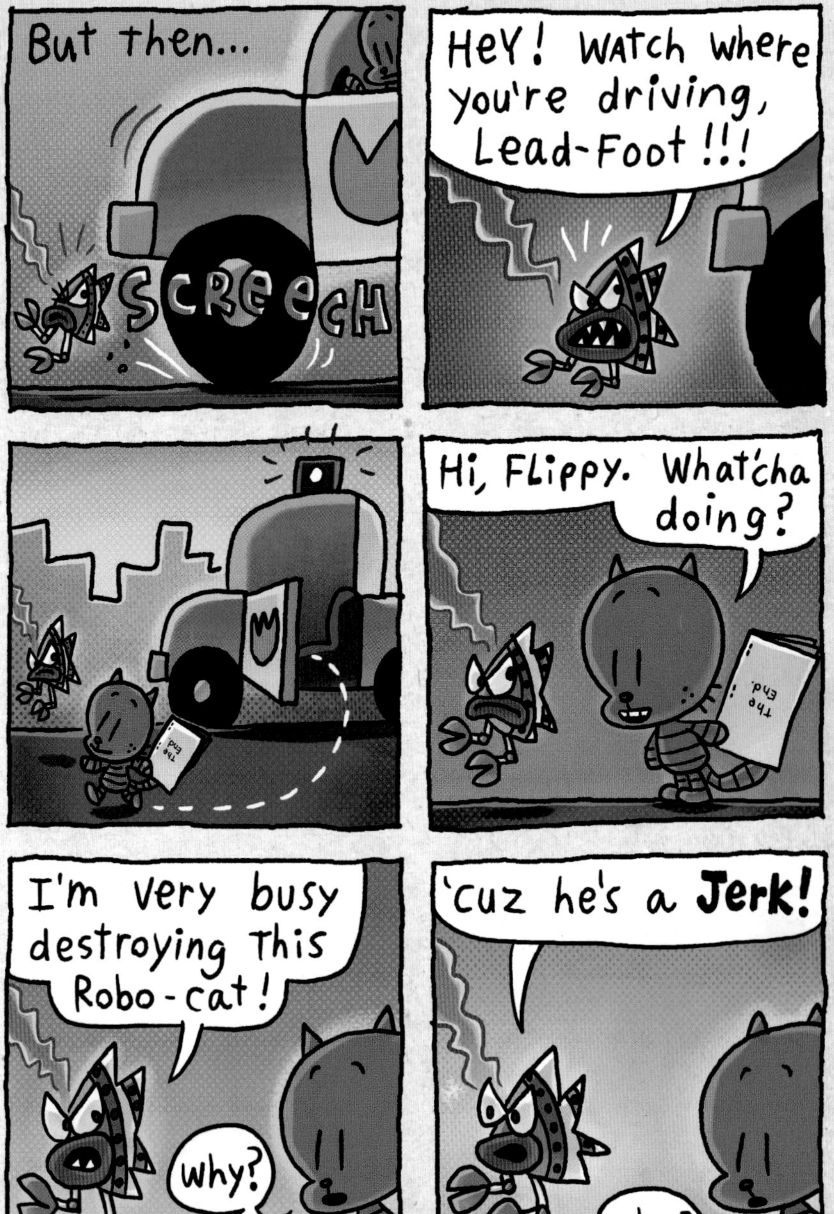
But then...
SCREECH
HEY! WATCH where you're driving, Lead-Foot!!!
The End.
Hi, FLippy. What'cha doing?
The End.
I'm very busy destroying This Robo-cat!
why?
'cuz he's a **Jerk!**
why?

208

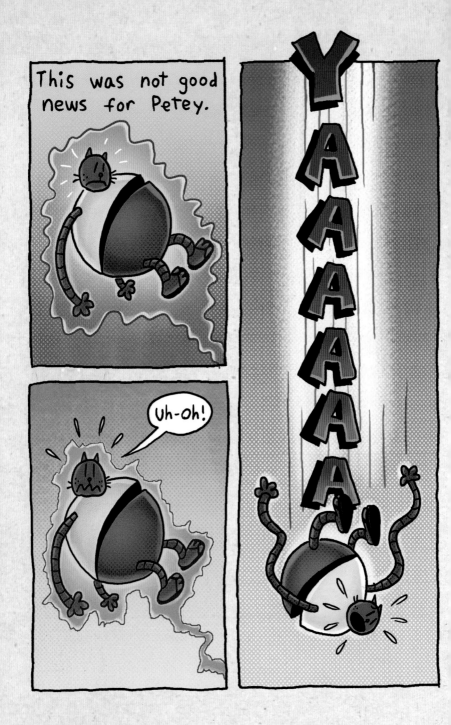

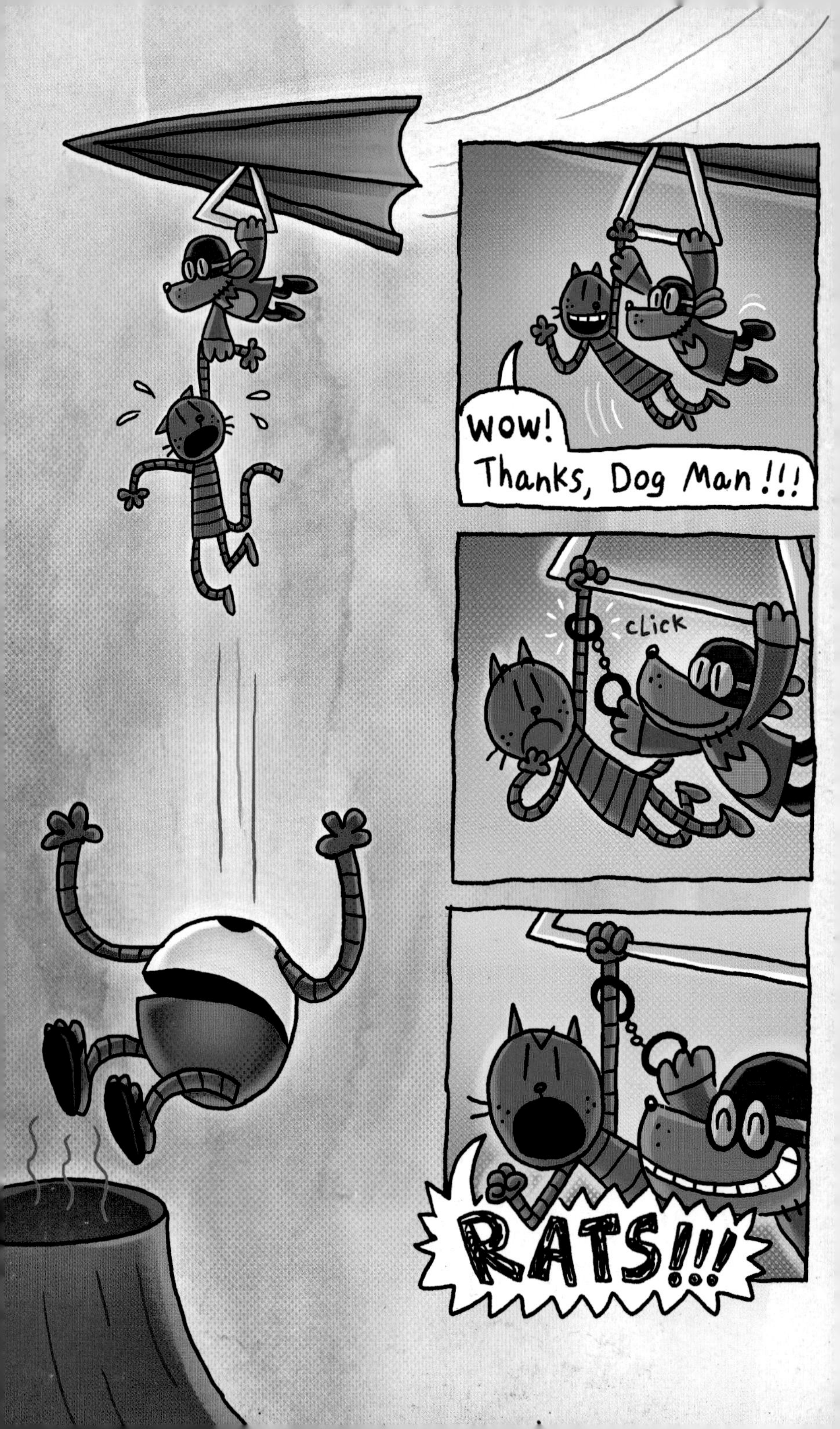
WOW! Thanks, Dog Man!!!
cLick
RATS!!!

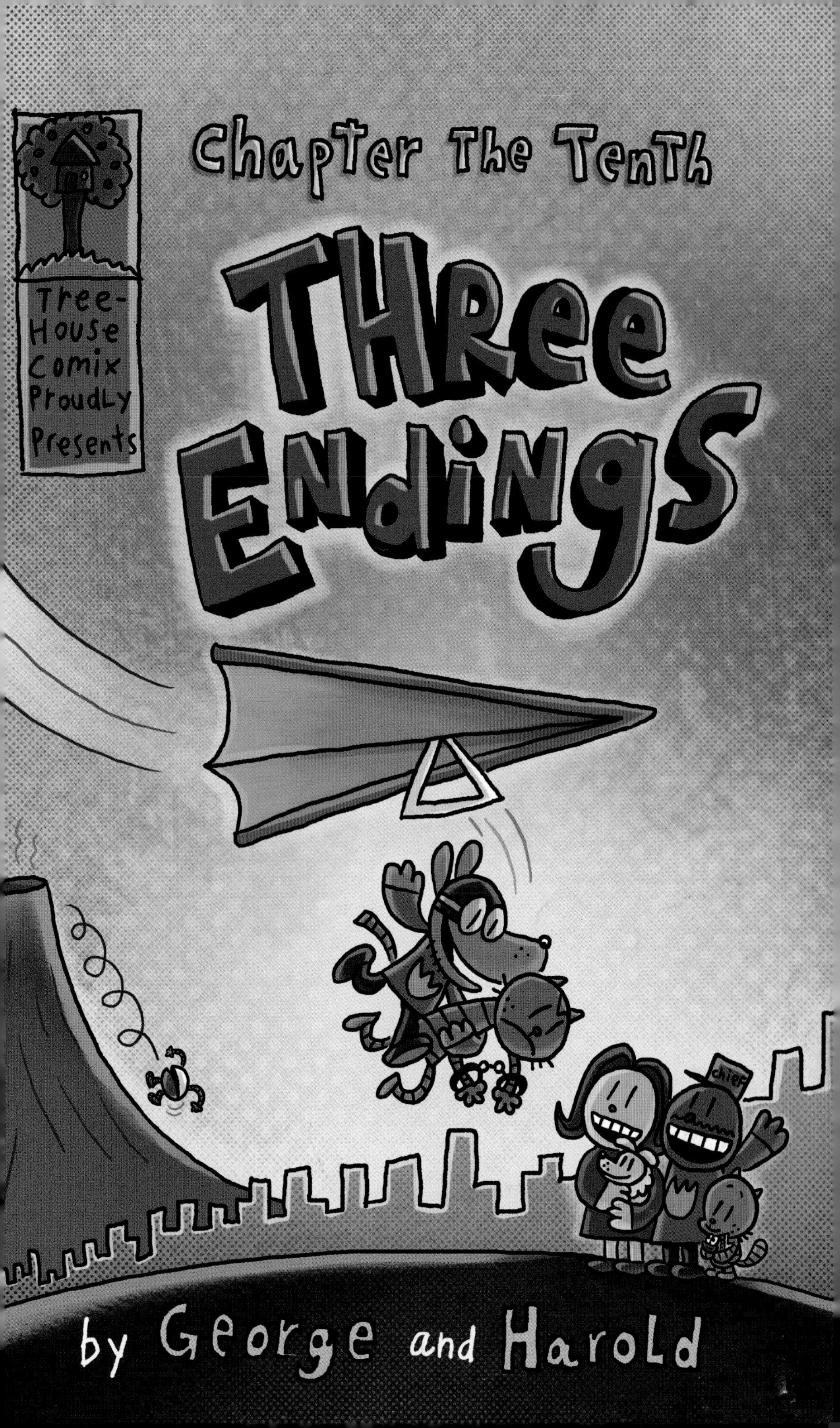
Tree-House Comix Proudly Presents
Chapter The Tenth
THREE ENDINGS
Chief
by George and Harold

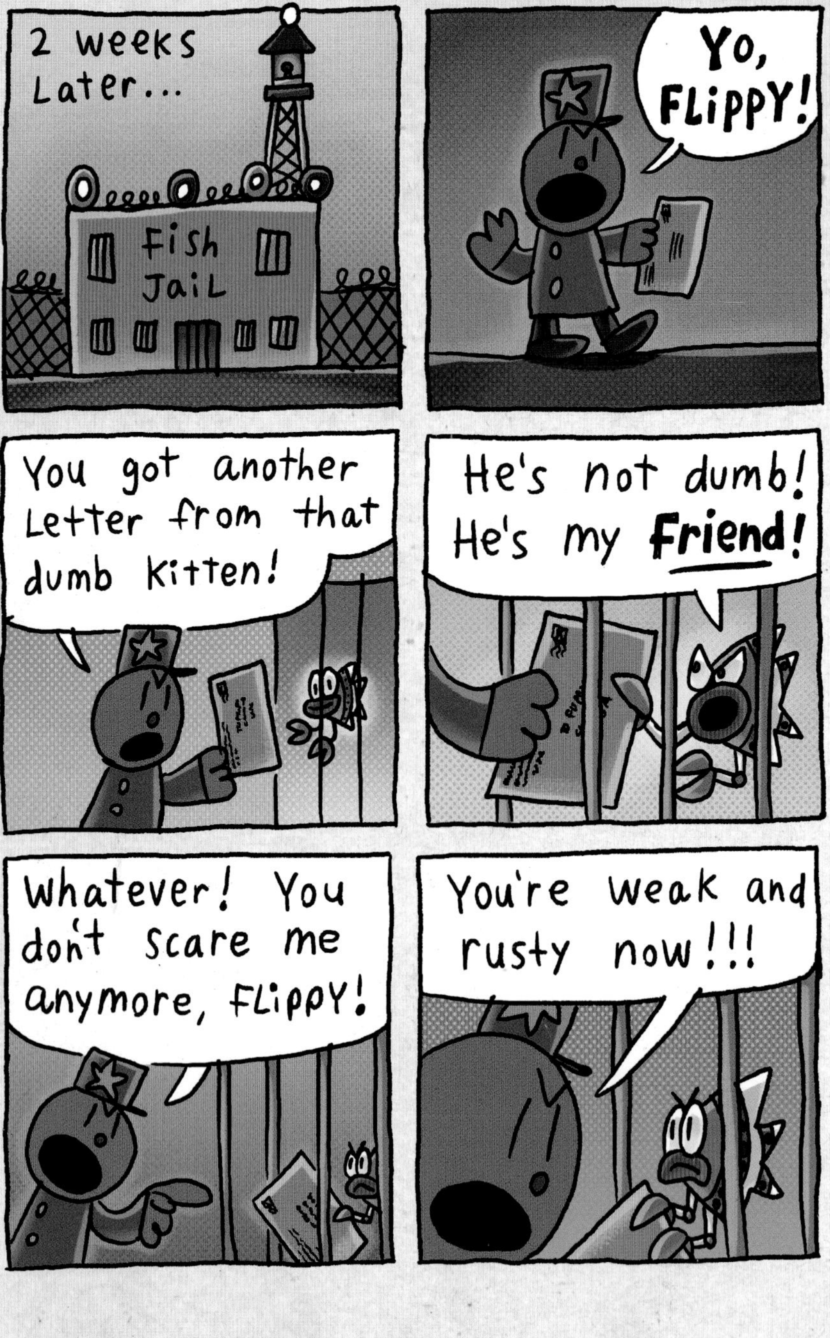
2 weeks Later...
Fish Jail
Yo, FLIPPY!
You got another Letter from that dumb Kitten!
He's not dumb! He's my **Friend!**
Whatever! You don't scare me anymore, FLIPPY!
You're weak and rusty now!!!

221

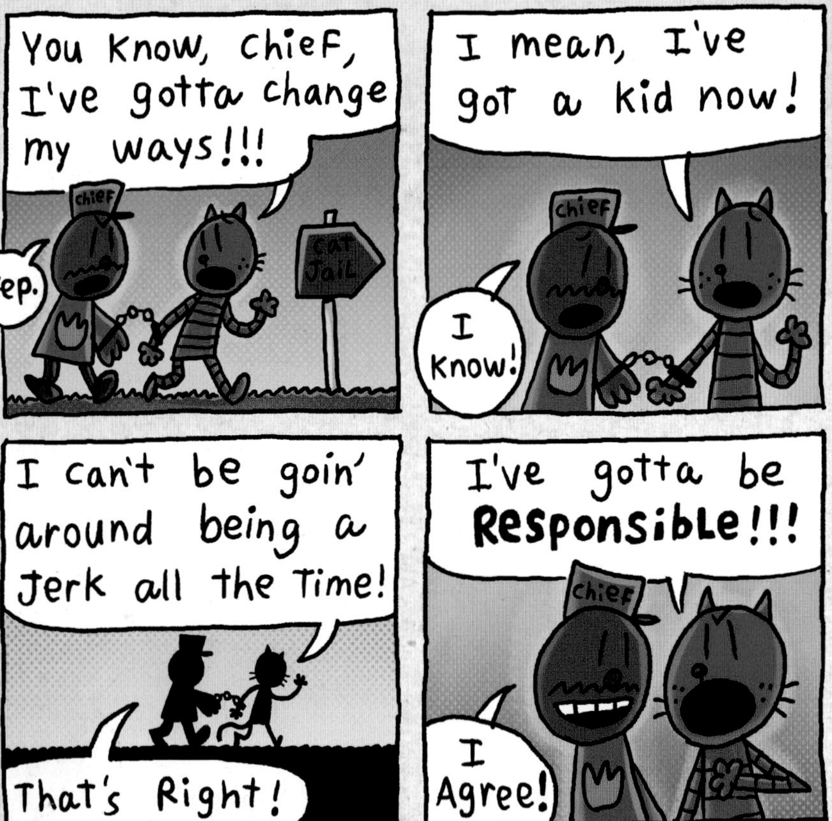
You know, chief, I've gotta change my ways!!!
Yep.
chief
Cat Jail
I mean, I've got a kid now!
chief
I know!
I can't be goin' around being a Jerk all the Time!
That's Right!
I've gotta be RESPONSIBLE!!!
chief
I Agree!
I've gotta be a ROLE MODEL!!!
chief
So true!
I've gotta be GOOD!!!
chief
ABSOLUTELY!!!

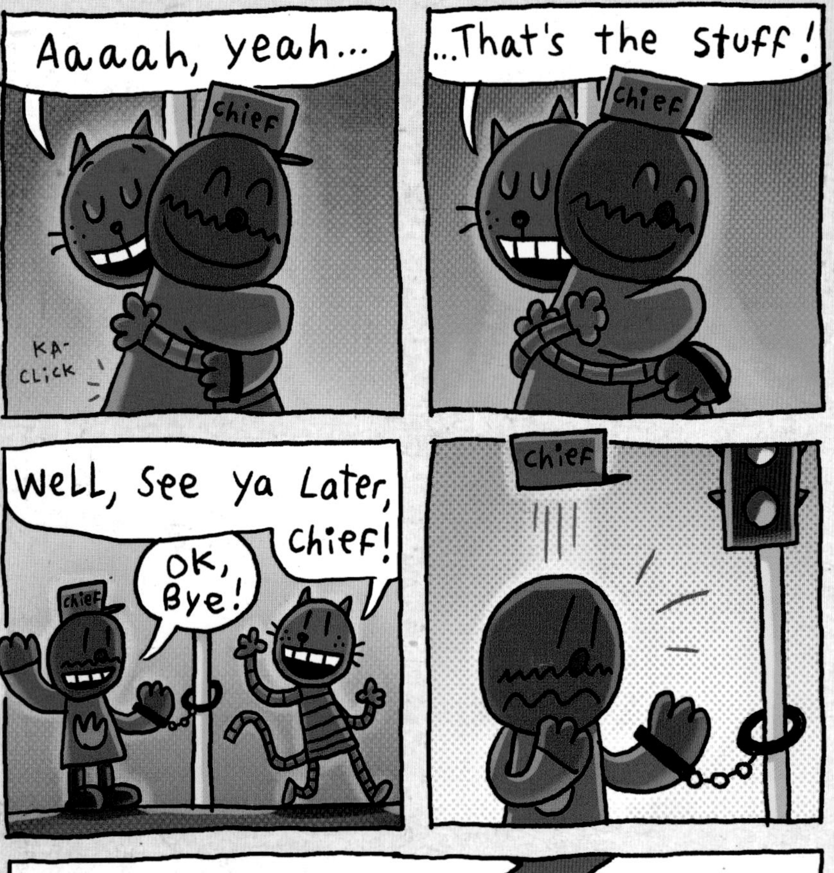
Aaaah, yeah...
chief
KA-CLICK
...That's the stuff!
chief
Well, see ya Later, chief!
chief
OK, Bye!
chief
PETEY!!!
Haw Haw!

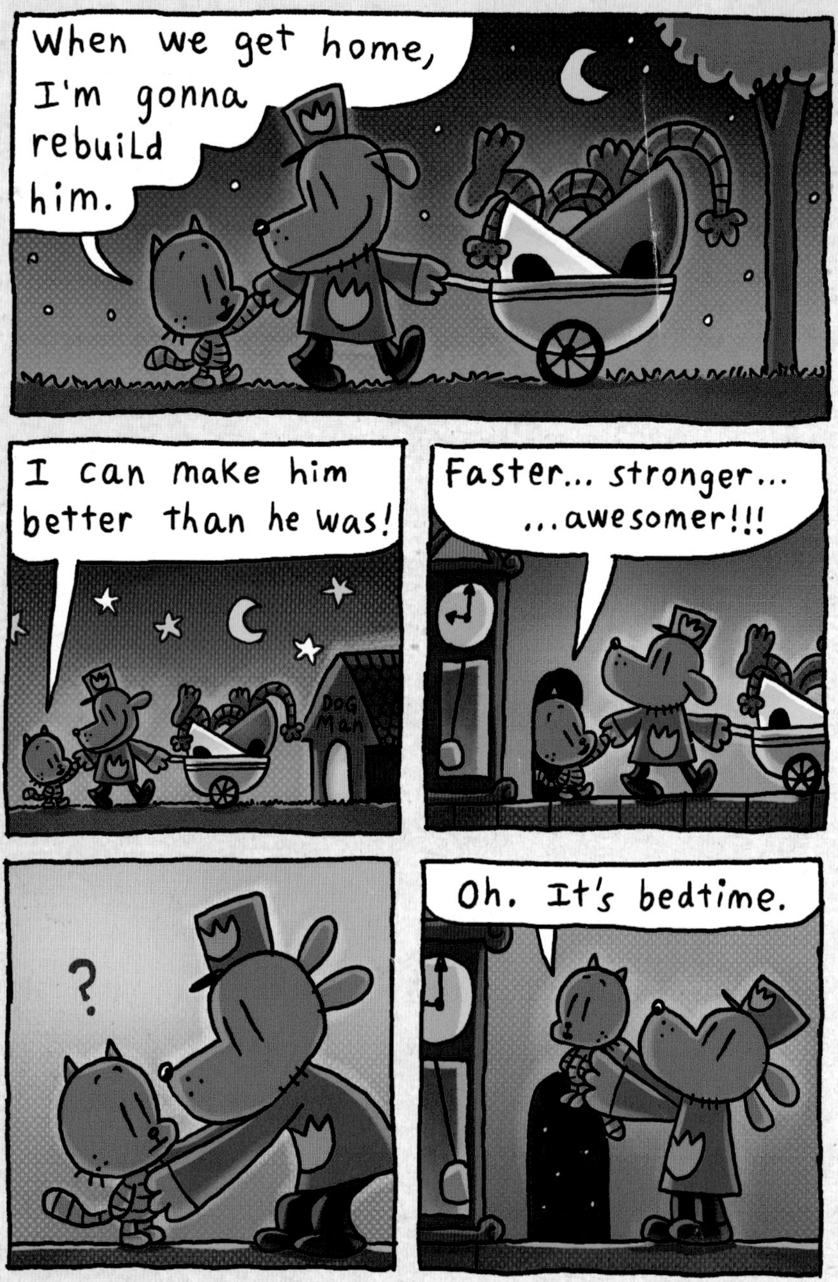
When we get home, I'm gonna rebuild him.
I can make him better than he was!
Faster... stronger...
...awesomer!!!
?
Oh. It's bedtime.

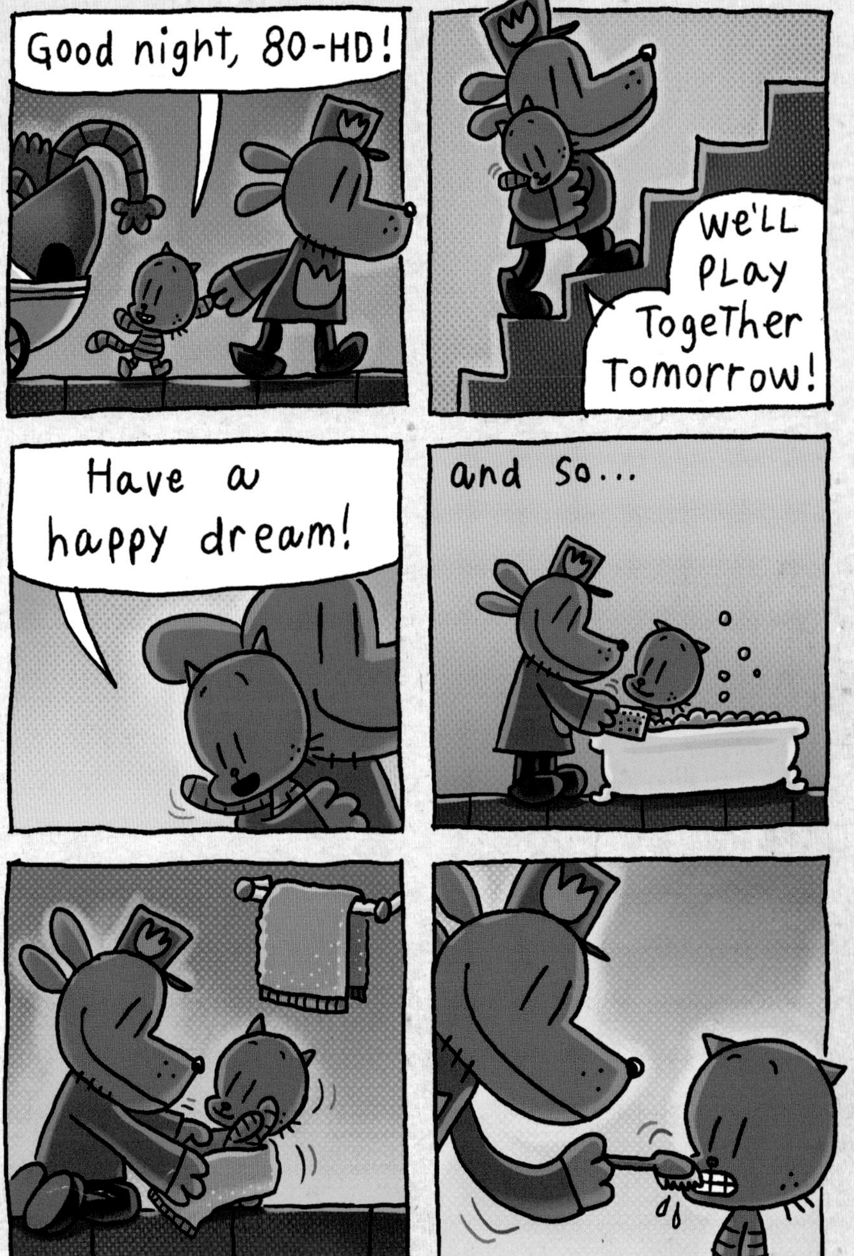

Good night, 80-HD!
WE'LL PLAY TogeTher Tomorrow!
Have a happy dream!
and so...

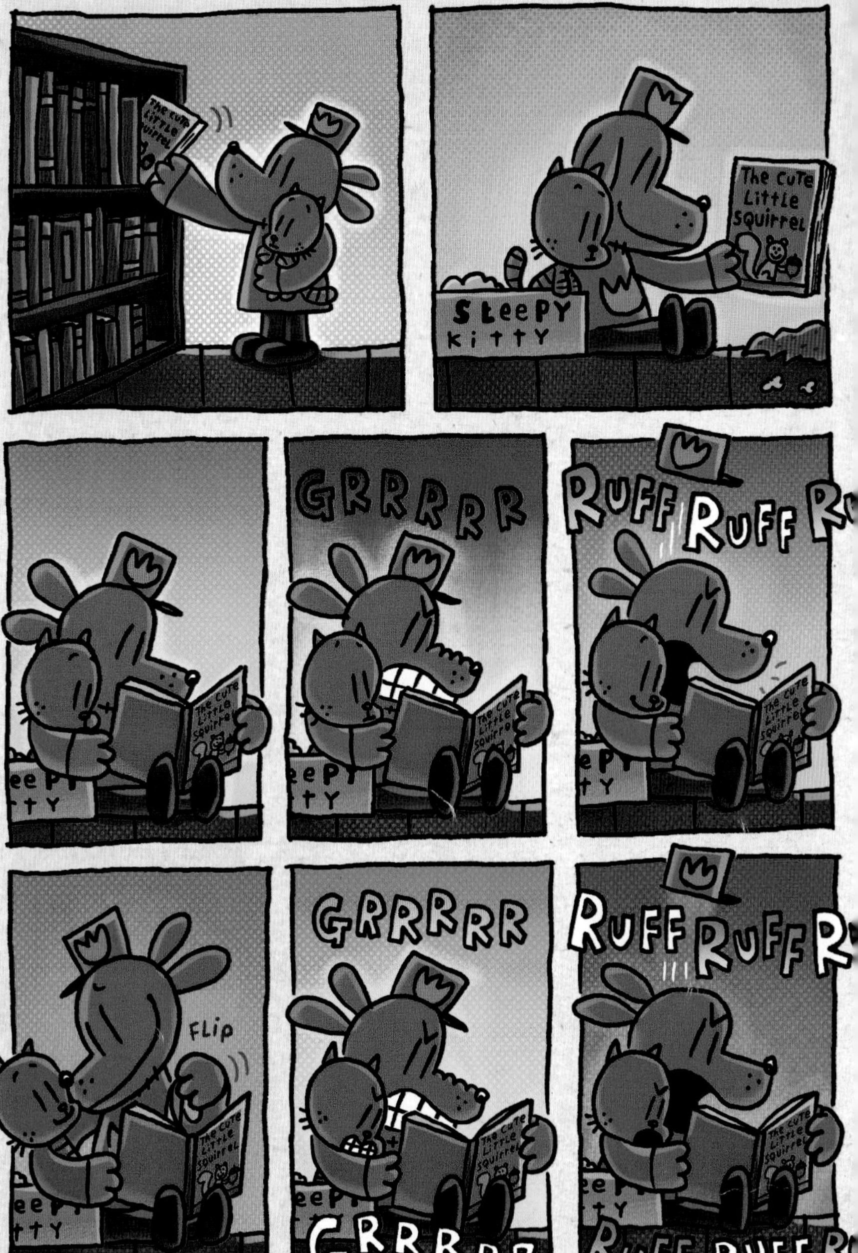

The Cute Little Squirrel
The Cute Little Squirrel
SLeePY
KiTTY
GRRRRRR
RUFF RUFF
FLip
GRRRRRR
GRRRRRR
RUFF RUFF
RUFF RUFF

RUFF RUFF RUFF
RUFF RUFF
DOG man
RUFF RUFF RUFF

RUFF
RUFF RUFF RUFF
RUFF RUFF

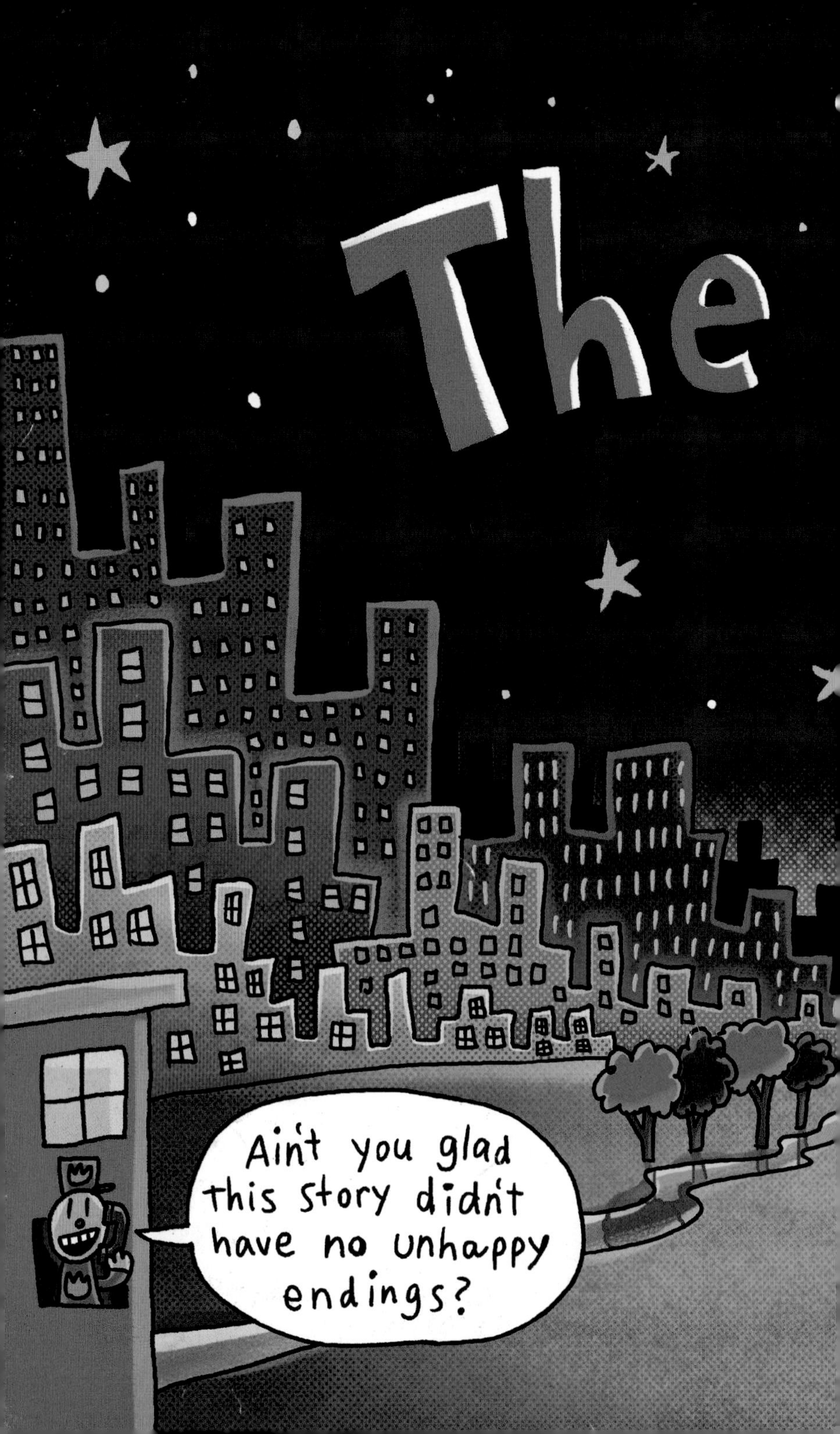
The
Ain't you glad this story didn't have no unhappy endings?

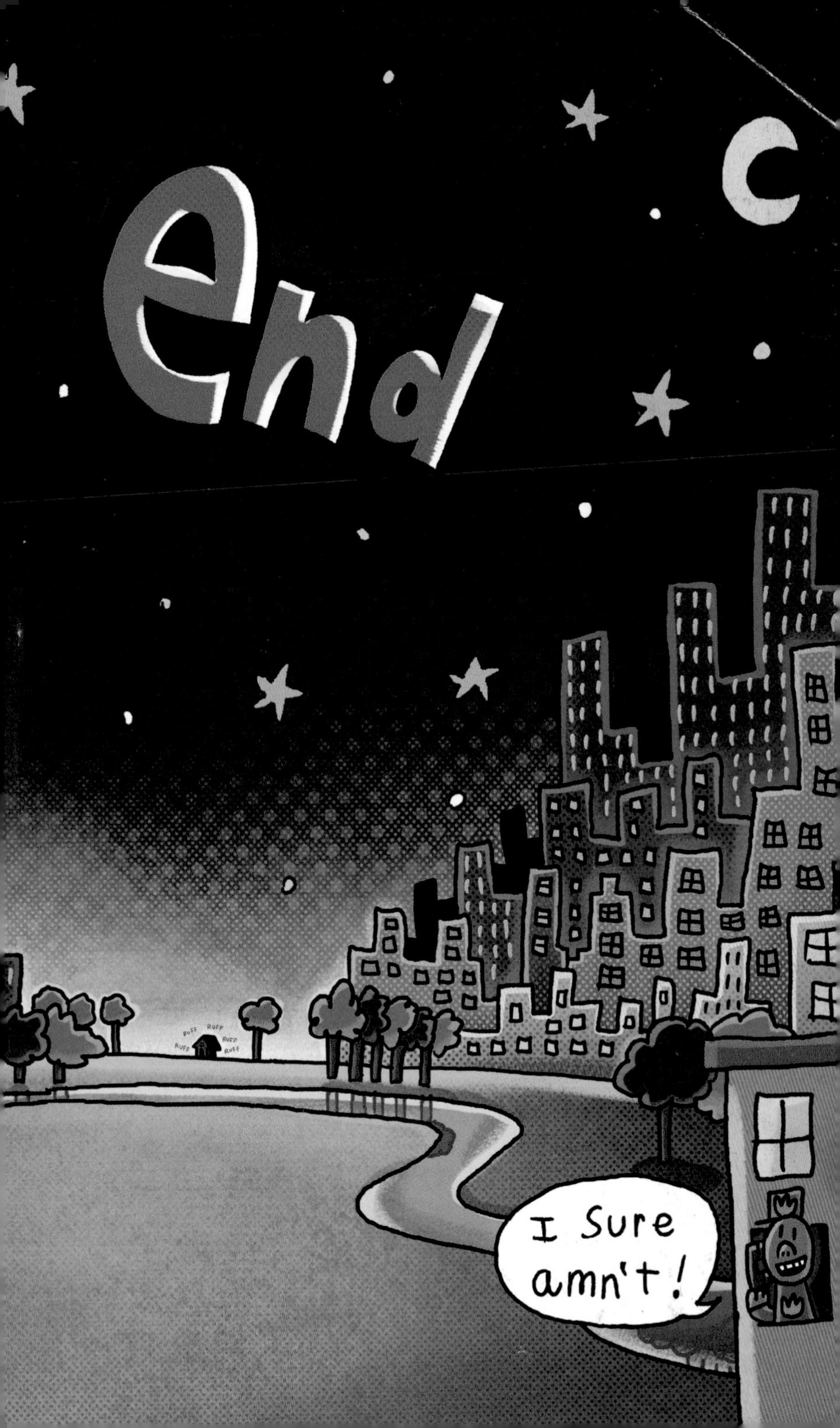
end
RUFF RUFF RUFF RUFF RUFF
I Sure amn't!

HOW 2 DRAW LI'L PETEY

in 20 RIDICULOUSLY easy steps!

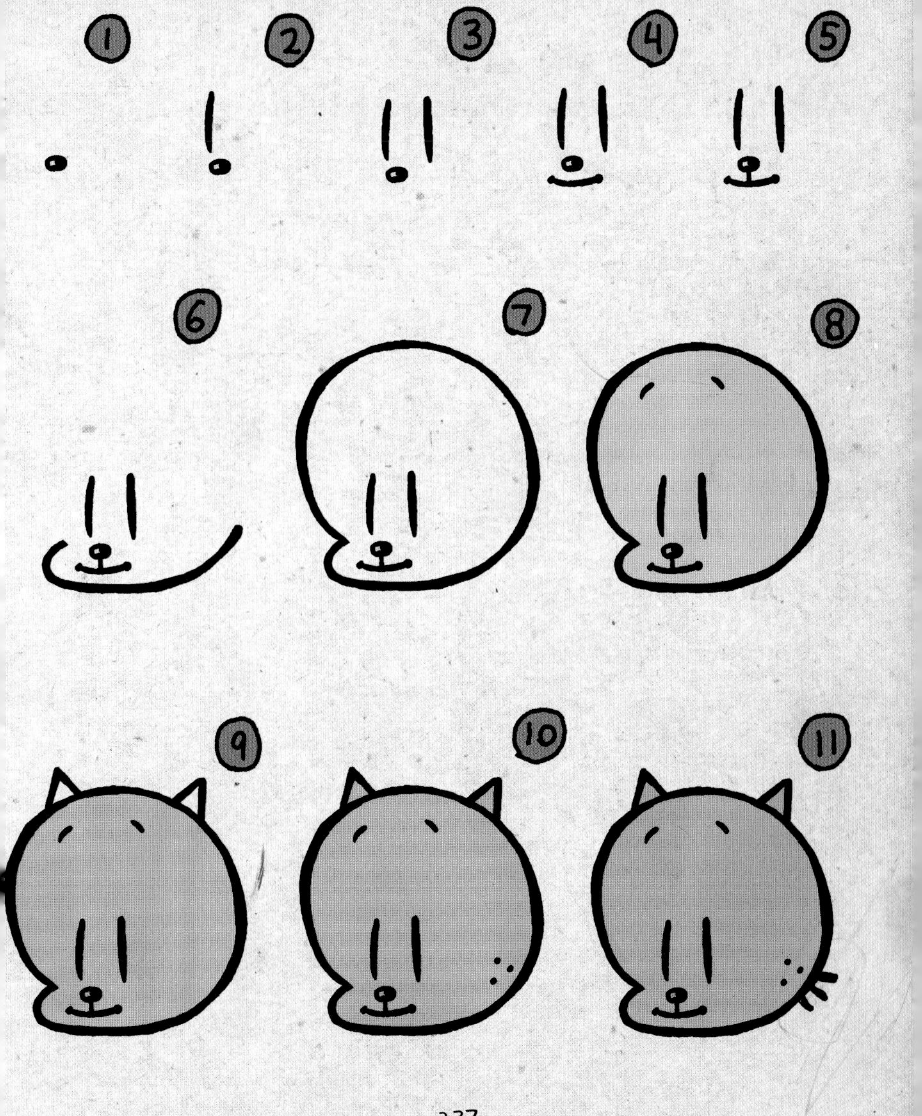
1
2
3
4
5
6
7
8
9
10
11

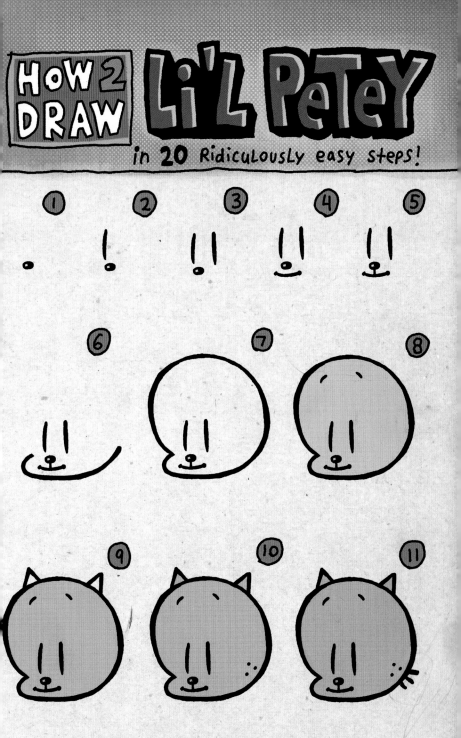

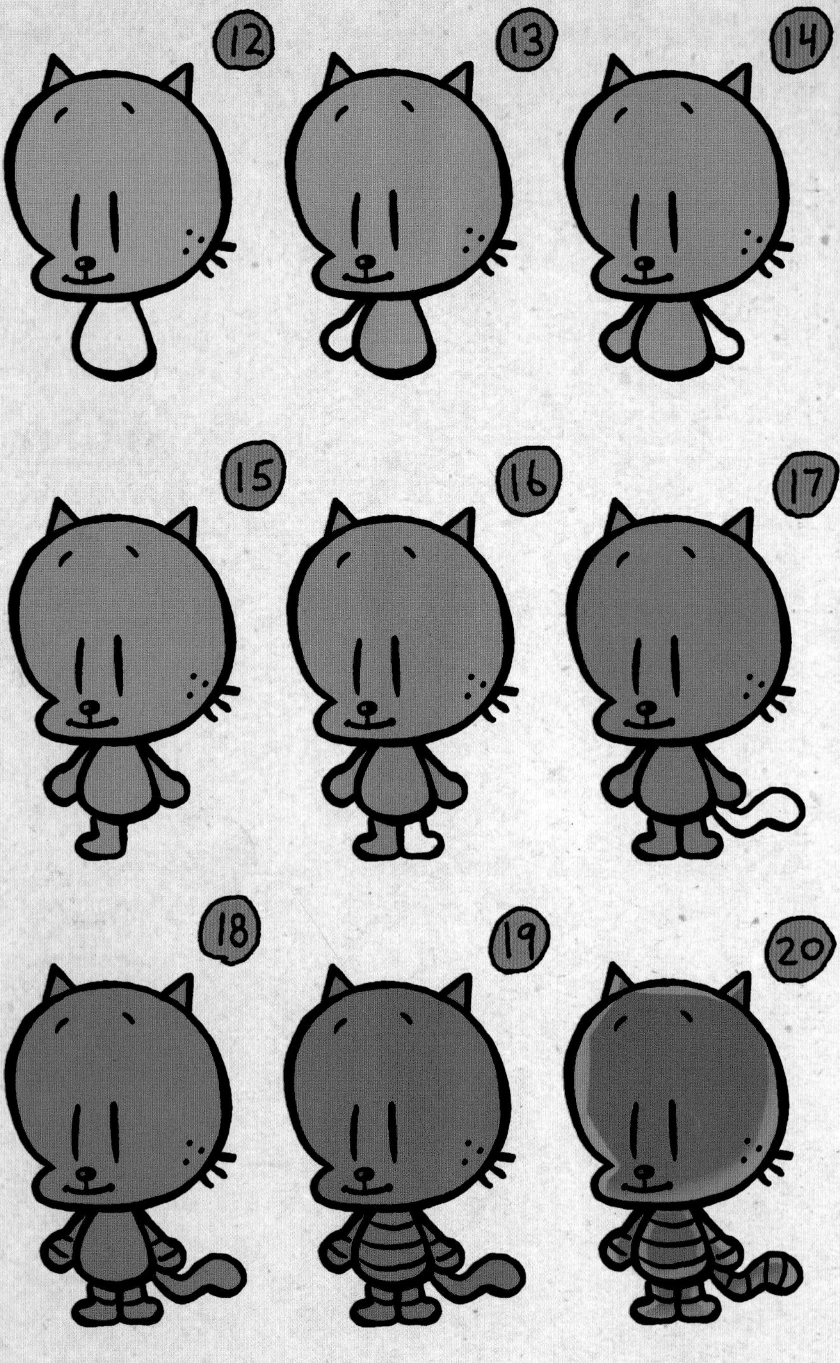
12
13
14
15
16
17
18
19
20

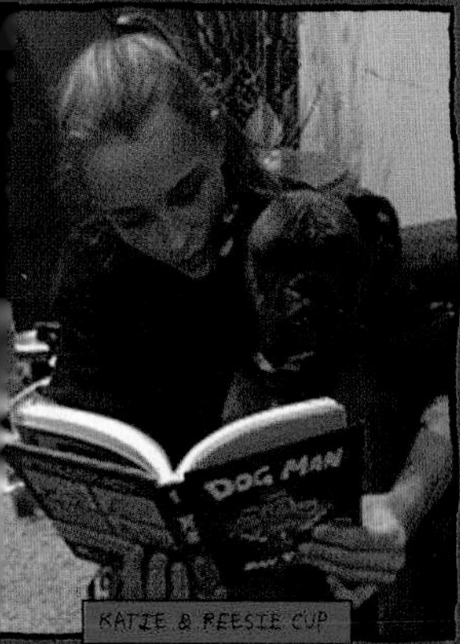

KATIE & REESIE CUP

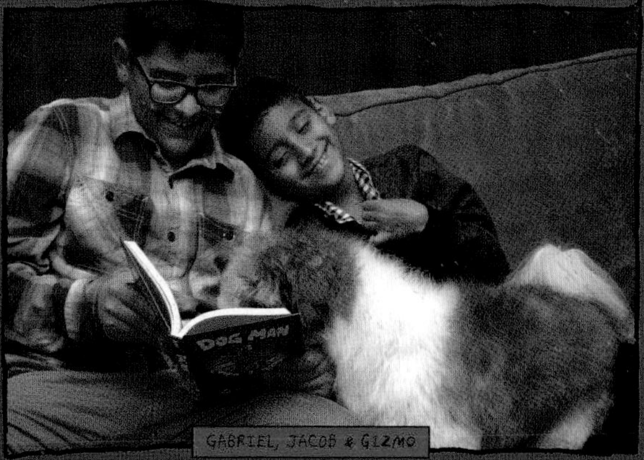

GABRIEL, JACOB & GIZMO

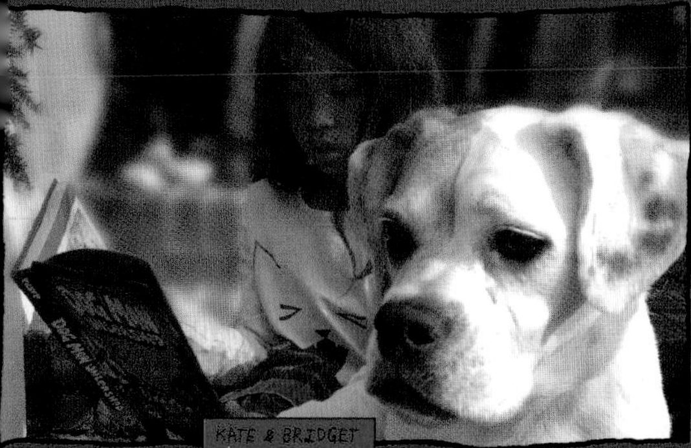

KATE & BRIDGET

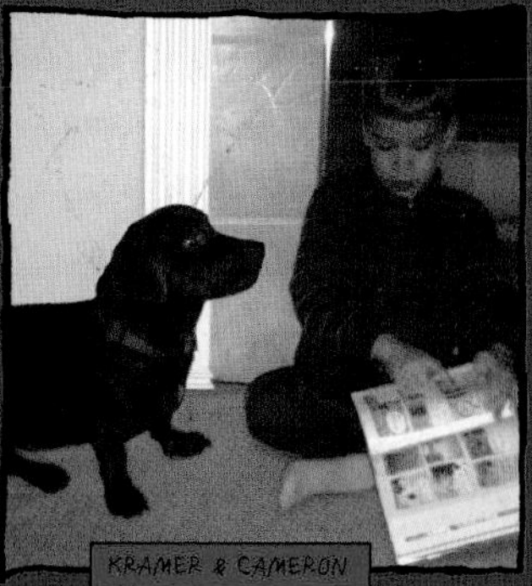

KRAMER & CAMERON

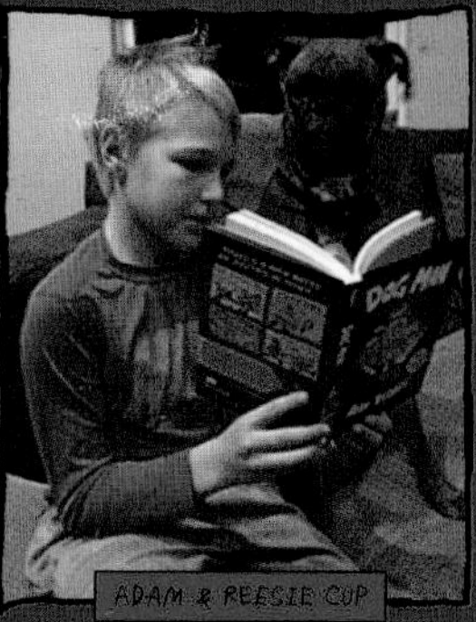

ADAM & REESIE CUP

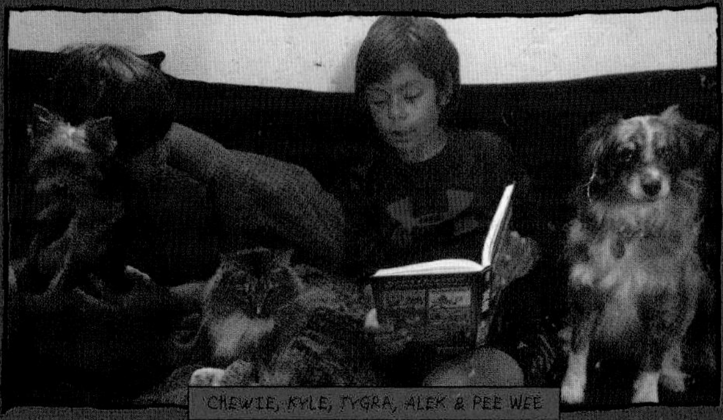

CHEWIE, KYLE, TYGRA, ALEK & PEE WEE

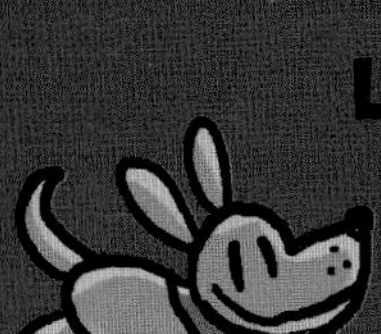

LEARN MORE AT PILKEY.COM!

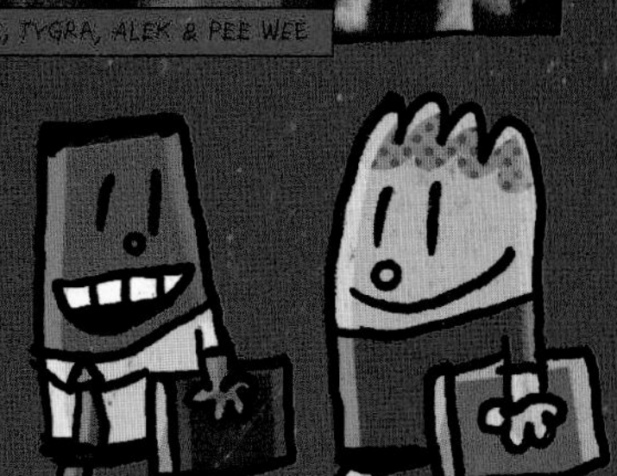

HOW 2 DRAW 80-HD

in 18 Ridiculously easy Steps!

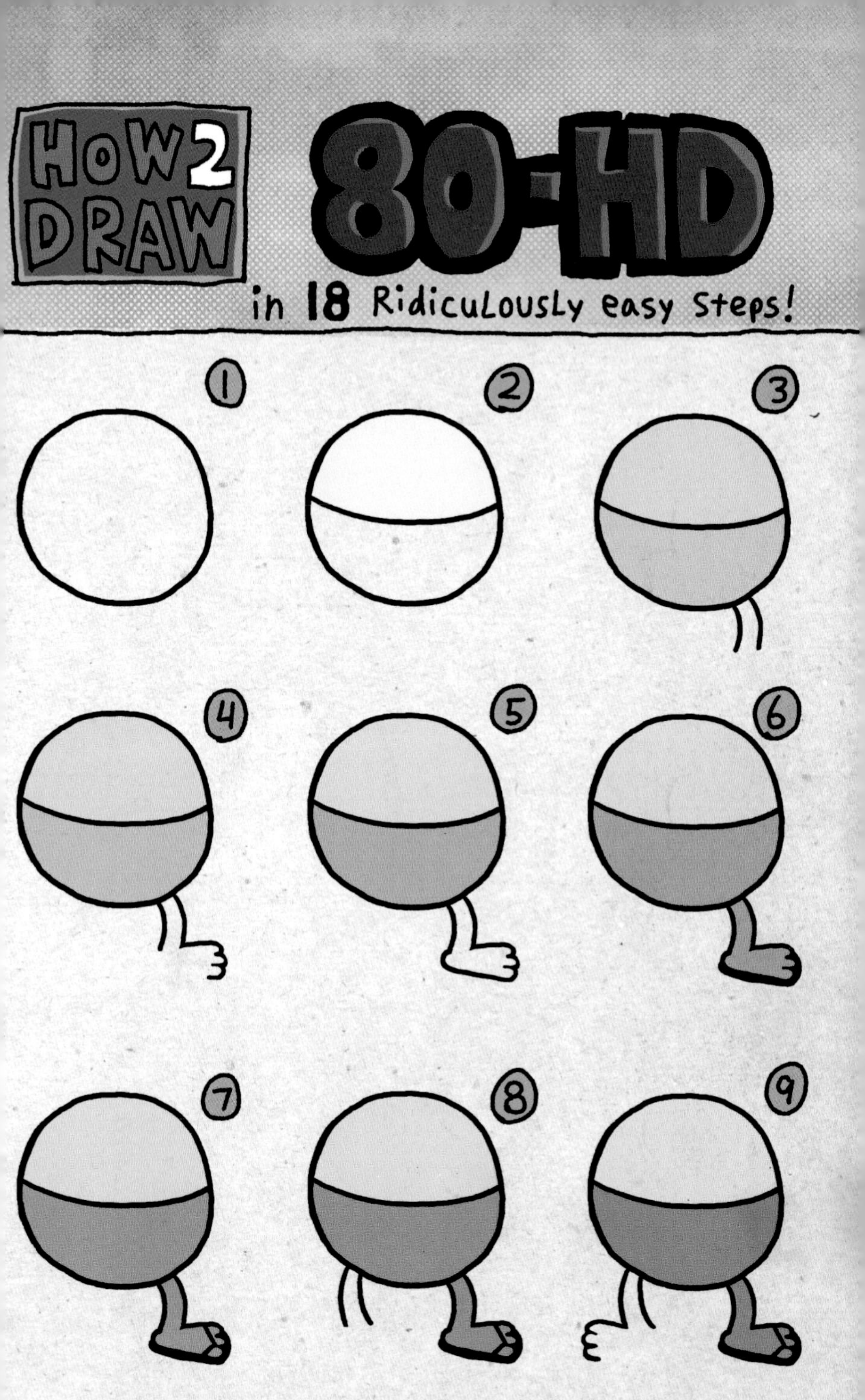
1
2
3
4
5
6
7
8
9

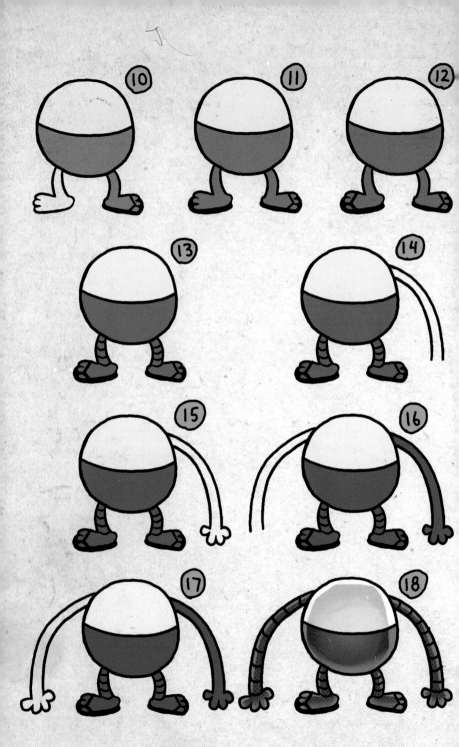

HOW 2 DRAW A BEASTY BUILDING
in 21 Ridiculously easy steps!

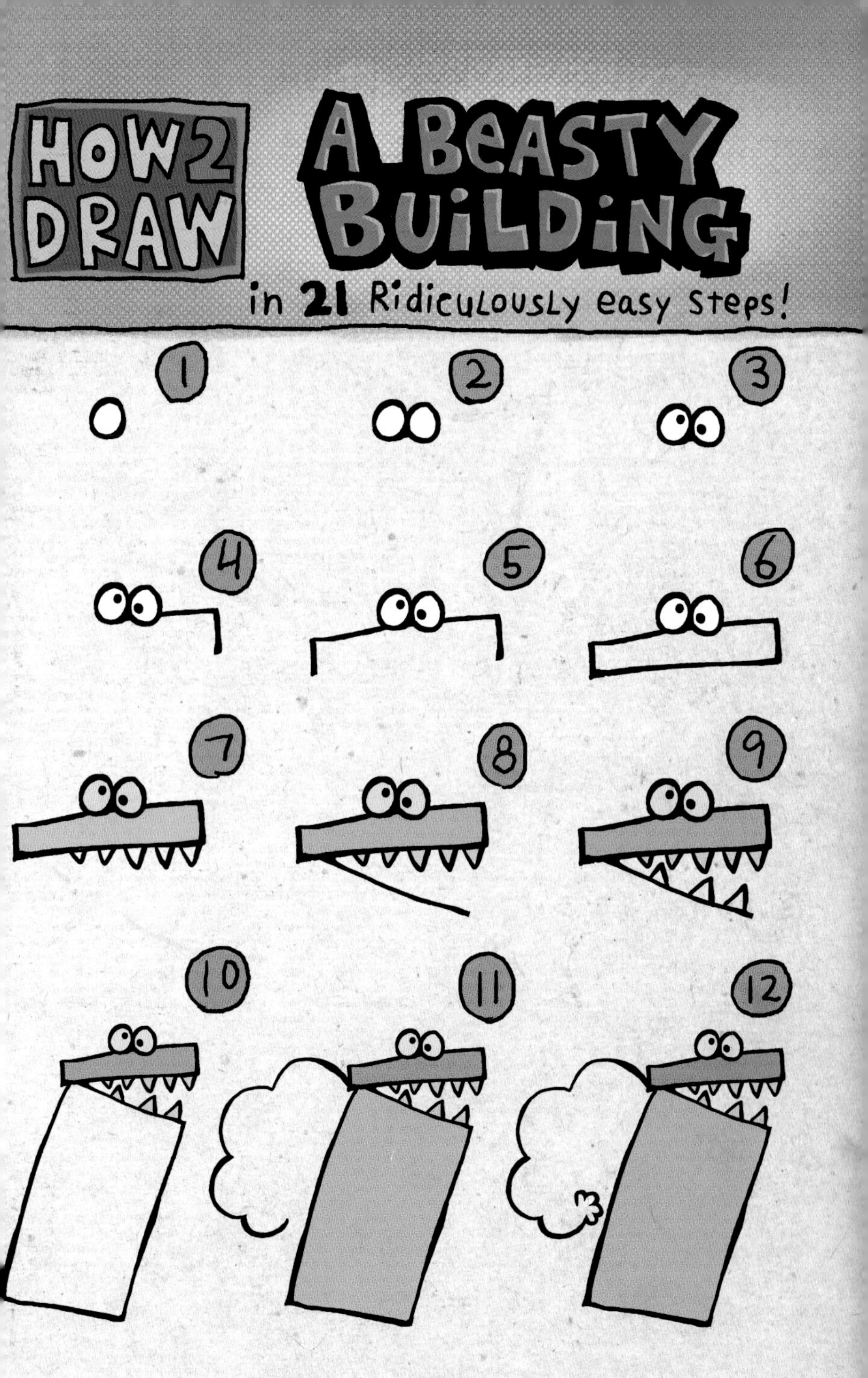
1
2
3
4
5
6
7
8
9
10
11
12

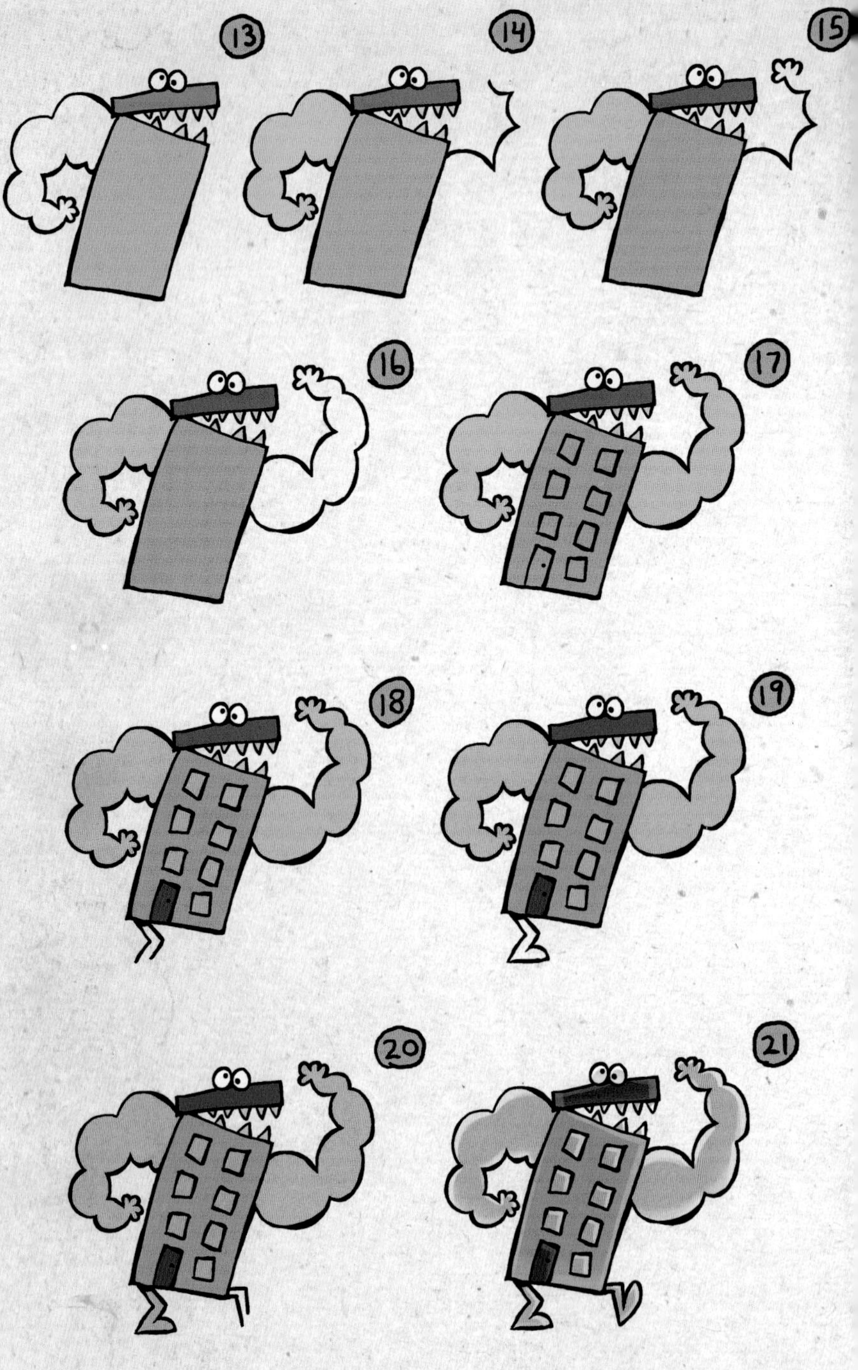
13
14
15
16
17
18
19
20
21

HOW 2 DRAW PETEY

in 27 RidicuLousLy easy Steps!

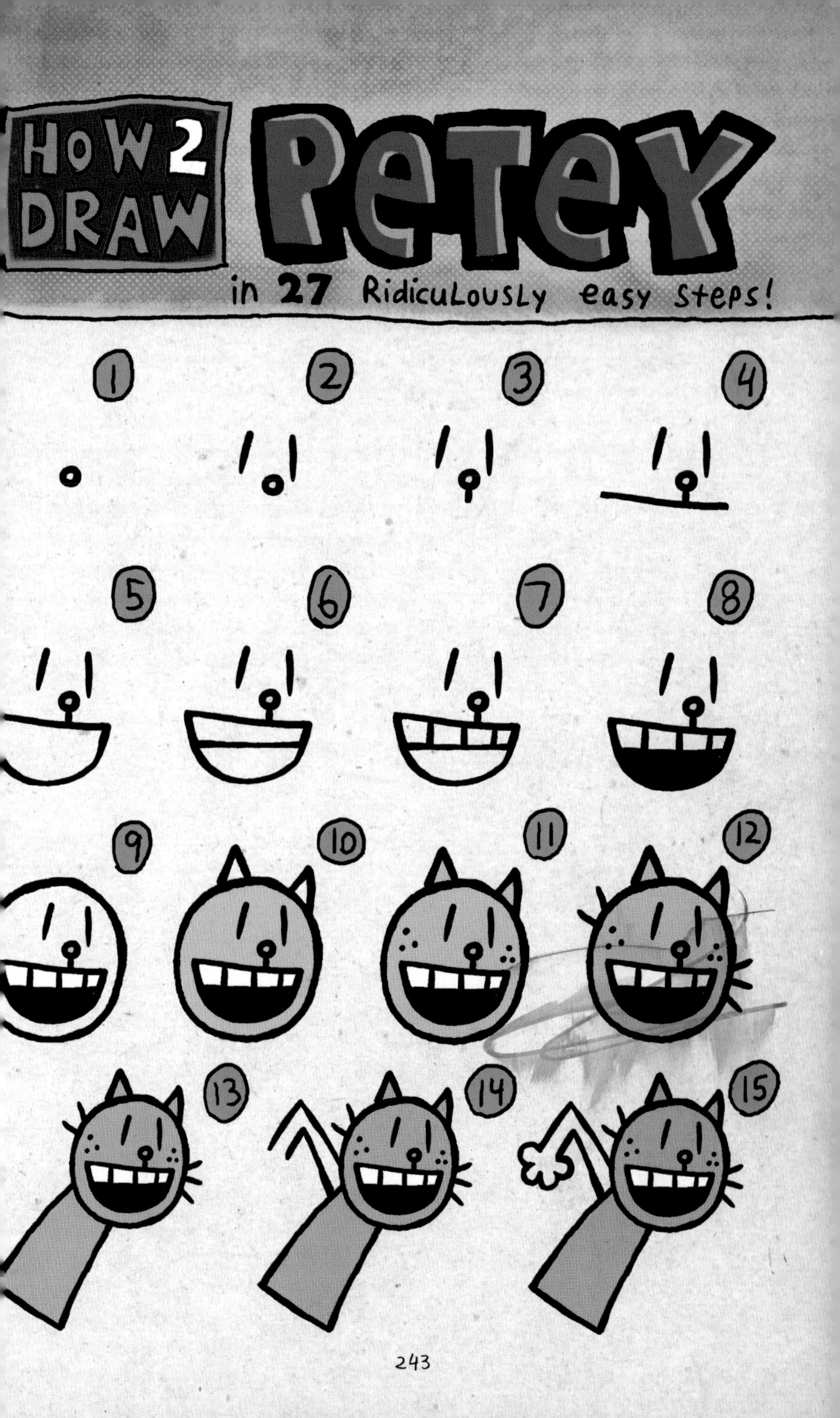

1
2
3
4
5
6
7
8
9
10
11
12
13
14
15

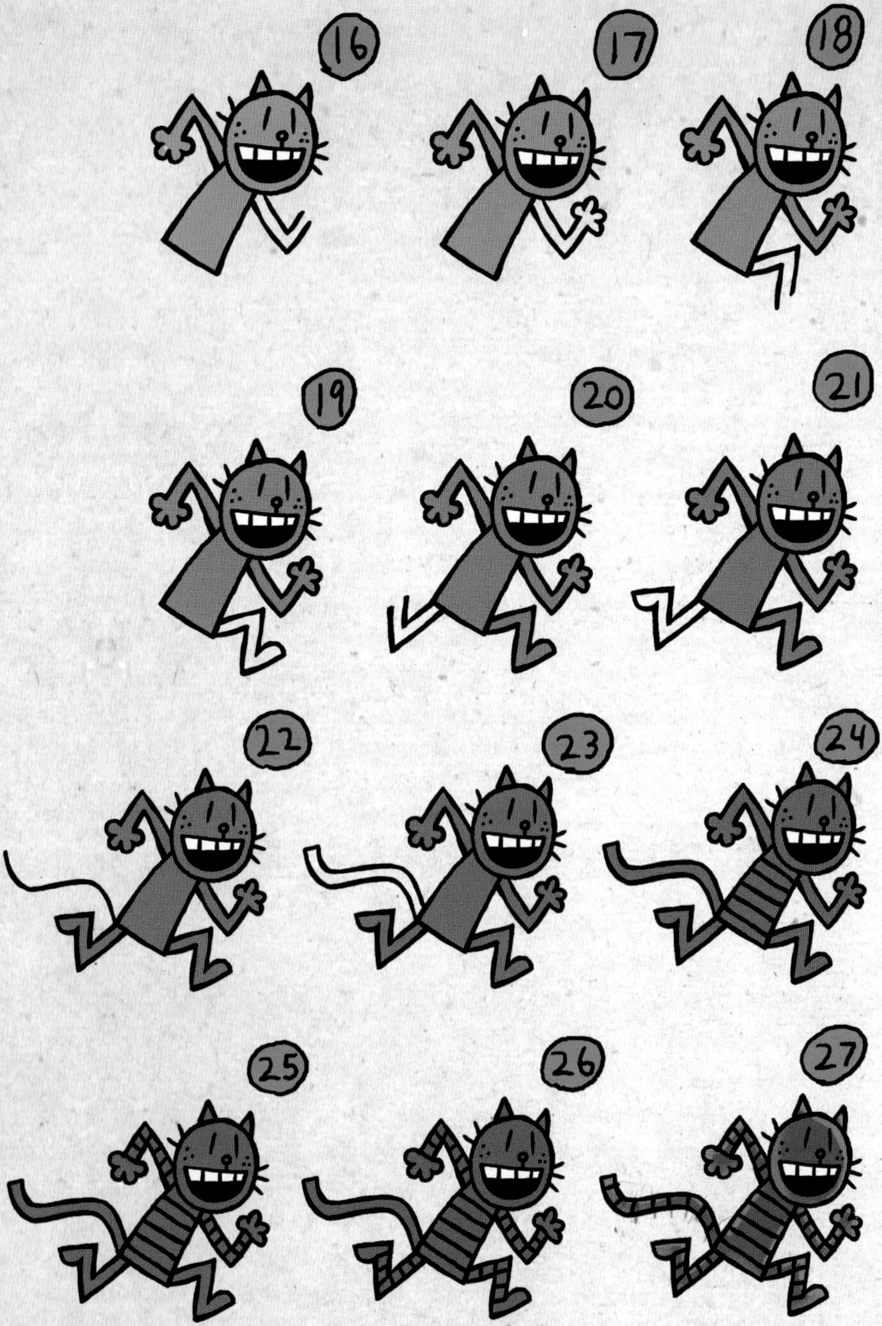
16
17
18
19
20
21
22
23
24
25
26
27

HOW 2 DRAW DOG MAN

in 34 Ridiculously easy steps!

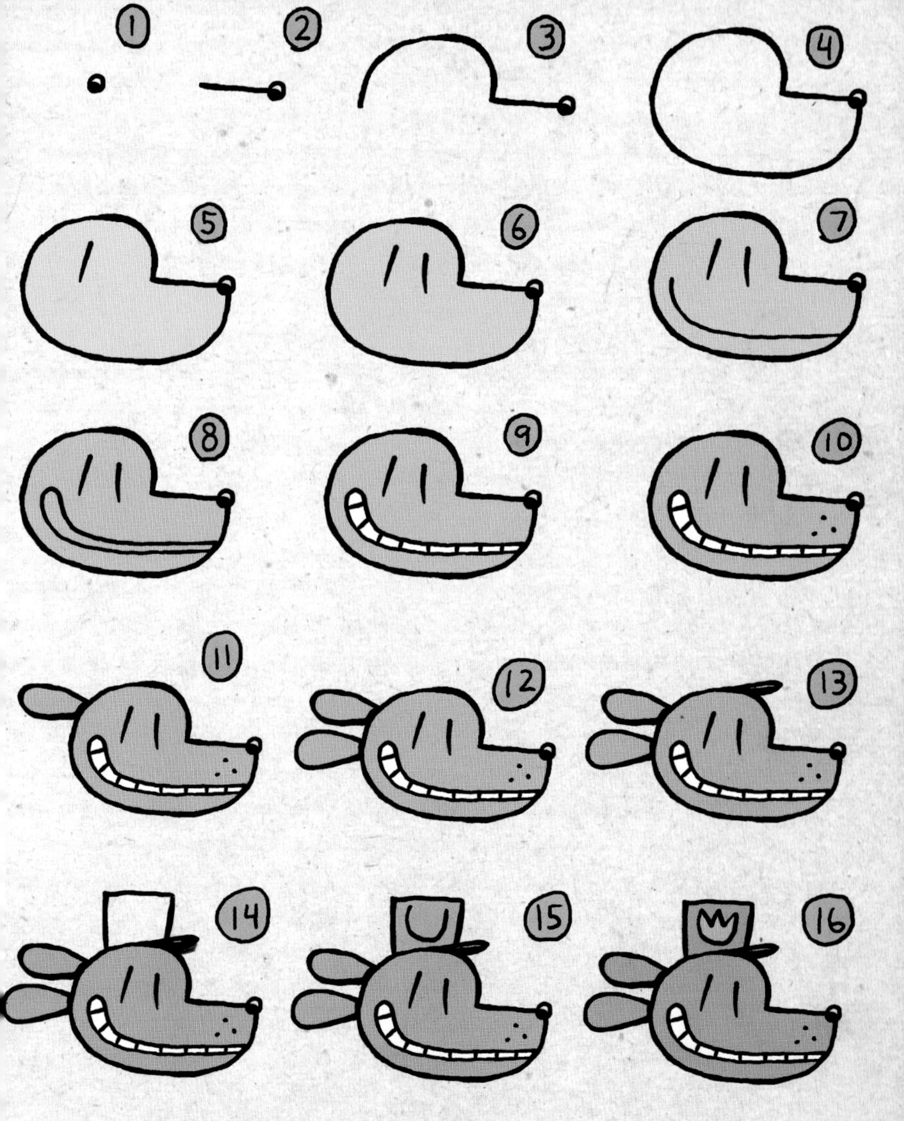
1
2
3
4
5
6
7
8
9
10
11
12
13
14
15
16

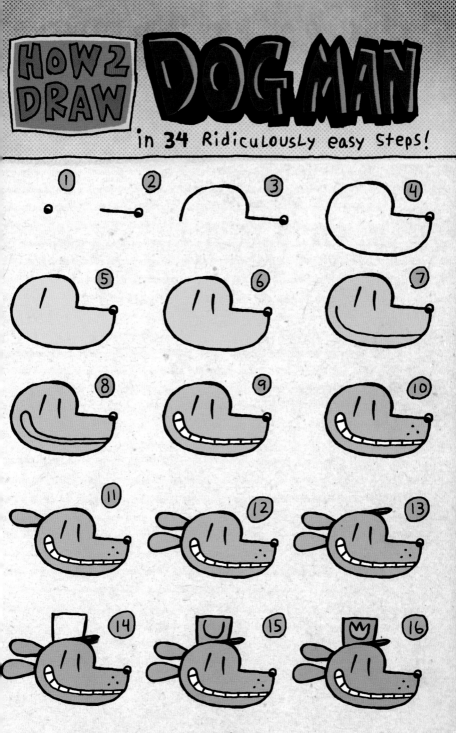

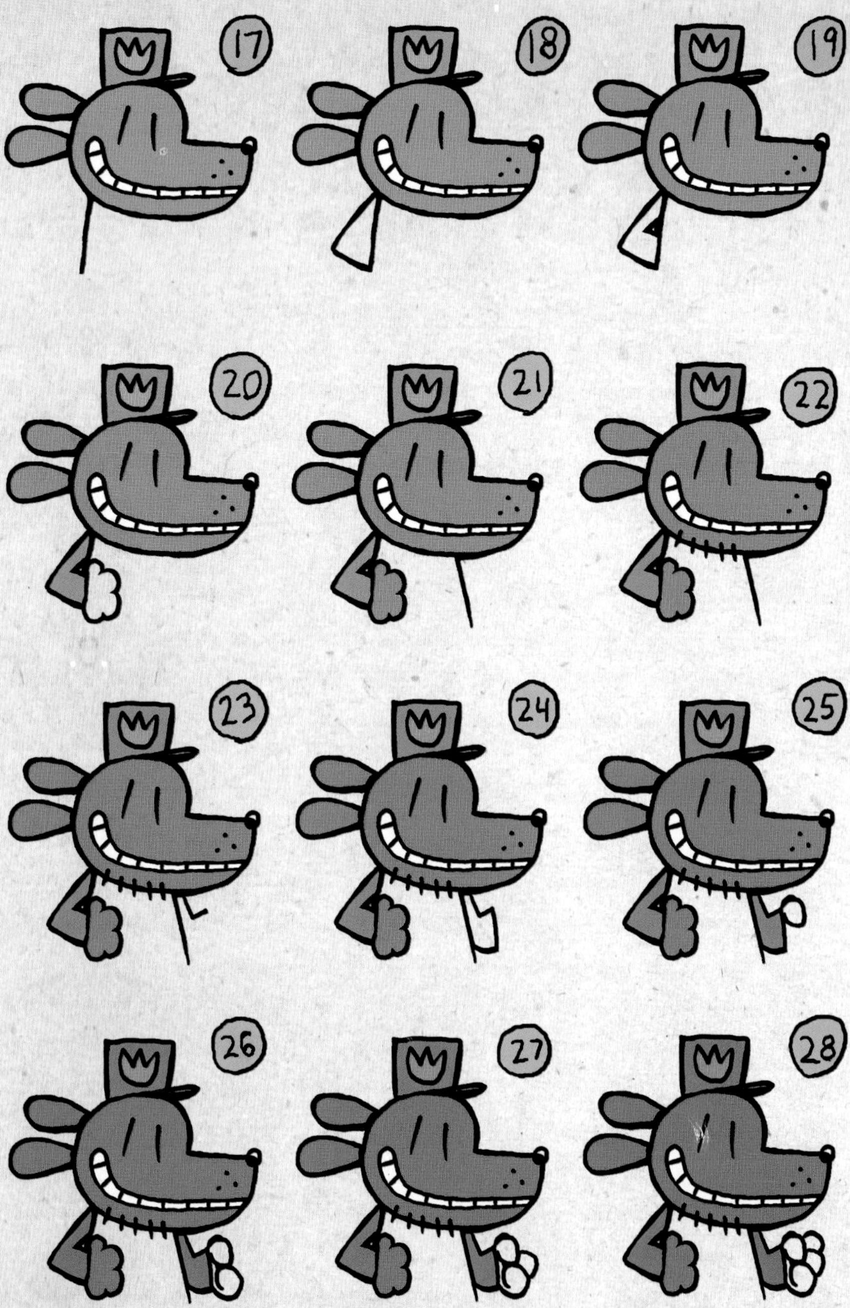
17
18
19
20
21
22
23
24
25
26
27
28

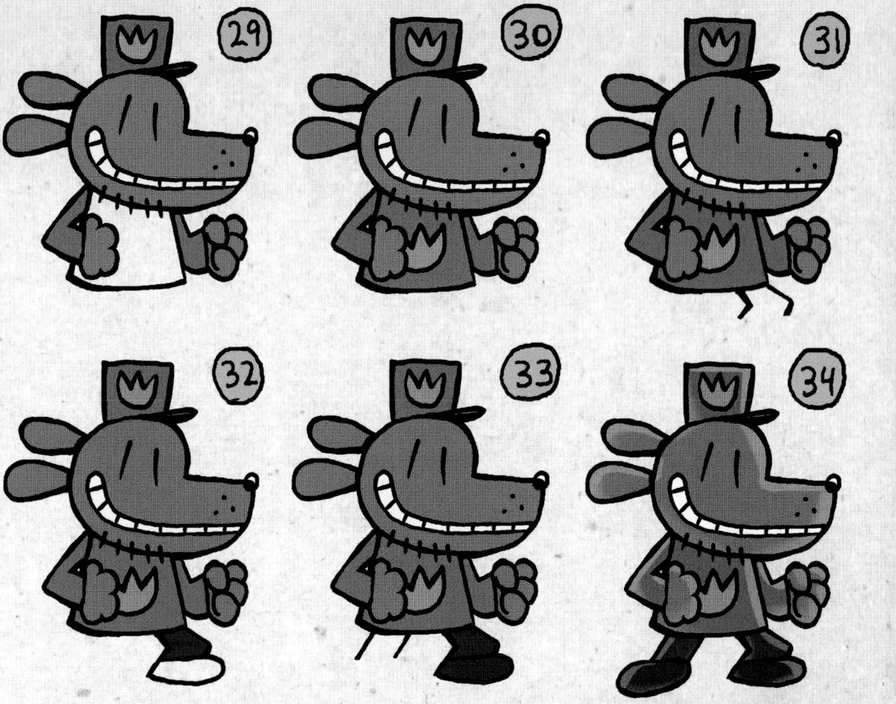
29
30
31
32
33
34

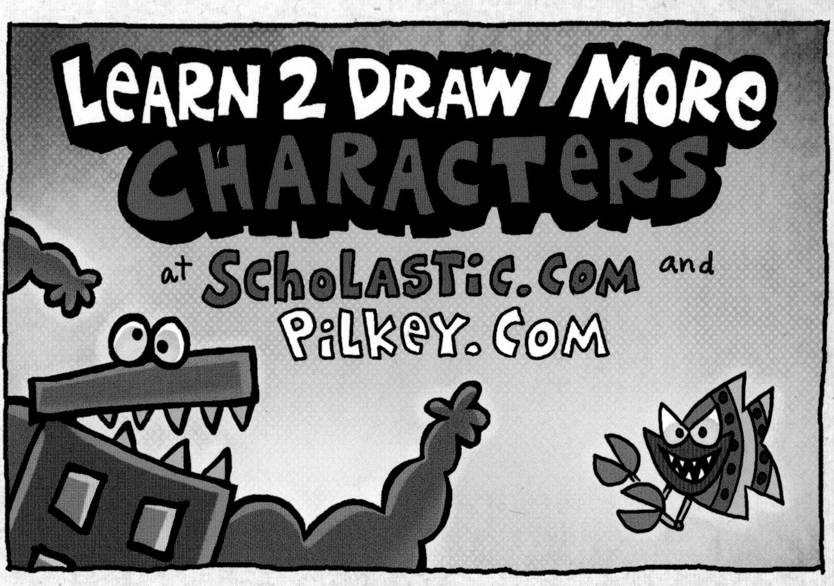
LEARN 2 DRAW MORE
CHARACTERS
at SCHOLASTIC.COM and
PILKEY.COM

READING TO YOUR DOG IS ALWAYS A PAWS-ITIVE EXPERIENCE!

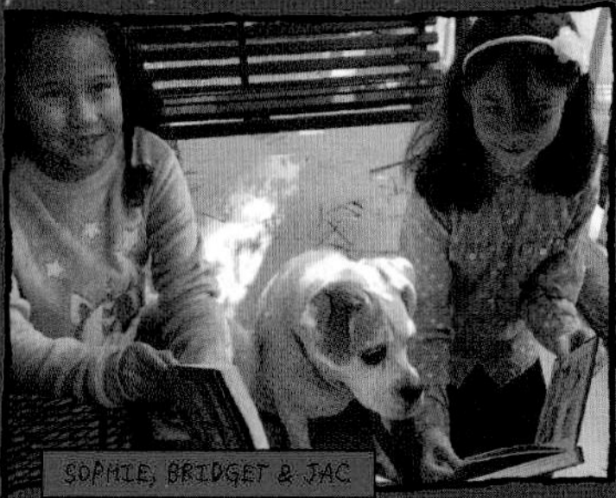
SOPHIE, BRIDGET & JAC

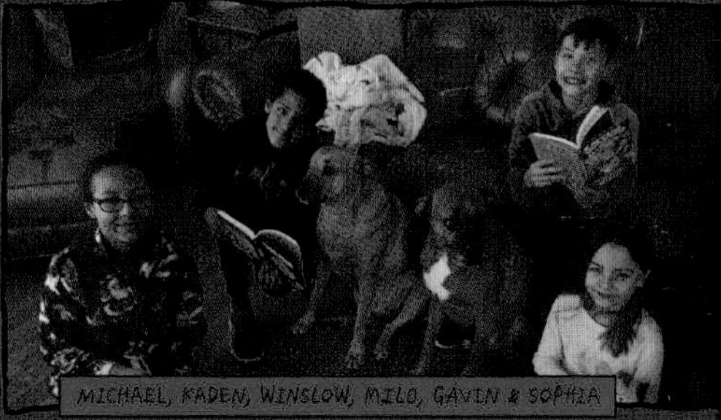
MICHAEL, KADEN, WINSLOW, MILO, GAVIN & SOPHIA

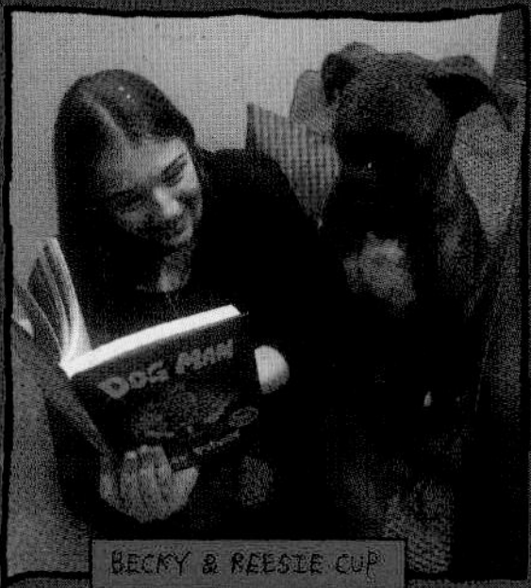
DOG MAN
BECKY & REESIE CUP

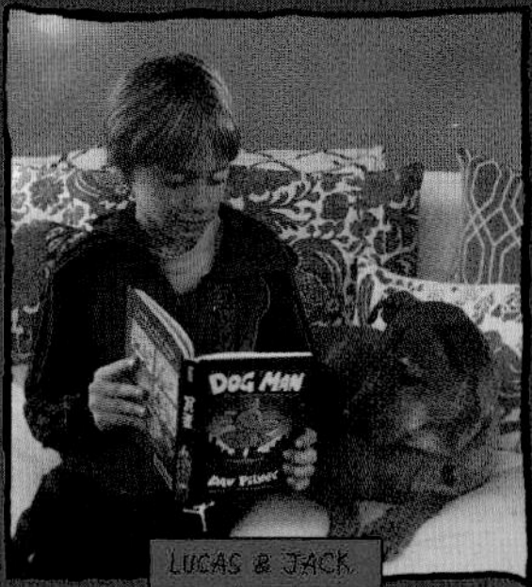
DOG MAN
LUCAS & JACK

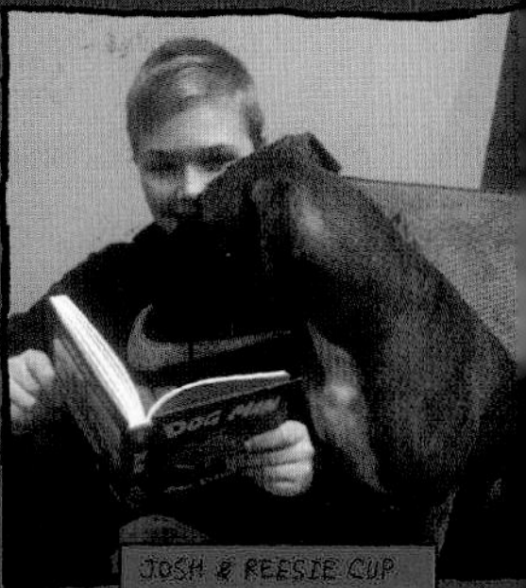
DOG MAN
JOSH & REESIE CUP

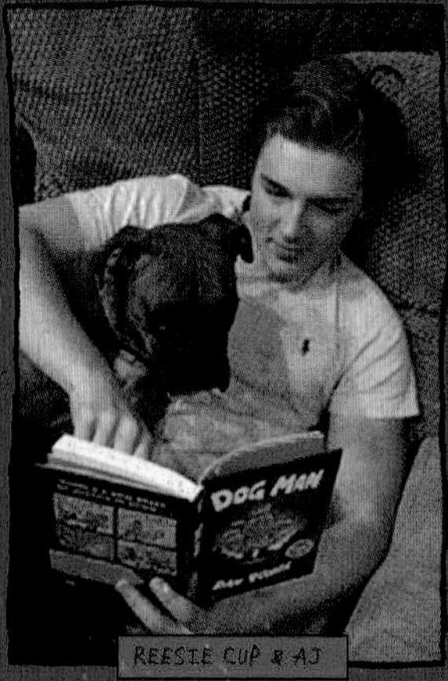
DOG MAN
REESIE CUP & AJ

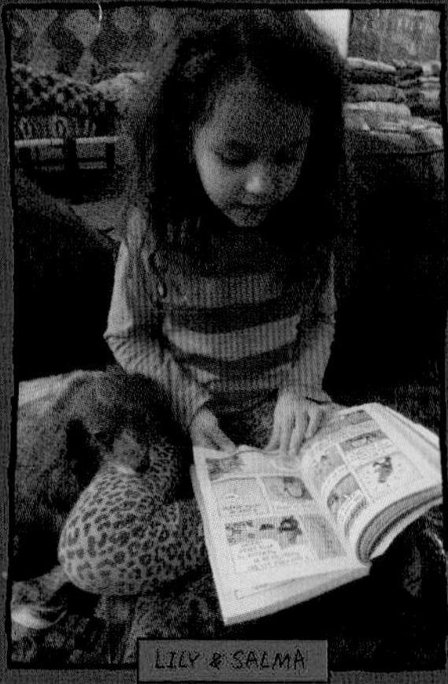
LILY & SALMA

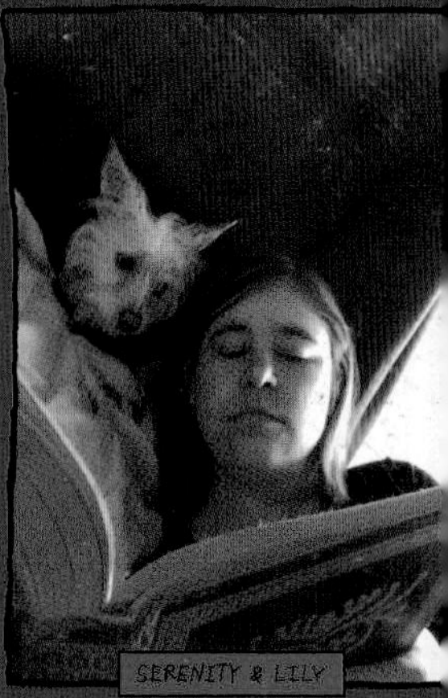
SERENITY & LILY

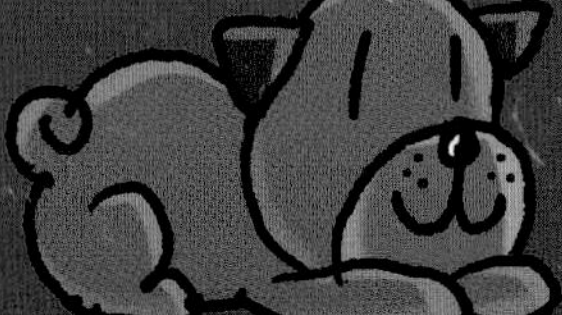

#Readtoyourdogman

ABOUT THE AUTHOR-ILLUSTRATOR

When Dav Pilkey was a kid, he was diagnosed with ADHD and dyslexia. Dav was so disruptive in class that his teachers made him sit out in the hall every day. Luckily, Dav loved to draw and make up stories. He spent his time in the hallway creating his own original comic books.

In the second grade, Dav Pilkey made a comic book about a superhero named Captain Underpants. Since then, he has been creating books that explore universally positive themes celebrating the triumph of the good-hearted.

ABOUT THE COLORIST

Jose Garibaldi grew up on the South Side of Chicago. As a kid, he was a daydreamer and a doodler, and now it's his full-time job to do both. Jose is a professional illustrator, painter, and cartoonist who has created work for many organizations, including Nickelodeon, MAD Magazine, Cartoon Network, Disney, and THE EPIC ADVENTURES OF CAPTAIN UNDERPANTS for DreamWorks Animation. He lives in Los Angeles, California, with his wonder dogs, Herman and Spanky.